INSIDE OUT

Alice Street Editions
Harrington Park Press

Judith P. Stelboum
Editor in Chief

Inside Out, by Juliet Carrera

Past Perfect, by Judith P. Stelboum

Forthcoming Titles
Alice Street Editions

Façades, by Alex Marcoux

Weeding at Dawn: A Lesbian Country Life, by Hawk Madrone

Extraordinary Couples, Ordinary Lives, by Lynn Haley-Banez
and Joanne Garrett

INSIDE OUT

Juliet Carrera

Alice Street Editions

Harrington Park Press
New York · London · Oxford

This is a work of fiction. No reference to actual persons, places, or incidents is implied or should be inferred.

Published by

Alice Street Editions, Harrington Park Press®, an imprint of The Haworth Press, Inc., 10 Alice Street, Binghamton, NY 13904-1580 USA (www.HaworthPress.com).

Cover design by Thomas J. Mayshock Jr.

Library of Congress Cataloging-in-Publication Data

Carrera, Juliet.
    Inside out / Juliet Carrera.
      p. cm.
    ISBN 1-56023-202-1 (alk. paper)–ISBN 1-56023-203-X (alk. paper)
    1. Lesbians–Fiction. I. Title.

PS3553.A76347 I5 2000
813′.6–dc21
                                                    00-036968

To my father, the most patient and unconditionally loving parent anyone could have had, and my mother for reading a little girl's first stories and crying in all the right places.

To Laura, my partner who made it easy for me to write about truth, passion and enduring love. You filled my life with all three.

ACKNOWLEDGMENTS

Thanks to Brian Morris, Linda Spadafina, Roe DeVito, Barbara Finkle, Susan Rainess, Yvonne Velazquez, Jeanne Killoran and of course, Aunt Pris for their help and encouragement along the way. Special thanks to Helen Mallon and Bill Palmer for making everything possible.

A Note to Those Who Read This Book

To me, writing is performing. The author's book is her show and the reader is the audience she wants to entertain. Any performer will tell you that the most thrilling part of a show is the feedback of the audience, particularly when that feedback is applause. Whether it's applause or not, I would very much like to know how you feel about this book, so I have asked the publisher to let me give you my e-mail address <julietcarrera@aol.com>. If you have any questions I will do my best to respond to them, as well.

It is my wish to know who you, my audience, are and to have you know me too.

I hope with all my heart that you enjoy reading this book.

J. C.

Sometimes, like angels we touch each other's lives in small but perfect ways and make miracles happen.

Prologue

Destiny

Destiny watched from the window as the low, sleek, red convertible pulled out of the driveway. She could see Nicole's long black hair being swept wildly around by the wind as the car picked up speed. Looking on as Sonia's hand left the steering wheel to affectionately brush the hair back off Nicole's face, Destiny was at once filled with a disturbing mixture of numbness and excruciating pain.

It seemed to take an eternity for the car to disappear from sight. Turning away, her eyes followed a reddish ray of late afternoon sun as it shed its light onto a framed picture of herself and Nicole. The photo was taken at a party about a year ago and had been sitting on an end table in the living room ever since. Picking it up, Destiny studied it more closely. This was the first time she noticed Sonia standing in the background. As she looked into the smiling faces peering out at her through the glass, she saw her own reflection and began to wonder if she had ever really found the peace she had sought. That thought made her hands tremble as a long-dormant rage erupted from deep inside her. Unable to contain it, she threw the picture against the wall. The frame seemed to explode on impact. Shattered glass landed everywhere, but the images remained intact, staring back at her defiantly.

Acknowledging defeat, Destiny slumped down to the floor, as tears welled in her eyes. Losing Nicole in itself wasn't what was causing this pain that grew stronger as the room darkened with the setting sun. Rather, it was knowing that she had lost her battle with the inexplicable emptiness she had tried so long and hard to overcome. But living with Nicole had only provided a shallow and temporary distraction from the hollow aching feeling that now left her sobbing in the dusky shadows of her empty home.

This was not the Destiny Anderson the public knew. This was not the woman who electrified audiences, sending them into screaming frenzies. This was the real Destiny Anderson; the one who was alone in the crowd. The one who had spent the past five years trying to build the life she hoped would make her feel complete, yet always knowing that there were pieces missing. The dream she had been chasing was as shattered as the glass that lay about her on the floor. There would be no refuge from the relentless, haunting feeling that something was missing from her life. Something . . . the memory of which had been long buried deep inside her and was now clawing and scraping its way closer and closer to the surface.

Andrie

The bedroom of Andrie LaStella's West Village apartment was dark. The white lace curtains were drawn and the lights had not been turned on as evening approached. A cold dismal silence occupied the room where Andrie lay in bed with Ann.

Bitterness and disappointment finally drove Andrie to breach the uneasy stillness. "Some people light up a cigarette after they make love . . . you announce your wedding plans. Do you really think that a wedding ring is what you need to win a congressional re-election? You'll have to live with Stuart, as if you were married to him. What about your life? Don't you care even a little about what this is doing to us?" Andrie asked, while she tried to suppress the vacant, abandoned feeling inside her. She had been crying throughout the evening and now she was doing all she could to hold back even more tears. Reaching over to the small antique table next to the bed, she turned on the light, hoping that the illumination would somehow improve the atmosphere.

Without looking at her, Ann responded in an unmoved tone, which had become typical for her. "You know that I have no choice. I need to . . ."

"I know, I know. You need to maintain a certain image . . .

reflect family values, right?" Andrie interrupted, making it obvious that she was all too familiar with the answer.

"I really don't appreciate the pressure you're putting me under. I told you that I have no choice with this. So, let's drop the conversation," Ann replied, as she lifted her wrist to the light and checked her watch, impatiently.

Undaunted by Ann's lack of tolerance for the topic, Andrie continued. "We've been together seven years. If it were legal, we would be married . . . and now you're going to marry someone else and see me on the side. I become the . . . whatever one would call someone like me . . . in a mess like this. I'm not going to allow that to happen. I've gone along with this engagement thing for too long . . . and I let it go this far, because you said that it would only last a few months . . . just to make it look good to the public. . . . But now, marriage? You can't ask me to stand by and look happy about this."

"Andrie, look at reality. I've gotten this far by representing traditional conservatism. I'm forty years old and I've never been married. I can't afford people to begin questioning that and speculating about my private life. My plans for the future mean too much for me to allow even the smallest rumor to get started. Ray feels that marrying Stuart would be best for my career . . . and frankly, I agree," Ann explained in a calm, detached tone.

"Ray told you to pretend that you were straight. Ray told you to get engaged. Ray told you to get married. . . . What's the next step? Will Ray want you and Stuart to start a family too? It amazes me . . . how much of our life you're willing to give up. You would even give me up, if it meant keeping your seat in Congress. When I try to remember back to when we met . . . I don't know if you were different then, or if I was just too naive to see the kind of person you were," Andrie said, turning away from Ann.

Nothing, not even Andrie's feelings, could deter Ann from whatever course she knew would help her get re-elected. She had learned well, from a father who taught her to go after what she wanted and to let nothing stop her. What she wanted now was to remain in Congress and to keep Andrie as her lover. "Andrie, you know that I hate this. It's this lousy world of politics that's doing this to us. Sometimes I hate it so much, for what it's done to us, that I want to walk away from it all. I want to just give up my career and the causes and projects that I've been fighting for, even Women's Way. Maybe I should. Maybe it's the only way that I know you'll stay with me." Ann knew the buttons to press to get exactly what she wanted from Andrie, or from anyone, for that matter. It was just one of many techniques she had mastered under her father's tutelage.

Without turning around, Andrie responded, "I don't want you to give up the Women's Way project or anything else you've been fighting for. I just want to have some kind of normal life with you. Maybe I'm being unfair . . . I don't know. It's getting late. You'd better leave before somebody starts wondering why you were here so long." There was a lump in Andrie's throat as she urged Ann to leave. She had always hoped for a stable, happy life with one person, but after seven years with Ann, sadly that dream had begun to fade.

Unaware of or indifferent to the sadness in Andrie's voice, Ann replied, "You're right, I have a late meeting with Ray and my father. I may just have time for a quick shower." With that she quickly kissed Andrie on the cheek and disappeared into the bathroom. She had neither the time nor the desire to concern herself with the fact that the kiss left the taste of Andrie's tears on her lips.

Chapter One

Andrie's feet and shoulders ached as she climbed the stairs to the third floor of her brownstone apartment. After twelve hours at the office all she could think of was shedding her clothes and relaxing in a hot bath. Reaching her apartment, she juggled her briefcase and groceries in order to pull her keys from her purse. As she leaned against the door to balance herself, it suddenly swung open. Andrie, along with her packages, pitched forward into the apartment.

"Fabulous entrance, darling. It's good to know all the money your parents spent on ballet lessons paid off." The surprise greeting came from her best friend David, who was in the habit of occasionally letting himself into the apartment with a spare set of keys that Andrie had given him.

"Thanks, this is just what I needed to complete my day," she sighed, with an annoyed look, as she knelt down to pick up some of the stray groceries that had been tossed out of their bags and onto the floor. Then, glancing around the living room, her expression instantly changed. "You cleaned my apartment," she observed in amazement, appreciating the fact that this would be one less job she would have to do that week.

"And it was no day at the beach!" David said, taking the groceries from her as he continued, "And let me tell you, *House Beautiful,* this was not. There was something growing in the drain of your kitchen sink," he recalled, cringing.

"Oh right. That's a tomato plant, I think . . . I was cutting up tomatoes a couple of weeks ago and . . ."

"Please don't tell me anymore." David recoiled at the thought.

"I just don't have the time to play Martha Stewart," Andrie replied, defensively.

"It looks more like you've been playing Morticia Addams," he quipped back.

The aroma of cooking suddenly struck her. "You made me dinner?"

"I made *us* dinner. Herb-crusted baked trout, asparagus with hollandaise, and for dessert, chocolate soufflé."

"You want something. What is it?" Andrie asked with suspicion in her voice.

"Let's eat," David suggested, as he pushed her toward the dinner table.

"This is a big one. I can tell. You brought over your own china and silverware," she said, observing the elegantly set table.

"What did you expect? All you had were two chipped cereal bowls and a package of styrofoam plates. By the way, you should know that they're not good for the environment . . ."

"OK. Tell me now or I'll never be able to enjoy dinner," Andrie prodded him, as he walked her to the table.

"Now couldn't I just want to have a nice little dinner at home with my dearest friend?" David mused, seating her, then commencing to massage her shoulders.

Despite the soothing effect of the massage, Andrie continued to probe for the answer to her question. "I know! Your cousin Beth from Baltimore is coming to New York and you want me to take her shopping again, right?"

"Taste the trout," David suggested as he shook out a white linen napkin and placed it on Andrie's lap, then sat across from her and filled her glass with a well-chilled chardonnay.

"It's delicious," Andrie exclaimed upon taking her first bite of the fish.

"So, how's Ann's campaign going? I've noticed that she's been getting a lot of good press lately."

"It's going pretty well. By this time next year, she'll be a shoo-in for re-election. It's just so hectic though. She was just elected last year and we already need to start on next November's campaign. Things would be a lot easier for me if a congressional term lasted longer than two years. . . . Oh, I meant to tell you that there's going to be a fundraiser for the Women's Way Project next week.

Harry and Elaine Stern are sponsoring it and Ann is hosting it with them," she mentioned parenthetically as she reached for the glass of wine.

"Harry Stern?" David asked.

"Yes."

"Destiny was telling me that he was having some financial problems. She's afraid that he might sell Cobra to get out of debt. You know, her career didn't take off until after he signed her to Cobra two years ago. Then her second album went triple platinum and Cobra's planning to put a lot of money into promoting her third album, when it's released. She's become pretty good friends with Harry and his wife, too." Then David paused in thought for a second as he filled his own plate. "I told you they were friends, right?"

"Every time his name comes up," Andrie replied with curt indifference.

"Does Stern know that you're friends with Destiny?" David asked.

"I'm not friends with her. And no, he doesn't know that she and I ever knew each other. The name Destiny Anderson has never come up in conversation. I see Elaine, his wife, pretty frequently, because she volunteers all her free time to Women's Way, but I've only met Harry a handful of times, through Ann. If Destiny's name ever did come up, there's really no reason for me to say that I ever knew her," Andrie answered him in a stiff, tense tone.

"Why are you hiding the fact that you knew her?" he asked.

"I'm not hiding it. I just don't want to talk about it. I've never even told Ann that I knew Destiny. That was too long ago to matter now . . . and besides, she would probably get all worried about the fact that I was once close with a very out-of-the-closet lesbian," Andrie explained with what seemed to be an unquestioning allegiance to Ann's sensibilities.

"I'm gay, and Ann knows how close we are," David said, trying to understand Andrie's reasoning.

"You're a gay man. People won't think we're lovers. On the other hand, Destiny's become the leader of the pack of celebrity lesbians. . . . And with her reputation, she makes them look like the Stepford wives. I can't afford the possibility of anyone suspecting that there was ever anything between Destiny and me, because of how that could reflect on Ann. She's in politics; anyone could use that against her," Andrie protested vehemently.

"Andrietta, dear, you're scaring me. I'm starting to hear Ann's voice when you open your mouth. You'd be a much happier woman if you started living your life for yourself, instead of worrying about who knows you're gay. Doesn't all this secrecy feel kind of *unnatural* to you?" David persisted.

"Look, Ann is under a microscope because she's a congress-woman. Could you imagine the field day her opponents would have, if we came out? My life is fine this way. I don't need that headache. I'm perfectly happy, damnit!" she replied impatiently.

"Oh, of course. Silly me. How could I not have noticed how happy you are?" David replied wryly, as he took a large piece of trout with his fork and admired it briefly before putting in his mouth.

Andrie had had enough of the conversation. She needed to change the subject. "Getting back to what I was saying before, can you come to the party next Friday? You'll be my guest, so you don't even have to worry about a donation."

"I think that it's a great cause. In fact, I'll buy a ticket right now, but please don't make me sit through it." David knew that aside from the main purpose of raising money for Women's Way, the party would also be used by Ann as an opportunity to campaign for her re-election. Over the years, David had successfully managed to maintain a polite, albeit cool, relationship with Ann whenever they had occasion to be in each other's company. However, he preferred to avoid such instances if at all possible.

"David, just come, even if it's only for an hour or so. I really get kind of lonely at these things and it would be nice to have you there," Andrie begged as she put down her fork and waited for a response.

"Every time I agree to go to these functions with you, you get all caught up mixing with the guests and campaigning for Ann."

"I know. That's my job. But this time will be different. It's not a campaign fundraiser, so I won't have to do that. Just say that you'll be there, please," Andrie petitioned him with a pout in her voice.

"OK. OK. Next Friday. I'll be there. . . . What would you do for company, if I ever get a life?" David asked with an exasperated sigh.

She ignored his remark. "Great! I really wasn't looking forward to going to this without you. You know that Ann's got to be with Stuart for the evening. She wants me to take a date, but I'm trying to hold out. She's pushing Jim Page. Remember him?"

David leaned across the table with a look of disbelief and annoyance on his face. "The doctor, right? Wasn't that poor guy in love with you? You can't do that to him. It's not right. I can't believe that she makes you date men to cover up the fact that the two of you are lovers. It's sick. . . . And now she's got herself engaged to Stuart Sottley, who is now her father's business partner in Atline Communications, which I find amusing. I'm tired of reading about them," David said, annoyed by the situation.

Andrie opened her mouth to answer, but she was cut off as he quickly continued, "Is she really planning to marry him, or what?"

"She has to." Andrie was becoming defensive.

"Why? Did she get him pregnant?" David's sarcasm rose from his dislike and distrust of Ann and his concern for Andrie. He had always felt that Ann's first love was power, and he feared that Andrie would become a casualty of her quest to attain more of it.

"I wish that you would just try to understand what she's up against. There are so many people who would use our relationship as a means of destroying her career," Andrie replied in Ann's defense, trying to convince herself, as much as David.

"I don't buy that one. You know damned well that there are successful gay women in politics," David argued.

"But how many of them are political conservatives in Congress? And Ann has bigger goals for the future," Andrie quickly responded.

"Look, all I know is that Ann Capwell better wake up to the fact that she's playing a dangerous game here. . . . And no matter what you say, I know that you can't possibly be happy with this situation. If the public finds out that she's been pretending to be something other than what she is, the shit is really gonna hit the fan." David was speaking from his heart. Although he didn't really care what happened to Ann or her career, he didn't want Andrie caught in the political crossfire. It was difficult for him to remain silent as he watched his best friend being forced to live a lie.

"And if Congresswoman Dearest does get re-elected and then walks down the aisle with Stuart Sottley, what happens to you? Do you continue as her assistant or does she move you in, as the upstairs maid? I mean, really . . . are you supposed to keep up this sham forever? You gave up a business that you worked hard to get started, just to become her assistant, because she thought people wouldn't question you being around her so much if you worked for her. But now, she's arranged this marriage thing with Sottley . . . I don't know . . . this whole thing is crazy. Does Sottley know that Ann's gay?"

"Of course he knows and he's kept her secret for years. They're very close," Andrie told him.

"Well excuse me if I sound like a *dumb bunny* here, but why the hell would he want to marry someone who he knows is a lesbian? I know that he's almost sixty, but he is a successful businessman. Couldn't he find someone to marry him for his money and give him a good time in bed too?"

"Stuart's been close friends with Ann for years and he wants to do this for her. That's it," Andrie answered curtly as she put the glass of wine to her lips.

David knew that there had to be more to this story. "Give it up honey, I can read you like a large print copy of *Valley of the Dolls*. Now what's this guy's story? You know that I've never repeated anything you've told me," he persisted, following Andrie as she got up and walked into the living room.

"OK, enough. You've made your point. I'll tell you what I know, but this is strictly between us. Stuart is . . . he has a . . . he can't . . ." Andrie stammered, as she awkwardly motioned toward her groin.

"Get it up," David filled in with a laugh.

"Ann just told me about this a couple of years ago. I have a feeling that it may be a contributing factor to his willingness to go through with this whole marriage thing. According to Ann, it happened when he was on an extended business trip in Sicily about fifteen years ago. While he was there he started an affair with a teenage girl who was working as his housekeeper. Apparently, her father found out about it and showed up at his door one day with a gun and a question."

"What do you mean, a question?" David asked, his curiosity piqued.

"Supposedly, he asked Stuart what he'd rather live without, 'his balls or his brains?' Next thing, you know . . . bang."

"Well if he's willing to marry Ann, I'm still not sure of what his answer was," David quipped.

Despite David's wisecracks, Andrie continued as she went back to the dining room to finish dinner. "He's always had this reputation as this big sportsman, he-man type. So when his wife left him, after all that happened, he paid her off so she'd keep quiet about the whole story. Especially, the part about his injury. He wants to maintain an image and so does Ann, so it's a mutually beneficial agreement."

"Hmmm, I guess it could work out for them, until he starts borrowing her dildo," David gibed, as he spun around and headed into the kitchen to check on his chocolate soufflé.

"I'm so glad that I have a sensitive friend who listens to my problems without making jokes or passing judgment." Andrie's tone was sarcastic but not truly angry. She was well aware of David's misgivings about Ann. She tolerated his frequent remarks, because she knew they came out of love and concern. He was her closest and most trusted friend.

"Angel face, I need a favor," David said with a sheepish grin, as he returned to the table.

"This is it, right? This is the reason for the dinner and the clean apartment," Andrie conjectured, as she waited for David to continue.

"Well, did you really think that I did battle with that sink from *The Little Shop of Horrors* for my health? Now, don't get all crazy on me . . . OK?" Without waiting for Andrie's response, he continued in a tone of voice that a therapist might use to calm an agitated patient. "Destiny is coming to New York next week. She asked if she could stay with me . . ."

"Why does she need to stay with you? Doesn't she rent hotel suites, so she can trash them like other rock stars do?"

"Come on now. You know she's not like that. All that star stuff is getting to her. Ever since her second album went triple platinum, she hasn't had a moment to herself. She just wants some privacy. She's been going through a really rough time the last six months, since Nicole left her for Sonia Gustafsen. You've heard about Sonia. She's the big blond Swede who won the Olympic gold medal for swimming and opened up that chain of sporting goods stores."

"Of course I know. You said that they were friends, right?"

"*Were* is the operative word here. That friendship's gone down the tubes, now that she took Nicole away from Destiny. It always amazes me how you girls will break up with each other and then go out with each other's best friends . . . or each other's ex-lovers . . . or Siamese twin . . . or something. It's so incestuous."

Cupping her hands around her mouth, Andrie pretended to shout, "Hello . . . can we please stick to one conversation at a time?"

"Well, Destiny said that LA is getting to her and she wants to get away for a while. She thinks that New York would be a good change of scenery and people. Apparently, she's working on some music for a movie that's supposed to take place here, so it just seems right for now. I guess losing Nicole to Sonia was really hard on her."

"She doesn't look too shaken up to me," Andrie said in an unmoved voice as she dabbed her mouth with the linen napkin, then impatiently shoved it under the edge of her plate, appearing ready to leave the table, annoyed by the conversation.

"What do you mean?" David asked, pulling Andrie's napkin out from under the plate and placing it back on her lap, as he pointed to her fork, encouraging her to continue eating.

"Come on, David, there are pictures of her in the magazines practically every week with a different woman. Actually, she looks like she's having a pretty damned good time," she said, angrily chopping at the fish on her plate.

David's tone became more serious. "You know her better than that. That's the way she reacts to pain. It's how she reacted when she had that falling out with you . . . that's why you still have angry feelings toward her. . . ." Suddenly David's words were cut off by Andrie.

"How can you attribute my dislike for her to a misguided puppy love thing, that began and ended over a winter break fifteen years ago?" Andrie snapped at David, then continued without giving him an opportunity to respond. "Destiny has never matured from the way she was back then. She's a grown woman who acts and dresses like a post-pubescent boy. And she's an exhibitionist too. . . . She finally makes a name for herself in music, but she's on the front of every tabloid in the country with her arms or lips wrapped around a different woman every time you see her."

"She can't help it if photographers take pictures of her with her arm around a girlfriend," David said as he tried to defend Destiny.

"I don't think that it's that innocent. Destiny couldn't make her splash as the first well-known, openly gay, woman musician, because there have been too many before her. So she's had to go beyond that to become the first well-known lesbian playboy."

Andrie's anger seemed fresh, almost as though it had been brewing just beneath the surface all the time.

"That's not how Destiny got where she is right now. She worked hard and sacrificed for years to make it. . . . You know that as well as I do. You never gave her a chance, after that winter break incident years ago. And as far as the way she dresses and carries herself, she may be a little rough around the edges, but it's her and it's honest. Don't be such a snob, just because you're with some poised and primped politician," David chided her.

"Oh, I'm a snob, because I prefer a woman with some culture and education to one who dresses like a Hell's Angel, sounds like Forrest Gump and rides around Los Angeles on a Harley." Andrie attacked the trout on her plate with her fork and began to chew vigorously as she glared at David.

"Hon, Forrest Gump was from Alabama. Destiny is from Kentucky; it's a different accent, hers has more of a twang. And she has a degree in biochemistry, remember? We were at NYU together," he reminded her.

"Oh that's right. She was in your fraternity, wasn't she?" Andrie replied sarcastically.

"Andrietta . . . far be it from me to bring up a subject that might embarrass you, but I remember a time when you felt entirely different about Destiny," David said with a cunning grin.

She flashed him a look of disgust, but he continued.

"Now, I know this may annoy you, but . . . what the hell, I'll remind you anyway . . . you were quite taken with Destiny, but you got scared and ran. I always felt that if you had been a little less concerned with what everyone else thought about you back then, things would be very different between you and Destiny today."

"You're out of your mind, if you think that I could have ever ended up with someone like Destiny Anderson . . . someone who doesn't give a damn about how she looks or acts or what she says in public. . . . How could you ever even think that I could–"

"Oh honey, cut the crap. We both know that you didn't always feel this way about her," David said, cutting her off abruptly. He derived a certain devilish delight in goading Andrie about Destiny, which was primarily because he had never stopped believing that they were made for each other. He had accomplished what he set out to do. He started Andrie thinking back to the way she felt when she first met Destiny. As David sat there at the dinner table with her, his mind, too, wandered back along the road of time to when he first met Destiny at a small gay bar on Seventh Avenue South. She had a steady gig, singing there every Wednesday and Friday. He remembered that from the first time he spoke with her, she seemed a paradox in every way. She was friendly and warm, smiling easily when David would engage her in conversation. Yet her wide dimpled grin was often not enough to disguise the sadness he saw hidden behind eyes that were so dark and soulful. Her Kentucky twang and wide boyish stride caused her to stand out in an environment full of far more urbane New York types. He could see that she was accustomed to not fitting in. Standing apart from the crowd might have contributed to her seeming lonely, yet at the same time she appeared to appreciate the distance she put between herself and everyone else. That was just another part of the paradox, David remembered thinking to himself at the time. There was an unaffected strength about the way she maintained her individuality, which he admired from the very beginning, having been an outsider so many times in his own life.

Despite the fact that Destiny rarely socialized with any of the groups of women who frequented the bar, David had noted that there were qualities about her that other women found attractive since she dated quite a number of them. Yet, no one more than three or four times before moving on to the next. As she became closer to him, Destiny confided in David that she was afraid that she would never meet that one woman that she could trust and love totally. This struck a chord in him and as his friendship and respect for Destiny grew, he found himself thinking that despite appearances, she had much in common with Andrie. That thought spurred his desire to have them meet.

Andrie was an extremely social creature who embraced life with both arms and an open heart and it amused David that she maintained a constant string of young male admirers, seeming to thrive on her own popularity, yet never to the point of conceit. Growing up with Andrie, it was obvious to him that her most prevalent shortcomings were a fiery temper and an intractable tenacity when it came to doing things her own way. But he also knew her as honest and fiercely loving. There was no one who knew Andrie better than did David. And as much as she loved her own brothers Michael and Nick, in many ways she was far closer to him. She wrote him every day from the time she left Brooklyn to attend Boston University. There had never been an emotion or a secret she kept from him . . . until her heart, mind and desires had been changed once and for all by Destiny.

That year, by winter break, David had convinced Destiny, who had graduated a semester early, to spend the holidays with him and his family before leaving for California, where she intended to break into the music business. At that time, he was still living with his mother and grandmother in a two-story brick house, next door to Andrie's family on a quiet, tree-lined street in Brooklyn.

He knew that Destiny didn't have much of a rapport with her family. She had often mentioned how much she wished that she had grown up with the love and warmth David had told her of when speaking of his family. It was for that reason that he wanted to share as much of his family and friends as he could with Destiny. He was particularly excited about introducing her to Andrie. David had spent a great deal of time telling each of them about the other. The one thing he told neither of them was that he had a feeling that they would be perfect for each other. The feeling didn't even make much sense to him, since Andrie had never been attracted to women. Perhaps what gave him pause to think was that Andrie had once confided in him that she was puzzled by the fact that she didn't seem to experience the same desires and satisfactions that most of her girlfriends described when discussing the intimacies of their relationships with their boyfriends.

At the time, his response had been that he thought she simply needed to meet the right person.

As David got to know Destiny, something told him that although she was a woman, she ·just might be that person. He was certain that his urge to match them up was a genetically inherited trait. He had seen his mother and grandmother try to fix up his cousins for years. Of course, this case was a bit different than his mother's setting up a blind date between her podiatrist and David's cousin, Irma, with the bad skin. But "who knows," he thought. It was worth a try. Besides, cousin Irma ended up happily married to the podiatrist.

At that point in their young lives, when David brought Andrie and Destiny together, he had no idea of the events that he would be setting in motion.

* * *

It all began that day in mid-December, as David ran slipping and sliding in the season's first snowfall to greet Destiny as she pulled up in her rusty old green Caprice. It was unusual to have such heavy snow that early in the season. The thick layer of soft white lent a pristine beauty to the lawns and row houses of the quiet little neighborhood.

"Welcome to Bensonhurst, Brooklyn," David said, tugging at Destiny through the half-open car window, as soon as she had parked.

"Howdy!" she greeted him, with a friendly Kentucky drawl, as she pushed open the squeaky car door and got out.

"Boy, are you ever gonna stand out in this neighborhood," David replied, teasing her about her southern drawl, while he emptied the back seat of her luggage, a battered green duffel bag, a small black case where she lovingly kept the fiddle her father gave her, and a maroon guitar case.

"So this is where you live. I like it. It took under an hour to get here. I was surprised it was this close," Destiny said as she looked around, taking in the feeling of the surroundings.

"Well, I've been trying to get you to visit here ever since we met, but you were always too busy," David replied.

"Give me a break . . . I had gigs every night and I had to study once in a while. In three and a half years, I never got to see much of anything. . . . Is that thunder I hear in the distance?" Destiny asked, as a somewhat muffled and remote roar could be heard around them.

"What? . . . Oh, that's just the *EL*. The *elevated* train. It's a few blocks away. I'm so used to it, I don't even hear it. After a day or so you won't either," David replied. His hands full, he turned back to tell Destiny to close the car door, but she failed to respond as she stood there looking past him. Realizing that his friend was captivated by something on the street behind him, he turned quickly to find out what it was. It came as almost no surprise that the source of Destiny's sudden preoccupation was Andrie, who had arrived home from school early the prior evening. Andrie was busy, alternately cleaning the snow off her father's blue and tan T-Bird and arguing with her brother over who would get to use the car next. She hadn't noticed David and Destiny watching her.

"Gimme a break, Andrie. My car's in the shop for repairs and I have a date with a girl from Long Island. I have to pick her up in less than two hours. What am I supposed to do?" said a tall, well built young man with dark wavy hair, as he slipped into the down vest he had been holding.

"Why don't you just ask her to pick you up? It is the eighties, you know," Andrie snapped back at him with annoyed eyes that reflected the winter sunlight.

"Don't be such a smart ass. I need the car. Look, it's snowing and I need to make it there in two hours," he persisted.

"So rent a dog sled! Look, we tossed a coin and I won. If you took better care of your own car it wouldn't be in the shop right now. So tough luck. I've got Dad's keys, and I'm using the car," she said, waving the snow scraper at him.

Something about the attitude with which Andrie dismissed her brother intrigued Destiny even more than her good looks. Without taking her eyes off Andrie, Destiny began to ask, "That's not . . ."

"Andrie? It certainly is." David completed her question and provided the answer. Appreciating Destiny's fascination, he continued, "She's something, huh?"

"I'll say," Destiny replied, as she watched the young man, frustrated by defeat, storm back into the house.

"Andrie!" David called out as he walked toward her, still holding Destiny's duffel bag and the two instrument cases.

"Boo Boo," Andrie called back, using David's childhood nickname as she dropped what she was doing and ran over to them. As she came closer, Destiny could see the downy, crystalline flakes of snow drifting through the air and landing lazily on her auburn hair.

Reaching them, Andrie smiled warmly at Destiny. "And this must be Destiny. Your ears must have been burning last night. David spent hours telling me what a fabulous musician you are and what a good friend you've been to him. He says that you're a cross between Billy Joel and Elvis. I can't wait to hear you play. By the way, I'm Andrie."

Destiny already knew that. She smiled back, silently. At that moment, speech was impossible for her. Something about Andrie's eyes–an expression . . . or perhaps the way the flecks of daylight danced in them–robbed her of words.

"I also told her that you're gay and out of the closet. You see, Andrie is a Republican; they don't approve of that," David added with a lighthearted sarcasm.

Smacking David lightly on the back of his head, Andrie argued, "In June I'm gonna be out in the work force and I want to make sure that the economy is thriving. That doesn't make me a bigot or a homophobe. Does it?" Andrie directed her remark toward Destiny.

"I don't know much about economics. But don't let David mislead you about me. I'm no big rebel. I just live my life the way I feel comfortable. For me that means not pretending to be somethin' that I'm not. David told me a whole lot about you too. But I don't remember him tellin' me that name you just called him."

Destiny's tone and easy way were immediately appealing to Andrie.

"Boo Boo? Oh, feel free to call him that whenever you like. . . . Especially in front of some of the neighborhood tough guys," Andrie jested, as she smiled coyly at David.

"She doesn't really mean that," David said, turning to Destiny.

"Don't you think I know that?" Destiny replied, surprised at David for pointing it out.

"Well, who can tell, with someone who yells 'Howdy' on a Brooklyn street?" he joked as he freed one of his hands to give a playful tug on Destiny's wind-blown, brown mane.

"Hey have you ever tasted strufelle?" Andrie directed her question at Destiny, knowing that David was already a fan of the small balls of honey-soaked fried dough.

"No. But if that's some kind of *Eyetalian* food, I'll probably love it," Destiny answered with innocent eagerness to experience the ethnic delicacy offered by this woman she found so enticing.

"Come inside and I'll make us all some coffee and you can try my mother's homemade strufelle," Andrie said, ushering David and Destiny up the front steps to her house. "By the way, you might get away with *howdy* in this neighborhood, but *Eyetalian* is never gonna fly," she joked as she held open the door for Destiny and David.

Once inside, Destiny noticed several arrangements of fresh flowers with cards attached to them.

"Is it somebody's birthday?" she asked as she looked around the neatly kept, yet comfortable-looking living room.

"Oh. The flowers. No. They're from a guy that I'm seeing. He's still up at BU. When I got home yesterday, they were waiting here. Then there was another delivery at dinner time. This morning . . . more flowers. He says that it makes him feel like he's here. He's supposed to stop by on his way down to his parents' home for

Christmas. They live in New Jersey. Anyway, I'll be taking these over to St. Jean's Nursing Home later today. I used to work there as a candy striper when I was a kid. So most of the time when a guy sends me flowers, I keep them one day, then they go straight to St. Jean's."

As Andrie finished speaking, the sound of a door slamming shut in the kitchen reverberated throughout the house.

"What's that?" David asked, somewhat startled by the noise, as he followed Andrie toward the direction from which it had come.

"I would say that it's probably my annoyingly immature brother, Michael, leaving the house by the side door," she told them, as she led David and Destiny into the kitchen. "He probably found my father's second set of car keys and is at this very moment starting up the car," Andrie explained with a cheerfully mischievous gleam in her eye as she slipped off her snow-saturated BU sweatshirt, revealing an equally saturated white cotton T-shirt underneath. The wet fabric sheathed her body closely, providing an almost transparent veil over the erect dark nipples that peeked through. She flashed a quick smile at Destiny, who stood frozen in place, not knowing where to direct her gaze.

Andrie was mercilessly flirtatious in those days. It came naturally to her. She did it without even thinking about it. Observing the dynamic, David couldn't help but wonder if she was intentionally flirting with Destiny. He thought it humorous that Destiny, who was usually in complete control when it came to matters of allurement and seduction, was now suddenly blushing and speechless as Andrie recklessly flaunted her charms.

"You were just outside, arguing loud enough over who would get the car that the whole neighborhood started taking sides, and now you're not even upset that your brother took it?" David asked as he tossed an oversized kitchen towel to Andrie and discreetly nodded toward her breasts.

"How upset can I be when I know that he's gonna have such a lousy time on his date?" Andrie answered as the towel hit her. Then, looking down, she quickly peeled the shirt away from her skin. Although she succeeded at somewhat obscuring the titillating sight, the image was already etched in Destiny's memory.

"How do you know that he's gonna have a lousy time?" Destiny interjected, trying to act as if she had not noticed Andrie's breasts showing through the wet T-shirt.

"How good a time can he have without money?" Andrie laughed, as she produced a worn black leather wallet. "He dropped this in the snow outside, while we were arguing. So, I thought that I'd hold onto it in case he decided to pull something funny." They all began to laugh, especially Destiny. To her, Andrie was everything David had described . . . and so much more.

All these years later, remembering that day in the kitchen, Andrie was still unsure if she had intended to be so flirtatious toward Destiny. As uncomfortable as it was for her to admit now, deep inside, she knew that from the second she had laid eyes on Destiny Anderson, with her careless chestnut hair, boyish walk and dark piercing eyes, something began to stir within her. It was as though some part of her, which had been sleeping all her life, suddenly woke up.

Now, sitting across from Andrie at the dinner table, David remembered her having an equally profound effect on Destiny from the very beginning.

Like the day after Destiny had arrived, when she offered to accompany Andrie in shopping for a Christmas tree. David, who had planned to go along, had something come up at the last minute.

"Are you sure that you really want to come along with me? It may take me most of the day and I don't like using a car to bring the tree home. It feels more like Christmas to carry it back," Andrie said to Destiny, as she stood in David's kitchen, slipping her hands into a pair of bulky, suede-palmed, raglan gloves.

"It don't bother me a bit, girl. Back in Kentucky, I used to find some big ol' dead trees and chop them down. Then I'd split the logs for firewood and haul it all home a couple of hundred pounds at a time, in a wheelbarrow. So, come on and let's find you a

Christmas tree," Destiny said, smiling widely as she opened the door for Andrie, following her from the warm kitchen into the brisk December air.

Three hours and several dozens of trees later, Destiny realized that Andrie wasn't the type to settle for just any tree. She knew exactly what she wanted and wouldn't stop until she had it.

"Are you this way with everything?" Destiny asked over a hot cup of cocoa in a small booth at a luncheonette where they gave their feet a brief rest.

"What do you mean?" Andrie asked back as she looked up from blowing on her hot cocoa.

"I mean that you won't settle for anything less than your perfect tree," she answered.

"That's funny, because no matter what tree I end up with here today, I'll feel like I'm settling," Andrie said as she rummaged through the pockets of the parka that she had placed next to her on the seat. Finally, she pulled out a folded up piece of paper and, opening it up, she handed it to Destiny. It was a page that had been torn out of travel brochure. "See this? This is the perfect tree," Andrie said, pointing to a towering spruce in the foreground whose branches were laden with thick layers of fluffy white snow. "That's in Montana, somewhere. No tinsel, no little lights. Just snow and pine cones. I want to live somewhere that I could look out my window and see a tree just like that someday. You probably think that's silly, huh?"

"No. I don't," Destiny answered. She wanted to tell Andrie how beautiful she was at that moment. She wanted to say how much she would love to be watching her, as she looked out that window at that snow-covered spruce. There didn't seem to be a single thing about Andrie that was less than perfect to Destiny. But she kept a tight rein on her words. She feared saying the wrong thing and seeming foolish, or even worse, predatory. She felt herself falling into Andrie's eyes. It was as if she were drowning . . . and there was nothing she wanted *less* than to be saved from her fate. She wondered what was making her feel that way. Surely, she had met beautiful women before. Yet she had never become captivated by them, she thought to herself, as she sat there drinking cocoa and looking at Andrie.

"David told me that you're a wonderful musician and that when you leave here you're going to the West Coast to look for work in the music business. He also said that you majored in biochemistry. Why not music?" Andrie asked, breaking in two the small round vanilla creme cookie that had come with her cocoa and dipping half of it.

"It's not as crazy as it sounds . . . or maybe it is. I don't know. It's because of a promise I made to my father. You see, when I was real little, he taught me to play a whole mess of instruments. There was the fiddle, the guitar and the piano. He was a preacher, but he loved music. He was the pastor of the Colton Corners Baptist Church. Colton Corners is the town I come from in Kentucky. It's about twenty miles south of Lexington. There were people who would travel from other towns on Sundays just to come to services at our church, so they could hear my dad sing. When I was about seven, he let me play the piano at services. After I'd been doin' that for awhile, I wrote a little song. I guess you'd call it a kinda gospel tune. He let me sing it for the congregation one Sunday at the end of services, and when I was done all these people started clappin' and callin' for me to sing again. I remember the feelin' that came over me when they did that. It was right then I knew I wanted to write songs and sing them for people. I know that's what I was put here to do. I was never real pretty and, Lord knows, I was never real popular, but that don't matter when I sing. Ya see, there's a kind of love that you get from an audience, any audience, when you perform . . . and I'm addicted to that. I need to sing like other folks need to breathe or eat. That's the thing I need to do in life. My daddy realized how singin' made me feel. One day he sat me down and said, *Rags* . . . that was short for rag doll, 'cause I always wrecked my clothes climbin' trees or fallin' off my bike and things like that. . . . Anyway he said, *Rags, if singing makes you feel as*

good as I think it does, then maybe that's what God meant you
to do in your life. But since I can't pretend to know what's in
the Lord's mind and the music business isn't easy to get into, I
want you to promise me that you'll go to college and find
something else that you can make a good livin' at, just in case.
Well, I promised him that I'd do that and he did everything he
could to help me with my music. He never made much money as
a minister, so he used to take photography jobs on the side. You
know, weddings, school pictures, freelancing for the local newspapers . . . all that. But no matter how hard it was on him
financially, he always paid for me to take piano and voice lessons
at a real music academy in Lexington. He took me there three
times a week until he died. So for the last four years when things
got tough between school and gigs I would remind myself of that
promise I made to him and somehow I'd get through."

"I thought David told me all he could about you, but I was
wrong." There was a quiet dignity to Destiny Anderson. It was
clear to Andrie now why David had become so close to her.
Despite her rough appearance and careless demeanor, she was a
surprisingly gentle person. They spent the rest of the day together
and even came upon a seven-foot Douglas Fir tree that seemed to
suit Andrie.

Thinking back, Andrie remembered how much had changed
inside her during that winter break. Desires stirred, feelings grew,
and so much conflict arose. She had never considered the
possibility of being attracted to another woman, even though she
had derived only the mildest physical pleasure from her sexual
encounters with men. Until she met Destiny, Andrie considered this
a temporary problem and attributed it to growing up in a rather
traditional Italian Catholic family. She had felt that eventually she
would meet that one right man who would make her feel what she
knew she was missing. But the more time she spent around
Destiny, the more Andrie had begun to question that assumption.

Every time they were together in a room, it would fill with a
kind of heat. As the days went by, there were exchanges of looks

and inadvertent touches between her and Destiny that caused flutters in her stomach and skipped heartbeats. It was like nothing Andrie had ever felt around anyone else before. It was the sort of thing she had always heard people call, a *chemistry*. All the passions that up until then she had only heard about, were becoming real for her.

Even after the fifteen years that had passed since, it was still alarmingly easy for Andrie to recall the fire that was ignited within her the first time Destiny kissed her. In retrospect, she was sure David had planned it all, just to give them the time alone.

He had explained that he was taking his mother and grandmother shopping that morning and asked Andrie if she could spend some time with Destiny, to keep her company. Without hesitation, Andrie agreed.

Hearing David's mother's car pull out of the driveway, Andrie ran out of her house and next door to David's. She entered through the side door. The sound of the piano filled every level of the large row house. She followed it down into the slightly musty-smelling, wood-paneled basement and stood listening in the doorway behind Destiny. The beauty of the unfamiliar melody struck Andrie as she listened silently. She felt herself trembling inside, as she watched the graceful undulating motion of Destiny's long agile fingers caressing the smooth white keys of the piano, drawing life and beauty from its loins. It was as though Destiny's gentle, powerful hands were delighting the instrument more and more with every stroke, until its music became a cry of ecstasy.

Andrie was captivated as her body began to pulsate in time to the music. She found herself becoming envious of the piano, as she imagined what it might be like to be pleasured by those hands, those talented hands. The music played on and on while her skin began to flush red and her breasts heaved with an unfamiliar need that so totally seized her, it felt as though some ravenous spirit had taken possession of her. Her body throbbed as each note Destiny played vibrated through her, until she dripped wet with a craving to be touched . . . to be taken by those hands. Then, without warning Destiny abruptly ceased playing. With her back remaining toward Andrie, she began to scribble down notes onto a sheet of paper.

Andrie could still remember how her heart raced and her breathing remained heavy as the room went silent. She also remembered how she decided to use surprise as an excuse to touch Destiny. So, creeping up behind her, she lifted her hand to tap Destiny on the shoulder. Then suddenly, without turning around, Destiny reached up and grabbed her wrist in midair. "Gotcha!" she chuckled, as Andrie gasped in shock.

Without letting go of Andrie's wrist, Destiny then stood up, facing her.

They were close enough to read the messages in each other's eyes and too close to speak in anything more than a whisper.

"How did you know I was here?" Andrie asked, allowing her hand to remain in Destiny's gentle grasp, as even that touch sent shock waves through her body.

"Your perfume. It makes me dizzy," Destiny answered, inhaling deeply as she lightly brushed her mouth against the soft smooth skin of Andrie's cheek.

As the heat of Destiny's words warmed her face Andrie murmured breathlessly, "I'm not wearing any."

Each could hear the other's heart pounding. They desperately needed to taste each other.

Destiny pulled Andrie to her and merged their lips in a full, passionate kiss. From the first second they met, every word, look, and touch had been leading to that moment.

They stood there wrapped in each other's arms only a few seconds, before a sound from upstairs disrupted the small world they had just created for themselves. It was David's mother coming through the front door and calling down to Destiny to let her know that she had decided not to go shopping with David and his grandmother.

"I have to go," Andrie said, frightened by the intrusion, as she pulled herself out of Destiny's arms.

"Wait. I'll go with you. We can go for a walk," Destiny said, as she reached for Andrie's arm and affectionately tried to tug her back.

"No!" Andrie replied sharply, then turned and bolted up the stairs and out the side door, leaving Destiny dazed and confused in her wake.

David was Destiny's sole confidant at that time and therefore the only person she told how much she wanted Andrie and how confounded she was by her. "I don't understand it. Every time I try to talk to her about what happened when I kissed her in your basement, she changes the subject. Yet she's still giving me little messages . . . with her eyes, and . . . oh I don't know," she complained to him, as she lifted up the hood of Michael's trouble-plagued red sedan and proceeded to examine what was under it. She continued to bare her feelings as she searched for the source of the car's problem. "I'm goin' crazy. I can't even be in the same room with her, without breakin' into a sweat. She keeps doin' things and sayin' things to make me want her. She knows it, too. Sometimes the moment is just perfect and she'll come real close to me and I'll move to try to kiss her and she pulls away. Believe me, I've been with enough girls to know that I'm not misinterpreting any of this," Destiny said from under the hood of the car. She had become friendly with the entire LaStella family, especially Andrie's two brothers, neither of whom knew nearly as much about cars as Destiny did.

"I know that you aren't misinterpreting anything. I've seen her with you. She's attracted to you and I guess she's handling it the only way she knows how. She's always been a big tease with guys, so maybe that's what she's doing with you . . . or she could just be scared because she's never been with a woman before," David theorized, as he hopped up and down in an effort to keep warm while he watched Destiny pull a screwdriver and a large half moon wrench out of the pocket of her brown leather bomber jacket. "You're really trying hard to win her over, aren't you?" he remarked, implying that Destiny was working on Michael's car as a way to get to Andrie through her brothers.

"Yeah, I guess I am," Destiny admitted with a little grin. "But I'm getting to like her family a real lot, too–I gotta convince Andrie to give me a chance."

"Do you think you can do that?" David asked, wondering if Destiny was beginning to lose patience with the idea.

"Well, I'll tell ya. Gettin' through to that girl is like tryin' to put stockin's on a rooster. It's damned hard. It's gonna hurt ya . . . but it ain't impossible." She told him in her most southern style. Then handing him the keys to the ignition, she said, "Here, start the car, when I give you the signal. I'm gonna be holdin' this air filter valve open."

As he slipped into the driver's seat David continued the discussion, in a slightly louder voice so Destiny could hear him from under the car's hood. "Andrie needs to be in control all the time and these feelings are probably throwing her for a loop. You've just gotta be patient. Besides, as much as I love her . . . and she's one of the kindest sweetest girls in the world . . . I know that she's never been a bed of roses for any of her boyfriends."

"A bed of nails is probably more like it," Destiny yelled out to him, as the car engine started up with a loud roar.

* * *

That evening, David, Destiny, and Andrie had gone to dinner at Rossi's, a quaint little Italian restaurant on the bay. Later, David claimed that he was sleepy from having had too much wine with dinner and that he wanted to go home to bed.

After dropping him off at home, Destiny and Andrie decided to go for a drive. It was a clear cold night. The midnight blue sky lent a perfect backdrop to the Christmas lights that shimmered here and there on the windows and house tops.

Destiny's shabby '73 Caprice convertible was drafty on the passenger's side because of a hole in the roof. Seeing Andrie pull the collar of her heavy wool coat up to cover her ears, Destiny motioned for her to move closer where it was less drafty. Andrie quickly slid over to escape the current as she gave Destiny directions to Shore Road Park. Aside from that, little conversation took place on the way there. The mixture of desire, anticipation, and a need to understand each other induced the gravid silence that made the ten-minute ride seem much longer.

"Where should I park?" Destiny asked, as they arrived at their destination.

"How about there?" Andrie pointed to a unlit area where a street light had burnt out.

The anonymity of the darkness appealed to Destiny, as she pulled the car into the shadows.

Shore Road Park was on a slight hill at the bottom of which they could see the glimmering water of the bay, stretching out like an infinite sheet of black glass.

"How about a walk?" Destiny asked, turning off the headlights.

"OK, but I don't know how long we'll last out there. It's much colder here by the shore."

The silence set in again as they walked through the park, along a path that brought them to the water's edge. Then, with an impulsive lack of delicacy, Andrie broke the silence. "If there's something that you want to say, just say it."

Destiny was dumbfounded as Andrie continued.

"I'm not blind. David hardly had anything to drink and you've had something on your mind all night. So tell me what it is," Andrie demanded, in a tone that sounded confident and in control.

It was obvious to Destiny that Andrie knew exactly what was on her mind and that Andrie in some way derived pleasure from seeing her blushing and speechless. But the patient southerner had reached her saturation point. She wanted Andrie too much to continue playing the game. "Why don't you just rest it for a while, little girl, because I'm really gettin' tired of you yankin' me around 'til I'm too dizzy to see straight," Destiny said in an annoyed tone.

"I don't know what you mean, or what's been bothering you,

but I'm not going to let you take it out on me. Maybe we should go back, now," Andrie answered sharply, as she turned to walk back to the car.

"What are you so damned afraid of?" Destiny asked, in a voice loud enough to cause Andrie to stop and turn around. She stood there stunned as Destiny continued, "You've been havin' a good ol' time for yourself, watchin' me wantin' you so bad that it hurts. You know the power you have and you use it to feed your ego. You know somethin', for somebody so pretty, that sure is a damn ugly trait to have. David said that you've always been like this with your boyfriends. Well, maybe it suits them, but it sure don't suit me. I've had enough of this *hide and seek* thing. I want you and I know that you want me too, but it scares you." Her angry tone had grown more gentle, as she moved closer to Andrie, who was still dazed and uncharacteristically silent.

She was unsure of how to react to what Destiny was saying, but for her ego's sake Andrie needed to stand her ground. "Nothing about you scares me," she announced defiantly.

"Prove it," Destiny dared, leaning forward and kissing her, slowly . . . and deeply, savoring the taste and touch of Andrie's lips and mouth. That kiss served only to whet their hunger for each other.

It caused a quivering sensation in Andrie, which started down below and seemed to rise, like a river about to overflow. There was no hope of controlling it. It was the feeling that had driven her to run away, the first time Destiny had kissed her. It was what she had waited to experience, yet feared to feel. It was desire.

"Don't let go of me," she said, resting her head against Destiny's chest, as the dark winter night cloaked them from the prying eyes of the few strangers who might still be walking through the park.

"Never. I'll never let go of you," Destiny answered, feeling like she had found everything she had ever wanted right there in Andrie's eyes. "You could make me forget that there's a world out there."

"Don't say that. The world out there holds too many dreams for you. And I'd never want to be the reason for even one of them not coming true," Andrie chided Destiny, knowing how much her music meant to her.

"You are my dream," Destiny said, holding Andrie close. "We should go back to the car. It's cold out here. I can feel you trembling," she said, taking both of Andrie's hands in her own and rubbing them, to stop her from shivering.

As they walked back to the car with their arms around each other, there was no one in the park to see them . . . even if there were, it would have changed nothing for them.

Reaching the street outside the park, Andrie pointed down to something on the sidewalk. "Destiny, look at that." There, on the ground, was a maple leaf, frozen to the concrete. Somehow, the way it was encased in the ice with the moonlight hitting it, the ordinary little leaf seemed to look as if it were made of silver. "Isn't it beautiful?" she asked Destiny, who was finding it difficult to take her eyes off Andrie long enough to notice anything else.

"I don't know how to say this without soundin' like some moonstruck, small-town hick . . . but nothing you could show me right now, could be near as beautiful as you."

"I think you're pretty beautiful," Andrie said, noticing how Destiny's dark eyes twinkled as they reflected the blinking red and green lights decorating a nearby house.

"Me? Beautiful? The only other person that ever said that to me was my dad," Destiny said, as she dismissed the notion with a grin.

"Your father was right. You are beautiful and you don't need to be on a stage for anyone to see that."

There was so much conviction in Andrie's voice that it made Destiny feel beautiful for the first time in her life.

"Tell me about your family. I want to know more about what made you," Andrie asked gently.

"Well, I told you about my dad some. Anything good in me, he put there. He always made me feel special. That's important to kids. When I was born, there was some trouble with the delivery. I think it had to do with the umbilical cord and the position I was in. Anyway, my dad told me that they almost lost me, but that I fought real hard to stay alive. He said that it looked to him like I had some kind of destiny to fulfill. That's why he named me Destiny. I was closer to him than anybody else in the world. Besides the fiddle and stuff . . . and how to fix a car . . . I learned how to be a person from him. He was the most honest, compassionate person I ever met. When I was thirteen, he had a heart attack and died while he was helping to put out a fire at a neighbor's house. He was a volunteer fireman. Two years later Momma remarried. I just felt alone. I didn't get along with her husband, Lloyd. He was a lawyer in town. He liked everything real clean and real perfect. He was into appearances . . . and he didn't like mine. He got along real well with my sisters, Lynn and Cheryl Ann. I guess they were perfect enough for him. I know they were too damned perfect for me. I'm gonna tell you somethin' that I've never told anybody but David; since the time I was a little girl and my daddy died, I felt like I had no family. I don't hate them. I just don't feel like I'm part of them. Since I've been here, I've seen how close and affectionate your family is and David's too and I want that."

Andrie kissed Destiny softly, hoping to soothe, even if only briefly, some of the pain she saw there in her. Then looking deeply into her eyes she told her, "I know that you probably don't think so now, but someday you're going to have all of that with your own family . . . because the person you'll love and spend your life with, will be your family. And that person will do everything they can to give you all the love you missed. You'll see." At that moment Destiny felt all the affection she could ever want coming from Andrie.

Andrie had recognized a loneliness in Destiny, but was only now beginning to understand its origin. "Do you ever visit them?" she asked.

"No. I don't contact them and they don't contact me," Destiny replied with a trace of what seemed to be either anger or pain, or both. "Right after my mom married Lloyd Flood, I vowed that I'd get as far away as I could from Colton Corners. So, I've been on my own since I was eighteen. I hated Colton Corners. I never really fit in there when I was growin' up. I was always different from all the other girls, especially Cheryl and Lynn. When they started liking clothes and boys, I started liking cars and girls. We were all a year apart and I was the middle child, but they had all the girl stuff in common, and I was . . . just different. It was real lonely for me. I didn't care if they didn't spend time with me, but they always went out of their way to make me feel even more different than I really was. They used to make fun of me, in real mean ways. They made me feel like a misfit. Like I wasn't a girl; I wasn't a boy . . . sometimes, I felt like I wasn't even a person. Right after my dad died, my mom said that she couldn't afford to keep sending me up to Lexington for music lessons. I couldn't let that happen. It was the only thing I liked about my life. I knew that it was my future. I still believe that. Anyway, I ran out and found a job as a groom's assistant on a horse farm. I lied and said I was fifteen. They believed me, because I was pretty tall for my age. I worked there after school, on the days that I didn't have music lessons. My job was to shovel horse manure most of the time. But at thirteen, I was lucky to have any job at all. Cheryl and Lynn would torture me about how I smelled after work and Lloyd made me shower in the basement, before I was allowed in the house. It sounds kinda funny now, but it wasn't when it was happening. I was about fifteen when Racine came home from boardin' school. She was the daughter of the man that owned the horse farm. She was a couple of years older than me and kinda wild. She was the first girl I ever kissed. She had been with other girls before and she had a steady boyfriend, too. We used to meet at Midnight Creek, it was real quiet there . . . and it was real dark, because of all the trees around it. . . . We never gave words to what we were doin'. It wasn't love, we knew that. It was sort of exploration and lust, I guess. We would call it *meetin'*. We *met* there just about every day for two years. By that time, my being gay was sort of an unspoken truth in town. I guess I didn't dress or walk the way most of the other girls did. It made things more strained at home, but we never discussed it. Then one day, someone saw Racine and me *meetin'* at the creek. After that, the whole town was talkin'. That's just part of the story. Anyway, when Lloyd found out, there was an ugly scene at home. The lucky thing was that I had just won a full scholarship to NYU. So, when he kicked me out of the house, I had a direction to travel in. The scholarship didn't pay for board, so I took every job that I could find, to get by. I hated how that town made me feel. Nobody should ever have to feel like that. People should have the right to be who they are. Someday, I'm gonna be famous and every small-minded, mean-spirited person from my past is gonna eat crow."

There was as much pain as conviction in Destiny's voice as she made that vow. Andrie read both in her expression. She saw that the quiet southerner's guileless and pleasant nature had been pushed to a point of bitterness. Stroking Destiny's thick brown hair, Andrie wished that she could somehow soothe her painful memories of Colton Corners.

"Do you think I'm crazy for believin' that I'm gonna be famous one day?" Destiny asked, wondering what Andrie was thinking about her.

Andrie's eyes locked in on her as she answered, "No. I don't think it's crazy at all. I admire you for feeling that kind of passion about what you want to do in life. I envy it. I still don't really know what I want. Sometimes, I think that I'm just wasting my time and my parents' money at school. It's like I'm waiting for some big change to come over me and give me a direction to follow. The only thing that I am sure of, is that I always want to be secure."

"Secure. How?" Destiny asked.

"Every way possible. Financially, family . . . every way." Andrie saw the puzzled look on Destiny's face, so she continued to explain. "You've seen my father . . ." Andrie paused.

"Sure, I really like Rocco."

"He's the best . . . and he loves my mother and my brothers and me more than anything. But he's not my real father, my natural one, I mean. That one left my mother when I was five. He left without any kind of good-bye or anything. He even cleaned out a joint bank account he had with my mother. He was a musician. I was really little, but I remember him playing the saxophone in the house sometimes, when he wasn't working. For the most part, he was away so much, I didn't even miss him when he finally left us for good. He wasn't much of a father when he was around. He was drunk a lot. My mother always said that she married him for all the wrong reasons. He was handsome, talented and he swept her off her feet with his charm. She said that her friends warned her not to marry a musician. They told her that musicians weren't stable and that he would probably cheat on her and leave her for someone else. He ran away with some woman who sang with his band. He'd been cheating on my mother from way before that, though. I remember one time when I was playing in his car and I found a pair of ladies' panties. I was too young to know what that meant, so I brought them into the house and gave them to my mother. I didn't understand why she started to cry. I didn't know that they weren't hers. He took everything when he left. We were so poor that we had to live in a one-room basement apartment that had no heat or hot water. If it weren't for some friends and relatives giving us clothes and food, I don't know what would've become of us. Every Saturday, my mother would go to the butcher and buy exactly one pound of chopped meat. She would make meatballs on Sundays for my brothers and me. She stretched out the meat so much that we were still eating meatballs for lunch on Tuesday. After awhile the butcher realized that my mom didn't have much money and that she had to feed three kids, so he started to do little things to help. So when mom would order a pound of chop meat, she'd get home there would be at least two pounds of it. Sometimes he would wrap up a couple of steaks and tell my mother that it was a gift for being such a good customer.

One Thanksgiving, he gave us a turkey. He delivered it himself. That was the first time I met the man that was going to be my father. My mother was lucky. She got a second chance at happiness for herself and for us. I'm gonna do whatever I can to make sure that I choose the right person the first time around . . . someone who's always gonna be there, and be stable, and won't leave. Nothing like my real father."

Just then, Destiny saw the hurt, frightened little girl that lived inside Andrie. She wanted Andrie to know that she would never hurt her. For some inexplicable reason, Destiny suddenly remembered the picture of the spruce tree in Montana. She wished that somehow, someday, she could give that spruce tree to the little girl inside of Andrie. For a few moments they just stood looking out toward the bay.

"Do you remember when I surprised you in David's basement the other day?" Andrie asked.

"When we kissed?" Destiny whispered, smiling, as she enjoyed the memory.

"Yes. Right before that, you were playing something on the piano. It was beautiful. Was it something you wrote?"

"It's something I wrote for you . . . but it's not finished yet. I'm fixin' to give it to you for Christmas." Destiny seemed proud and a bit shy about it at the same time.

"I wish that there was something that I could give you that was as beautiful."

"Sweetness, you already have," Destiny said, kissing Andrie tenderly on the face and lips, then taking her hand as they began to walk back.

Looking down, Andrie noticed that the ice which enveloped the maple leaf was beginning to melt. "Let's go before it melts completely. I want to remember it being silver."

All these years later, sitting in the dinning room of her apartment, Andrie remembered the enchantment and exhilaration of that night. Yet as quickly as the memory of those emotions came back to her, Andrie forced them from her mind. She believed that too much had occurred in the days, months, and years that followed that night.

*   *   *

Although so much had changed in all their lives since then, David could still recall how Destiny came home that night and told him about her evening with Andrie. She had burst into his room, waking him from a sound sleep. "Davey, wake up, man. I have to tell you what happened," she said, flopping down on the narrow bed next to him.

"Don't call me that. I hate it when you call me that," he replied sleepily with his eyes still shut.

Destiny continued without apology. "We had a beautiful night. We kissed. We talked. We walked. . . . What do you think?" She waited eagerly for a response.

"I think that my mother must be thanking God right now that I have a woman in my room in the middle of the night. By breakfast she's probably gonna ask if you'll convert to Judaism."

"Would you be serious and listen to me," Destiny insisted, as she playfully punched David in the shoulder.

"Ouch," he groaned, as he rubbed his arm. "Hey, watch it with that dyke stuff. I bruise easily. . . ." Then opening his eyes, he saw Destiny's face beaming with happiness. "So you kissed her again, huh?"

"Yep. And this time she didn't run. You know, she makes me feel like this whole world is mine. There's that part of me that I still carry around from Colton Corners and until tonight it used to pain me to think on it. But Andrie did somethin' to it. She touched it and it stopped hurtin' . . . I want to be able to do the same thing for her. She told me about when her real father left them."

"She told you about that? She never talks about that. Not even with me," David replied with a look of surprised satisfaction. He knew that if Andrie spoke about that to Destiny, she had to feel something very special for her. David was proud of himself for having brought them together. *Why not be proud,* he thought to himself, Andrie and Destiny were a much more attractive match than his cousin Irma and the podiatrist.

Then, pondering out loud, Destiny went on, "I don't think that she's crazy about musicians though. . . . You know because of her father . . . the one that abandoned them."

"Well, I'm sure that you're nothing like him, so don't worry," David assured her.

"I know that, and she's opened up a lot to me, but I think that she's still a little scared of letting someone get too close because of that," Destiny said, staring up at the ceiling in thought.

David, in turn, stared at her, becoming concerned as he realized that her observation was probably correct.

"If you think that there's a part of Andrie that's still afraid of getting too close to anyone, aren't you a little scared of her realizing how hard it is to carry on a relationship with another woman in this society? . . . Don't get me wrong, I believe that you're perfect for each other, but timing is important. Take it slow with her. As much as she may want this, it's a big change for her," he advised, with a maturity that went well beyond his twenty years.

"I'll give it time. I'm even thinkin' that New York isn't such a bad place to try to make it in the music business. Maybe I should forget about California for a while and keep trying here. Whatever happens, I know we'll be fine. Don't worry," Destiny replied, too wrapped up in the euphoria of the moment to consider his warning, as the distant rumble of an approaching train on the elevated tracks disturbed the calm night around them.

Destiny and Andrie spent most of the next few days together. During that time, David saw that Andrie seemed happier and more at ease than he had ever known her to be with anyone else, and Destiny was like a new person. The loneliness that once showed in her eyes had completely faded away. She was happy, down to the very core of her being. They seemed to fit together as though nature had tailor-made them for each other. As happy as that made David, his concern lingered.

Despite his warning to her to take her time, David saw Destiny falling deeply in love with Andrie. She was ready to love and be loved, totally. She had lived on her own and dealt with pain, disappointment and all the other elements a person needs to grow. But, he knew that Andrie had led a far more sheltered life. David worried about whether she was really ready to deal with her feelings.

In the years that had passed since then, David had become certain that it was this unfortunate combination of the two personalities, maturing at different paces, that doomed Destiny and Andrie's budding relationship. Their happiness was fated to vanish like the snow that's washed away by a late December rainstorm.

                              *   *   *

It was two days before Christmas and Destiny had gotten an early start on the day to peruse the myriad of shops and stands that lined the streets under the elevated train line that hovered above Eighty-Sixth Street. By late morning she had returned to David's house loaded with packages.

"What's all this?" he asked, opening the front door to let her in.

"Well, I did some Christmas and Chanukah shopping. I got your grandma a robe. I hope she likes pink," Destiny said, as she spread a bulky pink terry-cloth robe out on the kitchen table, then continued, ". . . and I got your mom a kitchen radio. It mounts under the cabinets. So when she's cooking she could listen to me on the radio . . . after I make it big, of course. I'll put it up for her before I leave."

"You didn't have to do all this," David replied, pointing to the packages, "but since you did, what did you get me?" he added as he plunged his hand deeply into the large white shopping bag, only to have Destiny immediately jerk the bag away and slap his wrist.

"You stop that now," she admonished him, in a maternal

fashion that, at times, came very naturally to her. "Be good and I'll give you your present," she said, producing a tiny narrow box with little blue and white menorahs all over it. "I had them wrap this in real Chanukah paper. Go on and open it," she said, handing him the small package.

Wasting no time, David stripped the wrapping paper off the package and pulled the top off the small box, exposing its contents. "It's beautiful. I love it," he declared, as he removed a polished teak wood pen from the box to look at it more closely.

"I had them engrave your initials on it," Destiny said, taking pride in her successful choice of a gift. "I wasn't real sure of what to get a future accountant, but I figured a good pen would always come in handy, since you'll probably be doin' a fair amount of writin'."

"I don't know what to say. It's perfect. Thank you. And who is that little package for? Could it be a Christmas gift for little miss 'A'?" David asked in a sly, suspicious tone, as he pointed to a small rectangular jeweler's box.

"Not exactly. Ya see, I wrote her a song that I'm fixin' to give her for Christmas. This was in a jeweler's window and it looked just like a frozen leaf we saw when we took that walk in the park last Friday," Destiny explained, as she opened the box and showed him the small silver maple leaf on a long handmade Spanish silver chain. "I'm giving it to her tonight," she added.

"That's perfect. I just saw Michael and Nicky. They said that they were going to a football game, tonight . . . and her parents just left, to visit her Aunt Rosanne in New Jersey. They'll be gone until real late. They never get back from there before midnight. So, it looks like the two of you will have the house to yourselves all evening . . . *Binaca* time, I love it," David said, rubbing his hands together in delight.

*   *   *

As evening approached, Destiny slipped the slim box into the inside of her brown leather bomber jacket and headed out the door of David's house.

"Wait, Des. Take this with you," David called after her, as he removed a chilled bottle of champagne from the refrigerator. "I thought this might be a nice touch," he added, handing it to her.

"Thanks . . . I mean for everything," Destiny said, taking the bottle from him. She headed toward the door, then stopped and turned to speak again. "This is special . . . she's special. You know, going with all those girls at school was never really what I wanted. It was just a way of feeling good about myself, after all those years of feeling like a freak in Colton Corners. This is different. I love Andrie," she said with a wide smile sweeping across her face as she walked out the door.

As David watched her heading next door to surprise Andrie, he realized that despite her durable, even boyish exterior, Destiny Anderson was every bit as vulnerable as any other woman in love.

A late afternoon snow flurry had left a thin coating of white over the sidewalk and steps that led to Andrie's house. Destiny decided to use the side door, since she wanted to surprise Andrie. She was too happy and excited to give any thought to either the footsteps in the snow ahead of her, or the presence of an unfamiliar car at the end of the narrow driveway. Slipping into the house, Destiny walked lightly across the kitchen and toward the living room. Her hand was flat against the kitchen door and about to push it open when she heard Andrie's voice. She remained quiet, assuming that Andrie was talking on the phone. Then she heard a man's voice, answering. Destiny stopped for a moment. The male voice was unfamiliar, sounding like neither Andrie's father nor brothers. Pushing the door open gradually, she was struck by the site of Andrie lying on the living room couch, her blouse opened, kissing and embracing a well-built young man with dark hair. Remaining frozen behind the door, she saw the couple get up and head toward the stairs. Destiny's heart was pounding so hard in her chest that she was afraid Andrie would hear it. Her body flushed red, as shock and anger coursed through her veins like a wildfire whose embers would remain smoldering, long after that day.

Destiny ran from the house and down the driveway toward the sidewalk, angrily tossing the bottle of champagne into the bushes, where, cushioned by the foliage and snow, it landed with a muffled thump. Reaching the pavement, she stood transfixed, staring up at Andrie's bedroom window, which faced the street. She was certain they were up there by then. She felt as though her eyes were penetrating the shades and ruffled cotton curtains, as a vivid image of the dark-haired man holding, touching and entering Andrie burned assiduously into her brain. In her mind Destiny could see him groping, sweating and thrusting, as he took his pleasure from the woman she thought was hers. Her face was red with rage and her body trembled as she brought to bear all her strength to keep from running back into that house and stopping at nothing to get Andrie away from this anonymous interloper. But she knew that she had no right to do that, so she remained riveted, never turning her eyes from Andrie's window as she continued to torment herself with visions of what was happening in that room.

Destiny realized that this was probably the boyfriend Andrie had mentioned when they first met. The one who sent the flowers and who planned to visit on his way to New Jersey. Brian . . . she remembered his name was Brian. It had come up once or twice in conversation. But Andrie had acted as though she wasn't even remotely interested in him, sexually. How could this nightmare be happening? Destiny asked herself . . . and how could she have been so misled by someone she trusted so much?

Slightly over a half hour had passed when the sky, which had been overcast all day, suddenly grew dark. In the distance, streaks of lightning crossed the dusky firmament. The approaching storm would be no deterrent to her, as she remained motionless and waiting, with her fists clenched tightly at her sides.

Then, from the driveway, she heard the sound of a car engine being started. The tall, attractive dark-haired man had exited the house through the side door. A few drops of cold rain had begun to fall. They did nothing to quench the angry fire inside Destiny, which burned hotter with every second she waited.

She would be confronting Andrie within the next few moments. The palms of her hands started to sweat and her stomach knotted, as she watched the car pull out of the driveway. She saw Andrie walk out to the curb and wave good-bye as it made its way down the block.

Before Andrie had a chance to turn and see her, Destiny began to walk toward her as though she had just come from David's house. She greeted Andrie with a smile, while pain and outrage tore at her like hungry animals, ripping her apart from inside. Destiny was no stranger to holding in her anguish. It was an ability she had perfected growing up in Colton Corners.

"Oh, hi," Andrie said, visibly shaken by Destiny's sudden appearance.

A crack of thunder rang out in the distance as they stood on the snow-covered street, facing each other with mounting tension.

"So what did you do today?" Destiny asked. All expression was temporarily absent from her face.

"Nothing much . . . I have a few things to do inside. Why don't you come over in about an hour? We'd better get in before it starts to pour. I'll see you in an hour. OK?" Andrie said, starting to turn away. A abrupt clap of thunder rang out directly above them as Destiny grabbed her arm. Andrie could see the fury suddenly blaze forth from Destiny's dark eyes.

"What kind of fool do you take me for?" Destiny asked in a tone that contained as much pain as it did anger.

Andrie was frightened by the expression she saw on Destiny's face. It forced her to face the reality of what she had just done. At that moment she couldn't even explain why she had slept with Brian. She wasn't in love with him. She wasn't even attracted to him. Yet, something inside compelled her to make love with him. Whatever it was, it felt nothing like desire. Andrie knew what desire was. She felt it for only one person, Destiny. As Destiny barraged her with questions and accusations, Andrie realized that there was no way to make her understand why this had happened, or how she felt. She didn't understand it herself.

Destiny's voiced cracked, as she did her best to keep herself from crying. "How could you do this to me? . . . I was just part of some game to you. You wanted to see if you had the same effect on a woman as you do on men, so you strung me along and made believe you cared about me."

"That's not true. I would never do that to you. I do care about you . . . I'm just not sure that I can do this, right now. You don't care about not fitting into society. I'm not like you. I don't think that I can be like that. At least not at this point in my life." Andrie's voice was trembling as her eyes filled with tears, but Destiny was too hurt to believe that there was any sincerity there.

"You seemed pretty sure about everything, until now. You played me the same way you did with the guys you've dated. You can't help yourself. I was just another person to give you attention. You never gave a damn about me," Destiny said with an accusing glare.

"You're wrong . . . can't you understand how difficult all this is for me. I never told you that I would stop dating men. There was no commitment between us."

The rain was now teeming down on them, but neither one reacted to it. The fleecy white snow that had coated the streets was rapidly transforming into mounds of semi-transparent slush under the pouring rain.

Destiny continued to bombard Andrie. "You told me how you needed someone stable and secure. Why? What stability or security do you offer anybody? I was falling in love with you. I thought that I could share my life with you." Destiny's voice was getting louder as tears mixed indistinguishably with the rain that rolled down her face.

"Please Destiny, let's go inside my house. The whole neighborhood shouldn't have to know about this," Andrie pleaded.

"Sure. Of course. Let's keep this great big, ugly mistake you made just between us," Destiny responded in a voice that was now just an exaggerated whisper as she continued to hold Andrie's arm in her grasp. "I was in your house once already today. That was enough for me."

"What do you mean?" Andrie asked.

"How do you think I found out about this? I saw you all over that guy when you were in the living room. . . . Then, I saw you take him upstairs."

"You came into my house and spied on me? Who the hell do you think you are? You had absolutely no right to do that." Andrie's tone became indignant.

"I wasn't spying. I was there to surprise you, but I got the surprise instead. You're only angry because you got caught." Destiny was beginning to raise her voice again.

"I told you before, I don't need everyone on the block to hear us. Do you know how my parents would feel if this got back to them?" Andrie said, nervously looking around the empty street, as the rain formed currents that coursed past them on the way to the sewer at the end of the block.

"Are you goin' to deny everything inside you and lie to the world just so you can go on pleasin' your family?" Destiny continued with a cutting intensity, staring angrily at Andrie.

Destiny's question angered Andrie even further.

"When I first met you, you said that you weren't a rebel, but that's not true, because you are. You want to change the world . . . I just want to live in it. Maybe I'm afraid because I care about what my family thinks of me. I'm trying to do what I think is right," Andrie tried to explain through her tears.

"You think that it's right to try to be something that you're not? You'll never be happy that way. You've gotta be what God made you, not what other people want you to be. That's just plain wrong," Destiny argued as she tried to keep her voice down for Andrie's sake.

"Don't you dare tell me what I'm doing is wrong. I care about my family and I don't want to hurt them. Maybe if you cared as much about your family as you do about your music you'd still have them."

Even as the words fell from her lips, Andrie already wished that she had never said them. She spoke out of anger and frustration. She didn't believe a word of what she was saying . . . but it was too late. The words fell hard on Destiny and cut deeply into her. She couldn't believe that she had trusted Andrie enough to have confided in her such personal feelings about her family and her dreams.

She released Andrie's arm as they both stood stunned in utter disbelief of the pain they had inflicted upon each other. The tears from both of their faces fell to the sidewalk between them and swirled around to blend together in a sad mixture by the force of the rain.

Nothing else was said. Destiny left New York and headed west that same night.

* * *

The years that passed since never fully erased the pain of that day, or the feelings of betrayal, frustration and guilt that went along with it. Somewhere inside each of them every lie, truth and shed tear lived on.

David had stirred up those memories for Andrie with only a few words. Yet, as she gazed briefly into the glass of wine in front of her, pride prevented her from admitting the depth of what she once felt for Destiny. Immediately, she returned herself to the reality of the moment and attempted to dismiss the topic.

"You're talking about something that happened when I was a kid in college. Well, kids do stupid things. I'm a grown woman now . . . and my tastes and sensibilities have matured. Whatever happened then means nothing to me now. I just happen to find the Destiny Anderson of today, a typical Hollywood type. Shallow, insincere, and promiscuous. What I'm saying is that I would rather have every tooth in my head extracted without the benefit of anesthesia than to spend one second in a room with her."

"Ophelia, darling, I fear you're protesting far too much. . . . If you asked *me,* I'd say you still hurt from that relationship."

"I don't know who you're making roll over in their grave more, Freud or Shakespeare." Andrie used her most sarcastic tone, but David continued, tenaciously.

"It seems to me that the way you react every time Destiny's name is mentioned is a sign of unresolved conflict," he said, taking another sip of wine, as he watched Andrie react to his prodding. As absurd as it seemed, he still harbored a flickering spark of hope to see the two people he loved so much find each other again.

"Why is it that everyone who's in therapy suddenly feels qualified to psychoanalyze everyone else who's not?" Andrie asked curtly.

"You're right. I admit that I've become a tad more obnoxious since I've been in therapy." David's frank admission caused them both to laugh.

He followed the brief moment of levity with a more sober, sensitive expression as he shifted the conversation back to the topic of Destiny. "Seriously, it's been a long time since you and Destiny and I got together."

"Every few years you get the bright idea that it would be nice for the three of us to get together . . . and it's always a disaster. You got in one of these moods a little over a year ago, right after she won that award for Best New Artist and I let you drag me to one of her concerts, remember?"

"Oh yeah. We were supposed to meet her in her dressing room but you were being pigheaded about meeting her there . . . so you waited outside while I went in."

"Yes . . . and I was attacked by two of her security gorillas." Andrie grew indignant as she recalled the incident.

"Darling, that was your own fault. You refused to wear the pass you were given and you stayed outside her dressing room, pacing back and forth while you waited for me. They thought you looked like some disgruntled, stalking groupie . . . and then you got snotty with them when they tried to escort you out."

"They were going to have me arrested," Andrie reminded him, in an irate tone.

"Well, you *did* take a swing at the guard. . . . Anyway, we identified you before it went any further . . . and Destiny even apologized to you," David snickered.

Still incensed by the memory, Andrie got up from the table and fumed, "She enjoyed it. She loved seeing me in handcuffs."

"Well, yes, she did say that she thought they were the perfect accessory for you," David mumbled under his breath, grinning as he remembered. Then he continued, "Look, nothing like that will happen this time. We're not meeting her at a concert. In fact, Destiny will be quietly staying right here in your apartment." Saying that, he closed his eyes and braced himself for the explosion.

"What?" Andrie screeched, as she stopped in her tracks and spun around. "You're kidding me. This is one of your obnoxious little jokes, right? . . . Say that you're kidding," Andrie pleaded, as her anxiety mounted.

"I was really hoping you that could help me out with this. I can't have her stay with me. Remember the massive flood I had in my apartment last week, when the pipe broke in my living room ceiling? Well, they're going to be working on my apartment the week that Destiny will be here. It's the only week they can paint my apartment and repair the plumbing and the ceiling. I can't even stay there myself."

Andrie shook her head and waved her hands in front of her. "No. No. No. She can stay in a hotel . . . or . . . or something. No!"

"Andrie, she's really hurting right now. She needs to have some privacy. I can't tell her to stay in a hotel. It's miserable for her in LA. She was almost in tears when she called me. She just wanted to get away from everything for a little while. The last time I remember her that down was when she left New York fifteen years ago." David's attitude was sincere and sympathetic when he spoke of Destiny's pain. It made Andrie remember the hurt she saw on Destiny's face, so long ago, in that driveway as it rained.

"Come on now. Destiny and I couldn't be in the same room for more than five minutes before we'd be at each other's throats. . . . Besides, if she stayed here, there would be groupies and reporters at my door in no time flat. I don't need that trouble," Andrie replied in a calmer, but still unyielding tone.

"Can't you just soften up this once and help her?" David persisted.

"Helping her is one thing, but you're asking me to set up house with her. Even if she were someone that I liked or that I got along with, I couldn't possibly let her stay here with me. What am I supposed to tell Ann? . . . *Honey, I have the most openly predatory lesbian of the twentieth century living with me for awhile and by the way . . . I was involved with her at one time.*"

"Predatory? You make her sound like a character out of an Anne Rice novel. Trust me, I'll hang garlic and crucifixes around your bedroom door. That should keep her away. Look, she's working on some songs for a film that takes place in New York, so she'll be so busy writing, she won't even have *time* to try to compromise your virtue."

"No. I simply can't do it. There's no way," Andrie said, shaking her head nervously.

"OK. I knew that you would react that way so I procured myself a bargaining chip," he told Andrie cryptically.

"What are you talking about?" she asked impatiently as she urgently searched her liquor cabinet for something stronger than the white wine she had been drinking.

"Well, I spoke with Paul Gowan and he's agreeable to the idea of doing a feature article on Ann and her work with Women's Way in an upcoming edition of *Profiles*. Just do this one favor for me and I'll make sure he does the feature," he said in a tone meant to tempt Andrie.

She knew that David's offer was genuine. He had been close

friends with Paul Gowan since college. She also knew that Paul trusted and respected David's opinion, since David was the only person that had faith and supported his idea to start the magazine two years ago.

Profiles was a weekly magazine, focusing on New York happenings and personalities. And although it was the newest weekly magazine to hit the stands, its sales were going through the roof. It would soon be *the* magazine to be seen in.

The idea of a feature article on Ann was more than appealing to Andrie. It was December, and Ann was up for re-election in less than a year. Andrie knew how important good press would be to her campaign in the coming months. She took a deep breath and agreed, with reservations, to David's proposition. "All right, but I have two conditions. First . . . I don't want the article done now. I want it to come out closer to election time. Second . . . no one is to know that Destiny is staying in my apartment . . . no one. God knows what Ann would think if she found out Destiny Anderson was staying here with me."

"I can agree to both conditions. In fact, Destiny's main concern is that no one should know where she's staying." David was beaming with satisfaction.

"Does Destiny know that you want her to stay here?" Andrie asked as she poured herself a Dewar's straight up.

"No. But I'll take care of all that. It's going to be so nostalgic for you," he bubbled, putting his arm around Andrie's shoulder as she threw her head back, emptying the glass of Scotch down her throat in one swallow.

Chapter Two

Friday at Kennedy airport was hectic with travelers leaving for the weekend. David stood at the gate impatiently searching the crowd of faces coming through. He became concerned as the last few passengers passed him by. He was sure that this was Destiny's flight, but where was she, he wondered. Suddenly, he was thrown off balance as he was playfully tackled from behind by a ragged green duffel bag. He turned to see Destiny's wide smile. For a split second, which seemed longer to both of them, he just looked at his friend. Her five-foot-six-inch frame had remained unchanged from year to year. Destiny was neither slim nor heavy, but somewhere in between, with large bones and strong muscular limbs. She was wearing the same brown leather bomber jacket, which had survived many winters since she first saw it in the window of a thrift shop on Canal Street, some sixteen years before. She also sported her standard faded jeans, brown suede cowboy boots and dark glasses. Her shoulder-length brown hair was carelessly pulled back in a ponytail, which protruded from the back of a black Chicago Cubs baseball cap.

A sudden rush of memories flooded David's mind. As they wrapped their arms around each other, both friends realized that nothing had really changed. It never mattered how much time would pass between meetings. The bond of friendship that they shared would always keep them close.

"You must have walked right by me and I never recognized you," he said with a surprised smile that lit up his face as he kissed Destiny on the cheek.

"I was the first one off. I've been havin' a good ol' time watchin' you there, lookin' for me in the crowd," she said, pulling off the silver-rimmed sunglasses and revealing the sparkle in her intense dark eyes, as she flashed him an amused grin.

"Is this it? . . . A duffel bag, a backpack and a keyboard case?" David asked with a look of distress, as he surveyed what Destiny had been carrying.

"This is actually overpacking by my standards," she observed with a nod.

"It looks like you're going on a survival weekend. Darling, with your money, couldn't you afford some real luggage . . . Gucci or Louis Vuitton, or something? Really, dykes don't know how to spend money." David shook his head in mock exasperation as he threw the bags over his shoulder. "And did you gain a couple of pounds?" he teased as he slipped his arm around Destiny.

"Did you lose more hair?" she countered, jokingly rubbing her hand over David's slightly receding crop of red hair, as the two headed out of the airport terminal.

The ride to Manhattan would take less than an hour. David needed to explain the change in arrangements to Destiny as soon as they settled into the back of the taxi. "We have a slight change of plans. I had a terrible flood in my apartment, so all the repairs are being done right now. Meanwhile, I'm staying at a hotel . . . but everything is fine, because Andrie suggested that you stay at her place while you're here." David almost choked on his lie.

"Wait a minute here. You're staying at a hotel and I'm staying with Andrie? This is a real bad idea. Maybe I should take my chances at a hotel."

"No, don't be silly. Andrie is looking forward to seeing you. Besides, if you checked into a hotel, it wouldn't take ten minutes before everyone you wanted to avoid would be at your door," David asserted.

"I can't believe this. How can I spend an entire week with that spoiled, hot-headed, obsessive closet case? You know, after all she put me through, it's amazing that I didn't go straight," Destiny said, pulling off her dark glasses and rubbing her eyes. She was exhausted from the flight and barely had the energy to continue to resist.

"Andrie's really mellowed. You know that she's been in a

relationship for seven years now." There was almost a twang of regret in his voice as David spoke of Andrie's relationship.

"Of course, Ann Capwell," Destiny said.

"Yes, and I still don't like the woman and I don't trust her either," David quickly added.

"Well now, if that woman has ever done anything wrong, I'm sure that she's been payin' her penance for the last seven years," Destiny told him as she stretched out her arms, placing one around David's shoulder. "So what's little Miss Andrie doin' these days. . . . Still playing gay in the bedroom and straight in the boardroom?" Destiny inquired sarcastically.

"She came to terms with all that a long time ago. Unfortunately, Ann is so uptight about family-values issues and her image that she's had Andrie date men, just as a cover. . . . In fact, Ann is actually planning to marry some guy, just to solidify her wholesome, all-American, heterosexual image."

"How does Andrie feel about that?" Destiny's tone and a barely detectable expression in her eyes betrayed some hidden concern for Andrie, which didn't go unrecognized by David.

"She'll never admit it to me, but I think that she's in a lot of emotional pain right now and no matter how she denies it, I'm sure that she's unhappy in the life she has with Ann. I don't know why she stays in that relationship. I don't know if it's pride or fear of being alone or what, but as hard as Ann makes her life, she won't leave. And she'll never admit that she's unhappy."

The taxi had almost reached its destination, the West Village brownstone where Andrie lived.

"So are you going to stay?" David asked hopefully, as they got closer.

"It sounds like Andrie's having a bad enough time with Ann . . . I can't stay in an apartment with them."

"They don't live together. You don't think that Ann Capwell would ever consider living in Greenwich Village, do you? . . . Andrie is lucky that Ann even visits her here. That's one of the problems with their relationship. So, you won't be getting in anyone's way."

Destiny thought about it for a moment. David tried to read her mind, as he told the driver to pull in front of a well-kept, three-story brownstone in the middle of the block.

"All right," she conceded with a smile. "I'll give it a try. If it doesn't work, I'll take my chances at the Plaza or something." With that, she put her dark glasses back on, pulled the cap's brim even lower on her forehead.

"Fabulous," he replied, as he paid the driver and stepped out of the cab with Destiny following him. The thin, swarthy driver smiled and thanked them in a heavy Mid-East accent, then proceeded to remove Destiny's luggage from the taxi's trunk.

David led Destiny up the front steps of the brownstone. "I wish that they would fix this door; the lock is always broken," he complained as he pushed open the huge six-panel oak door. Destiny followed him up the two flights of steps inside.

"Oh, I'll probably be out kinda late tonight. Andrie will be OK about that, won't she?" Destiny asked as they reached the apartment door.

"Of course. She figured that you would probably have different schedules." With that David unlocked the door and handed the key to Destiny. "So, where are you going tonight, anyway?"

"Well, I was kinda trapped into sayin' yes to a party," she replied, glancing briefly at the key in her hand, finding it hard to believe that she had really agreed to stay with Andrie.

"How did that happen? I thought that the only person who knew that you were coming to New York was Maggie, your manager."

"That was almost true, but I told Harry Stern that I was planning to get away for awhile."

"Why did you tell him?" David asked, knowing that Destiny had originally planned to tell no one at all.

"Well, he and his wife were really good to me during the break up with Nicole. They have a house right near me in LA. So, when they're out there they drop by a lot. I guess he was just concerned when he heard that I needed to get away."

"So how does all this end up in a party?" David was curious.

"Well, Harry and Elaine are really New Yorkers at heart and they're still involved in different causes and charities over here. So, when I told him that I was going to New York for a while, he invited me to some fundraiser they were sponsoring. It's tonight. At first I told him, 'no way,' because I didn't want to deal with the press and all that. But Harry said it was a closed party and there wouldn't be any reporters. So, I agreed to drop by."

"Did he say what the fundraiser was for?" David could hardly contain his delight when he realized that Destiny and Andrie were going to see each other even sooner that he had planned. He chuckled, as he wondered briefly if this were some sort of omen.

"It's for some kind of project to help abused women. I know where it is and the time it starts; that's it. I guess that I'll just bring a blank check with me and make it out when I get there."

Hearing that, David pulled a small dove-gray invitation from the left, inside pocket of his jacket and began reading from it. "Let's see, Club Vingtune at seven-thirty this evening. The cause is the Women's Way project and the fundraiser is being sponsored by Harry Stern and his wife, but it's being co-hosted by Congresswoman Ann Capwell."

"Ann Capwell? Andrie's Ann Capwell?" Destiny asked in disbelief, dropping her duffel bag down on the living room floor as she divided her attention between the conversation and her sudden urge to glance around the room for signs of the Andrie she remembered.

"The one and only . . . and Andrie's been helping the Sterns by arranging the guest list and so forth. She knows who to seat with whom and who needs to avoid whom, or whatever. I can't believe that she didn't see your name."

"Well, that's because my name never appeared on any guest list. I told Harry to keep it to himself that I was coming. I figured that I could drop in, write a check for whatever cause it was, have a drink and leave. Now, I'm really not sure if I should show up at all." Destiny was still gazing around the living room as she spoke. She noticed the way the sunlight played off the soft comfortable colors with which the room was decorated.

"Drop by for a few minutes. If you don't want to stay, the two of us can go somewhere else for a few drinks and catch up on everything in each other's lives, OK?"

"Yeah, that sounds OK . . . I can't believe this. I came to the East Coast to have some private time. I just wanted to do some writing and try to . . ." Destiny stopped in mid-sentence. She was distracted by a picture in a small Limoges china frame sitting on a narrow table behind the couch. She walked over and picked it up. "When was this taken?" she asked, looking at the picture of Andrie and three other people, in formal evening attire.

"A few years ago, at Ann's victory party, when she was first elected to Congress," David answered with a very noticeable distaste toward Ann. "That's her in the picture with Andrie and the two men between them are Stuart Sottley and Andrie's date *du jour* for that occasion," he added with a look of annoyance.

Destiny continued staring at the picture in her hand. She looked first at Andrie, than over to Ann and back again. Several seconds went by before she spoke.

"They look so disconnected from each other. . . ." The picture struck a chord in Destiny. There was sympathy and astonishment in her voice.

"Ann makes certain that all pictures of them look as platonic and heterosexual as possible," David explained in a cynical tone.

It was obvious that David maintained animosity toward Ann. Destiny knew how totally out of character this was for him.

"Does Andrie know how much you dislike Ann?" she asked, as she placed the picture back down.

"She knows that I'm not wild about Ann, but I try to avoid being too critical. Unfortunately, I don't always succeed. Listen, make yourself comfortable. Andrie made up the second bedroom for you. She's going to the party, directly from work," David said, changing the topic, as he led Destiny to her room. He dropped her duffel bag on the floor at the foot of the antique brass bed. Then, glancing around at the lace runners and delicate floral print fabrics that adorned the sunny little room, David couldn't resist the urge to comment, "I'd tell you to make yourself at home, but I dread to think of what you'd do to the decor."

"Very funny. For your information, I like pretty things," Destiny said with lighthearted indignation.

"Don't bullshit me. The only pretty things you like wear skirts," he quipped.

"Only 'til they're alone with me," Destiny replied, raising an eyebrow and grinning devilishly.

"You do sound predatory," David joked under his breath, remembering Andrie's remark as he headed back into the living room with Destiny following him.

Slipping off her heavy leather jacket, Destiny tossed it onto a nearby chair. "I think I'm gonna take a nap, that was a long flight. I'll meet you at the party tonight."

"Are you sure? I can come by here and we can go together, if you want."

"No, I may get there a little late. I want to relax. I may even do some writing when I wake up. I've really got to work on those songs."

"OK. But call me if you change your mind. Oh, they're predicting the first snowfall of the season tonight and I heard that it's going to be heavy," David warned her.

"Hey, I'm pretty hearty and I love snow. Now get outta here and stop babyin' me," Destiny ordered, with a laugh.

*   *   *

As David left the apartment, it occurred to him that he needed to let Andrie know that Destiny would be coming to the party. He could hardly wait to see how she would react to that little surprise.

Over the years he had seen Andrie mature and accept herself.

She had even come out to her parents, who eventually accepted the idea of their daughter being a lesbian.

It was ironic to him that Andrie should then end up with a woman who seemed to stifle her growth and care nothing for her feelings. He didn't understand why Andrie couldn't, or wouldn't, see how much of herself she had given up in order to hold on to Ann.

In the seven years that Andrie was with Ann, he had witnessed Andrie giving up so many things that were important to her in order to accommodate Ann's requests.

The one thing David was sure about was that Andrie's sacrifices seemed to be made less out of love than fear of losing Ann.

Exiting the building he scanned the street for a cab, smiling to himself as he thought of Destiny and Andrie spending a week in the same apartment.

Chapter Three

The sub-street-level lounge room of Club Vingtune was filled with well-dressed business types. Destiny, in a black leather jacket, dark sweater and faded jeans, looked out of place in contrast. Yet, she was able to remain unnoticed by facing a display showing the work of the Women's Way project. It allowed her to face away from most of guests as they meandered around with their drinks before taking the elevator up to the second floor dining room.

Most of the people attending seemed to be in their late fifties to mid-sixties. This probably contributed to the fact that Destiny was able to go unrecognized except for the maître d' and restaurant manager who had been told by Harry Stern to expect her.

The atmosphere was very reserved. She noted to herself that this wasn't the usual type of affair that Harry and Elaine would arrange. But it made sense to her as she remembered David mentioning that Andrie had planned the guest list.

Destiny was tempted to leave, but she knew that David was expecting her. As she stood there, deciding whether or not to stay, she heard a woman's voice carrying on a one-sided conversation. It was emanating from behind the display.

"You did hear me ask for a technician and not a magician didn't you? Because the man you sent me just disappeared and the video equipment I'm renting from you still isn't hooked up. So I would appreciate it if you would send someone here immediately."

Recognizing the voice and the attitude, Destiny walked around to the back of the display, where she saw Andrie. She was as beautiful as ever, in a cream-colored silk skirt and a matching jacket which hugged her petite but well-curved frame in the most flattering way. She remained on the phone facing the wall, unaware that Destiny was standing behind her.

The wheels in Destiny's head turned rapidly, as she wondered how to approach her. She laughed at herself when she realized how ironic it was that this encounter made her far more nervous than performing in front of thousands of people at a time.

Andrie finished the conversation, flipped the phone closed and twirled around only to gasp, shocked to see someone so close behind her. Although David had informed her earlier that Destiny would be attending the party, Andrie still felt a pang of surprise at seeing her pop up that way. For several seconds she merely observed Destiny's appearance. The first thing she studied was the deep-set, dark eyes, which still had a look of unpredictability in them, then she noticed the careless, sandy hair and overly casual clothes. Success, fame, and time all failed to change the way Destiny dressed or carried herself.

"So . . . here you are. You look good. Success agrees with you," Andrie said cordially.

Destiny tried to resist staring as she appreciated the allure of this beautiful woman whose eyes still captivated her, even after years of mutual antagonism. She wondered if Andrie's eyes had the same effect on Ann.

"You look good, too . . . real good," she said somewhat awkwardly, wondering if Andrie could tell how she felt at that moment. "So, how are your parents?" she added quickly.

"They're fine. Dad still owns the butcher shop. And since my brothers and I have been out of the house, they've done a lot of traveling."

"That's good. You should let me know if they ever come to LA. It would be great to see them again . . . I'd love to return the hospitality they showed me when I stayed at David's, way back. Although I don't know one LA restaurant that has a chef that can cook as good as your Mom," Destiny said, remembering dinner at the LaStella house, so long ago.

"Thanks. I'll tell them you said that," Andrie replied politely, as she wondered to herself why Destiny should make her feel as nervous as she did.

"So how are Michael and Nick? Is Nick still on the police force?" Destiny asked, recalling the two or three times she had seen Andrie's brothers at her concerts over the last several years.

"Yes. He loves it. He's been on the force for about seven years. But I wish that he chose something that wasn't so dangerous," Andrie answered, hoping that she didn't look as nervous as she felt.

"I know what you mean. But everyone has to follow their own path. I bet he's a great cop," Destiny said, smiling as she remembered how much she liked both of Andrie's brothers.

"He is . . . and Michael is doing really well. He works for a brokerage firm on Wall Street. He got married a few years ago and moved to Long Island. I don't see as much of him as I do of Nick," Andrie said. She thought to herself how normal a conversation this was for two people who liked each other as little as she and Destiny did.

"And how's Ann?" Destiny asked in an abrupt fashion that took Andrie aback.

"She's wonderful. We're all sure that she'll be re-elected. . . . Oh, so did you get settled in at the apartment?" Andrie asked, purposely changing the topic.

"Yes. Thanks for everything. Your apartment is really nice . . . very warm." The words seemed a little stiff. Small talk was never easy for Destiny and it sometimes showed.

"I have to ask you for a favor," Andrie said quietly, as she looked around the room to see if anyone was listening.

"Sure, what is it?"

"Ann is aware that I know you through David, but she doesn't know about what happened. It was so long ago, I never told her. I would just like to keep it that way. OK?" Andrie asked in a hushed voice.

"Can't you ever just live your life without hidin' big chunks of it?" Destiny replied with obvious disapproval.

"I just never thought to mention it before, since . . . it was . . . just something that happened when we were kids," Andrie replied, still whispering. "Besides," she continued, as her annoyance grew, "I'm sure that Ann would find it hard to believe that I could have ever been attracted to someone who feels it necessary to wear their sexual preference like a sandwich sign."

"You're right. Please, forgive me for not livin' my life in some closet and lyin' to the world about who I am," Destiny replied in a low, but angry tone. "I guess if I followed your example, I could be just as happy as you and your boyfriend and your lover and her fiance."

"You never change. It doesn't matter to you that people all have different circumstances in their lives. You still think that everyone else in the world should think and do everything exactly the way you do," Andrie shot back.

"And you still think that secrets and deceptions are the building blocks for a healthy relationship." Destiny's attack stung Andrie. She felt no choice but to bite back.

"Excuse me, but do you really feel qualified to lecture me about relationships at this point in your life? From what I've read in the papers, one night stands have been the mainstay of your existence ever since Nicole left you," Andrie retorted.

"You're really somethin' else. Tell me, did you study anatomy to learn how to go for the jugular like that? Or is it just one of the many wonderful qualities you were gifted with from birth?"

Destiny's reply seemed to break through to Andrie. She regretted the remark almost instantly.

"Can we at least call a temporary truce? I'm sorry. It was wrong of me to say anything about your relationship. It's just that I've been under a lot of pressure lately and when you started criticizing me and giving me a hard time about keeping our past to yourself . . ."

Destiny jumped in before Andrie could finish. "Andrie, in all these years I have never told a soul about me and you. I never even told Nicole . . . and that's gospel truth. I knew that you weren't ready to come out, so I never said anything to anyone." Destiny's tone was sober and sincere.

"I believe you. Despite everything else, I've always trusted you. I suppose that's the reason I didn't get too upset when David made that slip a few years ago and told you about Ann and me." Andrie's affect was softening.

"That was five years ago. It was when I told him that Nicole was movin' in with me. Maybe you should be warning David not to say anything to Ann. He seems to be the one with the loose lips," Destiny joked.

"Luckily, they don't usually entertain conversations with each other," Andrie laughed. She was certain that by now, David had made his dislike for Ann clear to Destiny.

Looking around, Andrie noticed that most of the guests had arrived. "We'd better go upstairs to dinner." With that they headed into the elevator.

"David told me that Harry Stern invited you here," Andrie said, as she led the way.

"Yeah, but I never even knew exactly what the party was for, or that you would be here, until David told me, this afternoon."

"Small world," Andrie commented, as she took the lead, walking ahead of Destiny as they left the elevator and strode toward the dining room.

Following behind, Destiny couldn't help but notice the way the silk hugged Andrie's body. She found herself staring at Andrie's legs and the way the short skirt revealed her smooth well-shaped thighs. Catching herself, Destiny wondered if Andrie knew that she was staring.

She *did*. As they reached the bar inside the dining room, Andrie smirked and rolled her eyes after turning abruptly to find Destiny still staring at her legs.

The bartender had just filled a tray of fluted champagne glasses. Andrie handed a glass to Destiny, then took one for herself.

"That's a very nice outfit," Destiny commented, pretending that it was Andrie's suit which had commanded so much of her attention.

"I *thought* you liked it," Andrie smiled condescendingly. She still knew exactly how to embarrass Destiny.

"So, what do you think of my outfit?" Destiny jested, as she took a step back and twirled around, as if she were modeling the clothes. Her well-worn brown cowboy boots and leather jacket drew a disapproving look from Andrie.

"We've been getting along peacefully for the last two minutes, so I won't screw it up by telling you what I think," Andrie replied, as she turned to briefly scan the room. "I've put you at my table, with David and the Sterns. It's number six . . . over there," she said, pointing to a large corner table at the opposite end of the room. Suddenly, a loud but friendly baritone voice broke in. "Destiny, doll. You made it. Wait till Elaine sees you." With that, Harry Stern, a gentle-faced, slightly rotund man in his early sixties, wrapped an arm around Destiny's shoulder and kissed her on the cheek. He then took hold of Andrie's arm and pulled her to his side as well. "It looks like you've met our little angel Andrie LaStella. She put this whole thing together for us. She's Congress-woman Capwell's assistant," he said to Destiny as he affectionately took Andrie's face in one of his hands and kissed her loudly on the cheek.

"Look at you. You're looking great. You lose some, huh?" Destiny said, tapping Harry's barrel-shaped belly. She wanted to get Harry started on his favorite topic . . . his health. She knew that if she didn't, he would soon start to pry about where she was staying while she was in New York.

Realizing what Destiny was doing, Andrie chimed in. "You do look thinner. What have you been doing . . . working out?"

"No. Elaine's on a new kick. . . . She's cooking dinner for us every night."

"So eating Elaine's dinners made you lose weight?" Destiny said.

"No. Avoiding them did. To be politically correct, my Elaine is what you would call domestically impaired," Harry explained as the three of them broke into laughter. After a little more small talk about his health, Harry digressed and began discussing Cobra business with Destiny.

"I'll be back in a minute. I want to see if I can find David,"

Andrie said, excusing herself, as she withdrew from under Harry's arm and headed across the room.

Both Harry and Destiny watched as she walked away. "I love that kid. She could go far, too," Harry said, his eyes following Andrie momentarily before returning to Destiny. "So, doll face . . . can you tell me why it has to be such a big secret that you're here in New York?" Harry's warm smile and his obvious concern convinced Destiny to address the unwelcome question.

"OK. I'll be honest and explain. But you have to promise me that you won't start asking me where I'm.staying. Do we have a deal?"

Harry knew Destiny was serious. She had always been in complete control of her life. He admired her for always being firmly grounded in reality, unlike so many other performers he knew. He trusted her judgment, so he agreed.

She looked him straight in the eye and began to explain. "Since Nicole left, I've really tried my best to get on with my life. I know that you've seen pictures of me with a lot of different women . . . and maybe I looked like I was having fun, but the pain was still there. I needed some time away from everything that reminded me of what happened with Nicole and Sonia. That was impossible for me to do in LA. Most of my friends there are friends with Nicole and Sonia too. So, New York seemed like a good place to clear my head. Anyway, I thought it would be a good idea to spend some free time here while I start workin' on those songs for Rena Samuel's movie. I wanted to do this ever since she showed me the rough cut. I'm not lettin' anyone know where I am, for one really good reason . . . Nicole. She's been callin' me at home. Apparently, Sonia's already seein' other women and it sounds like it's over between them. Six months is the max Sonia spends with any one woman. After that she moves on. Now, Nicole wants to move back in with me and I'm not interested in havin' her back. I just want to sort some things out for myself. If I told you where I was stayin', Elaine would pry it out of you. I love her, but you know how loose lipped she can be and I don't want Nicole to find out through the grapevine and start botherin' me here."

Harry laughed and nodded in agreement as Destiny went on, "I just need a little time to work on my music and not be disturbed. I'm sure you would love the person I'm staying with. So please don't worry. OK?"

Harry's curiosity had been satisfied. He would keep his promise to Destiny and not question her further.

Meanwhile, at the other end of the room Andrie had found David. She whispered to him, as he piled a hill of hors d'oeuvres onto a cocktail plate. "Destiny's here."

"Great, where is she?" he responded as he stuffed an herb-crusted shrimp into his mouth.

"She's by the bar, with Harry."

"So, is round one over yet?" David asked, his mouth still full.

"Very funny."

Before David had time to further annoy Andrie, Destiny came up from behind, greeting him with a friendly pat on the back. "Hey boy, I've been lookin' for ya."

He hugged Destiny and kissed her on the cheek. "I'm really glad you came. I was starting to think that the jet lag got to you," he said, smiling, as he looked from Destiny to Andrie and back again. "This is great. I'm together again with my two favorite women."

It was obvious that after a few drinks David was ready for a nostalgic stroll down memory lane . . . and he was taking Andrie and Destiny with him . . . whether they liked it or not. "Do you remember that old green Caprice?" he asked, then waited for them to acknowledge his question. Andrie and Destiny glanced uncomfortably at each other and nodded.

David looked at Andrie and continued, "Well, you remember what a rust bucket that car was. But Destiny kept it running for years." He nodded to Destiny and continued. "It finally bit the dust after she moved to LA. She couldn't afford to replace it right away, so she ended up walking to her gigs and using an old shopping cart to carry her instruments and sound equipment in. . . ." Then, turning to Destiny he asked, "Remember the time you got stopped by the cops because they thought that you were a bag lady?"

"Yeah, they offered to drive me to a women's shelter for the night, which would have probably been an improvement over my apartment at the time," Destiny added with a hearty laugh.

As they stood there talking, Andrie's mind began to wander. She thought about how all Destiny's dreams of success had come true. For a split second she questioned whether Destiny would have still found her fame and fortune if they had stayed together all those years ago. She grew uncomfortable as she wondered if the same thought had occurred to Destiny.

"There's Ann. I'd better get over there and fill her in on a few things, before she starts to circulate," Andrie said, extricating herself from a conversation she was afraid would lead to too many uncomfortable memories.

As Andrie walked away, David observed the way Destiny watched her.

Without turning her eyes from Andrie, Destiny responded to his thoughts, "Stop thinkin' what you're thinkin'. We weren't together five minutes before our first tussle. Anyway, there's the type she likes." Destiny nodded toward Ann. "Ya see, she's the polished, finishin' school type . . . and I'm real far from that. Besides, Andrie's not my type, either. She turned out to be a little too formal for me. I like more free-spirited women."

"Oh . . . I think you might still enjoy freeing up her spirit a little . . . hmmm?" David jested coyly as he sipped his champagne.

"Listen, it's been over fifteen years. I'm not interested in her anymore," Destiny protested, as she continued to watch Andrie speaking with Ann. She saw a well-built man with dark hair, who looked to be in his late thirties, approach them and slip his arm around Andrie.

"So, who's he?" Destiny inquired of David.

"You mean the guy who just put his arm around the woman you're not interested in?" David paused for a response, but Destiny simply rolled her eyes and smiled.

"His name is Jim Page and he's Andrie's date for the evening. Remember, I told you how Ann encourages her to date, so she appears to be a typical, single career woman, playing the field?"

"Does this Jim Page guy know that he's just a front?" Destiny asked.

"No. He has no idea and Andrie's worried that he's falling in love with her. They met at a party last year and Ann felt that he'd be perfect for the part. He's a surgeon and he lives in Philadelphia, so Andrie doesn't see him that often. It's ironic that Andrie finally admitted to herself that she's gay and she even came out to her family . . . then, she ends up with a woman who shoves her right back into the closet. It's all very fucked up." David studied Destiny's face for a reaction, but she simply continued to gaze at the scene across the room.

"Andrie's not stupid. Why does she allow Ann to do that to her?" she asked, her eyes still fixed.

"I don't know. I guess that sometimes, in certain circumstances, even the smartest people let their lives be ruined by people they think love them. . . . It happens insidiously. You fall in love, or you think you do. So, at first you don't see what this person is doing to you. . . . Then, as time goes on, you make excuses for it. . . . Eventually, you either go on living a miserable existence with that person, or you open your eyes to it and leave the son of a bitch . . . or they leave you . . . whatever. It's a hard reality to face, but you know that."

Destiny knew that David was referring to her breakup with Nicole. On some level, it helped her understand Andrie's situation.

"Destiny. . . . W-what are you doing here?" an eager voice spurted, as they were suddenly accosted by a slightly overweight, apple-faced blond in her early thirties, wearing an exaggerated black silk version of a nineteen-forties zoot suit.

"Oh . . . hi . . ." Destiny said, somewhat stunned to see the woman. Then, turning to David, she introduced her. "David, this is Bee Avery."

"Hi, D-dave," said the woman, as she vigorously shook his

hand. Bee Avery was a bit of an off-beat character. She had written and published several science fiction novels. All with lesbian protagonists. There was even talk of her latest book being made into a major motion picture. Destiny had met Bee several times before, through Sonia. Sonia loved throwing parties and Bee was always invited when she was in LA. She divided her time fairly evenly between New York and the West Coast, although preferring to do all her writing at her New York apartment.

Destiny had never understood what Sonia saw in Bee as a friend. There was something about Bee that never felt right to Destiny. It was her suspicion that there was another Bee hiding behind the superficial, party-loving, good-time girl. Destiny had also observed that Bee, who never had a relationship last more that a couple of months, had always seemed smitten by Nicole.

"So, how did you end up here tonight?" Destiny asked, sounding less cordial than she intended.

"I've b-b-been a supporter of Ann's since she first ran for city council years ago. I was really happy when she ran for Congress l-l-last year. I contributed enough to her campaigns to c-claim her as a dependent on my taxes. I guess that's why they invited me," Bee said with a laugh.

David had remained silent through their conversation as he observed Bee. He sensed that Destiny wasn't at ease with her, so he decided to liberate his friend from the situation. "Excuse me," he interrupted, "Destiny sweetie, I think we should go to our table now."

"Oh, OK. I'm totally beat, I just got in from LA this morning. I really do need to sit for a while. . . . It was nice seeing you again," Destiny said as David tugged her away.

"Sure. I'll see y-you later," Bee said, as she remained standing at the bar.

"That's what sh-sh-she thinks," David whispered to Destiny as they walked toward their table.

"Stop that. That's not nice . . . but thanks for getting me away from her."

"How do you know her?"

"She's a friend of Sonia's," Destiny replied as she looked around the room.

"Well, there's another strike against her," David responded curtly.

"She writes all those books about gay aliens from other planets," Destiny explained.

"I've seen her books. She spells her name B-e-e like in buzzing. Right?" he asked.

"Yeah. She once told Nicole that her mother called her Bee, which was short for Honey Bee," Destiny told him with a smirk.

"So I've just met a woman whose mother named her after an insect," David mused humorously.

As they approached their table, someone tapped Destiny on the shoulder. It was Andrie and she was with Ann.

"Destiny, I'd like you to meet Congresswoman Capwell."

Ann Capwell was tall, very tall, and slender. Though Destiny had seen pictures of her, meeting her, she was taken aback by the woman's height. Ann towered over Andrie, who was petite even in heels. Overall, Ann Capwell was far more attractive than her pictures in the newspapers, although not what one would consider pretty. Her short, conservatively coifed golden blond hair neatly framed her large, angular features, the most distinctive of which was a long aquiline nose.

"It's a pleasure to meet you. I'm really quite a fan of yours. I have all of your albums. I'm so glad that you could be here tonight," Ann said, cordially extending her hand to greet Destiny. Her tone was measured, almost calculated, as though her words had been chosen ahead of time. Not at all unusual for a politician, Destiny noted to herself.

"Thanks. I'm real glad to be here. I admire what you've done with the Women's Way project," Destiny responded, trying to remain polite yet honest. She was not one to give false praise.

"Thank you. I'm quite proud of it myself," the congresswoman replied.

As the polite little chat was taking place, Andrie and David glanced at each other and exchanged vague smiles; they could read each other's minds. They wouldn't feel comfortable until the evening was over and Ann and Destiny were no longer in contact with each other. Andrie broke in, "Excuse me. I'll be back in a minute. I have to greet some guests who just arrived," leaving Ann and Destiny to continue their conversation.

"It seems that you've also given a lot of your time to charitable causes. I've read about the benefit concert you did for the World Circle Children's Foundation. I admire that. It's so important for well-known artists to use their celebrity to advance vital issues," Ann said, employing her flawless politician's charisma.

"Harry actually spearheaded that benefit. I was just one of the seven Cobra label artists that did that concert," Destiny replied modestly. She was surprised that Ann was even aware of the small concert that took place on the West Coast several months ago, especially since it wasn't widely publicized. They continued to talk, but Ann's voice seemed to fade into the background as Destiny's mind began to wander. This was the woman who Andrie had been with for the past seven years. Something about Ann Capwell struck Destiny as being cold and unapproachable. It wasn't because of anything she said, but rather a feeling she seemed to exude, perhaps due to her overly poised manner. It was difficult for Destiny to picture her having a tender or affectionate side to her personality.

"She seems pretty busy," Destiny said of Andrie, who was deep in lively conversation across the room. It was her way of getting Ann to talk about Andrie. Destiny wanted to see if she could find some evidence of warmth in Ann's words or voice when she spoke about her.

"Well, this is all part of her job and she's very good at it. Actually, my entire staff makes one really great team. I'm lucky to have them. I'm sure it's similar to the way a performer, like yourself, depends on your band and crew," Ann answered, coolly and without any specific emphasis on Andrie. It both frightened and confounded Destiny to see how easy it was for the smug politician to conceal any special feelings she had toward Andrie. Their conversation was interrupted, again.

"Destiny, sweetie, Harry told me you were here. You look wonderful. . . . Look at you, you're adorable." The loud voice, raspy from years of smoking, belonged to Elaine Stern, Harry's wife. The tall, broad-shouldered woman, who seemed to be a cross between Auntie Mame and an NFL linebacker, was as friendly and good-natured as anyone could be. She loved to drink, especially at parties. Tonight was no exception. It was obvious that she had had a few already. Elaine was normally a rather garrulous type and drinking made her even more so. "So, I see that you've met our favorite congresswoman," Elaine said to Destiny, as she took hold of her hand. Then, turning to Ann, she added, "and you've met our favorite rock star."

"And Elaine and Harry happen to be my two favorite constituents." Ann smiled her patent, pearl-white, even smile, as she looked from Elaine to Destiny. It was the smile she employed for occasions such as this. It was her father's smile. Just then a staffer came by to inform Ann that there was a phone call for her.

"Excuse me, I've been expecting this call from my Washington office," she told Destiny and Elaine, then was spirited away.

Destiny glanced across the room again to see Andrie involved in a conversation with Harry Stern and two other guests. She couldn't help but notice how exuberant she was. As Destiny watched, she could see that Andrie seemed to be explaining something to the three men. At first, it appeared that they weren't in agreement with her. But, as the conversation progressed, it became obvious by their body language and facial expressions that Andrie had won them over. There was so much energy coming from her that, to Destiny, it seemed the men had no choice but to be persuaded to her point of view.

Meanwhile, Destiny was unaware that, as she watched Andrie, a very observant Elaine was watching her. Harry and Elaine had admired and valued Destiny as an artist, ever since she first signed with Cobra Records. In the few years that she had recorded for Cobra they had become her friends, as well. In many ways she had become almost a daughter to them.

"So what's so interesting over there? . . . And don't say it's Harry. I know better; I'm married to him," Elaine asked Destiny, who again found herself staring at Andrie.

Elaine's comment shook Destiny from her trance, as she turned to answer, "Nothing, I guess I'm just suffering from a little jet lag."

"Des baby, this is your Auntie Elaine. I've gotten to know you like one of my own kids. Except that I see you more than once a year. I know you're looking at Andrie LaStella."

"I was that obvious, huh?"

"Only to anyone with eyes, sweetie," Elaine responded with a compassionate chuckle. As she continued, she saw that Destiny seemed unable to take her eyes off Andrie. "You're really attracted to her aren't you? Honey, she's straight. Besides, she's very New York. She's not like the women you know in Hollywood." Elaine's tone was almost that of a mother giving dating advice to a son. "Oh, I just don't know if I would recommend it," she said, sounding perplexed.

"Recommend what?" Destiny asked, looking at her, somewhat bewildered by the statement.

Elaine continued, "Well, sweetie, even if Andrie wasn't hetero-sexual, you both have very different personalities. You would do better with someone else who's in the business. Someone who understands the world that you live in."

"Nicole was in the business," Destiny replied with a wry grin.

"Honey, Nicole was just the wrong girl. My Harry never thought she was right for you. Those things happen. You'll find love. Just go out, have fun . . . but remember, you don't need the ones that are just after you because of who you are. Someday the right girl is going to come along . . . you'll see. Oh God, I think I've had this talk with my son." By now, Elaine, finishing her fifth martini, was beginning to wobble a bit. Seeing this, Destiny guided her to a nearby table and helped her sit down.

"Elaine, how well do you know her?" Destiny asked as Elaine plopped down in the seat.

"Andrie?" Elaine asked, as she looked up from the chair and tried to focus on Destiny's face.

"Yes," she answered, as she gently took the martini glass from Elaine and placed it on the table.

"Well, I told you that she was heterosexual, right?" Elaine blurted as her speech became increasingly slurred.

"Right, right. But what else do you know about her?" Destiny continued prodding.

"I've been doing a lot of volunteer work with her, whenever I'm in New York . . . and I helped her plan this party. I like her. Harry even talks politics with her. She's a very bright girl. Harry said that he thinks she should be running for Congress. Ann would be totally lost without her. Do you know about the Women's Way project? It was because of that project that Harry and I became so devoted to her campaign."

"Yeah, I've read about it. It's a special domestic violence project."

"Well, it was the all-around appeal and success of that project that has made Ann so well known. Especially for a freshman congressman . . . woman . . . person . . . damnit. I have such a hard time with politically correct speech after four martinis."

"Five," Destiny reminded her with a sympathetic smile.

"Here. This has a little blurb about it somewhere. . . ." Elaine began clumsily flipping through the pages of one of the gold and white programs which had been set at each guest's place. Finding the section she was looking for, she began to read aloud to Destiny. *"Women's Way provides secure shelter for abused women and their children, while it assists them to find jobs or get job training. It also helps them with relocation if they need it. It's funded almost entirely by private donations and staffed by volunteers. There are a number of large businesses which have also supported Women's Way with generous grants* . . . and it goes on. The beauty of it all is that while it's helping these poor unfortunate women, it's not spending taxpayers' dollars. It's a brilliant idea. All these people from other cities around the country have been coming here to study it. My cousin, Faye, was married to a creep who abused her. The poor thing told nobody. Then one day she took too many tranquilizers. They said it was accidental . . . I think she wanted to end her suffering. She probably figured that he would have killed her anyway, given enough time." Elaine reached for her martini and took a large gulp, finishing what was left in the glass.

Destiny didn't try to stop her. She finally understood why Elaine, who was generally far more interested in shopping than voting, had become so involved with Ann Capwell's campaign.

After a several seconds of silence, she again tried to get Elaine to tell her about Andrie. She wanted to get an idea of what kind of woman Andrie had grown into.

"Elaine, I think that it's a wonderful program too, but what's it got to do with what I asked you about Andrie?" Destiny asked.

"Women's Way was all her idea. She thought it up and put it together," Elaine replied.

"How do you know that?"

"Honey, I was volunteering at Women's Way since it first started up. I've seen that girl spend every minute of free time she had on that project. She knows it inside out. She's given it her heart. . . . Trust me . . . I know it was her idea. When you've lived as long as I have, you learn to trust those feelings."

"Ladies, I thought that I'd come over and escort you to our table," David broke in as he approached them.

"Good idea," Destiny agreed and nodded to him to stand on Elaine's other side, as she helped her stand up. The three then walked over to their own table, where Harry had already been sitting.

"Harry, where's Andrie? Weren't you just with her?" Elaine asked.

"Let's see . . ." Harry said, jokingly checking through his pockets, "No, she's not there . . . Uh oh . . ."

"Oh stop," Elaine said as she jabbed him lightly with her elbow. Harry smiled and explained that Andrie had gone to find Ann. At that point dinner was being served so they all began to eat.

*   *   *

Outside the restaurant manager's plush office on the third floor, everything seemed calm. But behind the door was a different story. The office was on loan to Ann for the evening, as a courtesy since she had expected several calls from Washington. She and Andrie were trying hard to keep their voices down as they quarreled.

"How could you possibly support that? Aside from the fact that it's wrong and unethical, it'll hurt your career. It could destroy it. God knows, it'll destroy Women's Way." Andrie's voice was little more than a whisper but she argued her point fervidly.

"Look, the program has been running strong for over two and a half years. Everyone knows I started Women's Way the second I took office. There's no way it could look bad for me. I could even appear to be resistant . . . to a point, so I won't look like I really approve of this."

"I can't believe what you're saying. You'd fake a struggle to look good, while you allow a corporation to buy the Women's Way building and put a garage in its place." Andrie was incredulous as she listened to Ann's strategy.

"Cortronics is a growing company, which we need to keep in New York. If we don't let them buy that property for employee parking and unloading, they could easily relocate to outside the city or even out of state. They're already planning demolition dates. What am I supposed to say to them? *Sorry, we would rather house a group of women who have contributed nothing to this city, instead of a major business which provides jobs to hundreds of New Yorkers who need them?* I'm trying to keep their money here. This is a matter of economics." Ann maintained a cool indifference as she remained unmoved by Andrie's argument.

"What about the matter of human lives? There are women who might have been dead by now if it wasn't for this program." Andrie was infuriated by Ann's dispassionate attitude.

"Look, Women's Way has done a lot of good for the women that entered it. I know that. But I've weighed the issues and at this time I need to address the economic factors. I've discussed it with Ray and he feels that, as long as I handle this the right way, it won't have a negative impact on my re-election. People recognize that Women's Way was my program. They'll naturally believe that I oppose the sale of the building."

Andrie walked toward Ann, who was now leaning back against the massive mahogany desk.

"Your program? Don't you dare forget whose idea Women's Way was. Do you understand?" Andrie's voice had an almost threatening quality to it now. Despite Ann's slightly reclined position, there remained a stark contrast in size between the two women. Yet, Andrie's tenacity made her a more than suitable match for Ann. "You used to have integrity. At least I thought you did. I'd leave this job right now, but you need me to stay because I'm the only vestige of a conscience you have left."

Andrie's enraged stare penetrated Ann in a way that even her words were unable to do. Ann looked away, attempting to disengage from the penetrating eye contact, and made an off-handed suggestion: "You can try to find the program an alternate location."

"Sure, that should be easy. I'll just go around and ask, who wants to donate a building to us . . . rent free. You know that the only reason we got the building we're in now is because Stuart Sottley is your friend. He doesn't even care if he sells the building. He'd stop the sale if you ask him to."

"I'm only going to explain this one more time. This is a matter of keeping jobs here in New York. Many of these people could possibly lose their jobs if Cortronics relocates. Why don't you think about those families?"

"Why can't you work on helping Cortronics find an alternate site for its parking garage?" Andrie shot back.

"That's enough. I've told you what I want you to do in order to prepare for my meeting with the Cortronics people. I expect you to do it."

"I'll do it, but I'm also going to start looking for another location for Women's Way . . . and I'm going to use every resource we have, if I need to."

There was something about Andrie's eyes and her stance that made her look like a cat readying itself to attack. Ann had ceased listening to what she had to say. Instead, the rapacious politician became more interested in taking advantage of the privacy of the locked manager's office. Reaching out, she ran her finger along the neckline of the low-cut blouse that draped gracefully over the curves of Andrie's body. She could see the heaving motion of Andrie's full breasts beneath the pale silk as she breathed deeply, in her anger. The movement drew Ann, until she leaned forward and kissed the side of Andrie's neck.

Pulling back, Andrie turned her face away. "Stop it . . . I can't take this. I'm so sick of all the charades. When we're alone, you're all over me, but to the outside world I'm nothing more than an employee of yours," she said, hurt and disgusted by their situation.

Ann continued trying to caress her, and though Andrie remained reluctant to be touched, her tone became softer. "Don't do this . . . can't you see that this relationship is killing me?" Andrie asked in a voice weighted by pain.

Ann instantly became annoyed by Andrie's reaction to her overture. "I think that you're overdramatizing the situation. You knew that it would be like this. I have a political career to protect," she said, folding her arms and leaning back against the desk again.

"Protect this!" Andrie said, pushing Ann away with enough force to send her off balance, causing her to fall backward on the desk. Then Andrie turned on her heels and stormed out of the room, slamming the door behind her. Left alone in the office, Ann recovered immediately. She was unmoved by the scene that had just taken place. This was nothing new. She had no doubt that Andrie would cool off and be back in place by the end of the evening.

*   *   *

With all the momentum of a runaway train, Andrie headed out from the elevator and across the lounge. She was blinded with anger. She needed to get away from the party, at least for a while. Suddenly her pace was broken. Her body was jolted back as it recoiled from impact. For a second, all she could see was black leather.

"Are you all right?" a voice asked softly.

Andrie felt a strong grip on both of her shoulders as she looked up to see Destiny's face.

"I'm OK . . . really . . . I'm fine." Andrie was more embarrassed by her clumsiness than hurt from the collision. Of all the people to run into at this moment, why did it have to be Destiny, she thought to herself. Realizing that her purse had fallen, Andrie bent down to retrieve it and so did Destiny, never losing eye contact with her. Andrie quickly grabbed the purse, but it opened, spilling out some of its contents. She began to nervously recover some of the items–lipstick, a pen and a small address book–as Destiny chased after a set of keys that slid across the polished marble floor, ending up underneath a large armchair.

Retrieving the keys, Destiny looked to return them, but Andrie was already halfway out the door and making her way down the snow-covered street. Destiny decided to follow her. "Wait a minute, Cinderella," she shouted as she took off after her.

Hearing her, Andrie looked back at Destiny, who was jingling the keys at her. "I'll get them when I come back. Just leave them by my place at the table." She continued to walk away, picking up speed with every step. Although she had neglected to take her coat, the anger and frustration she felt fueled her hot blood, making her temporarily immune to the weather.

Still following her, Destiny called out, "Do you have a minute to talk . . . or do you have to get to your Ford before it turns back into a pumpkin or something?"

"It's a Toyota," Andrie replied without turning. Then, still looking ahead, she abruptly stopped walking until Destiny caught up with her.

The snow was falling heavily as Destiny reached her and handed over the keys. "Oh. A Toyota, huh. I guess they turn into sushi or something," she said with a wide grin that even made Andrie smile at the corny joke.

"Cute! But I'm not going to my car. Now, go back to the party and leave me alone," Andrie said as she turned to walk away.

"So where are you headed in this weather?" Destiny asked, undaunted by Andrie's demand.

"I just needed some air, that's all."

"Mind if I come along?" Destiny asked, looking down at a crushed paper cup that was lying flat in the snow on the sidewalk and nudging it with the toe of her boot.

"Well, I suppose it's better than having you follow me," Andrie said as she started walking again.

"How did you know that I would do that?" Destiny kicked the cup off to the curb and resumed tailing Andrie.

"Because I don't believe that you've changed much in the last fifteen years. You didn't give me any time or space to think then, why should you now?" Andrie snapped impatiently.

"If you would just hide your claws for awhile, maybe I could try to help. It's pretty obvious that something is bothering you. You really barreled out of that restaurant like you were on your way to a fire."

"I'm sorry; did I hurt you?" Andrie's affect softened. She realized that she was displacing her anger.

"No . . . not this time," Destiny said with a furtive grin. Destiny's vague reference to their past went unnoticed by Andrie, who was still visibly upset.

"Do you want to talk about it?" Destiny asked.

"No. . . . Even if I did, I wouldn't know where to begin."

"Then let's go for a walk and talk about something else," Destiny said, taking off her jacket and slipping it over Andrie's shoulders.

"I can't take your jacket; you'll freeze," Andrie said as they continued down the block. She hadn't seen this side of Destiny since before that day in her driveway, fifteen years ago.

"Let's walk, I won't be cold," Destiny replied confidently.

"Aren't you worried that people will recognize you?" Andrie asked.

"Not really. I can usually blend in with the crowd. Let's face it, I'm not that glamorous lookin'," she said with unaffected modesty.

Andrie noticed a cryptic smile on Destiny's face. "What's the smile for?"

"Us. I guess," Destiny replied shyly.

"Why?"

"Well, the few times we saw each other over the last fifteen years, we never had a chance to be alone like this. It just feels good to be talkin' with you, without the insults or the ornery looks. It's comfortable." Destiny's smile widened as she spoke. "I could use some comfort these days."

"You look pretty comfortable in all those pictures I've seen," Andrie replied with a chuckle.

"You're talking about me and all those women in the tabloids, hmm? I tried to make a life with Nicole. I needed to fill some kind of empty space inside me. But when she left, it just made me more aware that she had never filled that space to begin with. Those women were my way to dull the pain. Some people drink . . . I date. I did that same thing after you, fifteen years ago," Destiny reminded Andrie.

"I remember. I let David talk me into taking a trip to San Francisco, and the next thing I knew I was sitting in some little bar watching you play. I was hoping that we could talk or something," Andrie recalled.

"That was the time you threw the drink in my face," Destiny reminisced with a confused look.

"There was a good reason for that. We sat there all night and you never once came over to us, until after your last set. Meanwhile, you were flirting with those three girls that were standing around your piano." Andrie brooded a bit as she recalled the incident.

"Well, the flirting was part of the performance. It still is, sometimes," Destiny defended herself.

"You called one of them over and asked her out, while you were in the middle talking with us, after the show," Andrie responded, as some of the old wound reopened.

"So you . . . with your hot temper . . . threw a drink in my face."

"I was hurt," Andrie replied defensively.

"So was I. I needed to get back at you for what I saw in the driveway that day. It just seemed like the perfect thing to do," Destiny blurted angrily.

"Funny, that's how I felt about throwing the drink in your face," Andrie snapped. Their eyes locked on each other and after a few seconds of silence they both laughed as they remembered the scene.

"It was peppermint schnapps. I smelled like a bottle of mint mouthwash for the rest of the night," Destiny recalled as they continued walking.

"Did you go out with her that night?" Andrie asked without looking at Destiny.

"That girl at the bar? . . . Yeah . . . sort of . . . in a way."

"Sort of . . . in a way. . . ." Andrie repeated Destiny's awkward response.

"She had seen you throw that drink at me. So later on, when we were at my apartment, she called you a bitch. That bothered me, so I asked her to leave."

"Let me see if I understand this. You did all you could do that night to hurt me and make me regret coming there to see you.

Yet you ended a date with someone because she said that I was a bitch for throwing a drink in your face?'' Andrie said, shaking her head in astonishment.

"When she called you that, it hurt me." Destiny went no further to explain.

Andrie found herself somewhat bewildered by Destiny's response, but she felt that she should change the topic rather than pursue it.

"How's your family? Have things gotten better between you and them?" she asked, wondering if Destiny's family had changed their opinion of her, after the success she had achieved.

"No. Not really. Things are pretty much the same as always. My sister, Lynn, got married about a year ago. At first I was gonna go to the wedding, but then I decided to just send a gift. It's funny, I thought that I would want to go back to Colton Corners now and thumb my nose at all the folks who made me feel like an outcast back then . . . but I'd still find it hard to be around my family. You know, I thought by sending my sister an extravagant wedding gift that I'd have the satisfaction of showin' them how all the dreams they tried to make me feel silly for havin', came true. I thought it would be like that old sayin' about *success being the best revenge*. Instead all I had was a numb feelin'. It was like sendin' a gift to a stranger." Destiny's voice was sad and pensive.

"You still really miss your dad, don't you?" Andrie said, sensing Destiny's loneliness.

"I play the fiddle at least once at every concert, just to remember him. It was the first instrument he taught me. He never got a chance to be proud of me. He never got the chance to see me make it," Destiny said, swallowing back the painful lump in her throat.

"That's not true. I believe he's somewhere looking down and saying, *That's my girl. That's my little Rags*," Andrie answered softly.

"How did you remember that he called me *Rags*?" Destiny asked in awe.

"I don't know. I just remembered," Andrie said. She too was

surprised by the fact that such a small detail remained in her memory for so long. But what perplexed her even more was the fact that, despite the years of growing dislike between them, the sadness in Destiny's eyes as she spoke of her father still made Andrie instinctively want to hold and comfort her. That idea suddenly made her feel uncomfortable being alone with Destiny. "I think we'd better turn back now. I need to take care of a few things before some of the guests leave . . . and I hardly spent any time at all with Jim," Andrie said, as her voice now took on a cooler, more businesslike tone.

"Jim?" Destiny repeated, as she now followed Andrie back in the direction of the restaurant.

"My date for the evening," Andrie replied with an tone of obvious distaste for the idea.

"Oh. Him," Destiny smiled, raising her eyebrow slightly as she continued walking.

They maintained a thoughtful silence almost all the way back. Then, just as they reached Club Vingtune, Andrie spoke. "I'm sorry that I gave you a hard time about walking with me."

"That's OK. Thanks for what you said back there . . . about my father. That was nice of you," Destiny said in a grateful tone. Andrie responded with a gentle smile as she looked back at Destiny.

Chapter Four

Destiny had already been back at the apartment long enough to change into a pair of old sweatpants and a T-shirt. She even had time to fix herself a cup of tea, while she waited for Andrie to get home from the party. The kitchen light shed only the slightest amount of illumination into the adjacent living room. As she made herself comfortable on the living room couch with that day's copy of the *Times* and was about to turn on the table lamp next to her, Destiny heard voices in the hall outside the apartment. Realizing that it was Andrie and Jim, she was unable to resist listening as she remained there in the dim light holding the newspaper. She could hear the entire conversation between them.

"Aren't you going to invite me in?" he asked eagerly.

"No . . . not tonight. I have a friend from out of town staying with me this week."

"Andrie, I'm not expecting to have a night of wild sex. I just thought that we'd have a drink and talk. I really think we need to discuss where this relationship is going."

"Jim, please. Tonight's not a good time for me."

"Then, tell me when it's good for you, Andrie? I'm falling in love with you. I want to see more of you. I want us to spend lazy weekends together . . . to have breakfast in bed, while we read the *Sunday Times*. I want to make love to you, with soft music on in the background. I want to take you home to meet my parents. We're never alone. The only time I see you is when there's some kind of function, like tonight."

Destiny heard the tension in Andrie's voice as she tried to respond to Jim's plea.

"I'm sorry; I really am, but I can't talk about this now. Please Jim, it's late and I'm exhausted."

"OK. You're right. It's late and this isn't a discussion that we should be having in a hallway."

The silence that followed was accompanied by the muffled sound of two bodies leaning against the door as they kissed goodnight. A few seconds later, Andrie opened the door and flipped on the light switch as she stepped into the room.

"Hi," Destiny said, taking a devilish glee in startling Andrie.

Andrie gasped and jumped back. Then, regaining her composure, she admonished Destiny. "For the time that you'll be staying here, I would appreciate it if you would show me the courtesy of not sitting in my living room with the lights out, waiting to scare the living shit out of me when I come home."

"I'm sorry. I thought that you might feel a little uncomfortable if I was in here with the lights on, while you made love against the door," Destiny quipped, as she put the paper down.

"That was a friendly kiss goodnight. You haven't been here long enough to have your depraved habits rub off on me."

"Now don't go gettin' your pantyhose all knotted up, 'cause I made a little joke about you and 'Mr. Breakfast In Bed.' I know that it was only a kiss and that you're just using him. So, I still have the highest regard for your morals and sensitivity to others," Destiny answered in a sarcastic tone.

"You were in here listening to us? I knew it was too good to be true, when we went for that walk before. It was the first time in years that you acted like a normal human being." Andrie shook her head in exasperation, as she continued, "But you're still a spiteful, judgmental extremist, who wants everyone to think your way. It really takes gall to lecture me on morals and sensitivity when you're incapable of being with one woman at a time . . . or is that trick photography in the newspapers? You should know something; I don't care how many women find you appealing or respond to your fame. To me, you're still the same holier-than-thou radical, who loves to preach to everyone else on how to live their lives: *Come out. Don't hide in your closets. Be like me. Be counted!* Well that's bull. Not everybody lives and works in a world like yours. You can be different in show business and it's accepted. You've already had plenty of people forge the way before you. But that's not the case in business or politics. Maybe what I'm doing with Jim is wrong . . . but right now, I don't feel like I have much of a choice . . . and I don't appreciate your spying on me or meddling in my affairs. You've only been in New York a few hours and you've already insinuated your way into my work life and now I find you in the dark, eavesdropping on my private conversations." Andrie was uncomfortable with her own argument. She was ashamed of what she was doing to Jim. She found it difficult to look Destiny in the eyes, so she began sorting through the day's mail as the conversation continued.

"You said that I haven't changed. How much do you think has changed with you? You're still playing games with people's feelings. That guy is in love with you, but you're just using him like a pawn. . . . And let me tell you somethin', I never preached to anyone about comin' out. I know that it's hard in this world. I see what's happening to you and I just think that you could be happier some other way, that's all. By the way, you're not the only person in this world who's capable of being faithful and committed in a relationship. I was with Nicole five years and I never even touched another woman in that time. I want to share my life with just one person. So stop tryin' to make me sound like some depraved, obscene monster. Remember, it was me who found you with someone else fifteen years ago. You act like it was the other way around. Maybe if you stopped hiding from the world, you would see things differently. Maybe you would even see me differently." As Destiny said that, her tone softened, as though, in some way, she truly wished Andrie would see her in a different light.

"I doubt it," Andrie said flatly, as she pulled a copy of a celebrity magazine from the pile of mail she was sorting and tossed it into Destiny's lap.

The cover pictured Destiny with an attractive blond woman at a Hollywood party and the tag line read: "Destiny Anderson, Don Juanita." She looked up to respond, but she found herself alone in the room as the door to Andrie's bedroom slammed shut.

Sitting there in the dimly lit room, with only her thoughts to keep her company, Destiny wondered why she had antagonized Andrie the way she did, when things had gone so well earlier. She could have pretended not to have heard the conversation between Andrie and Jim, but some irrational part of her brain compelled her to do what she had done. As she looked down at the magazine's cover again, she realized how much it hurt her to think that this was the image Andrie had of her. She had observed that Andrie had never been impressed by her success, in fact there were times, like just then, when she felt Andrie disapproved of everything about her. She asked herself why Andrie's opinion should affect her as deeply as it did.

Destiny sighed as she slumped back lower into the green brocade couch. It was time to face an inescapable truth. After all these years and all the friction, fights and animosity between them, she had never truly been able to rid her heart of Andrie. There were times, even when she was living with Nicole, that Destiny would experience an emotion that felt akin to being homesick when she thought about Andrie. The idea that a part of her missed this woman, who had once hurt her so badly, had always puzzled her. But right then, sitting alone in Andrie's living room after all the pleasant and unpleasant encounters they had shared throughout the evening, Destiny felt almost engulfed by a sense of belonging where she was . . . there, surrounded by things that belonged to Andrie, her scarf with the scent of her perfume on it, draped over the arm of the sofa, her briefcase, leaning against the leg of a cherrywood table in the foyer . . . even the small touches to the room, like the dried wild flower arrangement over the counter that separated the living room from the kitchen. Andrie was all around the room and it felt wonderful. It seemed as though some veil had been lifted, allowing Destiny to see what had been there all along. She had always wondered why the anger had remained after fifteen years. Now she knew the answer; she never stopped loving Andrie.

Chapter Five

Morning's light illuminated every corner of Andrie's living room. Destiny had gotten up early and done some grocery shopping. By the time Andrie came out of her bedroom, Destiny was almost finished preparing breakfast.

"Do you like French toast?" Destiny asked in a voice that was louder and more robust than Andrie could stand first thing in the morning.

"Is there coffee?" Andrie asked in a sleepy voice, squinting as she looked around the kitchen.

"How about tea?" Destiny asked cheerfully.

"Fine." Andrie's tone was indifferent. She sat on a stool and leaned on the counter with her chin in her hand as she watched Destiny in the kitchen. "So, you cook?"

"Of course. You know that I've been on my own since college, that meant cookin' and cleanin' for myself," Destiny answered as she poured the tea.

"You don't look like the domestic type," Andrie groaned, still sleepy as she observed Destiny moving around the kitchen.

"I'm not. I don't do this a lot, anymore. I usually eat out, or order in, when I'm on the road. And when I'm home, I have Consuela. She's this really nice woman who cooks and cleans for me. You must really know how to cook. So what's your specialty?" Destiny asked, remembering the wonderful meals Andrie's mother had cooked.

"I've made a couple of sandwiches over the past few years, but I normally just order in," Andrie said in a grumpy morning voice.

"Girl, you should be ashamed of yourself," Destiny said as she waved a spatula at Andrie.

Andrie straightened up on the stool. "Why?"

"You're Italian. You should be a great cook. Your mom is a

great cook. I remember eating at your house that time I was down for winter break. After fifteen years I still dream about her homemade manicotti."

"It gets boring cooking for yourself," Andrie replied, reluctant to continue the conversation.

"What about Ann? Haven't the two of you ever had a quiet little dinner here?"

"No. She's never here that long. And when she comes over, it's not for dinner," Andrie replied, attempting unsuccessfully to embarrass Destiny into a temporary silence.

"That's too bad. I can't think of anything nicer than an intimate dinner and a glass of wine before making love," Destiny replied, seeing through Andrie's technique.

"I knew that it wouldn't be long before you'd introduce some crude remark into the conversation. Was that the type of line you use to charm those creatures you date?" Andrie said sharply.

Placing a plate of French toast in front of Andrie, Destiny proceeded to cut a large piece off with a fork. "Here, taste this, girl. Maybe it'll make you sweet," she teased, as she shoveled it into Andrie's mouth without allowing her time to respond.

As Andrie struggled to get the wad of French toast down, Destiny continued to talk. "I'm workin' on a couple of songs for a movie that's supposed to take place in New York. So, I thought that I'd sort of hang around the city and get the feel of it. I never get the chance to do that when I come here for a concert. Wanna come along?"

"No thanks. I really need to do some shopping," Andrie answered with her mouth still half full.

"You mean you don't have plans with Ann?"

"No. She's gone out of town for the weekend."

"Really, where?" Destiny asked.

"Not that it's any of your business, but she went skiing with Stuart Sottley."

"Oh . . . her fiance. Why didn't you join her with your boyfriend from last night?" Destiny asked with a smirk.

Andrie was becoming increasingly annoyed by Destiny's questions. She didn't want to be made to think about her lover being at some ski resort, pretending to be having a romantic weekend with a man.

"If I agree to go with you today, would you promise not to needle me or pry about my life with Ann for the rest of your stay?" she asked Destiny.

"I promise," Destiny said, putting her hand over her heart.

Andrie sighed and agreed to spend the day with her. It was quite obvious that she wasn't looking forward to the experience. But that had little effect on Destiny's enthusiasm.

"Fine. I'm going to take a shower. And you can decide where you want us to *hang around* today," Andrie said sarcastically, as she hopped off the kitchen stool.

"OK. Cool," Destiny chirped back, smiling.

"Cool?" Andrie repeated and rolled her eyes as she left the room.

Chapter Six

Saturday afternoons in Central Park bustled. New Yorkers seemed to thrive on the mid-December chill. There were parents out with their children, playing in the mounds of snow that were left behind from the night before, and every so often, a vendor selling pretzels and chestnuts.

The taxi ride to the park had been polite but lacking in conversation. It was clear to Destiny that Andrie wasn't in the least bit interested in entertaining a conversation with her and that she was there simply as part of their agreement.

Strolling through the park, Destiny ambled with a wide leisurely stride down the snow-covered paths, while Andrie took smaller, more hurried steps as if she were on her way to an appointment. They didn't even appear to be dressed for the same activity: Destiny in a pair of faded jeans, cowboy boots and her beat-up brown bomber jacket . . . while Andrie wore a snug black skirt and sweater with a soft black cashmere coat.

Close to an hour had passed, as they walked without more than a casual word, here or there. Yet both their minds were busy with thought, Destiny wondering how to make Andrie see that she hadn't become the person that the tabloids made her out to be, and Andrie trying to figure out why some part of her felt so comfortable spending the day with a person she had repeatedly proclaimed she disliked.

The sight of an empty park bench put an end to the uncomfortable silence. "Do you want to sit for a while?" Destiny asked, pointing to the bench.

"All right," Andrie agreed.

"I was hoping those little fellers would be hangin' around here," Destiny said, nodding toward a flock of pigeons with heads bobbing back and forth as they rambled around, exploring the

walking path for discarded crumbs of food. She dug into the
pocket of her jacket and produced a crumpled up brown paper
bag.

"What's that?" Andrie asked, with a puzzled look.

"Your French toast. These little guys love this stuff. When I was
in college, I used to go to Washington Square Park with David
almost every day at lunch time. I would play my guitar and he
would feed them pieces of my sandwich. By the time I was ready
to eat, my lunch was usually gone. Watch this," Destiny said as
she tossed a handful of slightly soggy mixture into the crowd of
cooing, gurgling birds. As it landed in their midst, they scattered,
running in all directions to escape the food. Then a split second later,
they scrambled back, even climbing over each other to get to it.

"Time and again." Destiny chuckled, shaking her head as she
watched frenzied birds. "That happens time and again and it
always makes me laugh. First, they run away from the crumbs
'cause they're scared of them. Then they run back to them when
they realize that it's food. It reminds me of people. Sometimes we
run away from somethin' that we need because we're afraid, then
we run back to it when we realize that it's right for us . . . and
you gotta hope that it's still there when you get back. Otherwise,
it's like some of these birds . . . by the time some of them go
back, there's nothing left. And what's worse is that people can be
just like these birds and make the same mistakes time and again,"
Destiny explained, never looking away from the pigeons.

"Did something like that happen to you?" Andrie asked, as she
watched Destiny feed the birds, who alternately ran, then returned
to the small chunks of bread that landed near them.

Destiny's voice and expression became somber and pensive as
she answered the question, "I don't know, I hope not," she said,
turning to Andrie. It had begun to snow lightly and she couldn't
help but notice the way the snowflakes landed on Andrie's face
and in her hair, making her look as beautiful as she did the first
time Destiny laid eyes on her.

*   *   *

By mid-afternoon, they had taken a cab from Central Park to SoHo, where they window shopped, then walked to the West Village where they decided to have lunch at a quaint little bistro.

The hostess immediately recognized Destiny as she removed her dark glasses after entering the restaurant. "Ms. Anderson, if you want some privacy, I have a lovely little table in the rear corner, over there." She pointed to a secluded little table by the fireplace at the rear of the restaurant.

"That's great. Thanks." Destiny was relieved that she didn't have to ask for a table where she wouldn't be noticed. She always worried about people misunderstanding her reasons for such a request. Destiny hated the idea of people thinking that she was trying to avoid the public. But there were times that privacy was important to her. This was one of those times.

Soon after they settled into their chairs they agreed upon a good French merlot that Andrie had chosen from the wine list. Neither was particularly hungry, so they almost immediately decided on a Caesar salad for two and a small plate of Camembert cheese and olives.

"So, I guess you always get the best tables in restaurants now," Andrie remarked, referring to the way the hostess had greeted them.

"It's not somethin' that I ask them to do." Destiny's response sounded almost apologetic.

"I have to ask you a silly question. Is that the same jacket you wore way back when I first met you?" Andrie asked with an embarrassed chuckle.

"Sure is. Why?"

"I just thought . . ." Andrie's voice trailed off, as she allowed Destiny to finish the thought.

"That I would have thrown it away years ago? This old jacket's outlasted every car, every job, and every relationship that I've ever

had. It's kinda like an old buddy and it aged better than I did too,"
Destiny joked.

Andrie stared at Destiny for a few moments, noticing time's
finely etched signature at the corners of her mouth and eyes. The
faint lines seemed less the legacy of age, than years of wide
friendly smiles and warm, hearty laughter. They were creases
Andrie knew would never mar Ann's face, with its well-planned and
calculated expressions.

"Well, I guess you really made all your dreams come true,"
Andrie observed.

"No. Not all of them," Destiny answered wistfully.

"What else did you want?" Andrie asked, wondering what career
goal Destiny had in mind.

"Don't you remember when we first met, I told you that I
wanted a family and you said that someday I'd meet the right
person and she would be that family to me?"

"My God. I do remember that, now." Andrie was shocked that
Destiny had carried those words with her all this time.

"I haven't made that dream come true yet."

"You miss Nicole, don't you?" Andrie was responding to the
sincerity in Destiny's words.

"I did for a while. But deep down I guess that I always knew
she wasn't the right one for me," Destiny answered in a reflective
tone as she looked across at Andrie and wished that she could take
back all those years they had lost.

The waitress arrived with their Caesar salad. Their conversation
stopped temporarily while the salad was being prepared at the side
of their table. Destiny smiled politely at the waitress, who seemed a
little nervous to be waiting on a celebrity. Destiny began to make
friendly small talk with her, so she might relax a bit.

Andrie observed Destiny. She knew that Destiny was trying to
make the waitress feel comfortable. It seemed a contrast to Ann's
polite but coldly formal behavior in similar situations. As Destiny
laughed at a story the waitress told, her eyes seemed to sparkle
and her broad smile transformed fine laugh lines into deep dimples,

making her face radiate a beauty that hid just beneath her rough exterior.

Sitting across the table from her, Andrie observed that there was undoubtedly a charm to Destiny Anderson, in an unpolished, unkempt sort of way. Remembering how she once felt toward her, Andrie needed to remind herself that this was the same Destiny Anderson who was constantly pictured on the tabloids flaunting her affection for various women and being dubbed "Don Juanita." Yet, she admired the sensitivity Destiny showed by being so nice to the nervous waitress.

Once the waitress left, Destiny pushed her fork into her salad and began eating.

Andrie couldn't help but comment. "That was nice of you," she said, nodding her head in the direction of the waitress's path.

"You mean trying to make her feel comfortable? There's no need for her to get all in knots, I'm working for a living, just like her," Destiny answered, looking up from her salad.

"You're doing everything you ever dreamed of. That's a little bit different than waiting tables or even being an assistant to a politician," Andrie added.

"You know it all used to be fun. People askin' for my autograph, takin' pictures of me, all of it. But after a while, you realize that the person they want isn't really you. It's the celebrity. That's OK, too, until you can't figure out if the people you want to be with, want to be with you or the celebrity. I can't date anyone without that thought in my head. I can't even make a new friend without wondering about it." For a moment Destiny put her fork down and turned toward the open fireplace. She stared into its blaze for a short while.

Andrie could see that she was troubled.

"So, you're surrounded by other celebrities who have the same problem. Haven't you found friends . . . or lovers . . . in that crowd?" Andrie asked awkwardly.

"I've found some people, who I got real close with and I have as friends. But looking there for a lover is pretty limiting,'' Destiny replied.

"I guess even having your dreams come true has its drawbacks.'' Andrie felt for Destiny. But she still wondered about all the stories that she had read lately. "You still date a lot despite all that. All those stories in the papers . . .''

"That's mostly hype. If I go anywhere with anyone, they make it into an affair. About a year ago I went to a football game with Nicole's cousin Carl, and because some reporter saw me there with a guy, a rumor got started that I was going straight. That really bugged me for a while. Pretty ironic, huh?''

"Are you telling me that all those women I've seen you with in magazines are just friends?'' Andrie asked skeptically.

"No. But like I told you last night, they were a way for me to ease the pain when Nicole left. . . . Can we talk about you for a while?'' Destiny asked, wanting to find out all she could about Andrie and her life now.

"You promised not to needle me, remember?''

"I won't needle you. But can I ask you some questions about your life with Ann?'' Destiny asked in a sincere tone, as she put her fork down and looked into Andrie's eyes.

"OK, but if I start to feel like you're taking shots at me that's it,'' Andrie answered, still feeling the effect of criticisms Destiny had made the night before.

"That's a deal,'' Destiny agreed, then leaned forward and asked, "Well, right now, while you're sitting here, Ann's pretending to be having a romantic weekend with some guy. Doesn't that bother you at all?''

"It comes with the territory. She needs to maintain an image. As far as how I feel, I guess I'm like you. My dream came true, but it has its drawbacks.''

"What do you mean?'' Destiny asked, wanting to learn all she could about Andrie's life with Ann.

"I always wanted someone who was stable, secure, respectable . . . Ann's all that. But since she's a politician, we have to put on this charade, for image purposes. No one seems to understand that. Not David and not my family. They all think that Ann puts her career ahead of me. I know that they only care about my happiness, but they only make things worse by not understanding her." There was sadness in Andrie's voice as she explained the situation.

It made Destiny need to ask, "Are you happy?"

"Are you?" Andrie replied. It was clear that she wanted to avoid the topic. She hoped that her response would discourage Destiny from questioning her further.

"Not completely. That's part of the reason I wanted to get out of LA for a while. Now, you still didn't answer my question yet," Destiny persisted.

"Yes." Andrie was lying. She hoped that Destiny couldn't see through her. She didn't want anyone to know how much pain her relationship with Ann was causing her.

"Last night, you had some kind of problem that made you run out of the party," Destiny reminded her.

"I had a disagreement with Ann, about the Women's Way project." There was an air of defensiveness in Andrie's answer.

"That project means a lot to you, doesn't it?" Destiny asked.

"It's helped a lot of women. It even saved some lives. I'm very proud of it," Andrie answered with a sad smile, as she put the glass of merlot to her lips.

"So what's the problem with it?"

"There's no problem with the project. The problem is with a company that wants to buy the building that it's in and turn it into a parking facility for its employees. If that happens, there won't be anymore Women's Way."

"Can't you just find another building?"

"It's not that simple. The project is funded solely from private donations and we're barely able to meet our expenses. We were given the building rent free by Stuart Sottley. No one else is ever going to let us have a building, rent free, in a good location. Stuart promised Ann the building rent free for seven years. In return she

introduced him to some very rich business investors from Asia he
had been wanting to meet."

"She must be pretty dedicated to Women's Way, to extend
herself like that," Destiny said.

"I'm sure that she cares about it," Andrie responded, ashamed
to admit that she knew that Ann's motives were far less altruistic.
Ann counted on the success of the Women's Way project to
improve her record in the area of social issues. Prior to Women's
Way, she had been considered an ultra-conservative politician who
did all she could to promote big business and reduce funds toward
social issues. Women's Way had given her national exposure as
being socially involved yet fiscally conservative. That was a winning
combination in the political climate of the day.

"So if she's so close to Sottley, can't she convince him to stick
to their agreement?" Destiny asked.

"He's not the one who's breaking it." Andrie proceeded to
explain the reasons why Ann was in favor of Cortronics buying the
building.

The story didn't surprise Destiny. It simply confirmed her
impression of Ann. However, she listened without commenting. As
long as Andrie was opening up, Destiny didn't want to alienate her
by saying the wrong thing. She saw Andrie trying to make sense
out of Ann's arguments in this situation. It was clear that the idea
of Women's Way becoming defunct was painful to Andrie.

Destiny wished that she could help, but a building of that size in
New York City was far more than she could afford. She wanted to
hold Andrie and help her through this. She hadn't seen Andrie
speak so candidly in years. Destiny was enjoying this cease-fire.
They both were.

"Let's talk about something happy, since we can't solve any of
our problems sitting here commiserating," Andrie said, forcing a
smile, then continuing, "Tell me about the songs you're writing."

"Well, I got a call from a friend of mine who's making a movie
that takes place in New York. I saw a rough cut of it, so I have a
feel of the theme. I thought that spending a few days here would

make it easier for me to give the music a more urban New York flavor. I think I needed a reason to get out of LA for a while, anyway. I always liked New York. It brings back a lot of memories."

"Do you remember how you used to dream about doing all the things that you're doing now? You really made it all happen," Andrie said with admiration.

"There are still things I haven't achieved yet . . . venues I haven't played and awards I'd like to win. I still have a lot of dreams left." As Destiny spoke, a familiar glow lit up her face. Andrie still recognized it after all the years that had passed. It was the look that would come over her whenever she would talk about her dream. Seeing it again, Andrie couldn't help but smile, knowing that there was still so much more that Destiny wished to achieve as she lived her dream.

"I'm glad that I came with you today," Andrie said, still smiling softly.

Those words and that smile triggered a sudden rush of euphoria which surged through Destiny like a dizzying drug. For a brief moment she saw the Andrie she had kissed so long ago on that clear dark December night.

Chapter Seven

The note on the counter read, *7:30 a.m. I was paged by DC headquarters. They need me to fax some papers from the NY office. I picked up some cranberry muffins and breakfast things this morning, so check the kitchen. I need to get some other work done as long as I'm there. I may be home late. Have a nice day. Andrie*

Destiny smiled as she read it. She decided to stay in and work on her writing. But first she would make breakfast. She found the bacon, cranberry muffins and orange juice Andrie had left for her and went to work cooking.

Moments later, the doorbell rang. It was David with a large bakery bag in hand.

"Here, I brought over some danishes and coffee," he said, entering the apartment and sniffing audibly as he walked toward the kitchen. "Cooking?" *sniff, sniff,* "Coffee? . . . What's going on here? Don't tell me that Andrie made you breakfast?"

"No," Destiny answered, as she moved around the kitchen.

David let out an exaggerated sigh of relief. "Thank God. For a second I thought that the pressure of having you around sent her over the edge," he joked.

"But she did go shopping this morning. So I was just cooking. Come on, have breakfast with me," Destiny invited him.

"Maybe she did go over the edge. She was out of bed before noon on a Sunday and she went shopping for food?" David remarked incredulously, as he walked over to the refrigerator and opened the door. "Jeffrey Dahmer wouldn't keep some of this stuff that's in this refrigerator," David observed with a nauseated expression, as he removed the foil that covered a glass bowl on the top shelf.

"Yeah, I thought that I'd clean that out for her," Destiny replied.

"Oh, where's my camera when I need it. Let's see, you can clean her refrigerator; Elton John can vacuum . . . I wonder if Madonna does toilets? . . . So, where is our little hostess from hell?" he asked, glancing around the room.

"She got paged this morning, so she had to go into the office," Destiny answered.

"Now that sounds more like her." As he spoke, David picked up the magazine that had the picture of Destiny with the "Don Juanita" article in it. "Hey, cute title. It's so endearing," he commented dryly, as he flipped through the pages.

"Dave, listen to me for a minute. I need to talk to you about something." Destiny slid a plate of bacon and scrambled eggs across the kitchen counter to him. "You know how there's been a cold war between me and Andrie for the last fifteen years?" she started.

David nodded curiously, as he took his plate and headed for the living room couch. He had no idea what she was leading up to, but he had a feeling that she was about to make a revelation.

Then Destiny continued, "Friday night all the pieces fell together. I want Andrie. I always have."

"Well, there goes the rest of my hair," David joked as he rolled his eyes and fell back on the couch in shock.

"That's where it happened on Friday night," Destiny said, as she pointed to the area of the couch where David was seated.

David quickly jumped up, holding his plate in one hand and brushing off his clothes with the other, as he mugged an exaggerated look of disgust.

"I don't mean that," Destiny said impatiently. "We weren't even near each other. In fact, we argued that night. But after the fight I was sitting here alone on the couch, thinking about Andrie and our past. Then I looked around the room at her things and I realized she's been the right one all this time. She had gone for a walk during the party and I went with her. She told me that the time she had come with you to San Francisco and saw me play in that little bar, she wanted to talk with me and iron things out . . . I always thought she was there to taunt me. I was too hurt to give her a chance."

"Look, I need to say something . . ." David said, putting his plate down on the coffee table. "I love both of you, and for a long time I thought it would be great if you got together. But after all this time, for you to come to this conclusion after spending just one evening with her seems a little too fast, even to me."

"I know it sounds crazy. I just wish that I was smart enough to have realized it years ago. But this was the first time Andrie and I have had time alone together in all those years. It was a matter of bad timing and too much pride. And I was afraid that if I gave her even the slightest chance, she'd just hurt me again."

"Your life has changed dramatically through the years," he said, pointing to the magazine with Destiny's picture on the cover. "Are you telling me that you want to settle down with one woman?"

"You don't have to illustrate your point with that stupid magazine. You know that as much I went through with Nicole, I never cheated on her. All the hype, including these pictures, started after Nicole left me. You know me. Don't buy into some exaggerated image that comes through in those rags. I'm still the same Destiny I was when you met me. Just a little older and wiser, I hope. For whatever reason fate had in mind, Andrie and I went in different directions for a long time. But I think that we were meant to be together. And now, fate is leading us down a new path. Maybe we needed to experience certain things separately before we could be together. I don't know. All I can say is that I know my life was meant to be with Andrie."

As much as David felt that Destiny was right about belonging with Andrie, something told him that fate had just as many obstacles in store for them now as it did then. "Des, you've got to remember that Andrie's been with Ann for seven years. Do you realize what you're getting into here?"

"I'm not tryin' to be a home wrecker. If I thought that Andrie was truly happy with Ann, I would walk away from this . . . as much as it would hurt me to do that. The fact is, I can see the sadness in her eyes and I would give my life to take it away."

Destiny was not one to waste words or exaggerate. David had always admired her for that. It was for that reason that he knew she was sure of her feelings.

"Well, it's not my place to say whether their relationship is right for Andrie or not. But I do know that the facade that Ann has them maintain causes Andrie a lot of pain. So, do you think she wants you, too?" he asked.

"She may not know it yet. But she wants me. And I don't care how long it takes or how much she fights it, I'm not gonna give up until we're together," Destiny said, with a determined gleam in her eye.

"Ooow . . . why are the best men always dykes? Sometimes you make me feel like I'm a lesbian trapped in a gay man's body," David said, as he feigned a swoon.

*   *   *

Andrie looked at the clock on her desk. It was almost 6 p.m. She had been working non-stop since eight-thirty that morning. It was almost as though she wanted to lose herself in work, in order to avoid thinking about Destiny. But throughout the day, Destiny's face would flash in front of her eyes. She didn't know why it was happening, but it worried her. If there was one thing her relationship with Ann didn't need right now, it was for her to be drawn to someone else. She felt her life with Ann becoming increasingly strained of late. Their disagreement about Women's Way and the pressure of the campaign added to the burden already presented by Ann's marriage plans. Andrie wondered if those factors played some part in her recurrent thoughts of Destiny. No matter what the reason was, Andrie told herself that she could not, under any circumstances, allow herself to become susceptible to the feelings she was beginning to experience toward Destiny.

As she packed up her briefcase to leave, Andrie instinctively reached for the phone to let Destiny know that she was on her way. After punching in the first few digits, she hung up the phone. She wasn't even sure why she decided not to make the call. Then, just before leaving, she looked at herself in the mirror and touched up her lipstick, which was something she never did when she was heading directly home.

*   *   *

Destiny had been playing her small keyboard and writing all day. She was happy with the work she had done on the first song. Taking a break, she realized that it was early evening. It had been several hours since David had left. She smiled as she remembered what he said on his way out the door, *"You're the best thing that could happen for each other."* His words gave her even more confidence that trying to win back Andrie's heart was the right thing to do. As she began to lose herself in thoughts of how it might feel to touch, and hold, and kiss Andrie again, Destiny heard the sound of someone coming into the apartment.

"I'm back," Andrie called out from the living room. The sound of her voice warmed Destiny inside as she walked out to greet her.

"Hi," Destiny called back casually, wanting all the while to take Andrie into her arms and show her how much she had missed her all day.

"Did you find my note this morning?" Andrie asked as she shed her coat, leaving it on the arm of the couch.

"Yeah I did. . . . Oh, thanks, you didn't have to go shopping."

"Oh, it was nothing. I would have burned you something, but I didn't have time," Andrie joked, then added, "I'm starving. How about Italian?"

"Fine, where?"

"There's a cute little place just down the block," Andrie told her.

"Is there someplace a little further? Someplace we could take a cab to?" Destiny inquired.

"This place is really pretty good. I think you'd like it. Why would you want to go someplace further away?"

"Ya see, if somebody recognizes me and we're close by, they're likely to follow us back here. But if we leave and get into a cab that probably won't happen," Destiny explained.

Andrie sighed deeply, tossing her head back. "Wow. There really are drawbacks to having your dream come true. . . . I'll tell you what, let's just call for a pizza and a cold antipasto . . . and we'll open a bottle of wine. That way I can get out of these heels and put on some lounging clothes. OK?" Andrie was wearing a forest green sweater dress, which clung and draped in all the right spots and came to an abrupt but appealing end about two inches above her knee.

"Sounds great. By the way . . . what you're wearing . . . it looks good on you," Destiny said. Her own awkwardness caused her to grin a bit. Although Destiny Anderson had been known to be able to seduce most women effortlessly since her college days, at that moment she felt like the shy young girl she used to be back in Colton Corners.

Andrie thanked her for the compliment and proceeded to her room to change out of her clothes. About five minutes later she emerged from the bedroom wearing an oversized, worn-out Boston University football jersey and white silk pajama bottoms. "I called the restaurant while I was changing, the pizza should be here in about thirty minutes."

"Great," said Destiny as she noticed that the change of clothes made Andrie looked very much like she did when she was twenty. There was still that little-girl quality there, which made it difficult for Destiny to forget how it felt to have her arms around her.

"So, did yesterday help you get the feel of the city that you needed for your songs?" Andrie asked as she slumped down next to Destiny on the couch.

"Yeah, I think it's comin'. I'm real happy with what I've done so far." They both had their feet up on the coffee table. Destiny stared at her worn cowboy boots next to Andrie's smooth bare feet and delicately painted toenails. She started to sway her feet side to side. Their movement forced Andrie to do the same.

"Can you play it for me?" Andrie asked.

"Sure, after I work on it a little more," Destiny told her.

"Remember that tune I heard you playing in David's basement?" Andrie asked, as she tried to recall the melody.

"Lord, do I remember that. I was fixin' to give it to you that Christmas," Destiny recalled.

"I know. You told me, that day in the basement. I thought that was the most beautiful present I could ever get. . . . Hey, how about some wine while we wait for the pizza to get here?" Andrie asked, jumping off the couch and heading to the kitchen, even before she could hear Destiny agree to it. It hurt her to think that Destiny never got the chance to give her that gift. She wished that the fear and confusion she felt as a young girl had not made her hurt Destiny and turn her back on her own feelings. Then, choosing a red Bordeaux from a modest collection under the kitchen counter, she drove the painful thoughts from her mind. "Come in here and open this bottle while I get us some glasses," she called out to Destiny.

Destiny gladly did as she was asked. There was something about puttering around the kitchen with Andrie that felt right, she thought to herself.

"How about a toast?" Destiny said with a smile.

"To what?"

"To finding happiness," she replied as she extended her glass toward Andrie.

"I am happy," Andrie replied in an annoyed tone as she put the glass to her lips. She was obviously irked by what she had inferred from Destiny's toast.

"Hold on a minute here girl, I just made an innocent little toast. I didn't say anything about your relationship and I'm sorry if you took it that way. But now that we're talkin' about it, I don't believe that you're happy being some deep dark secret in the life of a woman who denies you the passion you were put on this earth to feel," Destiny blurted out, knowing that she needed to bring her feelings into the light if she ever hoped to get through to Andrie.

Andrie's expression escalated from annoyance to outrage. "How dare you tell me what I was put on this earth to feel? . . . And how can you accuse Ann of denying me passion when you have no idea of how she feels for me?" Andrie responded in an angry, defensive tone, while inside other emotions were moving her. It was becoming impossible for her to avoid the memory of how Destiny once made her feel with little more than a kiss. Now, Andrie was fighting back thoughts of what it would feel like to make love with Destiny.

Her body jumped as Destiny unexpectedly slammed down her glass and began moving closer.

Andrie's head began to swim. All the thoughts and desires she had hidden, denied and pushed to the deepest parts of her memory were coming alive and seizing control of her body.

Something, maybe the expression in Destiny's dark eyes, told Andrie that Destiny was about to touch her. The anticipation made her quiver with excitement. The room around her was fading . . . all she saw was Destiny.

There was now almost no space between them as Destiny closed in on her.

"Ann encourages you to be with a man who holds you, who kisses you, who touches you . . . who does everything short of making love to you. Or have you taken him to bed, too?"

The accusation stunned Andrie. It wasn't what she had expected at this moment. Indignant with rage, she tried to push Destiny away from her, but Destiny wouldn't be moved. Rather, she persisted, as her heavy breathy voice caressed Andrie's face with every word, "You need someone who can love you with all the passion that's missing from your life now . . . someone who will tear down the gates and storm the walls that you've built up around yourself, until they penetrate every part of you . . . a lover who fills you with fire and passion and blood . . . until it becomes that one person alone who can reach into you and touch your soul." Destiny spoke the last of those words with her lips just touching Andrie's, who welcomed them longingly, as inside she faced the unavoidable truth: she had never stopped wanting Destiny.

Immediately, the sound of a loud knocking on the door violated their intimacy and shattered the moment. It caused Andrie to spring back with a gasp.

"Who is it?" she called, as she headed anxiously toward the door, her heart still pounding from desire and excitement.

"Pizza delivery," a voice called out from the other side of the door.

Andrie opened the door, still half dazed from her encounter with Destiny.

Looking on, Destiny could see Andrie searching the area around her for her purse. Destiny darted over with a fifty dollar bill which she promptly stuffed into the delivery man's hand as he stood just inside the doorway, seeming to look about the room, almost as if he were pretending not to notice their fumbling.

"Let me see here," he mumbled, as he stuck his hand in his pocket to make change.

"It's OK. Keep it," Destiny replied, and thanked him for the delivery as she started to close the door.

"Thanks a lot. Oh, by the way, the front door downstairs was open. That's why I let myself in and knocked on your apartment door. I hope I didn't alarm you," the neatly dressed, thirtyish man said.

"No. It was fine. See ya," Destiny replied, closing the door. Just then the phone rang. Destiny turned to see Andrie, who was still quite shaken, answer it.

"Hello . . . oh, Ann." Andrie tried her best to sound calm and relaxed. But, the storm of emotions which Destiny caused in her was still raging. Her voice was edgy with a mixture of guilt and surprise.

"No. I'm fine. I'm just tired. I was at the office all day. Frank Harris called from DC this morning. They needed your position paper on the flat tax issue for an article in the *Washington Post*. So, I had to finish the one I had been working on and fax it to them. Then, I ended up staying to get a few other things done. So, how was skiing?" she asked.

Ann's voice on the other end answered, "Good. I feel really relaxed. Listen I'm calling from the car, so I should be back in the city in about an hour. I'll stop by."

Andrie could feel her face flush red hot, as she tried to come up with a reason why Ann shouldn't come over. She didn't want to face Ann that night. "Well, I don't know. It'll be late by the time you get here and I'm really exhausted."

"It won't be that late and I can't stay long, anyway." Ann spoke quickly, almost impatiently.

"OK," Andrie replied hesitantly as she hung up the phone and tried to figure out how she would explain this to Destiny. She also wondered where Destiny could go while Ann was in the apartment.

"Ann's coming over, isn't she?" Destiny couldn't help hearing Andrie's side of the conversation.

"Yes . . . she should be here in an hour."

"How do you feel? Are you gonna be all right?" She realized that Andrie was upset and confused and that she was partly the cause. Destiny struggled with herself. She couldn't bear the idea of leaving Andrie alone with Ann, but she didn't have the right to oppose it. She would have to leave.

Shaking her head, Andrie whispered sadly, "This was wrong. I shouldn't have. . . ." Then her voice trailed off in resignation.

Destiny put her hands on Andrie's shoulders and looked deeply into her eyes. "I'm not gonna forget what almost happened here tonight. I don't think you are either. I'll go now, but we're not finished. We haven't even started." Destiny was determined to have Andrie face what they had both kept hidden from themselves for so many years.

At that moment, Andrie ached to feel Destiny, but that feeling was marred by the guilt and the confusion of the circumstances. She stood at the doorway of the guest room as Destiny walked in to get her jacket. Destiny began to put some of her things out of sight, but Andrie stopped her, saying, "You don't have to hide your things. Ann never goes in this room."

She walked past Andrie and headed into the living room, where she took a cursory look for signs of her presence there.

"Don't worry. She never goes in here either," Andrie assured her.

"Well, we don't have to worry about Ann finding traces of me in the one room that she does use, do we?" Destiny asked, as she felt herself being torn apart inside. The sarcasm of her remark betrayed her feelings. She would have given anything right then to be able to tell Andrie how she felt and not leave her alone with Ann. But she knew that Andrie wasn't ready to make that choice just yet. Despite the fact that she believed Andrie still cared for her, Destiny was still aware that Andrie had been committed to her relationship with Ann for the last seven years. No matter how agonizing it would be for her, Destiny had to hold back now or risk losing Andrie to Ann forever.

Andrie offered no response, as she quietly walked Destiny to the door. She searched Destiny's face as if she needed some answer to what was happening, but what she found there took her back fifteen years to that stormy evening outside her house in Brooklyn.

Embarrassment, confusion and, most of all, frustrated desire were in her voice as she broke her brief silence. "She has a bronze Infiniti. It'll be parked across the street in the no-parking zone while she's here, so you'll be able to know when she's gone," Andrie said, putting her hand on Destiny's brown leather sleeve as she stood in the doorway ready to leave. Then she asked Destiny where she was going.

"I'm not sure. I need to clear my head. I'll be back when her car is gone," she answered.

Andrie was relieved when Destiny told her that she'd be coming back, and it showed on her face. It was that look that told Destiny that, whether Andrie realized it or not, she still cared deeply.

As the door closed behind her, Destiny felt a sick, aching feeling in her stomach. Leaving the brownstone seemed next to impossible, as she forced her feet to keep moving one step at a time, further and further from the building. Had she looked back, she would have seen Andrie at her bedroom window, watching her as she disappeared around the corner.

*   *   *

"I can't stay long, I'm meeting with my father in about an hour," Ann announced, as she set foot into the apartment and tossed her coat on a small mahogany chair by the door.

"Do you want something to drink?" Andrie asked as she came out of the kitchen.

"I'd love a glass of white wine," she sighed.

"There's a bottle of pinot gris in the fridge."

"Good, let's bring it into the bedroom," Ann suggested as she all-too-predictably proceeded down the hall without waiting for Andrie.

Andrie lingered in the kitchen as she took out the bottle of wine and two glasses. All she could do was think about what had happened earlier. Her lips still tingled with the anticipation of being kissed by Destiny. As Andrie tried to regain her grasp on the reality of what had almost happened, she told herself that it was fortunate that Ann's call had interrupted them. As far as Andrie was concerned, her relationship with Ann was as binding as any marriage that existed between a man and woman. Yet, as much as she struggled with her conscience, her desire for Destiny remained.

"Andrie . . . I don't have all night. What are you doing?" Ann's voice beckoned from the bedroom, summoning Andrie deeper into the reality of the moment.

"I'm just looking for a corkscrew to open the bottle . . . I'll be right there." Her voice was tense and hesitant, but Ann failed to notice. Andrie would have to deal with the fact that once she went into the bedroom she and Ann would make love. She didn't know how she could be with Ann when she was still reeling from her encounter with Destiny. Heading down the hall to the bedroom, she wished that she could somehow vanish until the chaos within her had ceased.

"What were you doing . . . stomping the grapes?" Ann asked impatiently. As was her habit, she had already undressed and climbed into bed. It was a custom she defended with arguments about the time constraints of her schedule.

"I told you, I couldn't find the corkscrew," Andrie answered, as she poured the wine. "I'm really exhausted from this afternoon."

Then, taking one of the glasses from her, Ann asked, "Did you happen to work on that Access to Medical Treatment Act stuff?"

"You mean H.R. 2019. . . . Yes, I did. I also edited and proofed the speeches Ray wrote for you on H.R. 1951 and H.R. 598. One is the Food and Dietary Supplement Consumer Information Act and the other is the Pharmacy Compounding Act," Andrie said as she sat down at the edge of the bed and began to pour the wine.

"I know. Those are the ones all the health food fanatics keep writing me about," Ann replied in a disinterested tone.

"They aren't fanatics. They're average everyday people who realize that the pharmaceutical industry has been lobbying to prevent legislation that would support their right to seek other natural therapies, if they wanted to. They're people who think that you're representing them in Washington. They're people who don't see you getting wined and dined by lobbyists," Andrie said in a critical tone, as she watched Ann calmly sipping her wine.

"Well, now I know why Ray felt it best not to have you write those speeches. After all these years, you're still so naive about how the world works. I'm not about to shun the pharmaceutical industry in order to placate a small group of health food nuts. So, let's talk about something more interesting," Ann responded, sliding her hand across the bed and resting it on Andrie's.

"We've polled people in the district and most of them are in favor of these acts. So just keep in mind that you were elected to represent them," Andrie persisted. Privately, she had never been in favor of most of Ann's political views, but projects like Women's

Way and some other activities Ann was involved in gave her hope that one day the conservative congresswoman would mellow and become more moderate in her agenda.

Ann had enough of that subject. She told Andrie that she would discuss it with Ray.

Not wanting to prolong the argument, Andrie changed the subject. "So, how was skiing?" she asked, as she sat at the edge of the bed.

"Fine. By the way, we're closing in on a wedding date. We decided to make it one year from this February. I haven't chosen the exact date yet, but I thought it would be best to wait until after the election." For a moment, Ann sounded frighteningly like any other bride-to-be.

Although Andrie had been living with the idea of Ann intending to marry Stuart, hearing that they were this close to setting a date for the farce wedding made her feel vaguely nauseated. "I wish you didn't feel it necessary to keep up this lie. Wouldn't you be happier just being yourself?"

"I am myself, but you can't see that. Being *myself* means being a member of Congress, as well as being your lover. I'm both, but I have to hide one part of me from the public. If I don't, the other part could be lost. Keeping our relationship private doesn't mean I care any less for you," Ann explained with diminishing tolerance.

"This isn't a matter of keeping our relationship private. This is a matter of denying it altogether and marrying someone else as part of that denial," Andrie replied.

"Andrie, we just went through this argument the other night. I don't want to revisit it. I don't have time for this now."

"Do you know what I see here?" Andrie's question was obviously rhetorical, as she quickly continued. "I see two people in this relationship, but for the last seven years we've only been caring for the needs of one of them. I gave up my business because you thought that me being your assistant would be an effective cover for our relationship. You said that we couldn't live together. So I live alone and you drop by here when it's convenient for you. You even have me dating some poor soul who's now in love with me . . . and, like a fool, I've gone along with that, too. Now, you decide that you need to boost your all-American, family values image, so you're marrying some geriatric eunuch, and I'm expected to swallow that, too. Where does it end? When do my needs start to count for something?"

"Do you think any of this is easy on me? I never know who's watching me, or who knows about us and will use this against me in a campaign. But I'm here with you, aren't I? . . . So, let's just enjoy this time together," Ann said, as she moved across the bed toward Andrie. Her glass was empty, so she reached down and put it on the floor. Then she took Andrie's glass and set it down next to hers. Slowly, she drew Andrie down on the bed. There was a graceful flow to Ann's long, naked body, as it began to move around Andrie in an almost serpentine manner. Slowly, she slid her hand under the soft cotton jersey, peeling it back as she kissed Andrie's breasts and shoulders.

Andrie tried to respond by guiding Ann's face up with her hand and kissing her softly on the lips. There was a hesitancy to Andrie's movements, since they were motivated more by dedication than desire. She was doing all she could to drive Destiny from her mind, but the memory and the longing remained to torment her as Ann's lips and hands traveled her body. Lying there, her body entwined with Ann's, Andrie had never felt farther from her. As she felt Ann's hand slowly sliding down her thigh, a voice, so deep inside of Andrie that at first she could only hear it as an obscure and distant rumble, began calling out to her conscious mind. As Ann's cold hands wandered her body, finding their way to all the places that should have welcomed their touch, Andrie was consumed by the sound in her head, growing louder and louder . . . until she recognized it as her own voice screaming for Destiny. In that instant of discovery, Andrie abruptly pushed Ann away and drew herself up.

"What was that?" Ann asked, startled by a clamorous knocking sound that filled the apartment.

"Someone's at the door," Andrie replied, equally startled by the sound, yet relieved that the noise had distracted Ann from the fact that Andrie had pushed her away. "Keep this door closed and I'll go see who it is," Andrie added, reaching for her robe on the way out of the room. As she approached the door, Andrie could feel her stomach churn with anxiety. She wondered if somehow Destiny had returned without noticing that Ann's car was still parked on the street outside. Looking through the door's peephole, Andrie was relieved to see that it was only the pizza delivery man again. Her fears assuaged, she quickly opened the door.

"You guys must really like our food," he said as he handed over a large pizza box.

"I'm sorry, this must be a mistake; I didn't order this," Andrie said with a faint smile.

"Hmm . . . I'll bet I know what happened. We probably never pulled your order off the counter. I'm sorry to bother you. Listen, take the pizza. It's on us."

"No thanks, really. It's very nice of you, but we haven't even touched the first one yet."

"Please. You guys gave me a really big tip before. Maybe you'll want a midnight snack."

"All right. Thanks," Andrie conceded just to make him leave.

"Great. Have a good evening," he called out as he left.

"You too." She closed the door, set the pizza down and headed back to the bedroom to find Ann on her cellular phone. Andrie heard just enough of the conversation to know that it was about Cortronics and the sale of Stuart Sottley's building.

As Ann ended the call and put the phone back in her bag, Andrie questioned her. "What's that all about?"

"When you went to the door, I got a call from Fred Grey at Cortronics. He needed to know if we could reschedule tomorrow's meeting from 9 a.m. to 1 p.m. I didn't see any problem with that, so the meeting is at 1 p.m. . . . Who was at the door?"

"Oh, it was just a mistake. They thought I ordered a pizza,"

Andrie replied in a voice that was still shaking a bit from thinking that it could have been Destiny at the door.

Ann looked at her watch. "Damn. I knew this would happen. I have twenty minutes to get to my father's house for that meeting. We spent so much time arguing that now we have no time to be together." She sat up at the side of the bed and reached over to a chair, retrieving her beige satin bra and panties. She didn't try to hide her annoyance with Andrie. "You've got to resign yourself to the fact that this is the way things are for us. It's beyond our control." She got up from the bed and hurried into her clothes as she continued to blame Andrie for the evening's failure.

Andrie decided that it would be better not to respond. Instead, she stared out the window to the street below as Ann's voice disappeared into the background. A strange numbness had rolled in, like a fog, insulating her from Ann's words. She could see the bronze Infiniti still comfortably placed in the usual spot, despite the sign that read *no parking any time.* The car had rarely been ticketed, since Ann would usually arrive late in the evening and never stay more than an hour or two. Looking down at the car, Andrie wondered if Destiny was watching it, too, from somewhere down on the street. *These thoughts have to stop. I can't give in to this,* Andrie told herself. Then suddenly, the sounds of breaking glass and Ann swearing roused her from her thoughts.

"Shit. God damnit!" Ann shrieked.

Andrie turned to find that in her haste, Ann had lost her balance and stepped on one of the wine glasses, shattering it underfoot.

"Are you all right?" Andrie asked as she walked toward the bed where Ann was now sitting, examining the sole of her shoe for imbedded glass.

"I'm fine. I'm just wonderful," Ann's reply was quick and sarcastic as she got up and walked out of the room.

Andrie followed after her as she headed toward the apartment door.

"I'll call you later," Ann said, as she took her coat from the chair and finally made eye contact with Andrie once again.

"OK." The numbness was still there. It made Andrie seem distant, although Ann seemed not to notice.

"Perhaps we'll get along better over the phone tonight," Ann told her and gave a thin smile.

"I'll talk to you about eleven then?" Andrie replied.

"Between eleven and twelve." With one hand on the door knob, Ann leaned forward and kissed Andrie quickly on the lips, then left.

Andrie went into the kitchen and made herself a cup of tea. Noticing the open bottle of Bordeaux, she began to wonder where Destiny was spending this time. Catching herself, she tried to think of something else. She reminded herself that these thoughts and feelings for Destiny were wrong and would only complicate her life. She needed to think about something else, so she walked back into the bedroom, knelt down and began carefully picking up the broken glass and putting it in a wastebasket. She started to think about her life with Ann and tried to remember the last time she was happy. Ann's thirst for power and political success had always been an issue, but over the past few years Andrie had watched that thirst become insatiable.

Inspecting the floor for any remaining pieces of glass as she wiped her brow with the back of her hand, Andrie breathed a painful sigh of resignation, as she faced the fact that this wasn't the relationship she had hoped for, but it was the one to which she had committed herself. That meant she needed to resist her growing feelings for Destiny and banish them back to that dark place where they had been hidden for so many years.

As Andrie knelt there, carefully searching out the smaller fragments of glass that remained, she was too deep in thought to have heard the apartment door open, or the broad footsteps coming down the hall toward her bedroom. It startled her when she looked up to see Destiny in the doorway with her arms folded, watching her.

"Looks like you had a wild ol' time," Destiny said with a sardonic grin that failed to disguise the pain she felt, knowing that Ann had so recently shared the room with Andrie.

In an instant Andrie got to her feet, rushed to the tall oak bedroom door and slammed it shut with such force that the entire apartment reverberated. She wished that she could shut Destiny out of her mind as easily. But that night, on each side of that dense wooden barrier, neither were spared the thoughts, the tears, or the desires that fate meant for them.

Chapter Eight

The aroma of freshly brewed coffee enticed Andrie as she finished getting dressed. Although she was running late, she followed it out to the kitchen where Destiny had prepared her a breakfast of poached eggs and toast.

"You didn't have to do this," Andrie said, taking the cup of hot coffee Destiny handed her.

"It's a peace offering. I'm sorry about that obnoxious remark I made last night," Destiny replied, as she motioned for Andrie to have a seat at the kitchen counter.

"Do you realize that if you made me breakfast after every obnoxious remark you've ever made to me, I would probably be about a hundred pounds heavier." Andrie's observation broke the ice and made them both laugh. Just then the phone rang. It was Ann. The conversation was short and, as she hung up, Andrie rolled her eyes and grinned. "I've only been awake an hour and I've already gotten two apologies," she observed as she pierced the soft white egg with a wedge of toast.

"Can I be nosy and ask what Ann apologized for?"

"She was supposed to call me before she went to bed last night, but she forgot," Andrie replied nonchalantly, and continued eating.

"Oh," Destiny groaned, as she poured herself a cup of coffee and leaned on the counter across from Andrie. It was impossible for her to fathom the idea of ever forgetting Andrie. It was apparent to her that this wasn't the first time Andrie had been forgotten by Ann.

There was a brief and awkward silence as they both sipped the coffee and remembered the evening before. Then, looking up from her plate, Andrie spoke. "Listen, I'm sorry, too . . . about last night. I shouldn't have slammed the door in your face like that. You didn't get hurt, did you?" she asked in a repentant tone as she searched Destiny's face for bruises.

"No, I'm learnin' that I have to be quick on my feet around you," Destiny responded, remembering Friday evening when Andrie plowed into her as she rushed out of the Club Vingtune.

"Oh boy. I'm really running late," Andrie announced after glancing up at the wall clock behind Destiny. She wanted to tell Destiny that she knew they needed to discuss what had happened between them last evening, but she didn't feel comfortable bringing up the subject.

Then, as if reading her mind, Destiny made the suggestion. "I think we'd better have a little talk tonight, if you have some time."

Andrie nodded. "I know. How about when I get home?"

"That's good with me," Destiny agreed, putting the cup of coffee to her lips, without turning her eyes from Andrie. The stare gave Andrie the feeling that Destiny saw past her cool exterior to what she was trying so hard to conceal. Grabbing her coat and briefcase, she quickly left for work, hoping that the naked, transparent feeling would pass once she was out of Destiny's sight.

*   *   *

That morning was hectic at Ann's New York office. She was usually in Washington from Monday to Thursday, while Congress was in session. However, because of her business with Cortronics, as well as some other local issues which required her attention, she was scheduled to leave on a 11:30 p.m. flight out of Kennedy that evening.

Andrie's desk was piled high with the usual messages from community groups who were requesting Ann's presence at various functions, letters from constituents either pledging support for her campaign or petitioning her to act on one issue or another, as well as a couple of faxes from the Washington office, all of which needed to be addressed. Soon after Andrie sat down and began sorting through the mountain of paper, her phone rang. David's familiar cheerful voice on the other end brought a smile to her face.

"Hi, sweetie. What are you doing for lunch?" he asked.

"What did you have in mind?"

"My favorite, of course," he responded with impish glee.

"Dim sum in Chinatown," Andrie guessed, as she divided her attention between David and the pile of work on her desk.

"Ummm. How does twelve noon sound to you?"

"OK. Where do you want to meet?"

"I'll come to your office and we'll leave from there," David answered.

"I'll see you then." Andrie hung up the phone and continued sorting through the heap. By mid-morning she had worked her way through a major portion of the assemblage. She was able to accommodate many of the requests that fit into Ann's schedule and had begun phoning some of the others in order to determine if she, or someone else from Ann's office, would be able to fill in for the congresswoman.

Ann knocked lightly as she entered the small office where Andrie was working. "How are you today?" Ann asked in a matter-of-fact tone.

"Fine . . . and you?"

"Good, thanks. You know I have that meeting at one o'clock with the Cortronics people," Ann said, stepping into Andrie's office.

"I know. I really wish you would reconsider your position about them buying that building from Stuart," Andrie said, looking up from her paperwork.

Ann's response was limited to a vacant sigh which told Andrie that it was pointless to try to change her mind about Women's Way.

"Don't forget that you have to be at that TV studio at two-thirty today to shoot that public service announcement on drinking and driving," Andrie reminded her.

Ann nodded, "I know . . . oh, I brought the outfit changes that you suggested."

"Good, because when I last spoke to the guy who's producing it, he wasn't sure what the set was going to look like. I asked Ray to help you pick out the most appropriate outfit . . . I proofed the script copy and faxed them my changes. I'll give you a highlighted copy before I go to lunch. You can look at it on your way to the studio," Andrie said, as she leaned back and stretched the kinks out of her neck and shoulders.

"OK. I have to make a few calls. I'll see you before lunch then," Ann replied, looking at her watch.

*   *   *

The rest of the morning had passed quickly. David arrived as only David could . . . boisterous, lively and in devilish humor. "Let's get out of here before Congresswoman Dearest finds the wire hangers that I put in her closet," he joked, as he stuck his head into Andrie's office.

"Not funny," Andrie said, holding back a grin to make her point. "I just have to give Ann something before we leave." Then, as she pulled out the copy of the script, which she had promised Ann, her phone rang. "Damnit. This happens every time I want to leave, I'll make it short," she said apologetically, and reached for the phone.

David saw Andrie's face change almost immediately after answering the phone. A frightened look had come over her face. He knew that something was wrong. He stepped closer to her and put his arm on her shoulder. Even though he heard only her portion of the conversation, it was enough to tell him that Andrie's father had been hurt somehow and was in a hospital.

She hung up and turned to him. "That was my brother, Michael. My father's in the hospital, he's unconscious. He was on a ladder, adjusting a vent in the ceiling of his shop, and the ladder gave way."

Without saying a word, David put his arms around her.

"I've got to leave. I've got to go to him," Andrie told him in a shaken tone.

"I'm going with you," David responded instinctively. Rocco had always been like a father to him.

"I'll be right back. I have to tell Ann," she said, and raced from the room.

Rushing into Ann's office, Andrie's face was still pale from worry, as she quickly explained what had happened to Rocco and that she was headed to the hospital.

Ann got out from behind her desk and walked over to Andrie. "I'm sorry, I can't go with you. But it's too late to reschedule these meetings. I just got off the phone with Ray. He's at the TV studio, checking out the set. He feels that we should be finished by three-thirty. I'll have most of the day free after that, since my flight isn't 'til eleven-thirty tonight. I'll try to stop over at the hospital," she said in a reassuring tone.

Even in her anxious state of mind, Andrie recognized that this was the first time in the seven years they were together that Ann showed any sign of warmth or concern for a member of her family. But as she put on her coat and hurried out of the building with David, Andrie had only one concern: for her father to be well.

Chapter Nine

David kept his arm firmly wrapped around Andrie's shoulder for the entire cab ride to the Brooklyn hospital. Andrie barely spoke, but her face was white with worry and her body was tense. She couldn't love Rocco more if he were her natural father. To Andrie, Rocco was her only father.

Brooklyn Memorial was a moderate-sized community hospital. Andrie and her brothers had been born there. In fact, most of the neighborhood had been born there. As she and David stepped off the elevator and headed down the long green-and-white-tiled hall of the three east wing, Andrie spotted Michael and Nick standing at the horseshoe-shaped nurses' station. They were engaged in a conversation with a small man who was wearing a starched white lab coat.

Andrie began running toward them as David kept pace with her. The patter of her heels on the highly polished tile floor caused her brothers to look her way. Seeing her, they abruptly extricated themselves from the conversation and walked quickly toward her. Andrie felt a sick burning sensation rise from the pit of her stomach to her throat. It was fear choking her.

"He's OK. He's conscious," Nick called out to her, seeing panic in her eyes as she looked past him to the doctor. He repeated, this time in unison with Michael, "He's OK. He's gonna be all right."

Their words finally reached Andrie, as she came closer. A feeling of relief came over her. She could breathe again and she heard David thank God.

As the four converged, a flurry of kissing, hugging and tears of relief erupted. They all walked down the hall together, like a family of which even David was unquestionably an important member.

"Dad's OK. He'd already regained consciousness when I called you. But I didn't know that until after I hung up. I called your office back, but you had left. Then I tried your cellular phone, but I got that 'out of range' message. We were worried about your rushing over here while you were upset over Dad. I didn't know if you were driving or what. I'm glad you were with David," Michael said, leading the group back down the hall toward Rocco's room.

"Is Dad talking?" Andrie asked anxiously.

"Yeah. And he's gonna eat something too in a little while. He had a slight concussion. That's what they found when they did some x-rays and a CAT scan."

As they entered the doorway of Rocco's hospital room, Michael dropped back behind his sister so she would be the first one to enter the room. He knew that his father would light up as soon as he saw her. That's the way Rocco was about Andrie.

"Andrietta," Rocco called, his face beaming with delight at the sight of his daughter. As he opened his arms to greet her, Andrie knew that he would be all right. She rushed toward his bed and hugged him tightly as she began to cry tears of relief.

"It's OK. Don't cry. I was on a ladder to fix-a the light in the back of the store. I leaned-a over too far and I fall on my head. For people like me and you, that's-a our strongest part," Rocco said, recognizing his daughter's capacity to be as stubborn as he was.

Standing next to her daughter, Maria nodded in agreement, as Andrie turned to hug and kiss her as well. Before long it seemed like everyone in the room had hugged each other. That was the way of the LaStellas: warm, demonstrative, open and sincere. This was not to say that they always got along. There were many loud disagreements in the LaStella household throughout the years, but never a grudge or suppressed feeling toward anyone.

Then, Maria motioned to David. "David, come here. Thank you for coming with Andrie. You're so good; God bless you. You're like another brother to her," Maria said, grasping David's face in her hands and giving him a loud, affectionate kiss on the cheek. Then, taking his hand, she led him over to her husband, who was at that moment finishing up the story of how he fell off the ladder.

"Rocco, look who else is here." Maria interrupted the end of the story.

Rocco looked up at David and reached for his hand. "David. Please sit, sit . . . Maria, find him a chair," Rocco said, as he gave David a broad thankful smile for accompanying Andrie to the hospital.

The large white hospital room was lined with chairs. Since the other bed in the room was unoccupied, Michael had taken two chairs which were against the opposite wall and pushed them toward Rocco's side of the room, forming a semicircle around his bed. Laughter and conversation filled the room. Because of their varied schedules, the only time the entire family got together like this was during holidays. As Rocco talked in his loud friendly voice with David, the atmosphere seemed to take on a decidedly festive quality.

"You know, just-a this morning I tell-a Maria that I want to see all you kids together sometime soon. So, God hears me and here we are," Rocco announced with a satisfied grin.

Hearing that, David leaned over and whispered to Andrie, "I'm glad I'm Jewish."

"Why's that?" Andrie said, as she affectionately rubbed the top of his closely cropped red hair with her hand.

"You never heard of God pushing a Jew off a ladder to have a family reunion."

Andrie tried to hold in her laughter, but that was never easy around David. The hours had rolled by without anyone noticing that it had turned to evening. Although there were undoubtedly more preferable reasons for the LaStellas to have gathered, the fact remained they all benefited by each other's company.

At one point, the doctor had stopped by to inform Rocco that he would see him in the morning and, most likely, release him at that time. After that announcement, it seemed that the laughter increased and the conversation got even livelier. Nick excused himself to go out for a smoke. There was such relief in the room that neither Andrie nor Michael even chastised him for the bad habit, as was their usual reaction.

"So how's Ann's re-election campaign doing?" Michael asked, as he removed his charcoal gray pinstriped jacket and folded it carefully over the back of his chair.

"Pretty well. But she's the type that worries, right down to the finish," Andrie answered, as she began to wonder when Ann would be arriving.

"Is she still thinking of going through with that phony marriage thing?"

"Yes. She has to go through with it. But let's not rehash that now. OK?" Andrie knew that no one in her family liked the idea of Ann's impending marriage. She had explained it to the family weeks ago so they would be prepared if they heard about it in the news. Despite the strong front Andrie put up, they all knew that this had to hurt her deeply. Michael agreed not to pursue the topic further. He had no wish to upset the pleasant atmosphere.

Suddenly, bursting back into the room, Nick broke up the conversation with an announcement. "I'll give all of you one guess to tell me what famous chick is here to see Dad."

Hearing that, Andrie was thrilled that Ann was able to make it. Although it did seem odd to her that Nick would be so forward as to refer to Ann as a *chick,* since he had only met her two or three times in the last seven years. Nevertheless, a proud smile lit Andrie's face as she stood and took a step toward the door. With that Nick moved aside to clear the entrance as Destiny strolled into the room. Andrie's smile immediately disappeared as she turned to David with a stunned look on her face, seeking an explanation.

"Look. It's our big Rocking Rolla star." Rocco could never get some phrases quite right and that always provided his family with a laugh. This time was no exception. Even Destiny laughed heartily as she leaned over the bed and gave him a big bear hug.

As Destiny straightened up, she turned to Maria who threw her arms around her. "How did you know to come here?" Maria asked with her hands cupping Destiny's face as she sprinkled her with kisses.

"David called me before he left Andrie's office. You see, I'm staying in New York and I had dinner plans with Andrie, so David called to let me know that she wouldn't be able to keep them. I would have come earlier but I figured that ya'all needed some time alone together."

"Andrie why didn't you tell me that when I talked to you the other day?" Maria asked, turning toward Andrie, who responded by simply shrugging her shoulders and glaring at David.

Maria took Destiny's hand and led her to a chair. Neither time nor the outlandish articles she had read in the tabloids could diminish her affection for Destiny. "Here, honey, sit and talk with me. You're so famous now. I buy all the magazines that have stories about you, and Rocco calls me into the living room every time he sees you on television. I'm surprised that you can walk around like this without some big crowd following you for autographs."

"It's amazing what a baseball cap and dark glasses can allow you to do," Destiny said, holding up the two items as she spoke. Maria's warmth made her feel welcome. It always had, even from the first time they met. "Let's see; the last time I saw you and Rocco was when I stopped by to visit David's mom, right after my first album was released and I was on tour in New York to promote it. I didn't need any disguises back then," she recalled.

"David's mother has a beautiful picture of you on the coffee table. You look like a model in it. You're such a pretty girl; you should dress like that picture all the time," Maria said, as she brushed Destiny's crop of overgrown bangs away from her face.

"Oh, I know the picture you're talkin' about. . . . That picture was so airbrushed, I didn't recognize myself in it," Destiny laughed. She and Maria chatted nonstop for over an hour, with only the occasional interruptions from Nick quizzing Destiny about other celebrities she had met. The time continued to slip by easily and without anyone noticing that Andrie had kept one eye on the door ever since Destiny had arrived. As Maria and Destiny and Rocco and his sons were engaged in their respective conversations, Andrie nudged David and nodded toward the door, indicating that he should follow her outside, which he did.

"Why did you tell Destiny to come here? Are you out of your mind? What's going to happen if Ann shows up?" she asked him in a huff.

"Darling, take a look at that fancy little piece of Swiss mechanics on your wrist. It's eight-thirty. Visiting hours are over." No sooner did David make that unwelcome observation than it was confirmed by the stern announcement on the overhead P.A. system. When the anonymous voice had finished, David continued, "By the way, I never told Destiny to come here. This was her idea. She didn't even tell me. I was as surprised as you when she walked in. In fact, the only thing that would have surprised me more would have been if Ann showed up."

Ignoring David's barb, Andrie looked toward the room, which continued to buzz with friendly conversation. "Do you see the way they're treating Destiny, like she's a long-lost daughter. That should be Ann. They should be that warm with Ann," she observed.

"You're right. That should be Ann in there but it's not. It's Destiny, who cared enough about you and your family to come here. . . ." David replied in an exasperated tone, leaving Andrie alone in the hall as he turned and walked back into Rocco's room.

*   *   *

At Maria's urging, Destiny and David, along with Andrie and her brothers, went to the LaStellas' house for coffee after leaving the hospital that evening. Evelyn, David's mother, had been watching at her window and rushed next door the minute they arrived home. As everyone crowded into the LaStellas' kitchen, Evelyn rushed over to Destiny. "Let me give you a big hug," she said as she squeezed Destiny affectionately and kissed her on the cheek, leaving behind a large crimson lip print. Then in a more somber tone she added, "I was so touched when you called me and sent us that beautiful fruit basket after David's grandmother died."

"I was real sorry when David told me that she died. I would've come to the funeral, but I was in England at the time. You were both so nice to let me stay with you that winter break. I'll always remember that," Destiny explained, with genuine appreciation. Nick then grabbed her hand and dragged her over to sit at the table with him and Michael.

As everyone began milling around the kitchen, Evelyn and Maria busied themselves making coffee and setting the table with a tray of strufelle, a walnut coffee cake and an assortment of Italian liquors.

"I have a feeling that this is gonna be a late one," David whispered to Andrie.

"How do you know?"

"I don't yet. But if my mother runs next door for the ruggalech, it'll be an *all nighter*," he told her, with a grin.

Suddenly, the sound of Evelyn's raspy, smoker's voice filled the kitchen. "Does anybody want some nice ruggalech?"

Andrie looked at David and burst out laughing. The sound of her laughter was all but obscured by the rowdy sounds emanating from the conversation Destiny, Nick, and Michael were having at the table.

"I haven't seen you laugh like that in a long time," David said as Andrie tried to regain her breath.

"I guess I'm so relieved about Dad that I just feel really good. . . . Oh, about before, when we were at the hospital . . . I'm sorry about the way I reacted to Destiny visiting. It looks like everybody really enjoyed seeing her again."

As Andrie spoke, she turned to see Destiny laughing heartily with Nick and Michael. Again, Andrie couldn't help but notice that the fine creases at the corners of her mouth and eyes were evidence of Destiny's readiness to share her generous smile. At that moment, it was clear to Andrie that Destiny Anderson knew how to approach life. There was an honest unaffected charm about her that seemed to easily win everyone's hearts. It amazed Andrie that after so many years her family had remained so fond of the boyish Kentuckian.

"Would you look at that! Your brothers are thinking that Destiny is great *in-law* material. They're right too," David whispered with a chuckle and a wink.

"Do you ever let up?" Andrie replied, only slightly annoyed by the comment.

There was something in her expression that gave David the feeling that she was seeing Destiny in a new light, although he knew better than to expect Andrie to admit that. Before they could discuss or argue the point further, Nick had come over to their end of the table.

"Andrie, listen. I'm gonna stay with Ma tonight and bring Dad home from the hospital tomorrow. Everything here will be under control, so no arguments," he told her with the soft-spoken authority of an older sibling.

"Thanks, Nicky. I'll call tomorrow after I get to the hotel," she answered, just as David interjected.

"This is a great night to see the Christmas lights down on the shore," he observed in a tone that was obviously meant as a suggestion.

"David's right. It's a nice clear night; it should be beautiful by the water," Michael interjected as he joined the conversation.

"But it's too long a walk from here to the shore and there's supposed to be a storm later," Andrie said as she considered the idea.

"The storm's not due for hours. I'll be right back," Michael said, before disappearing momentarily and leaving Andrie, Destiny and David to wonder what he was up to.

"Here we go," he called out smugly as he returned jingling a set of car keys. When he reached the table, he stood next to Destiny and dropped the keys into her hand.

"Aren't you and Nick coming?" Andrie asked, as she tried to figure out the reason Michael gave Rocco's car keys to Destiny.

"No. We'll stay here and you guys go. We can't all leave Mom and Evelyn after they fixed up that whole table of cholesterol," Michael answered with a loud LaStella laugh.

Andrie noticed that Michael was in a rare mood. He was always the quiet, serious brother, who always had work on his mind. Yet tonight he seemed jovial and much livelier than usual.

"OK. Let's go," she said, as she stood up and looked at David.

Remaining in his seat, David looked up at her. "I'm going to stick around here for a while. I should use this as a 'mother visit.' She's been leaving messages on my answering machine lately to let me know that she's still at the same address. I'll give you a call tomorrow," he said, tilting his head to one side and smiling contritely.

Destiny looked at Andrie to see if she had changed her mind. But she remained eager, despite the distinct feeling that there was a conspiracy afoot to send her off to be alone with Destiny.

"Andrie, honey, are you leaving?' Maria asked, seeing Andrie putting on her coat.

"No. I'm just going down to the shore for a while with Destiny."

"Take your father's car. There's supposed to be a storm sometime tonight."

"Michael's already thought of that," Andrie said, pointing to the car keys in Destiny's hand.

"Andrie, you know that I would love you kids to come back here after you go to the shore, but the weather is supposed to get bad and you have to go to Washington in the morning, so I think it would be better if you went straight home from there. Nicky could pick up the car tomorrow," Maria suggested, then turned toward her son for assurance that he could do what she wanted.

"That's a good idea. I'll pick up the car tomorrow afternoon. You can let me know where you parked it when you call tomorrow," Nick offered readily. Then, taking the keys back from Destiny and reaching for his coat, which was hanging on the back of a nearby chair, he added, "I'll go warm up the car for you . . . I wanted to go outside to have a cigarette anyway."

As Nick left, Maria turned to Destiny who by then had donned her bomber jacket. "Destiny, honey, where did you say you were staying?" she asked, as she walked over and flipped up the collar of Destiny's heavy leather jacket.

Destiny glanced quickly at Andrie, who answered for her. "She's staying with a friend. Why?"

"She should stay at your apartment tonight, if the weather gets bad before you get back to Manhattan." Maria LaStella was an extremely intuitive woman. As soon as Andrie answered for Destiny, Maria knew exactly where Destiny was staying.

There was something in the tone of her mother's suggestion that made Andrie suspect that this was Maria's discreet way of saying that she knew Destiny was staying with her daughter and she approved.

Destiny put her arms around Maria and hugged her affectionately. "Maria, thanks for making me feel so welcomed. It was great seeing you again. Now take good care of Rocco when he gets home," she said. Then, turning to Andrie, she added, "I'm gonna go out front with Nick. I'll wait for you there."

After the exchange of several good-byes and kisses with everyone in the house, Destiny bounced down the front steps where Nick was sitting outside. She plopped down next to him and bumped him playfully with her shoulder, noticing that his mood had changed. He seemed pensive, even worried, as he took the cigarette he had been smoking from his lips, and tossed it into the street. They both followed its blazing tip with their eyes, as it arced through the dark night until, reaching the curb, it crashed down in a small flurry of cinders.

"I gotta talk to you about something before you go," he said in an apprehensive tone.

"OK. Shoot," Destiny said, with an easy smile.

"I always liked you. You know that. I know that you and Andrie didn't get along for all those years," he began.

"You knew about that?" Destiny interrupted.

"Sure. So did my brother. We figured something was wrong when she never went with us all those times you sent us passes to your concerts . . . and how uncomfortable you looked when you would ask us about her. Neither of us ever said anything to Andrie about it. We figured if she wanted us to know she'd tell us. But tonight things looked different . . . like whatever was wrong had changed. I'm glad about that. I figure that you're probably staying with her, too. Right?" he asked.

Destiny had no response as she smiled awkwardly.

"You don't have to answer that. I didn't mean to put you on the spot. . . . Do you know what the hardest thing is for me, about my sister's being gay?'

"What?"

"I don't know how to protect her. Ya see if she was dating some guy and something worried me about him, I could have a talk with him. I could tell him that I love my sister and I wanted them to both be happy, but if he ever hurt her, he would have to answer to me. I can't say that to a woman. It's a little screwed up, huh?"

"No. I understand what you're sayin'. I care about your sister . . . a lot." Destiny kept her voice low. She was afraid that Andrie might come out the door any minute.

"She cares about you, too. I saw the way she looked at you and stuff. I can read my sister. Her eyes show everything she feels inside. She was always like that." Nick glowed when he spoke of his sister.

"I know," Destiny said, smiling as she recalled that quality in Andrie.

"Andrie hasn't been happy in a long time. I don't think that Ann loves her. At least not as much as she loves being a congresswoman. My sister deserves real love in her life, not what Ann's been giving her. Anyhow, I'm telling you all this because . . . I saw something there between you and Andrie. And I think that it's real good . . . except for one thing," Nick said, becoming even more uneasy.

Seeing that, Destiny finished the thought for him. "You're worried about me having a lot of women . . . right?"

"You have more women than all the guys I know put together. You're always in the magazines and newspapers with them. I don't want my sister to leave one set of problems, just to get involved in something else that could hurt her. I don't think that you would mean to do that, but it could happen," he said with a troubled look.

Destiny knew what he was saying and she understood why he felt the way he did.

"I wish I could find the words to tell you how I feel about Andrie. If there was a door that I could open, so that you could see what's inside of me, you'd know that I could never hurt her," she answered in a voice that couldn't help but tremble from the emotions inside her. And although the years had made changes in her life, Nick saw that Destiny herself had remained every bit as sincere and candid as she had always been.

"You're a real special person . . . you always were. I hope my sister realizes that," he said, in a way that told Destiny that he knew she was telling him the truth.

She simply smiled in response at this LaStella for whom she had always kept a warm place in her heart. His innocent and generous soul had obscured his rugged, even intimidating appearance from the first time she met him years before.

"Look, would ya mind not tellin' Andrie that we talked about this. She'll just say I'm stickin' my nose where it don't belong," Nick asked.

"Don't worry. I won't say a word," Destiny replied, touched by Nick's concern for his sister. No sooner had she said that than Andrie emerged from the house.

Nick walked them to the car that he had left running at the curb. He kissed and hugged them both good-bye and stood at the curb watching as the tail lights faded into the distance.

*   *   *

As she maneuvered the car through the dark Brooklyn streets Destiny turned to Andrie and said, "You're real lucky to have a family like that. It's so easy to feel comfortable around them."

"It's not that easy for everyone," Andrie replied, as she gazed out the car window. The night sky still looked too clear to expect a storm.

"Doesn't Ann feel comfortable with them?" Destiny asked.

"No. They aren't very fond of her. They've never been," Andrie answered, still peering out at the sky.

"That's too bad. I don't mean this as a shot at Ann, but I can't picture the problem being on your family's end," Destiny remarked.

"Two rights, then go straight, until you see the park," Andrie directed her, then turned from the window and continued, "Well, the problem is really on both ends. They aren't rude to each other and they don't argue, but there's just a lack of warmth there. Ann's only met them a handful of times, so there was never much of a relationship established between them."

Destiny decided to change the subject. It was the only way she could be certain to avoid saying something about Ann that Andrie would find offensive. "I really enjoyed seeing everybody again. I think that they liked seeing me again too," she said, looking ahead as she continued to drive.

"They loved seeing you again. . . . By the way, thanks for coming to the hospital. You didn't have to do that."

"Yes I did. I was worried about you. I didn't know how badly Rocco was hurt," she answered.

Andrie smiled. She didn't know what to say in response. It struck her as painfully ironic that it should be Destiny, rather than Ann, who cared enough to have come to the hospital.

Reaching the park, Destiny pulled into a spot near one of the entrances. As she and Andrie got out of the car and looked around, they were both struck with the fact that this night was so similar to the first time they had come to the park together, so many years before.

Here was another clear dark sky, showing off stars that looked like a handful of brilliant diamonds scattered on a piece of black velvet. Across from the park, Christmas lights adorned the houses that faced out toward the bay, just as they had back then. Yet neither made mention of these similarities. Instead, they quietly began walking down through the park and toward the bay. All the conflict and animosity that had stood between them for so many years was absent, or at least temporarily dormant. Other feelings had begun to surface, for both of them.

"I have to leave for Washington in the morning." Andrie began thinking out loud. "And when I get back on Thursday, you'll be leaving for LA. . . . I was just starting to get used to your French toast too," she added with a sad smile.

"Girl, our timing has never been real good," Destiny said, returning the same sad smile.

"Do you miss Nicole?" Andrie asked as they continued toward the bay.

"Where did that question come from?" Destiny replied, chuckling incredulously at its inappropriate timing.

"I just wanted to know more about what happened between you and her . . . and since we don't have much more time together, I thought that I'd just come right out and ask," Andrie admitted bluntly.

Still somewhat stunned by the abruptness of the question, Destiny responded, "No. I haven't missed her for some time now. After five years of chasing a dream, I finally realized that I was living a kind of nightmare. I wanted Nicole to be that person I could call my family, but she had other ideas. Eventually, I knew that it would only be a matter of time before the relationship ended." By the sound of Destiny's voice, Andrie sensed that the easygoing southerner regretted the years spent with a person who was wrong for her.

"You don't sound bitter," Andrie observed, somewhat puzzled.

"I'm learning that bitterness grows out of deep pain . . . and that kind of pain can only be caused by someone you love in a very special way. I didn't feel that for Nicole."

"How did you end up living with someone for five years, who you didn't love in a special way?" Andrie couldn't contain her questions.

"It just kind of developed. About six years ago, I needed to make ends meet, so I was working a day job as a poolside bartender at one of the nicer hotels in LA. Anyway, Nicole was working there part-time as a waitress. She was auditioning a lot and she actually scored a couple of small parts, but nothing that really took off. I was attracted to her, but at the time she had been having an affair for a couple of years with an older guy. He was a pretty well-known plastic surgeon who used the hotel restaurant for parties once in a while. He promised to divorce his wife and marry her. I used to give her a lift home after work sometimes and she would tell me all about how she was waiting for this guy to leave his wife, but how he would always come up with reasons for putting it off. One day I was leaving the hotel and she was in the parking lot crying. He told her that he had left his wife and he was marrying some up and coming starlet. At the time, she said that she was through with men. She was making a lot of good connections in the business and she said that she was going to forget about finding love and concentrate on her career. She quit her job at the hotel and devoted herself, full-time, to her acting career. We stayed friends. Then one night she was over my place watching TV and she came on to me. After that we started to see each other pretty often, but she still dated a lot of other people too . . . men and women. So I continued to see other girls, too. I didn't want to just sit around and wait for her to commit to me. She taught me a lot about the business and introduced me to a lot of people she knew in it. She was really nice that way. I was lonely. I knew that there was something that I needed . . . something that was missing from my life, but I wasn't sure what it was. Nicole was the real lively, popular type. She helped me to ignore that need. Then one day, shortly after I had been signed by

Cobra, I was in Birmingham and I got a call from Nicole. She had hurt her back and broken her leg in a car accident on the freeway. She was never one to save money. Every penny she made was spent on clothes and rent. She told me that she was losing her apartment and she had no place to stay. So, I told her that she could stay in my place as long as she needed. When I got back, she was still there. She never left. Which was fine with me because it made me feel like I was connected to someone. I started doing better and better with my career, and our lifestyle changed dramatically in a short time. Nicole stopped dating other people, so I did too. Unfortunately, her career had never really taken off. So, after a few of years of nothing more than a few bit parts, she was pretty depressed. She started to spend a lot of time with Sonia while I was working. I actually encouraged it, because I saw that Sonia was able to cheer her up in a way I couldn't. They had a lot in common. They both enjoyed all the parties and the people . . . and neither one had an easy time being faithful to one person. What happened was inevitable."

"I'm sorry," Andrie said, as they began to cross a small cobble-stone foot bridge on their way to the shore.

"Don't be. I'm not religious, but I do believe that we're all put here to play certain parts in each other's lives. What happened with Nicole led me back here to you, so we could have a second chance. . . . My daddy used to say that there aren't any coincidences in life, just small miracles," Destiny recalled, as they both looked out over the side of the bridge. The sky was clear and storm clouds had yet to roll in over them.

"I don't believe in miracles anymore. I don't even remember when I stopped. I guess I've been hanging around politicians too long," Andrie said.

"That's too bad, sometimes miracles are the only hope we have and hope is what gets you through hard times."

"Is that something else your father said?" Andrie asked, smiling softly at Destiny.

"No. It's just something I learned livin' my life," she answered.

Then, leaning back against the stone wall of the bridge, she added, "Ya know, we need to talk about last night."

"I know," Andrie replied, as she continued looking out over the bridge. She was doing her best to avoid looking into Destiny's eyes. She knew that once she did, it would be impossible to resist her.

Destiny stood close beside her. "This morning I apologized for the stupid remark I made to you when I got home last night. I made it because I was jealous. But I'm not going to apologize for what I said before Ann called. I meant every word of that. I was about to kiss you, and we would have probably made love if she hadn't interrupted us."

"Then I guess we were lucky, because that would have complicated both our lives." Andrie knew that what she said and how she felt inside were two completely different things.

"Don't lie to yourself, Andrie. You know what's complicating your life," Destiny said, putting her hand under Andrie's chin and turning her head until their eyes met.

Andrie felt herself weakening as she stared into Destiny's eyes and held back the tears in her own. "I don't know anything anymore. My whole life, and everything I ever thought I wanted, is all changed. It's all inside out. Nothing makes sense anymore. I thought that Ann would be a constant. I thought that she'd be someone to depend on. Instead, she's got me dating men, while she's getting ready to be married. . . . Then, as if that's not enough, after I spend fifteen years of hating you long distance, you walk back into my life and my apartment . . . and within three days I find that I'm in . . . I . . . I can't stop thinking about you." With that Andrie turned away again. She needed time to sort out her thoughts, which was impossible to do while looking at Destiny.

Destiny took her hand, but Andrie refused to turn and let her see the tears in her eyes. Over and over again, she told herself that she was in a relationship and that what she now felt for Destiny was wrong. A part of Andrie wanted to run fast and far from that bridge . . . and not stop until she had put an incredible distance between herself and all the confusion in her life. At the same time, she felt that all the pieces of the puzzle that made up her heart were, at last, coming together.

Destiny slowly turned her around until they were facing each other. The park lamp above leaked its dim light onto the spot where they stood and was mirrored in Andrie's misty eyes.

Before either one of them could think, their lips were touching in a long, slow kiss that melted away all the years of pride, hostility, and denial.

Unable to hold back any longer, Destiny let her feelings free. "I love you. I always have, from the very first time I saw you . . . outside your parents' house, cleaning the snow off your father's car. I watched the way you moved and how you got snow all over yourself . . . on your clothes and in your hair. By the time we all went into your house, it had melted. Your face was all rosy and glowing and your jeans and shirt were soaked through. You were drying your hair with a towel and you looked up and smiled at me. I knew I had never seen anything more beautiful in my life. You robbed my soul with that smile . . . and you've owned it ever since." Destiny's voice was breathy and passionate. Its fire seared Andrie.

They held each other tightly. For that moment, the bridge, the park, the whole world outside them, ceased to exist. They never noticed the clouds gathering in the distance or the tide slowly gaining strength. The storm was indeed approaching.

Andrie touched Destiny's face tenderly. "I wish I hadn't been so scared and confused then. Things might have turned out so differently for us." Her voice was marked with regret.

"Andrie, you're scared and confused now. The only difference this time is the reason behind it. You think it would be wrong to be with me, because you're with Ann. What's really wrong is not to be where your heart is. . . . We've both been wrong for fifteen years. You can't run from it anymore. What should have happened between us then, is going to happen soon . . . maybe even tonight." As Destiny spoke a stray lock of her sandy hair crossed her face as the wind grew. Brushing it back, Andrie looked into her eyes.

"Let's go home," she said in a voice that was at once both determined and seductive. It was clear . . . Andrie had decided that neither fear nor confusion would keep them apart any longer.

*   *   *

Andrie turned on the lights as she entered the apartment. The drive from Brooklyn had been relatively quick, since there was little traffic that late in the evening. "It's chilly in here," she said, taking off her coat and adjusting the thermostat on the wall outside the kitchen.

Destiny shed her heavy brown leather jacket and followed her. "Does that work?" she asked, pointing to an ornately mantled fireplace in the living room.

"Yes. But I can't ever get the fire going, so I don't really use it." Andrie had no sooner answered before Destiny was kneeling in front of the fireplace, wasting no time in re-arranging the apple wood logs and stuffing crumpled-up pages of that morning's New York Times in the spaces between them. Within a few short minutes, the unfamiliar sight of a blazing fire had begun to shed its warmth and light on Andrie's living room.

"How did you get that going so fast?" Andrie asked, pointing to the flames that were dancing furiously in and around the logs.

"It's just one of those things that country girls are good at . . . like splittin' logs . . . ridin' horses and . . . well, you'll just have to find out the rest yourself," Destiny said with a devilishly seductive grin, as she stood up and strolled back across the room to Andrie. They stood wordlessly, staring into the reflection of the fire in each other's eyes. The silence was flawed only by the crackling of the fire. Destiny gently caressed Andrie's face with her fingertips, as if she needed to feel what she was looking at, to make sure that it wasn't a dream.

Andrie trembled inside, as the tender touch of Destiny's coarse fingertips sent shocks, like lightning bolts, throughout her body.

Every part of her had come alive and was crying out for more. Her lips, her tongue, her breasts, all craving to be touched and tasted by Destiny.

Now alone in front of the fire, the innuendoes, seductive looks, and rediscovered feelings had ignited the passion within them, until it bubbled and swelled like a long silent volcano ready to erupt . . . when suddenly the intruding sound of the apartment's intercom blared out at them from the wall.

The sound made Andrie jump. "It's eleven o'clock . . . who would be at the door now?" she wondered aloud as she moved to answer the intercom. "Yes?" she called abruptly into it.

"Andrie, it's me. Well, I'm glad to see that your intercom is working for once. Buzz me in, I'm on my way up." It was Ann's voice.

Andrie froze for a second before saying anything. Then she choked out a tentative "OK" as she turned to Destiny plaintively and apologized. "She's on her way up. . . . I'm sorry."

"What do you want me to do?" Destiny asked, the words sticking in her throat.

"Go in there for now," Andrie said, pointing to the guest room where Destiny was staying. "When you hear my bedroom door close wait a few minutes and then you can leave the apartment. She won't be able to hear you from the bedroom."

Frustration and anger filled Destiny as she looked back at Andrie. "This is the last time I'll ever do this for you." With that, she walked out of the kitchen and down the hall to the guest room, grabbing her brown leather jacket on the way. Just as she reached the room and closed the door behind her, Ann entered the apartment. Destiny could hear her voice as she walked past the guest room complaining about the fact that the front door had swelled up and was difficult to open. Then came the sound of Andrie's bedroom door being shut. Destiny winced, as an old familiar wound was suddenly ripped open once more. A thick ugly silence then ensued, allowing her to hear the angry pounding of her own heart as she stood, staring at the antique clock that sat on the heavy mahogany dresser. Its hands had been frozen in time for lack of winding, so she looked at the bulky stainless steel watch on her wrist. It was 11:06. Three minutes . . . three minutes was all she would wait before leaving the apartment. She looked into the dresser mirror and searched her own eyes for an answer to what was happening. The three minutes seemed interminable as she waited for them to pass.

Her hands were clenched tightly as she battled to control every natural impulse she had. Looking at her watch again, she saw that the three tortuous minutes had elapsed. She grabbed her jacket and opened the door of the guest room. At the other end of the hall, she saw Andrie's door. Everything inside told her to run down that hall into Andrie's bedroom and put an end to what was happening.

It tormented Destiny to know that she had no right to do that, since she still had no claim on the woman who had been holding her soul hostage for all these years. She pushed herself to open the apartment door and walk out. As she closed it behind her, she looked back one last time. Anguished by the battle being waged inside her, Destiny tore her hand from the knob and ran down the stairs. At the bottom she reached the massive oak door, which Ann had left ajar. In one brutal sweep, she yanked it fully open, causing it to crash into the wall behind it, as she entered the dark blustery night.

She ran down the stone steps and crossed the street. There, she was assaulted by the sight of Ann's illicitly parked car surrounded by the luminous circle of a street light. Then, looking up at Andrie's bedroom window, she saw a dim light filtering through the drawn, lace curtains. The fury within her grew beyond her capacity to contain it. She lunged toward a row of overfilled garbage cans and with all her anger and strength, kicked them over and over and over again, each time with increased rage and each time making deeper gouges into their sides, as their unpleasant contents hurled out onto the sidewalk. Finally, exhausted and tearful, she fell back against the cold brick wall behind the cans, her excess rage momentarily spent.

* * *

Inside the apartment, Andrie was fighting a battle of her own. Her feelings for Destiny were growing more powerful with every thought. She was beginning to realize that all these years could, and perhaps should, have been spent with her.

But now, tormented by regret and confusion, Andrie remembered how she often told Ann that their relationship was a marriage. She said that and believed it with all her heart. To Andrie, this was a marriage. A very troubled one, at that. Yet she had committed herself to it and she wanted to be strong enough to do what she felt was right and remain faithful to that commitment. It occurred to her that twice now, she and Destiny had almost made love, but were interrupted by something. Perhaps fate never meant them to be together, she tried to convince herself. Yet, she knew that those two unfinished moments had only made her want Destiny more. As she stood there looking at Ann, one thought alone dominated her mind . . . Destiny.

"What happened with your flight? Weren't you taking off at eleven-thirty?" Andrie asked.

"I had to reschedule for six-fifteen in the morning. Just when I thought that I was done, something came up with the Cortronics thing. And now I'm on my way to my father's house. He wants to have a campaign finance meeting with Ray and me. Speaking of fathers . . . how is yours doing?" she asked, as she took Andrie's hand and sat down on the edge of the bed with her.

"He's going to be fine. He had a slight concussion. They're releasing him tomorrow," she answered coldly. It angered her that Ann brought up the subject of her father as an afterthought. Again, Destiny's face appeared in her mind as she remembered how she had looked when she walked into the hospital room and how she sat laughing and talking, for hours, with Rocco and Maria.

"I'm glad that he's OK. I'm sorry that I wasn't able to make it to the hospital, but you can see how my schedule's been. I know that I should have called there to see how things were going, but I just didn't have a minute." As Ann spoke she reclined on the bed, still holding Andrie's hand. Her touch felt cold and cadaverous to Andrie.

"So, if your schedule is so hectic and you're on your way to a meeting at your father's house, why did you stop here?" Andrie asked in a flat tone, as she fought back a sick feeling in the pit of her stomach that started when Ann took her hand.

"I wanted to see how everything went at the hospital and I missed you. I thought that it would be nice if we spent a little time together," Ann replied, as she drew Andrie down until they were lying next to each other.

The sick feeling in Andrie's stomach seemed to worsen with that. Ann's reasons for not coming to the hospital, or even calling, were flimsy. Andrie knew that Ann could have found at least one minute to call, since they both had cellular phones. To Ann, it was a simple matter of priorities and Andrie had become accustomed to where she stood on that list.

The idea of Ann showing so little concern would normally have hurt and angered Andrie. But this time it didn't. The numbness had returned. At the moment, she was devoid of all emotion where Ann was concerned. She wanted no arguments, no recriminations. She wanted nothing more than for Ann to leave.

"What time is the meeting tonight?" Andrie asked, as she subtly retrieved her hand from Ann's grasp.

"They can start without me. I'd say we have about an hour," Ann replied, kicking off her chocolate-brown suede pumps. The plunking sound they made as they hit the wooden floor seemed to punctuate her words, emphasizing the fact that she had not just stopped by to find out how Andrie's father was.

She began to stroke Andrie's hair with her hand. "We both had a hard day. We need to unwind a bit," she said, using her most seductive tone.

"Listen, I don't feel like unwinding this way tonight. I've been through a lot today, rushing to the hospital and worrying about my father . . ." Andrie said, sitting up and moving to the edge of the bed.

"Well, that's why I'm here. I knew that you probably had a hard day and needed to relax," Ann replied, as she slid over to the edge of the bed where Andrie was sitting and again attempted to take her hand.

This time Andrie's entire body recoiled, as she stood up from the bed. "Please, don't treat me like a fool. You came here to make love. You weren't concerned about my father's condition or how I was feeling. If you were, you would have at least found the time to call me at the hospital. I'm not even angry about it. All I'm asking is that you don't try to give me a snow job, like you do everyone else," Andrie explained in a controlled tone.

"I told you how busy I was. I guess that I was foolish enough to think that you would understand. . . . Obviously, I was wrong," Ann responded in disappointment, as she sat up on the bed.

"I do understand . . . I always understand," Andrie told her, in a flat voice that seemed drained of emotion. She had no desire to argue. Across the room, the white lace curtains had come alive, flapping vigorously, animated by the chilly gust of wind coming in through the slightly open window. "There's a storm coming. If you're going across town, you should leave now, so you don't get caught in it," she added, walking over to the window and pulling it shut.

Ann realized that Andrie was right about the storm and it was obvious that her plans to make love had failed, so there was no point to remaining there. "You're probably right. What time will you be getting into DC tomorrow?" Ann asked, as she retrieved her shoes from the floor and prepared to leave.

"I should be reaching the office by late morning. I'm scheduled for a meeting to discuss increasing the media coverage for some of the events you'll be involved in between now and next November," Andrie replied, glancing back toward the window, as the distant rumble of thunder drew her attention and made Ann more inclined to depart quickly.

*   *   *

Walking with her collar turned up and her hands shoved deep into her pockets, Destiny had put several blocks between herself and the brownstone, while the wind and her desire to return to Andrie grew more powerful. Her chest alternately swelled and contracted, as she breathed deeply in an involuntary and futile effort to cool the rage within her. Thoughts of Ann's hands touching Andrie, and her lips and tongue caressing her, ripped sanity and reason from Destiny until she could no longer see the street or the night in front of her. She had become blind to everything but the image of Andrie wrapped in arms that weren't hers. She was stricken motionless by the thought, stopping dead in her tracks. Taking her hands from her pockets she tried in vain to rid herself of the vision by rubbing her eyes. She felt the small crumbs of bread still in her pocket from when she had fed the pigeons. In that instant, she realized that she was making the same mistake she had made fifteen years before.

"No!" she cried out to the dark empty street around her, her voice exploding with a fury far more fierce than the first sound of thunder announcing the arrival of the storm. She turned back and began running toward the brownstone. She would no longer be kept out. She would be with Andrie and she knew that Andrie needed to be with her. Nothing else mattered. The sky burst open with a torrent of pouring rain, instantly saturating Destiny and the pavement beneath her. As she ran, the rain beat down on her, keeping perfect time with the incessant drumming in her chest. The harder the rain pounded, the faster her pace became. She had become the storm.

Lightning flashed in her eyes, as she looked ahead to see Ann's car pulling away from where it had been parked. Whatever happened with Ann was done. Destiny vowed to herself that it would be the last time anyone's hands but her own would touch Andrie. Moving with the speed of the wind, within seconds she had reached the steps of the brownstone. She ascended them two at a time and hurled back the partially opened front door, bursting through it possessed by her one need . . . Andrie.

Inside, she raced up the two flights of stairs that led to Andrie's apartment. Out of breath, soaked from rain and sweat, her skin burning with anger and desire, Destiny threw open the door, crashing it against the wall. The thunder exploded. There in front of her stood Andrie in the dark, silhouetted by the glow of the fireplace.

Their eyes locked as a bolt of lightning flashed through the hall window behind Destiny, making her look like some powerful, redeeming angel. She rushed toward Andrie, taking her into her arms. Her rain-drenched hair and clothes dripped onto Andrie, as their bodies came together and their lips found their way.

At that moment, fifteen years of love, anger and need were unleashed. They were finally feeding each other's hunger . . . and this time they would not stop until their appetites were satiated.

Andrie felt Destiny's lips pressing on hers and the tongue that fervently searched her mouth. She had waited so long for this. She craved more of this woman . . . much more. She pressed her body even closer to Destiny. The short, tight, black skirt she was wearing rode up as she straddled Destiny's sturdy thigh.

Their bodies melted, one into the other, as they tumbled to the floor where they began tearing hungrily at each other's clothes. Destiny's hands slid up under Andrie's loose-fitting blouse. She unsnapped the black lace bra with one hand as her other rushed the blouse up over Andrie's head. The sight of Andrie's smooth full breasts seemed to propel her into an even more feverish state of excitement, the electricity of which ran from her body directly into Andrie's.

The sound of thunder and flashes of lightning raged around them as, layer by layer, what had remained a mystery for so long was now suddenly and furiously revealed. The storm was reaching its full fury as the lightning continued to fill the room in pulsating bursts.

Andrie pulled the soaked brown leather jacket off Destiny, then tore at her damp, worn-out denim shirt and plain white bra underneath. Destiny freed her arms from the shirt and bra in one motion. Her long, wet hair sprinkled Andrie with droplets of water as she knelt over her, kissing her breasts. Her hands explored Andrie's body with an almost fierce intensity until they found their way under the short black skirt, where the only barrier remaining was a pair of black silk panties.

Andrie's body writhed with pleasure and anticipation as she felt the motions of Destiny's hand between her thighs. Her arms thrashed out wildly. The fire that burned within her now raged uncontrollably. She whispered only two words: "Destiny, please."

Destiny heard the urgency of the plea. She knew what Andrie wanted. Taking the silk in her hand she swept it away with just enough force that the fine strings around Andrie's hips tore with ease, readily surrendering to what was about to happen. The slender fingers of Destiny's determined hand began to probe deeply into Andrie. Andrie's body throbbed, hot and wet with desire, as it responded to the invasion. Her hips moved, at first rhythmically with Destiny's hand, but then, as the passion intensified, their thrusts became faster . . . faster . . . faster until her body became totally engulfed in an unstoppable frenzy of excitement. She stretched out her arms, digging her nails into the rug beneath her, as her back arched off the floor. With that, her body, burning white hot, reached its pinnacle. It was as though an electrical current had charged through every one of her muscles, then suddenly stopped. Andrie fell back on to the floor, her body still entwined with Destiny's. She felt Destiny's lips on her neck. Slowly and tenderly they worked their way to her mouth, where the passion continued.

Andrie pulled back gently as if to observe Destiny, who lay atop her. She studied Destiny's face, especially her eyes. The combination of passion and tenderness that Destiny possessed was like nothing Andrie had ever experienced. She thought to herself, could this be the same woman that she had remained belligerent toward for so long? No one had ever made her feel like this. It was as if

Destiny knew everything about her, right down to where and how to touch her.

Every word that passed between them now was being spoken with their eyes. Destiny tenderly retrieved the hand that had just pleasured Andrie so intimately and ran its fingers slowly along her lips and tongue, savoring the sweetness that remained on it.

As she watched her, Andrie slowly unzipped Destiny's jeans and began pulling them down from her hips. Destiny pushed herself up onto her knees, balancing herself first on one leg then the other, as she kicked off the worn-out denim jeans. The sight of Destiny kneeling over her, with her thighs astride, enticed Andrie to reach up and run her hand through the thick tuft of dark hair that was now laid bare. Then Andrie drew herself up on to her knees, facing Destiny. She kissed her on the mouth, longingly, as she gently leaned into her, causing Destiny to gradually fall back onto the floor. She began to outline Destiny's lips using her tongue. She continued to her chin, her neck, then advancing downward to her chest and her breasts, where she lingered for a while, as her tongue danced over Destiny's erect nipples, before moving lower still. . . . Andrie's long hair caressed Destiny's body as she continued downward. Destiny felt as though she were being pulled under in a tidal wave as her senses seemed to be drowning in Andrie.

Working her way ever closer to her destination, Andrie made delicate circles with her tongue on the inside of Destiny's thighs. She heard Destiny murmur with pleasure, as each time she got closer to the throbbing, engorged lips that yearned for her touch. Unhurried, she relished the taste and texture of Destiny's smooth skin. Andrie was naturally artful at the sweet torment of foreplay.

Destiny's groans increased. Her hands were extended straight down as she squeezed, grabbed and caressed whatever she could reach of Andrie, her hair, shoulders, her breasts. Destiny had endured all she could. Every last part of her ached to be joined with Andrie. "Now. I want you, now," she groaned compellingly, as Andrie hovered alarmingly close to the heart of her fire. At the last breath of those words, Andrie's supple tongue entered Destiny, immersing itself with slow, deep, long strokes, which seemed only to add fuel to the flames. Destiny's body pitched to and fro with the fury of a ship being tossed in a storm.

Andrie increased her tempo to match Destiny's wild movements; she wrapped her arm around Destiny's thigh as the passion heightened. Any control Destiny had maintained until now was consumed by this fire that spread so uncontrollably throughout her. The energy of her body enveloped them both, until it seemed they moved as one.

The motion of their one perfect body escalated until all that had raged so long and ferociously within Destiny finally exploded in an ecstasy which left them both devastated in its wake.

Several minutes of motionless silence had gone by before Destiny, who seemed totally sapped of strength, reached down and stroked Andrie's head as it lay on Destiny's thigh. Although no words had passed, Destiny knew what Andrie was thinking and she needed to reach her now before the moment was lost. "It's right, Andrie. This was supposed to happen."

The gentle tone of Destiny's words drew Andrie up to kiss her. Looking into her eyes, Andrie knew what Destiny said was true. This *was* right. It was more than right. It was predestined, yet she couldn't help but wonder what was to happen now.

Then, as if she had been inside Andrie's mind, Destiny continued softly, "Don't worry about anything right now. This time should be only for us. In the morning . . . in the light, we can think about what we should do. Let tonight be ours, alone."

Andrie didn't respond, verbally. She simply began to kiss Destiny, slowly . . . seductively . . . again, yielding to a passion she had denied herself for so long.

*   *   *

It was well after midnight as the 762 from Los Angeles prepared for its arrival at Kennedy Airport. This was the first time in years that Nicole had traveled in coach class. As the plane made its

somewhat bumpy touchdown, she silently recollected all the traveling and luxuries she enjoyed with Destiny, and even with Sonia for
the short time that they were together. Comforts, elegant clothes,
and celebrity were important to her, even if she didn't earn them
herself. She was determined to live that life again, but to do that
she needed Destiny to take her back, just as she had done in the
past.

An unexpected phone call from Bee Avery had provided Nicole
with the information that Destiny was in New York. It took little
encouragement for Bee to convince Nicole to agree to hop a flight
to New York and stay at her place while there. At the time of the
call, Bee hadn't told Nicole exactly where Destiny was staying, but
she promised to have that information for her by the time she
arrived.

On her way to the luggage claim Nicole hurriedly searched the
large, amorphous leather shoulder bag she was carrying for her
cigarettes. Long flights were hell for her because of the no-smoking
rules. As she lit up and took a deep, relieving drag, she thought to
herself that she was nervous enough about finding Destiny and
rekindling their relationship, without having to suffer six hours
without a smoke. With the cigarette dangling from her lips, Nicole
once again rummaged through the huge disorganized purse, first
pulling out her cellular phone and finally retrieving a crumpled
piece of paper with Bee's New York number on it. She promptly
fingered the keypad and stood poised for Bee to pick up on other
end. Instead, she heard the tinny sound of Bee's answering
machine: "*Hello. This is Bee. I'm not available right now, but if
you leave a message, I'll get back to you as soon as possible. . . .
If this is you Nicole, I have good news for you. I've located our
friend. See ya soon.*"

"Perfect!" Nicole marveled, as her cranberry-colored lips formed
a toothy smile. Bee, who was never known for her reliability, had
kept her word.

Having picked up her luggage and placed it on a cart, Nicole
headed out of the terminal to the taxi stand. New York's early

winter weather was a shock to her Southern California system. Jumping into a waiting cab, she instructed the driver, through chattering teeth, to put her bags in the trunk.

Moments later the cab was making its way from Kennedy to Bee's apartment in Gramercy Park. The ride would be long enough for Nicole to go over what she would say to Destiny and prepare herself mentally for the encounter. She was, without a doubt, on a mission.

Chapter Ten

The morning sun slowly tore the lovers from the fleeting refuge that the night had provided them. Andrie had been awake to witness the dawn breaking. The rude, intrusive light made her cling even more tightly to Destiny's smooth, powerful body as it rested still entwined with hers.

The fragrance of Destiny's hair and skin was mixed with the sweet lingering scent of the love they had made. Andrie made a conscious effort to let her senses become inundated with the sight, smell and feel of Destiny in her bed. She watched Destiny, as she continued to sleep after the night of endless and strenuous passion that had begun in front of the blaze of the fireplace.

Feeling her stir, Andrie looked up to see Destiny staring lovingly at her.

"How long do we have before you leave?" Destiny asked in a sleepy voice, as she brushed Andrie's hair away from her face and tenderly kissed her on the forehead.

"I have a car picking me up in a couple of hours," Andrie responded in a soft morning whisper, as she took Destiny's hand in both of hers, kissing every finger, then holding it to her face. The small calluses on Destiny's fingertips made Andrie's skin tingle. It was a sensation that reminded her of how hard Destiny worked at the art of making music. A dreamy and contented smile crossed her face, as it occurred to her that those hands that made so many instruments come alive in concert halls, had spent all night proving that they were blessed with far more intimate talents. Without letting go of Destiny's hand, she sat up and pulled the soft white cotton sheet to where it just barely covered her breasts. A feeling of warmth and security filled her as she realized that everything she had ever wanted, or ever could want, was lying there next to her in bed. Andrie knew that Destiny was her world, at that moment and for the rest of her life.

Destiny sat up, feeling no need to cover her full bare breasts. She moved closer until she was sitting behind Andrie with her arms and legs wrapped around her.

Andrie leaned back against her, and began to speak again. "I've been up thinking about this ever since the sun came up. I can't be without you anymore. You were right. For years, I told myself that you were everything I hated. But right from the beginning, you were everything I ever loved . . . I just didn't want to face it, because I thought you hated me after you found me with Brian. I knew that I had hurt you, even though I never meant to. Every time I remembered the expression on your face that day, I became more certain that you could never forgive me for what I had done, so I tried to convince myself that we were wrong for each other," she said, resting her head softly against Destiny's chest.

"None of that matters anymore. What matters right now is that something I thought was impossible, is happening," Destiny said, realizing that her search for what was missing had come to an end.

"What did you think was impossible?" Andrie asked. There was an innocent curiosity in her tone, as she looked deeply into Destiny's eyes.

"To hold a dream in my arms," Destiny answered with a sigh, gently pulling Andrie even closer to her. The morning was slipping away, as Destiny counted and savored every minute they had left before Andrie had to leave for Washington.

Andrie wished that she could clutch every second, every minute that was vanishing from their morning. Yet there was a bittersweetness to the passing of this time for her. She knew that the sooner she ended her relationship with Ann, she and Destiny could start their life together. "As soon as I see Ann in Washington, I'm going to tell her about us. I'm going to resign from her staff as well. When I get back, I'll be free . . . totally," she said, affectionately rubbing her face against Destiny's bare shoulder.

"Oh no, you won't. You'll be mine, forever. Neither of us will ever be free *that way* again," Destiny replied softly, as she climbed around to face Andrie again, then once more unleashed the feral craving inside her and began to tenderly devour every part of Andrie.

Unwilling to yield to the cold light of day, they fed on each other, body and soul, until the very last moments before the car arrived to take Andrie to the airport.

* * *

The hotel stood towering like a dark gleaming monolith over Capitol Hill. As the transparent plexi-glass elevator began to rise, Andrie looked down at the large atrium lobby shrinking away below. All the usual faces, who greeted her each time she arrived, were still smiling from behind the front desk as she made her ascent. Washington had always been a friendly, comfortable place for her. She had considered it her home-away-from-home ever since she had started working for Ann. But this time was different. This time she knew that she had only one home and that was with Destiny. It didn't matter if it were in New York, Los Angeles, or anywhere else in the world. Andrie had never felt so completely enveloped by another person . . . so attached and secure.

Exiting the elevator, she smiled to herself as she felt her body still throbbing from Destiny's long, sculptured musician's fingers probing all her secret places. The pleasure of the memory undulated inside her with every step she took, until her thighs weakened, as her body begged to be visited by Destiny once again.

Reaching her room, Andrie opened the door and was struck by the fragrance of flowers. To her shock, as she looked around, every flat surface was covered with dozens of roses. The room was alive with the reds, pinks, whites and yellows. In vain she searched each arrangement for a card. Then, looking over to the bed, she noticed an envelope sitting on the pillow. She tore it open and read, *Andrie, You are the soul that gives my body life. Wherever you go, look no further than yourself to find me. Love forever, Destiny.*

Her heart began to race, and below she could feel her body

continuing to yearn for Destiny. Just then the phone rang. Certain who it was, she grabbed the receiver before the second ring.

"Hello," she said into the phone.

"Hi, sugar. I miss you somethin' awful," Destiny's voice groaned on the other end.

"I miss you too. I can't wait to be with you again. I can't wait to start our life together," Andrie said, falling back on the bed.

"Baby, we already have, and it's gonna get better every day. So did you get my flowers?"

"Did I get them? There's no room for me in here, with all these roses. You must have bought out an entire florist shop. They're beautiful."

"I wanted to surround you with them, so wherever you looked you would think of me," Destiny's voice explained in a soft tender tone.

"I don't need flowers to think of you. I don't need anything to do that. You're the only thing I think about. I can barely remember why I'm here. All I can do is miss you. I can still feel you from this morning."

"I can taste you . . . I want you so bad." Destiny's fervor burned through the telephone line until Andrie felt her heat at the other end.

"I took one of your T-shirts with me, so I could sleep in it," Andrie confessed.

"Don't wear anything else with it. I want it to be like me touching your bare skin." Destiny's breathy whisper resonated inside Andrie, making her whole body quiver.

"OK I promise, just your shirt and nothing else. I'll call you when I'm ready for bed," Andrie said, as she touched the petals of one of the roses next to the bed.

"I'll be waitin'. . . . By the way, I remembered that you used to bring all your flowers to that nursing home years ago. I figured that you still like to do that, so I arranged for them to be sent to one of the nursing homes down there after you check out."

"I love you," Andrie sighed. Her body was weakened and drained from desire and lack of sleep.

"I love you too baby . . . I always have." Destiny answered softly.

"I'll talk to you tonight," Andrie said, blowing a kiss into the phone before hanging up.

At the other end, Destiny held the receiver for a few moments before hanging up, as the sound of Andrie's parting kiss lingered in her ear. Then, abruptly, the apartment intercom blared out, commanding her attention. Still happily distracted by thoughts of Andrie, Destiny smiled, as she answered the intercom. "Who is it?" she asked cheerfully.

"Des, honeybunch, is that you? It's freezing out here. I just hate New York weather." As the familiar voice crackled back over the intercom, Destiny stood there, in a state of shock, temporarily unable to answer.

"Des, honey, it's freezing out here," the voice called out.

"Nicole?" The name caught in Destiny's throat.

"Of course, Des, sweetie. Now let me in, OK? . . . Oh never mind. I didn't realize that this door isn't locked. I'm on my way up."

"No . . . Nicole . . . shit," Destiny called out, but there was no response. Exasperated, the arteries in her neck pulsed as her blood rushed and her mind raced with questions. How could Nicole have found her, she wondered. Destiny loathed the idea of her showing up like this and violating the privacy of Andrie's home. But before she could think further about it, she heard Nicole knocking at the door.

Destiny stomped furiously to the door and opened it. Her dark eyes turned cold as she angrily greeted Nicole. "How did you know where I was? . . . And why are you here?" Destiny wasn't a person given quickly to anger, but it enraged her to see that Nicole had shown up at Andrie's door.

"I was in town and I heard . . ." Nicole began to explain, as she walked in and quickly surveyed the surroundings.

"Don't lie to me. Who told you that I was here? Give me an honest answer or in one second I'm gonna kick you out, bodily," Destiny interrupted impatiently.

"What's happened to you? This isn't like you at all," Nicole replied.

"If you're not going to answer me, I want you out!" Destiny grabbed her arm and pushed her toward the door.

"Wait. I'll tell you," Nicole said, pulling her arm free from Destiny's grip. "Bee told me. . . . She had seen you at some party on Friday night and I guess that you both left at the same time."

"So she followed me?" Destiny asked, glaring furiously at Nicole.

"No, that's not what happened. Bee said that she happened to leave the party about the same time you did and she decided to go to a bar that's not far from here . . . so you had both headed the same way and she happened to notice that you got out of the cab in front of this building. That's all. So when I phoned her on the weekend and started talking about how much I missed you, she told me where she had seen you . . . and here I am." Nicole was nervous as she spoke, not knowing what balance of truth and fallacy would keep Destiny from growing angrier. There was trembling in her voice. She saw Destiny's expression growing colder and more impatient.

"Why are you here?" Destiny asked in an icy tone.

"Oh honey, I really miss you and I needed to talk to you, about us," Nicole answered with the same assumed sweetness that she had always found effective to manipulate those around her.

"I'm gonna save you a heap of time then. . . . There is no us, Nicole. I'm not mad at you anymore for what happened with us, but I'm real mad about you comin' here like this . . . so I want you to leave now." With that Destiny took a broad step toward the door and pulled it open. She was leaving no room for further discussion.

Nicole saw that Destiny was immovable. She knew Destiny well enough to recognize that something had changed tremendously, and she had lost the effect she once had on her. For Nicole, there was no choice but to leave. As she walked out the door in absolute defeat, she turned and apologized. "I'm sorry about coming here like this. Whoever she is, she's very lucky." Her words were sincere; reality had set in for her. She was now as anxious to leave the brownstone as Destiny was to see her gone.

It took Destiny a few minutes to recuperate from the encounter and begin to sort out her thoughts. She wandered into the living room and dropped onto the couch. As her mind cleared, it occurred to her that, although Nicole was told where she was staying, she didn't know with whom. Destiny now knew that her instincts were right about Bee. She was a gossip and a sneak. But Destiny concluded that none of that would matter, since the whole world would soon know that she and Andrie were planning to spend the rest of their lives together. She picked herself up off the couch and headed into the bedroom to continue working on the songs she was writing.

*   *   *

Andrie's meeting with Ray Dalton went well, despite the fact that her mind kept wandering back to Destiny and the love they made just before she left that morning. The primary focus of the meeting was the very heavy schedule of appearances that Ann would be making over the next few months. Among these would be a number of television and radio shows. Most would be of a topical nature and a few would be interviews. The latter were usually cherished as a chance to allow Ann to present herself and her views to the voting public, with little opposition, assuming she had the right interviewer. Generally, Ann had a policy of being too busy to be interviewed by anyone with a reputation for being contentious.

By the end of the meeting, Andrie had her work cut out for her. Together, she and Ray had compiled a list of topics about which she needed to brief Ann, prior to any of these engagements.

Andrie knew that the responsibility for these briefings would probably fall back to Ray once she resigned.

It was almost 6 p.m. and outside the city was dark, except for the street lamps and the brightly illuminated monuments. They had worked through lunch and neither realized it until now.

"Do you want to catch a bite?" Ray asked as he packed his briefcase.

"No thanks; I'm supposed to have dinner with Ann this evening," Andrie responded in a polite, but faraway tone. She was sure that Ray would attribute her decline of his informal dinner invitation to the fact that she had become less than comfortable with him, ever since he developed the notion of Ann marrying Stuart for appearances. Although that *had* been true, it wasn't any longer.

Whatever Ann would decide to do as a result of Ray's, or anyone else's, suggestions was no longer Andrie's concern. If she sounded distant when she answered Ray, it was because she *was* distant. Her heart and mind were back in New York . . . with Destiny, but she wasn't about to announce that to Ray, at least not until she had broken the news to Ann, as she planned to do that evening.

Aside from Stuart Sottley, the rotund, ruddy-faced, mid-fortyish Dalton was the only other associate of Ann's who was privy to the fact that she was gay. Underneath his overstuffed, teddy-bearish appearance, Ray Dalton was a cunning and calculating PR man, whose savvy was essential to Ann's success; therefore, few secrets were kept from him. As he and Andrie finished shuffling their papers and stuffing their briefcases, the office phone rang. He reached across his desk and answered it. "Hello . . . Ann . . . sure, hold on, Andrie's right here." Then, handing the receiver over to Andrie, Ray picked up his briefcase, said goodnight and left the office.

"Ann, where do you want to meet?" Andrie asked, tucking the phone under her chin, as she maneuvered her way into her heavy tan trenchcoat.

"Oh. I'm sorry about this, but I'm going to have a dinner meeting with Paul Hoberly and Diane Atwater." Hoberly and Atwater were two senior members of the House whose friendships Ann had been courting. "How about dinner tomorrow night?" she asked Andrie.

Andrie stopped wriggling into her coat and took the phone into her hand again. "I was really expecting to have dinner with you tonight. I need to discuss something very important with you," she said, hoping that Ann would offer to change her plans. She didn't want to wait an extra minute to explain things to Ann and begin her new life with Destiny.

"What is it that's so important? . . . Did any problems come up at the meeting?" Ann began to sound impatient.

"No, it's nothing like that. It has to do with me . . . and us," Andrie tried to explain.

"Well, I'm sure that this can hold for tomorrow evening. We'll talk then," Ann replied, sounding pressed for time.

"OK, we'll talk about it tomorrow night then. Enjoy dinner." With that Andrie hung up and headed out of the office. Now she would have to wait until the next evening to break her news to Ann. Although she felt frustrated by this delay, she decided that it would at least allow her more time to find the most gentle way of saying what she needed to say.

As she left the building and walked to the corner to hail a cab, it began to rain lightly. As the cool drizzle hit her face, it reminded her of the night before and how Destiny burst into her apartment, drenched with rain, wetting Andrie in so many ways, as they combined their bodies. Thinking of that, she could hardly wait to get back to her hotel room to call her.

Chapter Eleven

The flamboyant decor of Bee Avery's apartment was appealing to Nicole. She had made herself at home from the moment she arrived the night before. The guest room was large and just as the rest of the apartment did, it clearly reflected Bee's eccentric tastes. The headboard of the king-sized bed was fashioned from highly polished branches of a petrified oak. It had a menacing look to it, as if it were about to reach down and crush in its grasp whoever slept there.

Nicole reclined on the bed with no such fear. As she leafed through the pages of one of Bee's earlier novels, she was preoccupied with the fact that the Destiny Anderson chapter of her life was at an end. She didn't like being alone. It was difficult for her, both emotionally and financially. There was no malice in Nicole. She was simply someone who depended on others in order to live the type of life that suited her rather exorbitant tastes. She envisioned herself as a yet-undiscovered star.

Both Destiny, and later Sonia, had not only supported her, but each did all they could to promote her acting career. The results of both their efforts amounted to a few roles in B movies and a commercial here and there.

Nicole was grateful to them and harbored no anger toward either woman after their relationships ended. But now she needed to move forward with her life and her career. Reclining snugly in her posh surroundings, Nicole decided that she was ripe for a new relationship, with the right woman . . . someone else with money and connections to all the right people.

"How are y-y-you feeling?" Bee stammered, breaking the spell of Nicole's pensive state.

"OK. I'm just trying to sort things out," she replied inattentively, as she continued flipping the pages of Bee's book.

"I'm going to a party at Louis Aimes's apartment tomorrow night. W-w-would you like to come?" Bee asked, with the enthusiasm of a schoolboy inviting a girl to a dance.

"Louie Aimes, the director?" Nicole asked, suddenly showing an interest in the conversation.

"Y-yes. You don't have to worry about clothes. It's c-c-casual," Bee answered encouragingly. "He gives a lot of these g-get togethers."

"OK. I'd love to come," Nicole replied cheerfully. The wheels in her head were already turning, as she wondered whom she might meet at the party.

Bee was elated. She had been attracted to Nicole since they first met at one of Sonia's parties, a couple of years before.

Nicole jumped off the bed and began searching through the clothes she had brought with her, for just the right outfit. As she did, she made a alarming discovery. She wasn't wearing the diamond tennis bracelet that Destiny had given her for their third anniversary. She never took that off. It was like a part of her. Bee helped her as they both scoured the room for it.

"Check the bed. Maybe it came off while you were s-sleeping," Bee suggested.

Nicole wasted no time as she frantically hunted through the sheets and under the pillows, but it was to no avail. The bracelet wasn't there. Suddenly, it occurred to her. She remembered the way she pulled her arm from Destiny's grasp when she went to see her earlier. Nicole was certain it was then that she lost the bracelet. Since neither she nor Bee Avery had the phone number of the apartment, it was clear that Nicole would have to return to the brownstone in the morning to look for the bracelet.

*   *   *

Destiny was busily working on the songs for Rena's movie. Everything felt so right, the melodies, the lyrics . . . the emotions. She smiled with satisfaction as she took a break from the keyboard and started to dig through her duffel bag until she retrieved a battered, dark reddish brown, leather wallet. She opened the tiny flap of one of its compartments and removed a flat, tarnished piece of metal. Holding it at eye level, she smiled, then she began rubbing with her flannel shirttail. After several minutes of rubbing, parts of it began to shine, revealing some of the original beauty of the small, silver maple leaf. She had never given it to Andrie, and yet was never able to discard it. She remembered how she had rationalized keeping it with her for the last fifteen years, by telling herself that it was a momento of her college days in New York. She chuckled and shook her head, as it became clear to her that she had never let go of her love for Andrie.

Removing the silver chain she was wearing around her neck, Destiny carefully slipped the small leaf onto it, then put it back on. She looked in the mirror and admired the delicate charm and she imagined how it would look against Andrie's smooth fair skin. She intended to see that on Thursday, when she planned to place the necklace on Andrie, where it was meant to be from the beginning. Summoned from her thoughts by the ringing of the phone, Destiny was elated to hear Andrie's sleepy voice on the other end.

"I'm in bed and I'm wearing nothing but your shirt, just like I promised you," Andrie murmured.

"I want to hold you so bad." Destiny breathed the words into the phone.

"All day I could still feel your hands all over me . . . everywhere you touched me," Andrie said, still losing some of herself in the sensation.

"I wish that I could touch you and hold you right now. It's gonna be hell to only see you for a little while, in some restaurant after all this. If there was any way that I could postpone this meeting back in LA, I would do it in a shot." The last thing Destiny wanted was to have to leave New York the afternoon that Andrie returned. But her meeting with Rena Samuel had been tightly scheduled on a day that Rena would be leaving for Europe, so there could be no changes.

"I would never let you do that. I know how important your work is to you. Don't worry, we're going to be fine. As soon as I tell Ann everything, I'll be able to start looking for positions in LA and eventually, I can open a marketing business. I promise that as soon as I get a job out there, I'll move, so we can be close enough to see each other all the time," Andrie promised.

"Whoa, wait a minute. You're not moving close by. You're moving in. I want you in my life, morning, noon and night. That means the same house and the same bed. Ya hear me?"

"I hear you. I just didn't know if you were ready for that yet. That's all," Andrie explained.

"Now listen. As soon as you finish things with Ann, I want us to be together. We already lost too many years together to worry about some kind of long engagement. You know my bad points. . . . Lord knows, you concentrated on them for fifteen years. And I already know that you're hot tempered and hard headed, among other things. So the worst is out between us. We don't need a gettin' acquainted period, we just need to be together."

"I agree . . . except the part about me. I'm not hard headed or hot tempered and if you say that again, I'll punch you. And what did you mean with, *among other things?*" They both began to laugh.

"Sugar, I'm serious. I really want us to live together as soon as possible. No more wasted time," Destiny persuaded.

"I really want that, too. Listen, I wasn't able to talk with Ann this evening. She already had other plans, so we rescheduled for tomorrow night."

"Do you know what you'll say?" Destiny asked.

"Not the exact words. I just have to tell her the truth. I'm also going to tell her that I'm resigning from her staff. I'll finish out this week, since I have meetings on Thursday and Friday, but after that I'm out. . . . Which reminds me . . . I have the perfect little place for us to meet on Thursday, before you head back to LA. It's called Lilly's. It's on Hudson Street. There's a matchbook that says 'Lilly's' on the kitchen counter. It's got the exact address on it,"

Andrie said, as she stretched, lazily sliding her limbs over the smooth, cool white sheets that covered the bed under her.

"I wish that there was a way I could postpone this meeting with Rena and her production people, so I could stay here until you were ready to come to LA," Destiny said, shivering inside from the sound of Andrie's breathing over the phone.

"I know. I'm sorry that I can't just leave with you on Thursday. These meetings are especially important, since I'm resigning. I'll need to tie things up with the rest of Ann's staff.

"But, after that it's just you and me babe, and I can't wait to get my hands on you." Andrie sighed the words seductively into the phone, knowing the effect it would have on the woman she loved.

The talking and teasing went back and forth in their conversation, as they tried to come as close as they could on a long distance line.

Then, in a soft, mellow voice made slow by her southern drawl, Destiny took Andrie on a sensuous journey, which would bridge the gap of the miles that separated them. "Oh, baby, I'm so hungry for you, it reminds me of this real hot day, when I was a kid in Kentucky. I was walkin' through this peach orchard one afternoon and I could smell the clean, sweet smell of the fruit. I just kept breathin' it in, 'cause it smelled so damned good. Then I eyed this peach. It was hangin' there on one of the lower branches. It was full and round and alive with swirls of pink and red. I reached up and just held it in my hand for a second before I plucked it from the tree. Its skin was like velvet when I rubbed my face against it, and I could feel its plump body underneath. It was so ripe and ready . . . it was just beggin' for me to eat it. But instead, I ran my tongue real light, back and forth over the sides of the crease that curved from its top to its bottom. I could feel its soft nap getting wetter and wetter, as I licked it. That little peach lay there so ready and waitin' in my hand, that I knew it was time to break through its smooth, willin' skin and taste the sweet juice that was waitin' for me inside. So right there, I opened my mouth over it and pushed through 'til I felt the smooth slick fruit underneath. With each mouthful I took after that, my lips and my face dripped wet with the warm syrup that flowed out. I couldn't stop. I entered deeper and deeper, into the sweetness that had been hidin' there, just beggin' for me to taste it. . . . Sugar, I just can't wait to get you alone."

Chapter Twelve

Destiny looked out the window of Andrie's bedroom at the clear, dry, brisk morning. It was a welcome departure from the on-and-off rain of the past two days. She touched the maple leaf charm that hung from her neck. Although Andrie had never worn it, somehow it made Destiny feel closer to her. An early phone call from David drew her from the window and her thoughts. David loved to have his morning coffee with a chat. He tried to convince Destiny to join him in person, but she had other plans. He agreed to stop by later in the morning, since he didn't have to be in his office until mid-afternoon that day. He also explained that he had a business meeting at a hotel near Kennedy airport the next day, so he planned to meet her in the VIP lounge, before her flight.

It was still early when they hung up and Destiny decided to go out and enjoy the sights and sounds of the city morning. She had been to New York countless times over the years, yet there was something about this morning that reminded her so much of that morning in Brooklyn, so many years ago, when she had bought the silver maple leaf charm and rushed home to David's house, anxiously waiting to give it to Andrie. The feeling alarmed her at first, as she remembered how that day had ended. But the apprehension fled as quickly as it set in. At the moment, Destiny had no room for anything but happiness.

The songs that she had been working on were just about finished and as she ambled down the concrete pathways that stretched out in front of her, Destiny was satisfied that her music reflected the city that was home to the woman she loved.

She had spent the night thinking about Andrie living with her in Los Angeles. There was something about the idea that had begun to bother Destiny, and it didn't take long before she figured out what it was. LA had long ago ceased being a place she wanted to call her home, and despite the fact that Andrie was ready to live anywhere with her, Destiny sensed that LA wasn't a favorite of Andrie's. She also knew that although they would be spending a lot of time in New York since it was home to Andrie, and her family lived there, they needed a special place, away from the big cities and the crowds . . . a place that was just for them, where they could get away from everything and everyone but each other.

She began to think of all the beautiful places she had been and tried to imagine where Andrie would be happiest. It was a problem . . . a wonderful problem. And, as she walked down the chilly December streets, Destiny hoped to herself that all the problems she and Andrie would face could always be as pleasant as this one. Turning the corner of University Place and West 12th Street, she immediately noticed that the air was filled with the scent of pine. There, lined up like tall green soldiers, were several rows of balsams, Douglas firs and scotch pine trees, all waiting to bring the spirit of Christmas to apartment dwellers throughout the West Village. Watching the young Asian man wrap twine around one of the taller balsams he had just sold, her mind drifted back to that winter break when she first met Andrie. Destiny recalled how she and Andrie trudged from vendor to vendor, until hours later and half frozen, Andrie discovered just the right Christmas tree.

She remembered stopping for cocoa at a little luncheonette and how Andrie pulled out a picture of a gigantic spruce tree, which she had torn from a magazine article on Montana. Suddenly, parts of the conversation came rushing back to her in a stream of recollection. She recalled a dreamy-faced Andrie telling her how that snow-covered spruce was the perfect Christmas tree and that someday she wanted to live in a place where she could look out her window and see a tree just like that. Making that dream come true for Andrie was something Destiny had fantasized about over and over again during that winter break, along with her own dreams of fame and fortune.

Continuing down University Place, it suddenly came to her, like being hit by a snowball . . . a big white Montana snowball. She could give Andrie her spruce tree and everything that went with it. That would be the place for them. Elation surged through her. It was as though she was the Destiny of fifteen years before, and her fantasy had come true. She could do this. She could make that dream come true for the girl she loved so long ago who lived inside the woman she adored today.

Destiny abruptly turned around and headed back to Andrie's apartment. Within minutes, she was sitting cross-legged on the living room floor, phone in hand, as she described what she had in mind to a Los Angeles realtor who handled large out-of-state properties. The realtor promised that she would do some research and provide Destiny with the pictures and listings as soon as possible.

Hanging up the phone, she reached across the coffee table for a magazine, when she noticed something on the floor near the door, brightly reflecting the late morning light. As she looked closer, she saw that it was a piece of jewelry. But it wasn't until she had it in her hand that she realized its origin. She had all but forgotten Nicole's visit until this. "Shit, I don't believe it," she muttered, stuffing the bracelet in the pocket of her red plaid flannel shirt. She wondered if Nicole had intentionally left the bracelet, so she could come back for it.

Whether it was left intentionally or not, Destiny knew that Nicole would be showing up soon to retrieve it.

                              *   *   *

Sliding clumsily into the backseat of the cab next to Nicole, Bee stammered out the address of the brownstone to the driver. Then, turning to Nicole, she asked, "Are you s-s-sure that you w-w-want to do this?" as she shifted around, attempting to prevent the gray silk jacket she was wearing from getting wrinkled.

"Of course. I want my bracelet. It won't take long. I've already said everything I could to her," Nicole replied. Then after a short pause, she continued, as she felt the need to explain herself to

Bee. "You see, I have had my head turned a few times since we've been together, but Destiny had always taken me back. I used to think it was because she loved me so much. But now, I'm starting to understand that it was just because she didn't care that much about what I did. . . . Who knows? When I first met her, she was no angel. I never saw anyone go through so many women as she did. It was like she was trying to find something that none of them had. She stopped all that when we got together. I was never sure why. It wasn't like I was what she was looking for . . . I always knew that, because there was always this really sad look in her eyes, even when we were having fun. Maybe that's why I didn't feel like I had to be faithful. But yesterday, when I saw her, I knew something was different. Even though she was angry, and her eyes showed it, that sadness was gone from them. I think she found the right person to take it away." Nicole's tone was melancholy and her manner was far more sedate than Bee had ever seen it. She seemed thoughtful, even sensitive.

"Were you in love with her?" Bee asked, realizing that there was a side to Nicole she had not seen until now.

"I don't know if either of us was in love with the other. We needed things from each other. I loved our life together. The friends, the parties, the fame. She loved having me to flaunt around like an award. But there was always a part of her that I couldn't reach. . . . Well, maybe, I didn't care to reach it. I don't know. I think, even at the best point in our relationship, we were both searching for something that we couldn't give each other."

Now, even Nicole seemed surprised with her newly found capacity for introspection. Bee slipped her hand over Nicole's and gently curled her fingers around it. It was her way of letting Nicole know that she sympathized with her. It was also a way of making some headway in her pursuit of Nicole.

Bee was physically unattractive by most standards and had a fairly obnoxious personality. Most of her life she had gotten by on her parents' money, and she was not averse to the idea of using it to attract Nicole.

As the brownstone came into sight, Nicole prepared herself for her next encounter with Destiny by checking her makeup in a small mirror that she pulled from her purse.

"I'll wait h-here in the cab," Bee said reassuringly, as she kissed Nicole on the cheek.

"Thanks. I won't be long." With that, Nicole walked up the stairs and into the building. She didn't bother using the intercom since a workman was standing around and the front door was open. When she reached the second floor, she approached the door slowly, almost tentatively. Rather than using the doorbell, Nicole knocked lightly on the door and waited.

On the other side, Destiny, sure of who was at the door, took her time to walk over and open it.

"I'm sorry to bother you again, but I think . . . ." Nicole began to explain immediately, but Destiny cut her off by pulling the bracelet from her pocket and dangling it in front of her.

"This is what you're here for, isn't it?" Destiny asked, with a skeptical look.

"Thanks. . . . Look, I'm sorry that I had to come back here today. I know that you probably think that I planned this. But I didn't. I promise not to bother you anymore. I know you meant it when you said that there was no more us. You probably won't believe this either, but I really do want you to be happy." Nicole's voice was serious and sincere.

Destiny's expression softened a bit, as she could see that Nicole was telling the truth. "Thanks. I'm sorry if I acted cold to you. I didn't appreciate being tracked down, and I needed to make you know that this wasn't gonna be like the other times," she told Nicole, in a more patient tone.

"I know. And I'm sorry about all of that," Nicole responded regretfully, as she put the bracelet in her purse.

"Look, you don't have to be standin' out there in the hall. You can come in if you want," Destiny opened the door wider and stepped to the side, to allow Nicole in.

"OK. I'll just stay a minute. Bee's downstairs in a cab, waiting for me," Nicole explained, smiling appreciatively, as she stepped into the apartment.

"So what are you gonna do now?' Destiny asked sympathetically.

"Well, for the immediate future, Bee's offered to let me stay with her. That's as far ahead as I like to plan. Most of my things are still at Sonia's place. How about you? Are you going to be bi-coastal now or what?" Nicole asked.

"I'm not sure yet. We need to do some long-range planning." Destiny saw no reason to discuss those plans with anyone until she spoke with Andrie.

"This is serious, isn't it?" Nicole asked.

"It's real serious. Maybe sometime down the road I'll tell you more about it," Destiny answered with a little smile, considering a time when she and Nicole would be able to discuss their lives like two old friends.

"Wow, I turn my back for six months and the next thing I know, I'm replaced. . . ." Nicole punctuated the remark with a laugh, so there would be no doubt that it was said in jest.

Destiny smiled. But inside she knew that the parting was more painful for Nicole than she was willing to admit.

Knowing that Bee was waiting outside in the cab, Nicole moved toward the door. "I'd better leave."

"I'll walk you out," Destiny said, reaching for the door.

Once outside, Nicole saw that the cab had moved several car lengths down past the front of the building because of the traffic on the narrow one-way street. This made her less uncomfortable about saying good-bye to Destiny there on the street.

"Well . . . I don't want to keep Bee waiting," Nicole said, still feeling somewhat awkward.

"You'd better get that clasp fixed on that bracelet, before you lose it for good," Destiny chided warmly.

"I will," she said, smiling back.

"Nicole, if you ever need anything or whatever . . . call me.

OK?" Destiny was offering her friendship to Nicole and the offer was appreciated.

"Thanks, honeybunch . . . I just wanted to call you that one more time," Nicole answered, with a sentimental look in her eyes.

They gave each other a brief, awkward hug, as they stood there on the front steps of the brownstone. Then, Nicole turned and descended the remaining steps. Reaching the sidewalk, she suddenly stopped and looked up at Destiny, who was still standing at the top.

"I was always a better friend than I was a lover. . . . I hope she's the right one. You deserve the best," she said.

Destiny knew how hard it was for Nicole to say those words. She walked down the steps to where Nicole was standing. The awkwardness had disappeared as they embraced each other, hoping in their hearts that they would always remain friends.

At that moment, David turned the corner and came upon the scene. As he continued down the block in their direction, Nicole and Destiny were still holding each other and unaware of him. They slowly came apart from each other as the cab's horn sounded.

"Bee's getting impatient," Nicole said, glancing in the direction of the cab.

"Take care of yourself and remember what I said. . . . Call me if you need anything," Destiny reminded her.

"Don't worry. You know I can be a tough cookie when I have to be. I'd really like to meet her, someday."

"You will. I'll explain everything to you then." Destiny watched as Nicole walked toward the waiting cab. She saw the door swing open as Nicole reached it. They exchanged a final wave good-bye before Nicole disappeared into its backseat.

Destiny stood looking on as the cab pulled away.

"What in the world was that?" a friendly, but curious voice inquired.

She turned to see that David was also watching the cab drive off.

"It was Nicole," she answered.

"I could see that. But why was she here? . . . And why were you holding her like that . . . and what's going on with Andrie? You know . . . I was hoping that by now the two of you would have finally come to your senses." David would have continued to rattle on, but Destiny stopped him.

"Whoa, whoa, whoa. Slow down boy," Destiny said. She felt emotionally exhausted from her encounter with Nicole. Although their relationship had been dead for months, she had just experienced the birth pangs of their new friendship. "Come on up. We'll have a cup of tea and I'll explain the whole thing," she said, putting her arm around his shoulder as they walked past the workman who had been at the top of the steps the entire time.

On their way up, David's questions continued. "Just answer this. Did Andrie know that Nicole was coming here today?"

"No. Nicole forgot something when she was here yesterday, so she dropped by to pick it up," Destiny replied, as she walked up the stairs.

"Oh. Of course. That explains everything," David shot back sarcastically, as he continued, with his voice becoming breathless from the trip up the stairs. "Does Andrie know that she was here yesterday?"

"No. I haven't had a chance to discuss this with her yet," Destiny said, opening the door to the apartment and heading into the kitchen.

"I'm confused. Tell me the whole story from the beginning," David persisted, as he followed her into the tiny kitchen.

"I really don't feel like talking about all of this right now, but I know that you won't give me a moment's peace until I do. OK. Here's the short version. Nicole showed up here yesterday. She wanted to see if I had softened about getting back together. Of course, I told her that I wasn't interested and I asked her to leave. This morning, I'm sitting in the living room and I see something shiny over there." Destiny pointed to the spot on the hall floor where she found Nicole's bracelet. "Then I recognized it. It was a gift I had given Nicole a while ago. Apparently, the clasp was broken, so it must have fallen off her yesterday. Anyway she came back this morning to pick it up."

"How did she know where to find you in the first place?" David still looked puzzled.

"This part isn't real easy for me to swallow. . . . Remember when we were at that fundraiser the other night?" Destiny asked him.

"Yes."

"Well, I introduced you to that blond woman, named Bee. Remember?"

"Y-y-yes, I r-remember," David answered, doing his poor impression of Bee's stutter. Destiny flashed him a disapproving glance and then explained what Nicole had told her about Bee leaving the party at the same time she did. Even as Destiny told the story to David, she found it hard to believe . . . and so did he.

"That sounds like a line of bull to me," David announced, as he searched the refrigerator out of habit.

"I know. But I think that Nicole believes it and if I started arguing about it, she would probably still be here and that's the last thing I wanted. So there you have the whole story, in a nutshell."

"And that's exactly where it belongs, because it's nuts. First of all, you should have told Andrie that Nicole was here as soon as she left yesterday. Second of all, you should be furious that she hunted you down like this, with the help of that blond heifer, B-b-bee."

"I'm plenty mad. Not so much with Nicole. I think we have a good understanding now. But I'm gonna have a talk with Bee after I straighten out some other more important things in my life . . . like where Andrie and I should live, after she gets back from Washington, where's she's breaking up with Ann," Destiny announced.

"What? When was I supposed to find this out, when Liz Smith reported it?" David was elated and indignant all at once.

"We had so little time before she left . . . things just kinda happened. And then, I wanted to wait until Andrie got back from

Washington, so we could tell you together. But when you showed up today and started askin' a heap of questions, I knew I had to tell you. So now, you're officially the first to know that we are together," Destiny told· him, leaning back against the kitchen counter, sporting a proud smile as the tea kettle let off a loud whistle and David threw his arms around her.

"Forget the tea. This is a champagne moment. I'm calling my office to tell them that I'll be late . . . I want to know all the details," David demanded, returning to the refrigerator where he knew Andrie always kept a bottle chilled.

What was left of the morning drifted gently into afternoon, as Destiny spoke to David, at first in a proud brassy voice, with broad smiles and laughter . . . and later in a soft earnest tone of life and love . . . and Andrie.

Chapter Thirteen

It was early evening and the small Japanese restaurant was almost empty except for a young couple at the sushi bar, and Bee sitting alone at a table in the corner. Her eyes were on the door as she sipped hot sake from a dainty stoneware cup. She pushed the cup aside when she saw a slightly built blond man in his late twenties enter the restaurant. Seeing Bee, he immediately headed in her direction.

"I'm just about finished with it. Here's a draft and a few of the pictures that were taken." He slid a manila folder across the table to Bee, who eagerly scooped it up, shuffled through the pictures, then began reading.

The man ordered an Absolut and cranberry juice on the rocks as he waited for her to finish reading. There was a curious expression on his face as he watched her read.

Finally, looking up from the folder, Bee displayed the contented look of someone who had completed a long-time ambition. "This is wonderful, Ed. I love it. It's amazing how some things just f-f-fall together by coincidence," she said, caressing the page melodramatically.

"Bee, I don't know what the hell you're talking about and I still can't figure out what's in this for you," he said.

Bee's face, which normally displayed an eager-to-please smile, had suddenly transformed into a dark vindictive mask. "Ed, when will this hit the s-stands?" Bee seethed, as she intently locked in on the blond man's face.

"Tomorrow. You know, I was working on it right until I left to come here. The investigator called me this afternoon with an update. He said that there should be more pictures waiting for me when I get back to the office. The story will be on page nine. In fact it will take up most of page nine. That's our *IN THE LOOP* section. We put our more interesting, well-documented trash about celebs and public figures on that page. If the story has legs, then it'll make it to our news articles. This story has legs. And it'll probably be picked up by every other paper in New York, as well."

"I'm counting on th-that. What's in this article right now w-won't be conclusive evidence that she's gay, but it *will* stir up enough controversy that the credibility of her ultra-conservative, family-values platform will be a j-joke. And the fact that her fiance is impotent should cast doubt on her reasons for getting m-married. Once her opposition gets wind of this, I can sit back and let them dig up more stuff on her private life," she said, tapping the papers with her finger.

"By the way, thanks again for the private investigator. That's not usually how I gather information for my stories, but it made things very easy for me. Do you know that he actually got into Andrie LaStella's apartment twice. The first time he paid off a pizza delivery guy who was on his way up to the apartment, and he delivered the pizza himself. That's when he saw Destiny Anderson there. Then after he saw her leave, and Ann Capwell go up to the apartment, he bought another pizza and made another delivery to the apartment, pretending that it must have been an error at the restaurant. He even had somebody at the brownstone for two days, posing as a repair man. That's how we got all the shots of Ann Capwell coming and going from there." As Ed spoke, it was clear that he was grateful to Bee for her help, yet he was still puzzled about her motives. Ed Gold worked for a newspaper that had a liberal editorial policy and an editor who would jump at the chance to expose Ann Capwell as the hypocrite she was. He counted himself lucky that Bee called him a few nights ago, after she met Destiny at Ann Capwell's fundraiser. But now that the story was written, he was compelled to find what was at the root of Bee's desire to obliterate the career of a woman who in many political circles was regarded as one day being a possible candidate for the presidency.

"Bee, I know you now for what . . . about two years . . . and

I've never seen you like this. I'm glad you gave me the story and I don't want to look a gift horse in the mouth, so let's just call it my reporter's curiosity. . . . You've got to tell me why you're doing this!" By now, he was leaning halfway over the table, his pale blue eyes squinting with inquisitiveness as he probed Bee for an answer.

Bee looked back at him without saying a word. Then she leaned forward until there was little space left between them at the table. Taking a deep breath she slowly began to speak. She seemed to draw upon some internal reserve of strength to control her words so that her stammer appeared to vanish, if only temporarily. "I need to completely obliterate Ann Capwell's political career . . . I don't want there to be anything left of it, Ed . . . not anything." The words flowed from her with chilling, unfettered clarity.

Ed needed to know, "Why is Ann Capwell's career such a threat to you? God knows, there are other powerful conservatives out there who have just as much to hide about their sex lives?" he asked pointedly.

Bee leaned back in her chair and made herself more comfortable. The muscles in her face appeared to relax, as she considered the idea of telling Ed the reason the secret hatred had long dwelt deep inside her, waiting like a caged animal to be let out.

"I'll tell you but I don't w-w-want this to be in tomorrow's paper," she said, her stammer once again punctuating her words.

"I wouldn't do that. First of all, it would mean revealing my source. Secondly, I consider you my friend and I'm asking you what your reasons are, because I've never seen you like this before. Whatever you tell me stays right here . . . I promise." He smiled gently as he looked across the table at Bee. It was obvious to him that she needed to tell her story and he wanted to hear it.

"I never told anyone this, but my father was in p-politics when I was a kid," she began. "He wanted to try to ch-change things that he thought were wrong. That's the w-w-way he was. H-h-he loved this country. He said there wasn't another place in the world where a poor guy, who was an immigrant's son, could become a millionaire just b-because of determination and h-h-hard work. He started out mixing cement for a construction company and he ended up becoming one of the top c-c-commercial developers in New York. It bothered him that there were people who couldn't get work because they weren't the right color or religion and he wanted to help change that. So, right around the time I was born, he r-ran for state assembly and he won. After four years as an assemblyman, he had become pretty popular in New York. A lot of people said that he would make a great r-representative and his party encouraged him to run for Congress, so he did . . . he ran against Robert C-c-capwell. Capwell was the incumbent.''

"Ann's father?" Ed interrupted, quickly becoming engrossed in the story.

"Yes. C-capwell was old money. He never held a real j-job in his life, he went to the Ivy League s-s-schools and knew all the right people. His family owned everything and e-e-everyone in this city. They were considered big philanthropists. . . . On the other hand, my father was from a working c-c-class background and went to the school of hard knocks. Capwell's problem was that voters were identifying with Arthur Koswaski. That was my father's name.'' Bee ran her finger around the rim of the sake cup as she spoke. "Anyway, C-capwell knew that it didn't matter how many of his rich friends supported his campaign if he couldn't get the average citizen's vote, and my father had a l-l-lock on that. Capwell needed to destroy their trust in my f-father. He couldn't do it with the issues. So he dug into my father's past, hoping he could find something he could use against him. He h-hired private investigators to uncover anything they could and eventually it p-paid off. They found out that my father had an affair with another woman while he was married to my mother. It w-w-was early in their marriage and he had only slept with the w-w-woman once. . . . He felt s-so guilty that he told my mother about it right after it happened. They had w-w-worked things out years b-before Capwell uncovered any of this. Capwell didn't stop there, though. His investigators found out that the woman was a socialist and she had written some kind of pro-socialist book. She was a part-time secretary in the office of the construction company where my father first worked. He met her at the company's Christmas party. He had too much to drink and this w-w-woman was there. . . . He ended up going back to her apartment with her. It only h-happened once. My father didn't know anything about her book or her politics until C-capwell took that information and turned it into h-headlines that claimed my father was having an affair with a c-c-communist. He made it seem like my father was a communist s-s-sympathizer. It was the sixties and the Cold War was still on. He tried to get the facts out, but nobody wanted to listen. It was just the way things were at the time.

"That story destroyed my father's campaign, his business and even his m-m-marriage. My mother couldn't take the public ridicule, so eventually sh-she told him that she was divorcing him. I was a kid but I knew something was wrong. At the time we lived in a three-story brownstone in Gramercy Park. My mother had taken some kind of tranquilizer that the doctor gave her since her nerves were sh-shot. She was out like a l-light in her bedroom, on the second floor. My f-f-father was in his study on the first floor. The housekeeper was on the third floor in the sewing room, wrapping gifts. The next day was my s-s-sixth birthday. I was watching TV in the living room across the way from the study. It was almost seven p.m. It was almost time for me to go to bed, so I thought that I'd go inside and h-h-hang out with my father for a while. I knew that whenever the housekeeper found me with my dad at bedtime, he would convince her to let met stay up a little longer. He used to let me listen to his s-speeches and I would imitate him. He always got a big kick out of that. Don't laugh; he said that I was a natural p-p-public speaker. I didn't have this trouble with my s-speech back th-then. This didn't happen until that n-night before my b-birthday."

Bee paused, momentarily arrested by the memory of that night. Ed knew by the expression on her face that she was no longer seeing him in front of her eyes, but some horrible frightening vision of the past. She took a slow pensive sip from her sake cup, then continued. "My father had s-spent most of that day in the study with the door closed. He didn't even eat with us that evening. I remember thinking how, even though he was around, I s-still missed him. I knew that there was a problem. I was just h-hoping that it would go away. . . . Anyhow, I got up from in front of the t-t-television, and went to the study. As I opened the door I saw my father sitting at h-h-his desk. He didn't even notice me open the door and come into the r-room. He was holding s-something up in front of his face . . . and as I walked toward him it e-e-exploded. I screamed. There was blood everywhere. Since the housekeeper was on the third floor it took a few seconds for her to get down there. . . . My mother didn't hear anything since she w-w-was out cold from the tranquilizer. In that time I r-ran over to my father and tried to . . . I don't know what I was trying to do. I j-j-just wanted him to be alive and t-t-talk to me or something . . . I don't know.

"When the housekeeper came in, she s-started to scream. Then she carried me out . . . like everything else in the room, I was c-covered in my f-f-father's blood." A brief pause followed her story, as Bee finished the sake remaining in her cup and filled it once again from a short brown carafe that sat next to it.

Ed needed time to digest what he was being told, and by whom. He didn't recognize the Bee sitting across from him now. She wasn't the Bee that always sparkled with titillating gossip and congenial conversation. In front of him now was a dark, tortured soul, bent on revenge. The pain and loss that Robert Capwell caused her as a child had transformed her very soul. And, in the years that had passed since, she had prepared to focus with deadly accuracy on her target of destruction. Bee Avery was more a weapon than a woman.

"To you, it might sound like my father committed s-suicide . . . but as far as I'm concerned, Robert Capwell k-killed him. It was fortunate that my father had a lot of friends in the p-police department. They knew that my mother had suffered enough already, so it was reported as an accidental d-death. They even tried to tell me that it was an accident."

"Bee, you were a kid at the time. Are you really sure that it wasn't an accident?" Ed asked, as if reluctant to believe the tragic story.

"I know what I saw and my father left a n-note behind. My mother didn't tell me about the note until years later. I was about fourteen when she married Ivan Avery. I guess she thought that t-t-telling me the truth with all the d-d-details would be a good way of closing the chapter on my father when Ivan adopted me. I already knew the truth, I just didn't know the reasons. She explained everything and then I asked to see the note. I was sure she had it, but she wouldn't show it to me. She would only tell me that it said how much he loved us. She would never talk to me about it after that. About twelve years ago she and Ivan were k-killed in a c-car accident. Going through her things, I found the note. It was hidden under a pullout drawer in an old jewelry box. At first I didn't know what it was. She had wrapped it in a lace handkerchief. I unfolded the handkerchief and there it was . . . s-s-stained with my father's blood. I guess he didn't realize how much blood there would be. It was short and there were some words that were totally blotted out with his b-blood. It just said that he was sorry for all the p-pain and embarrassment he had caused us. . . . And how much he loved me, but that as long as he was alive we would have to l-l-live in the shadow of what had been done to him. So, this was the only way he could protect us from that." There was sadness in Bee's tear-filled eyes, but her jaw was tight as she clenched her teeth in anger at the man who caused her father to take his own life.

"I don't know what to say to you," Ed said as he reached for his drink, which had sat in front of him, neither disturbed nor noticed until now.

"There's nothing to say. I'm doing what I n-need to do. Robert Capwell is retired from politics because of his age and his health, but his ambitions for his daughter's career are what keep him g-going. Ann and her career are the only things he cares about. I w-w-want to see him suffer the way my father suffered. I want to see him stand by helpless and humiliated as his daughter loses what's most important to her . . . power. I don't think that I would have been able to carry all this out, if Ann had turned out to be a different kind of p-person. But she didn't. She's just like him, a power-hungry hypocrite who would stop at n-nothing to get what she wants."

"But you're using the fact that she's gay to destroy her. You're gay too. Doesn't that bother you?" Ed was still trying to assimilate everything he had heard.

"No. She's spent her whole political life being a s-s-self-righteous hypocrite. She's voted against anything that she c-claimed wasn't consistent with her f-family values beliefs. It wasn't just a simple matter of her being in the closet," Bee answered with a derisive grin.

"How long have you known that she was gay?" Ed asked, as he finished his drink.

"About ten years now. But it didn't mean anything to me when I first found out, because she w-w-was in the private sector practicing law. I had seen her at a friend's party. She wasn't with anyone at the t-t-time, and the host wanted to fix me up with her. Naturally, I declined. In fact I left the party before we were even introduced, but that's when I started keeping t-tabs on her. Sometimes I would even use a private eye to do it. But you know that, from the reports that were in the folder I gave you the other day."

Bee had shown Ed reports and compromising pictures of Ann with other women that were taken even before she met Andrie. She was ready to use them if Ann attempted to deny the validity of the article. But she preferred to start by simply stirring up some well-founded rumors first, so she could watch Ann Capwell suffer as she became the subject of ridicule. It would be far more painful and embarrassing to Ann if she at first denied the gossip and then was proven to be a liar when Bee released more definitive proof. Bee did not intend for this to be a quick political death, but rather a slow and tortuous one.

Ed still had questions. "You knew that Andrie LaStella was her lover for seven years now. You could have blown her career away when she was on the city council, years ago," he said, perplexed by Bee's timing.

"It wasn't enough of a career to lose at the time. It's been hard for me to wait this long, but I w-wanted her to have enough success that she'd have a longer way to fall, once I p-p-pushed her. I've even contributed m-money to her campaigns, j-just to make sure that she'd have more to lose when the time came. Besides, over the years she became a conservative icon, with all her family values s-speeches. That's what makes this information so p-perfect to destroy her; she'll be disgraced in her own party." Bee signaled for the waitress to bring them another round of drinks. The small restaurant started to fill up as time went by, making both Bee and Ed speak in quieter tones.

"What about these other people involved in the story, like Destiny Anderson and the LaStellla woman?" Ed asked, playing devil's advocate. For him it was hardly a matter of conscience. He had no allegiance to the other people who would be included in the story. In fact, he had done everything he could to make the article sound as sensational as possible.

"I have nothing personal against any of them. I don't think that this story is going to cause them a lot of harm a-a-anyway. Destiny Anderson has never kept her sexual p-p-preferences a secret. She's been *out* her whole career. As far as this goes, it's just one more time that her name is in the p-p-papers. She knows gossip is all part of the package with fame. As far as Nicole Bonham is concerned, I think she'll appreciate her name being in p-print anywhere. It could only do her career good. Since she left Destiny for Sonia, her n-name hasn't shown up anywhere."

"What about Andrie LaStella?" Ed pressed, as the waitress came by with their drinks.

"I thought about that one. I met her for the first time the other night at the fundraiser. I had always wondered what she would be like. I knew that she was with Ann for seven years. I knew where she l-l-lived. I knew all the things that the private investigator told me about her, but I didn't know her. I didn't know what she w-was like. I used to think she had to be a lot like Ann, to stay with her for so long. But, after ·meeting her, I don't think that anymore. She seems lost, like she's somewhere that she doesn't want to be, but she doesn't know how to get h-h-home. When I mentioned Ann's engagement to her, I could see that she was trying to hide her feelings about it. I think that if Ann splits with her b-because of this story, I'll have d-d-done Andrie LaStella a big favor." Bee needed to rationalize what she was doing to the innocent people involved in her story, because her conscience, although dulled by her thirst for revenge, still caused her some amount of guilt.

"It doesn't seem like Ann Capwell has any idea that Destiny is staying at Andrie LaStella's apartment. Both times Ann showed up, Destiny left and she didn't return until Ann had gone," Ed told her.

"I know. I read it in your draft. I think that the n-news should really be a k-kick in the head t-to Ann Capwell. In the same article that outs her, she reads that her lover is having an affair with another woman. It's all falling into p-p-place so perfectly." Bee lifted the small cup of hot sake to her lips and began to sip, as she beamed with satisfaction at the way her plans were coming together.

Chapter Fourteen

Andrie sat alone at the table waiting for Ann to arrive. *Le Provençal* was a small but elegant French restaurant and a favorite of Ann's. Andrie had always liked the staff better than the food, which she often found too rich.

Henri, the maître d', would often entertain Andrie with pleasant conversation as she waited for Ann, who was frequently late. This time Andrie hoped that Henri would be too busy to stop by and chat with her. She had too much on her mind to make light conversation and she knew that in a short time she would be telling Ann that she was in love with Destiny. There was no way to predict how Ann might react. For the first time, Andrie admitted to herself that there was a part of Ann that she feared. It was the part that refused to lose at anything. It was most likely that fear which prompted her to choose this place to tell Ann everything, rather than in the privacy of Ann's Georgetown apartment.

"Mademoiselle LaStella. The congresswoman is late again, hmm . . . I'm going to bring you a special champagne cocktail while you wait. Albert at the bar devised a new secret recipe for it. It's wonderful," Henri said, then turned and headed toward the bar.

Andrie smiled at the tall, sixtyish Frenchman who had always been kind and discreet. She was sure that he had probably surmised that she and Ann were lovers a long time ago. Perhaps it was something he may have picked up on by talking with her so many times while she waited to meet Ann at the restaurant . . . or it could have been a careless expression or her body language. The only thing Andrie was sure of was that if Henri did suspect that they were lovers, it wasn't because of anything in Ann's behavior. Ann was far too careful to ever let that happen.

"You must try this. Albert is quite proud of it," Henri said as he returned and put a slender, fluted glass filled with a ruby-colored liquid in front of Andrie. He took a step back to observe her reaction.

She tipped the glass to her mouth and took a sip. "Hmmm . . ." she crooned as the bubbly red elixir traveled across her palate.

"Albert calls it a *rosebud*. But he's not ready to tell me what's in it," Henri explained.

Andrie took another sip and added, "It's my new favorite. Tell Albert that I'll never drink anything else."

Henri promised to do that as he left, satisfied that Andrie was so pleased.

Running her finger over the rim of the glass, Andrie hoped that the kindly Frenchman wouldn't notice that she had little desire to finish the drink. She wanted nothing to impair her as she concentrated on how to break her news to Ann. The problem so occupied her that she didn't notice that Ann had arrived and was heading toward her table.

"This has to be a quick dinner. I need to be back to work as soon as we're done here." With that, Ann sat down across from Andrie and picked up the menu.

"Look, I need to discuss something with you. It's important." Andrie said with a determined look in her eyes.

"If this is about the wedding again I really don't have time for it," Ann replied in a low annoyed voice as she looked up from her menu. Just then a waiter came by to take their orders. She told the waiter that she had very little time and that she needed to be served quickly. She handed him her menu and told him she would have the poached salmon. Andrie immediately added that she would have the same.

Before the waiter could say another word, Ann brusquely waved him away and motioned impatiently to Andrie to get on with what she had to say.

"First of all, this has nothing to do with your wedding. In fact, it may make your plans easier in that area, because I won't be bothering you about that anymore," Andrie began to explain.

"In that case I'd love to hear what you have to say," Ann said, squinting skeptically at Andrie. Then, abruptly distracted, she turned away, realizing that she forgot to order a drink. "Damn. Where's the waiter?" she grumbled, as she summoned him to return. "You neglected to ask me if I'd like a drink when I ordered. Bring me a double vodka martini, extra dry, straight up." Ann's intolerance, as well as her taste in liquor, paralleled her father's closely. After ordering her drink, she nodded to Andrie to continue.

Andrie's momentum was shaken by the interruption. Her voice became tight with nerves as she started to speak. "It's about us."

"Oh no. I can already tell that this is just another tactic to discourage me from going through with the wedding. I told you that I'm . . ."

"Listen to me!" Andrie's demand was controlled in volume but potent in its insistence. "I told you . . . this has nothing to do with that." Her voice softened slightly as she continued, "It's time for us to realize that we have no future together. It's not your fault; I've been coming to this conclusion for a while now. But recently, something happened to me that made me need to tell you right away. I realized that I'm in love with someone else." Having said that, Andrie momentarily felt a great weight lift from her shoulders. She then paused, as if to regain the strength to finish what she had to say.

Ann's face showed annoyance and disbelief. She turned away from Andrie and fixed her eyes on the waiter who was walking toward her with the martini. Without looking back at Andrie, Ann responded, "I know what you're trying to do and you should just give up. This tactic is really beneath you. I'm surprised at you, I really am."

"What in the world are you talking about? Have you even heard one word I've been saying?" Andrie asked incredulously.

Ann picked up the martini as quickly as it had been placed in front of her and took a sizable swallow.

"I know that you're getting desperate to stop the wedding, but this is ridiculous. Can't you understand that I'm doing this, no matter what you think. If you just accept it, you'd make it a lot easier on yourself. My marriage won't change anything between us. We'll go on just as we always have," Ann assured her smugly.

"It's Destiny Anderson. We're in love with each other. Please, just listen to me and forget about the marriage thing for a while, because that's your own business now."

The self-assured smirk she had been wearing suddenly left Ann's face. It was replaced with an expression which quickly transformed from annoyance to anger, as she began to digest and believe the information that confronted her. "What are you trying to say?"

"I'm in love with her, and . . ." Andrie was unable to finish, as Ann cut her off with a barrage of questions and accusations.

"Are you crazy? Are you becoming some kind of rock star groupie? You hardly know her. . . . Oh, wait a minute . . . that little faggot David. . . . He's behind all this, isn't he?"

"How can you be such a hypocrite? You rationalize taking a public stand against gay rights, because you claim that's how your constituency wants you to vote. You've built your image on supporting policies that deny rights to people just like you and me. You call my best friend a *faggot* when you're every bit as queer as he is. You know, I'm ashamed of myself for accepting all the garbage I have from you. All this time, I tried to believe that you had good reasons for denying the fact that you're gay. I know how much prejudice is out there. . . . It was your choice to live in a closet rather than deal with that. For seven years you kept me in the closet too. It's funny really. . . . We weren't even in the same closet. I kept hoping that things would get better between us. I lied to my family about how happy I was with you. I guess I thought that if I said it enough, I would start to believe it myself. But it didn't work that way. Don't blame David or Destiny for this. Even if this didn't happen, I would eventually have had to leave you. I couldn't survive like this much longer." Andrie was hoping for this confrontation to be over as quickly and painlessly as possible.

Ann leaned back in her chair. Her tone was low, exact, and seemed to lack the emotion that would be appropriate for the circumstances. "Never mind the melodramatic attacks. I'm a politician. I'm immune to them. Just answer my question. . . . How do you figure that you're in love with someone whom you hardly know?"

"I never spoke about this, but Destiny and I met when we were about twenty. David went to college with her and he introduced us. We became involved. In fact we were falling in love, but I was too young and confused about what I was feeling and how to deal with it. So, it didn't work out for us then." The regret in Andrie's voice was obvious to Ann.

"You realized that last Friday night at the party?" Ann's question was heavy with sarcasm and disbelief. She was still unsure of whether Andrie was telling her the truth or using some new type of tactic to keep her from marrying Stuart Sottley.

Andrie continued, "Through the years, I had seen her on a few different occasions, because she and David had stayed close. But it wasn't until now that we realized that we were in love. She was staying in New York, so we've been seeing a lot of each other ever since the fundraiser. I didn't want to be dishonest with you. I wanted to tell you about this as soon as possible. I was going to tell you last night, but you had to change our dinner plans."

Ann was finally convinced by Andrie's tone that this wasn't a ploy to discourage her from marrying. She was no longer interested in the whys and hows of what Andrie was saying. Her questions ceased. Her face grew colder and angrier. The look in her eyes told Andrie that she had made the right decision by choosing to break this news in a public place. It forced Ann to control the anger of her reaction. "Another double vodka martini," she ordered in a strained, harsh voice as their dinner arrived at the table.

"I need to tell you something else," Andrie continued with slight hesitancy. "I have to resign from your staff . . . I think that it would be an uncomfortable situation for the both of us if I stayed. You see, I'll be moving out to the West Coast very shortly . . . I'm sorry, Ann. I wish that there was a better way to tell you this," she added as she began to nervously push the food on her plate around with her fork.

Having finished her first martini, Ann was now growing anxious for her second as she glared at Andrie. "You little piece of trash. I knew that I was asking for trouble when I got involved with someone like you. I should have known that eventually you would seek out someone like Destiny Anderson. No matter how you tried, you could never shake off the dirt of that sleazy Brooklyn neighborhood . . . could you? . . . This really shouldn't surprise me . . . you're just seeking your own level with Destiny Anderson. You're perfect for each other. You both come from similar backgrounds. You were born in a basement in Brooklyn and she comes from some hick town, down south. I suppose some might call that a match made in heaven. Destiny Anderson is just trash with money and believe me, that won't last. She's just another flash in the pan. In five or ten years she'll be a *has been,* living in a trailer park somewhere . . . and I suppose that you would want to be right there with her, where you probably belonged in the first place." The words spewed forth from Ann's mouth with an accustomed ease.

Andrie was transfixed with shock. She was only now realizing what had remained just under the surface for the last seven years. The attack temporarily dumbfounded her, as Ann continued venomously.

"Do you know why we're together? It's because you fit certain criteria for me. I was physically attracted to you. You have that trashiness in bed that I've always found an appealing quality in certain women. . . . Women who come from your level of society have a tendency to be more in touch with their animal nature than women with more highly developed sensibilities. I would imagine that's what makes so many of them successful prostitutes. You would also be easily bought off. . . . You see if I were to break up with a woman of means and she wanted to be vindictive, I couldn't change her mind with a check. I tried to confine our personal relationship to the bedroom, since we had little in common in any other area of our lives. That's one of the reasons I never had the time to associate with that family of yours . . . I grew up with servants that showed far more refinement."

Andrie had heard enough. She emerged from her state of disbelief and fired back. "You're sick. You're so sick. I can't believe that I blinded myself to this side of you for seven years. I should have seen it. It was obvious that you were no saint. I knew that you were pompous and class conscious, but I had no idea that you were pathological about it. You really are your father's daughter. Whatever you think about me is no longer material. So, I'm not going to stoop to your level and attack you. In a way, you've made leaving you a lot easier for me. I'll have a messenger deliver my letter of resignation before noon tomorrow. . . . Don't worry about me ever mentioning our relationship to anyone who doesn't already know. It's something that I would be ashamed to admit." With that, Andrie stood up and began to turn away from the table, but she stopped for a moment when Ann followed up with a question.

"How do you think Destiny will feel about you when she finds out that because of this relationship, her career was blown out of the water?" Ann seethed.

Andrie was ready to walk away, while inside she suddenly felt that something terrible was about to happen. She tried to remain cool and adopted a defiant attitude. "What the hell are you trying to say?"

"Stuart Sottley . . . my fiance, has just purchased a controlling fifty-four percent of the Cobra record company . . . and if I instruct him, he can cease promotion of Destiny Anderson and her latest album."

"Harry Stern wouldn't let that happen," Andrie shot back in disbelief.

"He doesn't have the power to stop it. Stern had some very serious tax troubles and needed to get his hands on a rather large amount of money right away. So Stuart was able to help him by purchasing a little more than half his company, with the agreement that he would have to sell it back to him at a moderate profit if Stern is able to buy it back within two years. If Stern can't come up with the money within that time, Stuart retains permanent control of Cobra," Ann replied smugly.

"Even if that's true, Destiny could sign with another label. Any of them would kill to get her."

"It's not that simple. We can have her in court for years and meanwhile, she's prohibited from signing with anyone else. She has only had two albums released. And although her second was extremely successful, she isn't what one would consider an established name yet. At this point in her career, that kind of interruption could finish her. . . . So you see, I can have the name Destiny Anderson drift into obscurity with one phone call. How do you think she would feel knowing that she lost everything she struggled so long for, because you wouldn't let her go. She might not care in the very beginning, but later as the romance wears off, she'll begin to resent you . . . you'll see."

"You're telling me that you're planning to destroy Destiny's career, just because I'm in love with her. I don't understand. What purpose does that serve for you?" Andrie felt like her world was suddenly falling apart around her, so soon after the pieces had finally come together. She sat and listened as Ann continued talking in a cold, steady, calculated tone.

"Have you ever known me to lose anything to anyone else? I'm simply not going to let Destiny Anderson just enter my life and take you, when I still want you around. . . . If she does, she'll have to pay dearly for it," the congresswoman threatened coldly.

Andrie knew that with Stuart Sottley holding the controlling interest in Cobra, Ann had the power to carry out her threats successfully. Suddenly, her priority had shifted from leaving Ann to protecting Destiny. "If you try anything like that, I'll make sure that everyone at every newspaper and TV station knows about our past seven years together. It would make for a great story. *Ultra conservative congresswoman, who espouses family values, has been having a lesbian affair for the last seven years.* That would just about finish you, wouldn't it?" Andrie asked defiantly.

"It might if you were able to substantiate your claims with tangible evidence. Remember there's no way that Ray would corroborate your story. In fact he would probably jump at the chance to make you look like nothing more than a disgruntled employee. He hasn't been too happy with your reaction to his idea about me marrying Stuart. All that aside, Stuart would still be controlling Cobra and I would have even more reason to destroy Destiny's career. . . . And trust me, he'll do anything I tell him to. Quite a while ago I realized that I would need someone to act on my behalf in certain business matters that might be viewed as inappropriate for me to be involved with. Stuart had lost a great deal of money in the market . . . so I arranged this little partnership with him, way back, before I ran for council the first time. So Stuart Sottley's money is really my money. Therefore, among other things, I own fifty-four percent of Cobra Records."

"Let me guess, you also own the building that Women's Way is in. Right?" Andrie asked with disgust in her voice.

"Yes, and now that I'm fairly well established on Capitol Hill, I don't need to breastfeed a program for women who should have been more selective in their choice of husbands and boyfriends. Cortronics is offering quite a nice price for that property. You see, I feel that I can tell you all of this and trust that you won't leak it to the press. If you did, Destiny's career will come to a very abrupt halt. No records. No tours. Nothing. . . . Now, I suggest that you tell that hillbilly dyke that you've changed your mind and that you decided to stay with me."

"She would never believe that and you'll never get any pleasure out of someone who can't even stand to look at you," Andrie said, as she felt herself become nauseated at the sight of Ann's smirking face.

"You have no idea about the things that give me pleasure. By the way, I really have no intention of resuming our physical relationship at this point. But it's nice to know that you'll be there if I decide to change my mind, in the future," Ann said, grinning cruelly as she watched the color drain from Andrie's face.

"So, this is the type of tactic you learned from your father. You're right about one thing; we were brought up very differently. I was taught to be honest and treat people with respect. And you were taught to use everyone to your best advantage. People are just *things* to you. You treat them like they're not human, but you're the one who isn't human. I don't know what you are, but whatever it is, it's ugly." Andrie paused and thought. She knew that there was little choice for her. But, before she agreed to Ann's terms, she needed assurance that the vindictive congresswoman wouldn't do anything that would hurt Destiny's career. "How can I be sure that you won't try to hold back on Cobra's promotional plans for Destiny's next CD?" She asked cautiously.

"She's a moneymaker for the company. I have no intention of destroying that, unless you make me," Ann replied as, seeing the waiter returning with her drink, she looked at her watch as though she had been timing him.

"Cobra is a small label. The money you make from owning it is insignificant to you," Andrie said, pressing further for a reason that would assure her that Destiny's career wouldn't be damaged by Ann.

"You're right and you're wrong. The money I make from Cobra is insignificant. However, the money I make from selling it to Cortronics would be quite significant. They wanted to buy it outright from Harry Stern, but he didn't want to let go of it completely. That's how he ended up selling me . . . I mean Stuart . . . fifty-four percent. So in two years when Stern can't come up with the money, the company will be mine and I'll sell it to Cortronics for an extremely healthy price. Now you can see why I want the company to look as good as it can. But if you make me, I will make that sacrifice and put Destiny Anderson on the shelf." Ann's eyes looked dead. Indeed, at that moment Andrie knew that no soul lived behind them.

"Everyone saw through you. David, my family, everyone except me. How could I have been so wrong?" Andrie felt as though she were in some terrible nightmare and couldn't wake up.

"My father wasn't so happy about you either. I had to assure him that our relationship was strictly physical."

"Your father knows about us?" Andrie was shocked by the revelation.

"Of course. He has from the beginning. He was the one that advised me never to give you anything in writing or anything that you could use to prove that we were ever lovers," Ann told her in a cold, detached tone.

"All these years I've tolerated your father treating me like a servant, while he knew that we were lovers . . . and you allowed that," Andrie said in disbelief.

"No one held a gun to your head and forced you to stay in this relationship. Whatever happened to you, was allowed by you," Ann said, looking at her watch again. Then, after taking a long slow sip of her martini, she added, "Oh my, this conversation was more interesting than I thought it would be. It looks like I'm going to be late after all."

Filled with disgust and hatred, Andrie was unable to sit there another minute. She stood up. "For now you'll have your way. I'll end things with Destiny tomorrow. . . . But someday, all your lies, all your cruelty . . . everything . . . is going to come back to you. And when it does, it's going to destroy you and that monster you call a father." With that Andrie abruptly turned and walked away from the table.

As Henri saw her approaching the coat check area, it was obvious to him that something was wrong. "Can I call a taxi for you?" he asked sympathetically.

"No thank you, Henri. I need to walk." Andrie forced a smile.

"Can I drive you somewhere?" Henri's concern was genuine. He read the look on Andrie's face as he helped her with her coat.

"That's so kind of you. But I really need to walk."

Henri opened the door for her and stood outside, watching Andrie until she had faded into the night.

Chapter Fifteen

A black leather jacket, a worn pair of jeans, a pair of sweats and some underwear had already been tossed randomly into her green canvas duffel bag as Destiny took a last look around Andrie's apartment. It was difficult for her to leave, but as she picked up the matchbook with the address of Lilly's on it, her pulse began to race with anticipation. . . . In a little more than an hour she would see Andrie. The only sadness that could touch her now was from knowing that she would only have a short time with the woman she loved before she had to leave for LA. She kept reminding herself that Andrie would be joining her there soon and nothing would ever separate them again.

As she phoned a limousine service to request a car and driver for the rest of the afternoon, Destiny kept imagining what it was going to be like when she surprised Andrie with that special place in Montana . . . complete with a giant spruce tree. She planned to meet with the realtor the second she got back to California. Hanging up the phone, she touched the small maple leaf charm that lay hidden under the red flannel shirt she wore. Feeling the smooth, rippled metal warmed from lying against her body, Destiny whispered to herself, "It's not a dream. It's not a dream."

* * *

Ann's New York headquarters was small and cramped. There was one small space in the center where three steel desks were located. Each was occupied by either a staff member or a volunteer, busily stuffing envelopes or typing. Andrie's office was located to the rear of the space and although it was modest in size, it was private. She had never been affected by its tiny size until today, when it began to remind her of a prison cell.

Looking at the clock, she realized that it wouldn't be long before she had to face Destiny and do what seemed impossible. There was no choice. Breaking up with Destiny was the only way she could protect her from Ann.

Destiny had worked and sacrificed all her life to achieve her success and Andrie didn't want to be the cause of her losing it. She could only hope that someday her prayers would be answered and she could be with Destiny the way she had planned. Struggling with the reason and the words that she would use when she saw Destiny, Andrie's concentration was interrupted as a newspaper was tossed onto her desk. She looked up to see Ann, whose steely eyes were wild.

Ann began to speak to her through gritted teeth. "Page nine. Turn to it. Now!" she demanded. Andrie opened the paper and turned the pages, tentatively. Intuition told her it had something to do with Destiny, but she had no idea how. Then reaching page nine she saw in bold print a caption that read, *Destiny Anderson Linked to Ultra Conservative Congresswoman in Romantic Triangle.* Under it was a picture of Destiny and a woman identified as Nicole Bonham, holding each other. The background was familiar. It was the brownstone where Andrie lived. She looked up at Ann, plaintively, as if seeking an explanation from her. But Ann's response was a brusque command to read the accompanying article, which Andrie began to do. The words followed, one after another, in a succession that assaulted Andrie's senses, until she felt the room spinning around her. She rose out of her chair still holding the paper, as she continued to read.

The article reported Ann's frequent late-night visits to Andrie's apartment. It also quoted supposedly reliable sources in New York and Washington as saying that it was obvious that there was a romantic relationship going on between Ann and Andrie. It mentioned the names of restaurants where they were seen having what were described as cozy dinners together.

Andrie froze when she read the exact words she had said to Ann, during the private argument they had at the fundraiser on Friday night. *"Stop it . . . I can't take this. I'm so sick of all the charades. When we're alone, you're all over me, but to the outside world I'm nothing more than an employee of yours. . . . Don't do this . . . can't you see that this relationship is killing me?"* An impeccably reliable source was credited with witnessing that conversation and claimed to have explicit and incriminating pictures to prove that Ann Capwell had always enjoyed the romantic company of women.

In an obvious effort to further its claim that Congresswoman Capwell was a lesbian, the article then linked her indirectly with Destiny Anderson, whom it cited as a well-known lesbian. It reported that Destiny was staying with Andrie and having her ex-lover Nicole Bonham pay her romantic visits while Andrie was out of town with Ann.

It was humiliating to Andrie to have to read this and look at the accompanying photo as Ann watched with sadistic pleasure. "Pictures don't lie," Ann taunted.

Andrie pretended to ignore her. She finished the article and pushed the paper back at Ann. "So. It seems that you must finally have an opponent as underhanded as you are," Andrie said, as she tried to appear unaffected.

Ann threw the paper down and glared at her. "Is that all you have to say? This is all your fault. You little slut. If you didn't have that dyke living with you, this story would probably have been far less newsworthy."

"Don't try to pin this on me . . . or Destiny. And let me ask you a question. If you're calling her a *dyke*, what do you call yourself, or the woman you've had sex with for the last seven years? Now that this is public knowledge, you won't be able to throw anymore stones at anyone from that glass house of yours . . . or should that be glass closet?"

Andrie's attitude was not what Ann had expected. It frustrated and infuriated her that Andrie didn't seem to be hurt by Destiny's apparent infidelity.

"It sounds like you're trying to ignore the fact that you've been cheated on by that white trash lover of yours. Tell me, how does it feel to be used by her, like just another easy piece of ass?" Ann was seething with hatred.

"I don't know why you ever use other people to write your speeches. You have such a pleasant way with words," Andrie replied, as she folded her arms and stared defiantly into Ann's face.

"Illusion is the soul of politics, so don't think that you can play that game with me. I'm far better at it than you could ever be. I know that right now your whole world is caving in on you, because you realize that Destiny Anderson was simply using you as a temporary diversion, and didn't give a damn about you," Ann said, doing her best to twist the emotional knife in Andrie.

"You have a habit of judging everyone else by your own standards. For your information Destiny Anderson has more decency in her fingernail than both you and your father could ever hope to have. I don't have an explanation for that picture, but I know that I trust Destiny and that she would never do anything to hurt me. That's no illusion. That's the truth," Andrie declared confidently.

Ann's rage was building. She knew that it was really her own world that was caving in and she was determined not to be the only casualty. "Just remember one thing. . . . This story changes nothing. If you continue to see Destiny, I'll finish her career."

"I don't doubt that for a minute," Andrie replied, as she noticed the phones outside her office were ringing wildly. "Listen to those phones," Andrie said, pointing out her door. "You'd better put a call in to your spin doctors. It sounds like you'll need an emergency house call."

Ann turned, slamming the door as she left.

Once Andrie saw the door close, she sunk into the oversized high-back chair behind her desk and began to cry. A knock at her door forced her to temporarily regain control, as she asked who it was.

"It's me, sweetie. David," he answered, slowly opening the door. Andrie looked up at him. There was no need for words, he knew that she had read the story. In one sweeping motion, David locked the door and rushed toward Andrie to hold her in his arms. He could feel her body shaking as she sobbed uncontrollably.

"Oh, honey, it's OK. It really is. I was there. Destiny's not carrying anything on with Nicole. Haven't you talked to her about this yet?" he asked, wiping the tears from her face with his handkerchief as he continued, "Damnit, I tried calling Destiny at your place, but she must have left already. . . . I don't know who did this but they're all wrong about her and Nicole. I was there. Destiny planned to tell you that Nicole showed up but she didn't want to waste time discussing it with you while you were away. She didn't want to waste the little time she had on the phone with you, talking about this. She planned to tell you about Nicole showing up when you got back from Washington. She'll explain it all to you. Please honey, don't cry anymore. There's no reason to. She's so in love with you, she can't even think about anything else."

Andrie just shook her head and continued sobbing. It wasn't because she didn't believe David. She knew how much Destiny loved her and nothing could diminish her faith in that. But now as David stood there trying to explain the situation to her, she suddenly realized how she would end her relationship with Destiny. She would use this story as the cause. She would have to pretend not to believe Destiny's explanation. Andrie would have to make Destiny believe that her faith in her was so weak that she would let this come between them. She said nothing about this to David as her tears refused to cease.

David felt confused and helpless. He had never seen Andrie like this. He stopped talking and just held her as she continued to cry. There were so many questions that he wanted to ask her . . . like how Ann had reacted to the article and how she felt about Andrie leaving her, but now was not the time. As her tears eventually began to subside, he could see that there was something going on inside her. "I don't know what you're thinking, but I know that you're too smart and too much in love with Destiny to believe this crap. . . . So just snap out of it. Now fix your face, so you don't frighten her to death when she sees you," he said with a faux sternness that he hoped would add a small amount of levity to the circumstance.

Using all the restraint she had Andrie began to calm herself down enough to speak. "Do you remember how you got me to agree to let Destiny stay at my apartment?" she asked him with an intent look.

"Yes, with a feature article on Ann in *Profiles*, I promised you," he answered, bewildered by the question.

"Forget that we ever made that agreement. . . . Forget your promise . . . please," she told him, grabbing his hand tightly.

David agreed readily, putting his arms around her once more, before she left the office to meet Destiny.

* * *

The shiny, jet-black limousine cruised carefully through the streets of lower Manhattan, as Destiny reclined in its back seat with her feet up. She was the picture of contentment as she anticipated seeing Andrie again. Every now and then, she would reach for the silver maple leaf that dangled from her neck, and wistfully rub it between her fingers as she remembered that first walk with Andrie, so long ago.

As the chauffeur pulled over in front of the unassuming entrance of Lilly's, Destiny drew herself up and opened her door before he could even get to it.

"I'll be right here waiting, Ms. Anderson," he said, jumping out of her way as she rushed from the limo to the door. She flashed him a smile to say thanks.

It was almost two and the restaurant was fairly quiet. Its warm, comfortable ambiance was inviting to women, particularly lovers. Ornate Victorian love seats and curio closets decorated its ground level bar. The owner and proprietor, Lilly Stockholz, was an imposing, yet gentle, figure of a woman. Her physical appearance was as memorable as her warmth. She stood close to six feet tall, with an unavoidably large bosom and a physique that would threaten most professional football players. Her thick straight blond hair was slicked back in a short, severe coif, which seemed to emphasize her heavily made up, pale blue eyes. Those who knew Lilly well were aware that she was gifted with an uncanny ability to see into the future. She claimed that it was not a power she had command of at all times, but rather, it would come and go. She was never known to use it for entertainment or profit, and only advised people when she felt the need. Her slight Austrian accent assigned her an air of formality, which was quickly dispelled upon getting to know her.

As Destiny entered the restaurant, Lilly was at the door, ready to greet and seat patrons.

"I'm meeting someone. I was wondering if she's here yet," Destiny said, looking at Lilly through her dark glasses. They exchanged smiles.

"No. Actually you have the place all to yourself right now. Don't worry. As soon as she arrives I'll show her to your table," Lilly replied in an friendly, assuring voice, as she ushered Destiny down the staircase. Once downstairs, Destiny removed her dark glasses. The dining room was romantic and dimly lit. The fireplace in the corner added its amber glow to the muted light of the wall sconces and the candles flickering on the tables. As Lilly turned to seek Destiny's approval of a small table against the far wall of the room, she recognized her face. "Destiny? Destiny Anderson, right?"

"Yeah," Destiny confessed with a smile.

"I like your music very much," Lilly said in a deep monotone voice, the sincerity of which was clear.

"Thanks. I like the way you've done your restaurant. It's got a very cozy atmosphere," Destiny replied, looking around her.

"I'm meeting someone real special. It would mean a lot to me to have it be as private as possible," Destiny said, almost whispering her request.

Lilly understood immediately. She had seen too many lovers come to the restaurant not to recognize the signs. "Don't worry about a thing. I'll make sure it's exactly the way you want it," she replied confidently as she seated Destiny.

"Thanks. I really appreciate it," Destiny said, looking up at the blond mammoth of a woman, who ran her establishment with a velvet fist. Lilly responded with a warm smile and asked if Destiny wanted a drink while she waited.

"Just a mineral water with lime, for now," she answered and thanked Lilly.

"I'll have it brought right over," Lilly assured her as she turned and walked toward the stairs.

Destiny sat watching the stairs, eagerly awaiting Andrie. She had no idea that all the happiness she had found with her was about to be taken away by Ann Capwell.

*   *   *

The cab was just a few blocks from Lilly's. Andrie stared out the window at the people on the street. She saw a sidewalk Santa ringing his bell in the midst of a crowd of passing Christmas shoppers and pedestrians. Watching the scene she wished that she was any one of those anonymous faces . . . anyone but herself. Again, she began to practice in her mind the words she would use to tell Destiny that it was over. She wondered how she could sound convincing, when she wanted to be with Destiny more than anything else in the world.

She had to keep reminding herself of what was at stake. Ann was ruthless and powerful. If anyone could destroy Destiny's career it was Ann Capwell. Andrie couldn't allow herself to be the reason Destiny's career would be ruined. Ann's statement about how Destiny would grow to resent her kept repeating in Andrie's head. She couldn't selfishly make a decision that would cause Ann to rob Destiny of everything she worked so hard to achieve.

Folding up the copy of the newspaper she had brought with her, Andrie started rummaging through her purse as the cab stopped in front of Lilly's. She paid the driver and pushed open the heavy passenger door of the yellow cab. As she entered the restaurant, she was greeted by Lilly, who seemed instantly to know that she was the woman for whom Destiny had been waiting.

As Lilly led the way downstairs, Andrie felt as though she were being led into the center of hell. Her heart felt as if it were about to burst, as she suppressed her overwhelming instinct to dash down those stairs and into Destiny's arms. Reaching the bottom of the steps, she saw Destiny at the far end of the dining room. Destiny rushed toward her, wrapping her arms around Andrie and pulling her close as Lilly stood nearby pretending not to look.

"I missed you so much," Destiny sighed as she kissed Andrie on the lips with a passion controlled only by the fact that they weren't alone. She felt like a child opening a long-awaited Christmas gift.

Andrie silently absorbed every bit of Destiny she was receiving, like drops of water on the parched ground. She savored these last touches and kisses. But she guarded closely the pleasure and desire they stirred in her. Since Lilly was present, she was able to allow Destiny to show this affection, with the excuse that she didn't want to cause a scene in front of anyone.

Destiny's initial excitement at seeing her caused her not to notice Andrie's modest response.

Lilly excused herself from them as Destiny led Andrie to their table, never fully releasing her from the embrace.

Once seated and alone with Destiny, Andrie felt her heart pounding and the air beginning to get thin. She was losing her courage to go through with this lie. Everything she wanted and waited for in this life was sitting across from her and loving her through dark, gentle, honest eyes. She needed to do it now, before Destiny asked any questions or said another word. Feeling as though she were about to throw herself off a tall cliff, Andrie took a deep breath and closed her eyes briefly, as she pushed the newspaper across the table with an affected anger. "What did you say? . . . You missed me? . . . Funny, but that's not what's in here."

"What do you mean? What's this?" Destiny asked innocently, as she looked down at the paper.

"A newspaper. It reports what's been happening around the world and in your own backyard. Open it to page nine. There's a really flattering picture of you there." Andrie's sarcasm tore mercilessly into Destiny. She knew that anything short of that would fail to be convincing.

Destiny quickly turned to the page and was confronted with a candid shot of herself and Nicole hugging. Without reading the accompanying text, she began to explain the picture with relieved laughter punctuating her words. "Sugar, this is all my fault. I wanted to tell you that Nicole found out where I was stayin' and showed up, but I didn't want to spend time on that nonsense when you had so much on your mind, especially telling Ann about us. I figured that I'd tell you when you returned from Washington, so we wouldn't waste our time talking about this while we were apart. I never expected some reporter to take a misleading photograph. I'm real sorry. I should have told you as soon as it happened."

Andrie leaned forward and began a relentless attack on the woman she loved. "First off, I don't believe pictures lie. . . . Secondly, If you would read further, you would realize that all of Nicole's visits to you at my apartment are reported in the story."

"The first time Nicole showed up, I was real upset that she was able to find out where I was stayin'. She tried to get me to take her back and I told her to forget that. I lost my temper and I grabbed her arm to push her out the door. I guess her bracelet fell off then, but I didn't realize it until the next morning. Anyway, she returned the next day to pick up the bracelet. By then she had realized that I meant what I said about not getting back together with her. She even apologized for the way she acted the day before. We had a little talk and she wished us the best. That was it. So I walked her out and I hugged her good-bye. That's the God's honest truth, honey. I swear. I'm sorry about the article. I'll do whatever you want to help make it better for you."

"Then go back to LA and leave me alone." Andrie forced the words from her mouth.

"What? You don't mean that. What's goin' on with you? Why don't you believe me? Andrie, you have to know that I would never lie to you." Destiny tried to touch her hand as she spoke, but Andrie pulled it away.

Their waitress arrived, carrying a bucket of ice with a bottle of Cristal protruding from it, along with two fluted champagne glasses. "This is from Lilly," she said in a quiet friendly tone, placing the glasses down in front of them.

Andrie stared at Destiny for a moment. Neither of them had any desire to sip champagne right then.

"Please, tell Lilly that I said thank you. This was real thoughtful," Destiny said, forcing a smile. Then, seeing the woman pull the bottle from the ice, she stopped her from opening it. "Could you come back in a little while to open it?"

"Of course. Would you like to order now or wait a bit?" the woman asked, as she placed the bottle back on ice.

"I think we need a little more time," Destiny said in a worried tone, still shaking her head in disbelief.

"I'll come back in a little while," the woman replied, then promptly left.

Destiny turned back to Andrie, who had taken up her purse and seemed ready to leave.

"Wait a minute," Destiny said, as her confusion and desperation grew. "Why are you doing this? . . . Answer me. . . . Why?" She pleaded for an answer.

"Because I don't trust you. This kind of thing may be fine in your world, but there's no room for it in mine," Andrie said, pointing to the picture of Destiny and Nicole. "Please . . . don't try to contact me ever again." With that she stood up and turned to leave. But Destiny jumped up and stood in her way.

"I'm not gonna let you go like this. Somethin's going on. I don't know what it is, but I know that this isn't you. Would it help if you spoke with Nicole? You can ask her about everything that happened. I'll do anything you want, to get us through this . . . but please, don't tell me that you're leaving me when we finally found each other," Destiny said, moving to put her arms around Andrie, as they stood there at the back of the empty dining room.

Andrie ached for what Destiny was offering her, yet she knew that accepting it could eventually be devastating to the woman she loved so dearly. She pushed Destiny away with both hands. "Don't touch me . . . I mean it. Leave me alone . . . please." The words cut as deeply into her as they did into Destiny.

Destiny was reeling with shock, as she tried to make sense out of what was happening. "This is exactly what you did to me fifteen years ago. You let me fall in love with you . . . and just when I think that we can be together, you pull away and leave me. I know that you don't believe that story in the paper, because you know me too well. You're using this as a convenient excuse for leaving me again."

Destiny's insight shook Andrie, but she refused to admit the truth. She loved Destiny too much to hold on to her. "Believe whatever you want. Just stay out of my life," she responded, as she turned and headed out of the dining room. But Destiny grabbed her arm as she reached the stairs.

"You're doing this because you're afraid of something. . . . What is it?" Destiny said, pressing for an answer.

"I told you, I don't trust you. I can't spend my life with someone who can't be left alone for a couple of days without acting like an alley cat in heat."

"That's it, isn't it. You never told her. . . . You decided to stay with her. Didn't you?" Destiny's affect suddenly began to change. The thought that Andrie had strung her along and then decided to stay with Ann caused an angry fire to begin to rage within her. Destiny had now been hurt deeply by her, for the second time. It was something she thought could never happen again.

Andrie was silent as she wondered if letting Destiny believe that she still had feelings for Ann would cause her to let go more easily.

Destiny's dark eyes pierced her, demanding a response. "Answer me. Did you tell her about us?"

"No." Andrie's voice shook as she lied to Destiny. But that only served to make the lie more convincing. It made her appear nervous about being forced to admit that she never told Ann that she was leaving her.

"Why?" Destiny asked angrily. "Tell me . . . why?" Her voice was getting louder.

Andrie didn't want their quarrel to cause Destiny further embarrassment by ending up in the next day's gossip column. "Please, Destiny. Everyone upstairs will hear you."

"I don't care who hears me. I didn't care who heard me when you did this to me fifteen years ago. I want you to tell me why my world is falling apart . . . why you didn't tell Ann about us?" Destiny demanded to know as she held Andrie against the side of the staircase.

Andrie felt herself weakening, as Destiny's body leaned against hers to keep her from leaving. She felt herself slowly and instinctively melting into Destiny, ready to surrender at any moment. Her heart was at odds with itself. There was nothing in the world more important to her than Destiny and no one she loved more, yet that was the reason she needed to let her go. Andrie would do all she could to prevent Ann from taking away everything that Destiny had worked all her life to achieve. That gave her just enough strength to tell the last and most crushing lie, the taste of which would linger in her mouth like bitter vomit, long after she had spat it out. "I can't leave Ann. I still love her."

Those words tore into Destiny as though they had teeth. She backed away from Andrie as she stared deeply into her eyes in disbelief. "No. That can't be true . . . not after everything that you said . . . not after what happened between us."

Andrie straightened up and pulled herself away from the side of the staircase. "It's true. That's the way I feel."

"Are you really that cold hearted? I can't believe that I let you do this to me again," Destiny said. Her jaw tightened as she tried to control both her tears and her rage.

Andrie was seared by the fire in Destiny's eyes. She looked away from her and attempted to climb the stairs. "No," Destiny commanded. Her voice was urgent and powerful, as she pulled Andrie back roughly and again pinned her against the wall. Then, clutching her with an angry, violent passion, she arched Andrie's head back and breached her lips with a fierce, penetrating kiss.

Andrie was taken off guard. She offered no resistance. She felt Destiny's energy, as it surged through her for as long as the brutal kiss lasted.

Destiny could feel Andrie's body melt under the heat of her attack. Then, with a crude abruptness, Destiny pulled away. "This time, I'll leave you wantin' more," she said, as she turned and walked up the stairs, while Andrie remained at the bottom, barely able to stand.

Reaching the top, Destiny looked back at Andrie and shook her head, as her eyes glazed over with the tears she had been holding back. Then, seeing Lilly, Destiny attempted to pay her. But the kind Austrian politely refused, surmising that something had gone terribly wrong between the two lovers. Her pale blue eyes easily expressed her sympathy toward Destiny. Destiny nodded and thanked her. "You were very kind. I'm sorry for the inconvenience. I just have to leave," she said, pushing the door open and hurrying into the privacy of her limousine, where she let her tears find their way out. Without questions, the driver quietly pulled away and started toward Kennedy airport.

*   *   *

In the dim light at the bottom of the stairs, Andrie stood alone, crying. She was empty. She had nothing left. Taking a tissue from her purse, she wiped the tears from her face as she tried to pull herself together. The bar upstairs had filled up since she had arrived and she didn't want anyone to see her like this.

Suddenly, the staircase vibrated and the sound of someone

running down it caused Andrie to look up. She saw Lilly quickly heading toward her.

"Come sit with me for a few minutes, honey. You can't go out looking like that." Lilly's tone was warm, almost maternal.

Andrie saw her reflection in the mirror above the fireplace and decided that Lilly was right. They sat at the same table she had shared with Destiny.

As the waitress passed by on her way to the kitchen, Lilly called out after her, "Tracy, bring us some tea–my private blend–and a bottle of Irish whiskey."

The young woman nodded, acknowledging Lilly's request.

"Really, you don't have to do that. I should be going now," Andrie said, obviously embarrassed by the fact that Lilly, a stranger, had seen her like this.

"I don't believe in ignoring other people's problems . . . if I can help, even a little bit. I can't let you leave without calming your nerves with a cup of tea," Lilly said, with a soft, kind smile.

"Trust me, I need more than a cup of tea for this," Andrie answered, her eyes now red and puffy from crying.

"That's what the whiskey is for. I learned this from my first lover. She was an Irish gypsy I met on holiday one summer. I was very young. She taught me so much. Until I met her, I had no idea that there were gypsies in Ireland." The small talk was Lilly's way of making Andrie feel more comfortable. However, it wasn't working as quickly as Lilly had hoped.

"I'm sorry. I appreciate what you're trying to do . . . really. But I should leave now." As Andrie attempted to stand, the waitress returned with the tea and whiskey.

"Oh. You see it came just in time. This means that you were meant to stay here for a while." With that, Lilly poured out two small glasses of whiskey.

In resignation, Andrie settled back down in her chair. Perhaps a dim room and a drink would help to numb some of her anguish, she thought to herself. Following Lilly's lead, she picked up the glass and put the clear amber liquor to her lips. Immediately, she felt it burning a path down her throat and into her empty stomach. Having eaten nothing since the day before, the whiskey would have no trouble finding its way into her system.

"You are very much in love with each other," Lilly observed.

"It's not meant to be," Andrie said as she continued to drink what was left in the small shot glass.

"That's not true. I don't feel that." Lilly pushed the full cup of tea toward Andrie with a gesture that encouraged her to begin drinking from it. Meanwhile, she refilled Andrie's whiskey glass.

"It's true, believe me," Andrie insisted as she sipped the hot tea. "There are just too many obstacles between us."

"Obstacles are life's growth stimulants. You need them to develop," Lilly chided.

"Not as many as we've had," Andrie said, shaking her head as she picked up the whiskey glass and took a large gulp.

"Do you believe in fate?" Lilly asked.

"I don't know . . . maybe. Maybe it's my fate to be alone. I'd rather do that than be with anyone else but her."

"She feels the same way too," Lilly assured her.

"She does? But how would you know that?" Andrie asked, curious as to why Lilly sounded so certain about Destiny's feelings.

"I could see that by how happy she was when she was waiting for you . . . and then how hurt she was when she left. It was obvious that she was expecting to have a wonderful lunch with you, but that you surprised her with some terrible news that prevented her from staying with you."

"I know. I shouldn't have told her here. I should have told her somewhere more private. I wasn't thinking," Andrie thought out loud, as she finished off the last of her tea and reached for her whiskey again.

"You told her what you had to tell her, where you were meant to tell her. You see, I believe in fate. Nothing happens without a purpose." As Lilly spoke she reached for Andrie's empty tea cup and began to study the muddy sediment which remained at its bottom. "I see two possibilities for your future."

"You're reading my tea leaves? I heard that you have a special talent for this type of thing, but, honestly, it's not something that I have any faith in. I don't mean to sound like I don't appreciate what you're doing but . . ."

"Please," Lilly cut in. "Let me tell you what I see. I don't ask you to believe in what I say. . . . Just remember it, when it happens."

"I'm sorry. Please, go on." Andrie saw that Lilly was doing what she felt was helpful. She decided that stopping her would be rude.

"The leaves show me that your future may take either of two paths. However, you will have no choice in the matter." With that Lilly stood up and walked over to the fireplace, where she removed a small, square, ornately carved, wooden box from the mantel and brought it back to the table. She removed the top to expose a smooth, clear, orb-shaped crystal.

"A crystal ball?" Andrie noted aloud, trying not to sound incredulous.

"I use this to focus my concentration," Lilly said, as she began to stare into it. After a brief silence she started to speak again. "Yes, there will be two different ways your life may turn out. I can tell you about each, but I can't see which way will be chosen," she explained, glancing up briefly. Then, returning her gaze to the ball, she continued, "There is a very wealthy man who will be passing from this earth, sometime within the next twelve months. Even now he is in frail health. His life has been misguided by bitterness for many years now. His only daughter has been affected by this. He must come to terms with an issue that has prevented him from giving her the love and guidance he owes her as a father. If he is able to do this, it will start a chain of events that will lead you and Destiny back to each other and you will remain together for the rest of your lives. But, if he chooses not to confront his bitterness and denies his daughter a father's love, then you and Destiny will remain apart forever. Those are the two ways. Nothing you can do or say will affect which way will be chosen." Lilly looked up from the ball, caught a glint of cynicism in Andrie's eyes and addressed it. "I don't expect you to believe . . . until it happens. When you hear that this wealthy man has passed on, you will know that the path has been chosen for you." Lilly took up her whiskey glass and drank. She seemed exhausted from her deep state of concentration.

"Thanks. If any of this ever does happen I'll let you know. It was very kind of you to spend this time with me. I should leave now," Andrie said, standing up and pushing back her hair, as she glanced into the elaborately framed mirror on the wall behind Lilly.

Lilly got up and walked her upstairs. She offered to call a cab for her, but Andrie declined.

"No thanks. I can flag one down when I get outside. I shouldn't have any trouble getting one at this time of day. Thank you again . . . for everything." Andrie started to push open the door.

"I'm hoping that your future takes the happier path and that you and your lover will find each other again. In fact, I'm going to place that bottle of champagne aside for you, just in case." Saying that, the tall, sturdy blond leaned over and gave Andrie a comforting hug.

"If it ever does work out that way, we'll be back to share it with you. I promise," Andrie declared as she smiled warmly at Lilly and went out the door. Heading down the street, she prayed that someday she and Destiny would return to Lilly's to open that bottle of champagne.

*   *   *

Nicole turned the pages of the Thursday paper, between sips of hot, black coffee. It was almost 2:30 p.m. and she had just pried herself out of bed after accompanying Bee to the party at Louis Aimes's apartment the night before. They ate, drank and danced into the early hours of the morning. She loved every minute of it, despite the fact that she was now suffering from a very predictable hangover. She had enjoyed Bee's company much more than she had expected, and had even found herself looking at the round-faced, slightly pretentious author in a new light.

Groggily leafing through the paper, she thought to herself that she might eventually give Bee a chance in the romance department, if nothing more promising came along soon. Meanwhile, she considered asking Bee to go back to LA with her, to help move the rest of her belongings out of Sonia's place. She knew that Bee would jump at the chance to help her do that.

Suddenly, in the midst of that thought, Nicole stopped cold. There, on page nine, was the picture of her with Destiny. Nicole picked up the paper, as if a closer look might change what she was seeing.

She began to read the accompanying story. "Oh, my God," she exclaimed, when she reached the part that described her visits to Destiny as romantic rendezvous.

"Bee . . . Bee, come in here, quick," she called as she continued to read.

"What? W-what's wrong?" Bee came running out of the shower, dripping wet, wrapped in a bath towel. Speechless, Nicole, held the newspaper up for Bee to read. But that wasn't necessary. Bee immediately realized what the fuss was about. She picked up the paper and pretended to be surprised by what she was reading. "This is incredible. I can't b-believe they're calling it a romantic r-rendezvous. W-w-what are you gonna do?" Bee asked.

"I don't know. I don't really care what they say about me. As far as I'm concerned, this could only help me, by reminding people that I still exist . . . but Destiny . . . suppose she thinks that I had something to do with this shit?"

"D-do you really care?" Bee asked.

"Of course I do. We may not be lovers anymore but I'll always be her friend. I care about her and I don't want to see her hurt by this. I need to talk to her. I have to see if she's OK . . . I'm going back to that brownstone." Nicole seemed determined.

"Suppose they still have someone watching it? You'll just be feeding into a misleading s-story," Bee advised her, not wanting any of the innocent people in the story to suffer further. Her only target was Ann. She had no desire to have anyone else hurt by her plot . . . especially if it didn't add to her cause.

"I don't know. I'll have to think it out." Nicole was confused. She wanted to help Destiny if she could, but she wasn't sure how to do that without making things worse.

Meanwhile, Bee silently read the article through. A feeling of self-satisfaction charged through her as she tried to imagine how it was affecting Ann. Closing her eyes briefly, she imagined the scene that was taking place at Ann's office because of this.

*   *   *

Destiny sat slouched in a chair by a large window in the airport's VIP lounge. Her dark glasses now did more than simply conceal her identity. They kept everyone from seeing how red and swollen her eyes were. Her Chicago Bulls baseball cap was pulled low and hair hung down from it, falling like a ragged brown mop around her shoulders.

She stared out the window, replaying the scene with Andrie over and over in her head. Every ugly, painful word repeated again and again, causing her still more anguish.

A lounge attendant asked if there was anything she wanted. She ordered a vodka and cranberry juice, without ever looking away from the window. Several minutes had gone by when she finally came out of her trance-like state. In that time, her drink had arrived and was sitting in front of her. Destiny wasn't sure why she even ordered it. She had no desire to drink it.

"Well, this certainly isn't much of a disguise to me. If you really don't want anyone to recognize you, you should wear some lipstick and a dress . . . I'm sure your own mother wouldn't know you like that," David teased as he approached her table. He was hoping that by now everything had been straightened out between her and Andrie. But, seeing her lack of reaction to his teasing made him acutely aware that nothing had been resolved. He stood over Destiny and lifted up her dark glasses. Her eyes confirmed his suspicions. "Oh honey, look at you. What is going on here? Did you explain to Andrie that that article was totally untrue?" he asked.

"Of course I did, but it was no use. I don't think it mattered to her. Her mind is made up. She's not leaving Ann. She ended everything with me, so she could stay with her. She said that she still loves her." The words caught in Destiny's throat as tears rolled down from behind her glasses.

"That's horse shit. She loves you. There's no way on God's green earth that she would choose to stay with Ann, rather than be with you. Something is very wrong with this." David suspected that there was another dynamic at work here.

"Look, maybe we both have to admit that Andrie just hasn't changed as much as we thought she did. Maybe she's always gonna be as confused and thoughtless as she was when I first met her," Destiny told him, as she continued to stare out the window.

David remembered how Andrie's sobbing seemed almost out of control that morning in her office. She had seemed untouched by his assurances that Destiny had not been cheating on her. It was as though the reason she was crying had nothing to do with the idea of trusting Destiny.

Looking at Destiny across the small, round cocktail table, David hoped that he would somehow be able to get to the bottom of this before too much time had gone by. At the moment there were no words that he could say to soften her pain. He moved his chair next to hers and put his arm around her as they waited silently for her boarding call.

Chapter Sixteen

Destiny closed the front door after the driver deposited her bag inside the house. The ride from LAX to her home was uneventful. It was about a quarter past seven and the temperature was in the mid-60s. Far more comfortable than the cold climate she had left behind. She had gained three hours from New York time. Time zones always fascinated her. For a moment, she fantasized about a time zone that was far enough away that this afternoon in New York had never happened. She headed into the living room of her spacious hacienda-style home and picked up the phone. As she held it in her hand, Destiny wanted desperately to call Andrie. She wondered what Andrie was doing at that moment. Was she alone? Or was she with Ann? Suddenly, she felt disconnected from everything and everyone. It was the same isolated feeling she had when her father died. There was no one with whom she could share her feelings and desires. It was the kind of loneliness that would follow her everywhere. Putting the receiver back on the hook she lay down on one of the huge, tawny, leather couches in the center of the room. She remained there the rest of the night, staring at the ceiling until her eyes began to close and she drifted off to sleep, only to find that even her dreams were unable to provide her with a refuge from her torment. They were plagued with images of Andrie, always beyond her reach . . . always fading into the darkness before Destiny could touch her.

*   *   *

Andrie arrived at the office later than usual on Friday. Her eyes told a story of a sleepless tear-filled night. David had called her after seeing Destiny off. He wanted to discuss what was going on, but Andrie managed to put him off by promising to explain things at dinner that evening. She wasn't sure of how she would handle him, but she had several hours to worry about that. Right now, she was distracted by a strange atmosphere that hung over the office. The staff and volunteers seemed solemn. It was like someone had died. Andrie wondered if they could be mourning over Ann's career, which had been dealt a mortal wound by yesterday's newspaper article.

The door to Ann's office was closed, but the sound of muffled voices could be heard coming from the other side of it.

"Who's she got in there?" Andrie asked Trudy, a young secretary who prided herself on knowing who all the major players were in New York and DC.

"Well, she's had Ray in there from before I got in this morning. Then, about a half hour ago, Hal Gottfried arrived. Are you going in?" Trudy asked, ready to admire Andrie's courage if she said yes.

"No, not right now," Andrie answered as she headed into her office, closing the door behind her. Hal Gottfried was the biggest public relations spin doctor around. Andrie didn't have to be in the room to know what was being discussed. Simply knowing that Gottfried was in there said it all.

Inside Ann's office, conversation was feverish, as Hal Gottfried began to deal with damage control.

"We have to be careful with this guy. We can't just demand to know his source. We have to assess how much validity there is to the story and how much proof he has to support it. After we know that, we can plan a strategy," Gottfried advised a nervous Ray Dalton.

"But we need to act right away before this goes any further," Ray urged, lighting a cigarette.

"You need to think before you jump here. This is my game. Let me do what you are about to pay me handsomely to do . . . OK?" Gottfried was confident and in control. He looked over at Ann, who had said nothing beyond greeting him since he walked in. "Ms. Capwell, you are presently unavailable for comment. You're also unavailable to all your party's big wigs and anyone else that wants you to talk. Right now, you talk only to me and you tell me only the truth. Until this all comes to a satisfactory conclusion, I will be your mother, your father, your husband, or in this case wife, I am your only link to the world. You communicate only through me . . . and I'll tell you again . . . you will tell me the truth about everything. If you can't do what I've told you, then I walk away. Am I clear?" Gottfried's affect was that of a Marine commander.

Ann detested being told what to do in this manner, yet she had no choice but to endure it. She knew that Hal Gottfried was the best PR man in the business. He was the only hope she had of salvaging her political career. She agreed to all his demands.

"Now, how much of what this article says about you is true?" Gottfried asked, looking Ann keenly in the eye, awaiting her response.

It took her several seconds before answering, "All of it." Her voice was uncharacteristically timid.

Ray looked on as the questioning progressed. He couldn't imagine anyone being able to save Ann's career now . . . not even Hal Gottfried.

After nearly four hours of questions and answers, Gottfried had the information he needed to begin his work. He knew every detail of Ann's private life and loves . . . from her first kiss all the way through her relationship with Andrie.

The process proved to be an excruciatingly embarrassing ordeal for Ann. Not only did Gottfried want to know with whom she had been, but what type of activity she had engaged in with each individual.

He explained that he needed to know who else could start talking to the press and corroborate the facts in the article. After assimilating the information, he looked at Ann and Ray. They were both pale, worn, and very nervous, as they awaited his advice. Gottfried suggested that Ray, who had been standing to the side of Ann's desk, take a seat. But, being too nervous to sit, Ray declined.

"I don't have to tell you that you have one hell of a mess

here," Gottfried said, as he crossed his legs and leaned back in the burgundy leather armchair that faced Ann's desk.

"So now that you know the facts, what do you think?" Ray asked anxiously.

"As long as what the article says about you is true, denying it will only make things worse for you. They've alluded to other, more incriminating, pictures and information. You don't want to stir that up. There's one way we can salvage your career and give you a fighting chance in the polls. It's a risk, but if it works, you'll be back on top again," Gottfried said, as he looked directly at Ann.

"What if it doesn't?" Ann responded.

"If it doesn't work, I don't see you being any worse off than you are right now . . . except for what you pay me." Gottfried's confident tone went a long way in calming his client's anxieties.

"Do you really think that we can get the public to believe us?" Ann was already regrouping emotionally.

"They should, since we'll be telling them the truth," Gottfried answered with curt aplomb.

Ann was puzzled. "I don't understand," she said, with her cold blue eyes searching Gottfried's face for an explanation.

Gottfried leaned forward, resting his elbow on her desk as he clarified his statement. "You're going to have to 'fess up to everything and tell the truth. Come out, as they say. . . . It's your only hope."

"Are you out of your mind?" Ann shrieked as she jumped up from her chair and stared down at Gottfried, who remained calmly seated.

Ray, who was now standing silently in the corner of the room, appeared incredulous as he shook his head and slumped down into the chair behind him.

"As I said, it's your only hope. If you do exactly what I say, you'll have a chance . . . I think you'll have a good chance. It'll be a matter of cutting your losses and re-posturing your stand on some major issues. Right now you're finished politically. You really don't have anything to lose."

"Her constituents will never go for that," Ray interjected from his seat in the corner.

"She's going to have to go after new constituents. She's going to be politically reborn." Gottfried responded to Ray's argument without moving his eyes off Ann. He could see how desperate she was not to lose her power. He continued, "You need to sort some things out . . . like how committed are you to any of your current positions. You'll have to ditch most, if not all, of them and adopt new ones. You'll have to change your political affiliations. You'll have to champion some causes that up 'til now you've opposed . . . and it won't stop there. You'll have to eat a lot of crow, but if we do it right, you'll be stronger than ever. The public has a short retention span. Eventually, they'll look at you as if the ultra right-wing conservative Ann Capwell never existed. In the process, most of your old colleagues will become your new enemies. That's OK, though, because you'll be garnering support from new camps. I can go on and on explaining the game plan, but your phones are ringing off the hook and the press is bound to catch up with you soon. So you need to make your decision, right here and now. If your answer is *no,* I'll wish you luck in your new field of endeavor and I'll leave. If it's *yes,* we start working now. Remember, either way, there's no turning back." Gottfried watched Ann, as she turned from him and stared out the window of her office. He could hear the wheels turning in her head. She looked over at Ray for advice, but he simply shrugged his shoulders in a gesture implying that the decision was hers.

"You really believe that this is the only way?" Ann asked as she turned to Gottfried.

He nodded affirmatively.

Ann knew he was right about her having nothing to lose. Political power was everything to her. She knew of no way to live without it. . . . It was her life. "All right. Tell me what we do first."

*   *   *

Outside her office, the troubled congresswoman's phones were ringing relentlessly. The staff were doing all they could to fend off the reporters. The front door had been locked since shortly after Andrie arrived, giving the office the atmosphere of a military headquarters under siege.

Andrie had been on the phone most of the morning. She had spoken with both of her brothers and her mother. It was obvious that her family was deeply concerned about her. She told them that she was fine and that she was sorry if the article had caused them any problems. The LaStellas didn't care about other people's opinions; they cared about their family. If Andrie was in trouble, the rest of the family wanted to help. It took hours of persuasion to convince her parents and brothers that she was OK and that they needn't worry about her. When they asked about Destiny, she could only tell them that she would have to explain that to them some other time.

Putting her head down on her desk Andrie thought about what Destiny was going through. She searched her imagination for some way out of this, some way she and Destiny could be together and not have to worry about Ann's vindictiveness. Suddenly she was startled by the ringing of the phone on the desk next to her. She quickly sat up, then hesitated for a moment before answering, "Hello."

"Andrie?" the voice on the line asked. It was David.

"David. Hi," she said, relieved that it wasn't a reporter or her family with more questions.

"I know it must be crazy there today, so I won't start this now. But I need to talk to you about what you're doing to your relationship with Destiny. When I spoke with you last night you said that we'd talk at dinner tonight . . . so how's my place at seven? I'll order in, since I'm too upset to cook."

"Fine. I'll see you at seven," Andrie conceded, then hung up the phone. Just as she did that, Ann walked into her office.

"Don't you believe in knocking?" Andrie asked in a blunt tone.

"I don't need to," Ann answered coldly, before she went on. "I've been in a meeting with Hal Gottfried all morning. We've come up with a strategy for handling this situation. But you'll have to cooperate . . . which I know you'll do." It was clear that Ann's emphatic tone belied a threat.

At that point, cooperation was Andrie's only option. "So what kind of lies do you want me to swear to now?" Andrie asked with indifference.

"Actually, we're going to be telling the truth . . . about everything," Ann said, as she closed the door behind her and sat down next to Andrie's desk.

"Everything? What do you mean?" Andrie inquired, certain that Ann would never consider coming out.

Without hesitation Ann explained the strategy that Gottfried had plotted out for her.

After several minutes of sitting and listening in astonishment, Andrie asked, "So why do you need my cooperation? Am I supposed to stand there and say, *Yes it's true, I can attest to the fact that Representative Capwell is indeed a lesbian?*" Then she stood up and moved across the room from Ann. Even the scent of Ann's perfume now sickened her.

"Gottfried believes that when I do admit to everything, I should look as settled as possible in my life. I shouldn't give the impression of being out on the prowl. Having been with the same woman for seven years will give me the appearance I need to have. . . . And if anyone asks you any questions about the Destiny Anderson imbroglio, you simply explain that she happened to have been staying at your place for a few days . . . and I knew all about it. We have no secrets from each other."

"How long are we supposed to keep up this farce?" Andrie asked in a cynical tone, making no attempt to disguise her loathing.

"As long as necessary. It all depends on Hal Gottfried. I'm letting him call the shots with this. By the way, I've assured him of your complete cooperation. That means you will agree to every-thing that he suggests . . . everything."

"You want me to act like we're lovers . . . partners. People are going to see right through this. It could backfire on you and make things even worse," Andrie tried to reason with Ann.

"I'm sure that if you remember your motivation, you'll be very convincing. Don't forget, I have my hand around Destiny Anderson's throat. . . . Don't make me squeeze," Ann said, reinforcing her threat to destroy Destiny's career.

Andrie stared at her with contempt, shaking her head in disgust as she spoke. "No heart . . . no soul . . . you have so little in common with a human being." Saying that, she walked out of the room.

Left alone in the wake of Andrie's scornful exit, Ann realized that her physical attraction for her was as strong as it had ever been. It made her consider using her threats to maximize her gains in all areas where Andrie was concerned.

* * *

The room was dim. It had been raining for most of the afternoon and little light filtered through the heavy brocade drapes that dressed the windows of Bee's outlandishly decorated apartment.

Nicole had packed most of her things and sat at the edge of the bed, waiting for Bee to complete their travel arrangements. She picked up the day-old newspaper and read the article again. She stared at the misleading picture of herself with Destiny, and thought to herself that there had to be some way she could help, or at least let Destiny know that she had nothing to do with this.

"Are you ready? We'll be picking up the tickets at Kennedy. Our flight leaves at 8:10, s-s-so we have about three and a half hours. I h-h-have a limo picking us up at 6:45. I still don't understand why you have to leave t-tonight. You're s-so hot h-headed," Bee said as she walked in and dropped herself down next to Nicole. The weight of her hefty body sunk into the mattress where she sat, causing Nicole to tilt sideways until their shoulders were touching. That small contact made Bee flush red with excitement.

Nicole began to think out loud, oblivious to the fact that Bee's round face was glowing. "I just need to get back to LA. I should have never come here. If I wasn't trying to lure Destiny back, this would have never happened. I ruined everything for her."

"That's n-n-not true. You don't know if her lover believes any of this. Besides, you've given her a lot. Everybody knows that you helped her when she was first s-s-starting out."

"All I did was introduce her to some people and give her a few tips. She had talent and they saw that. I didn't really do anything for her. I couldn't. I was nobody then . . . and I'm still nobody," she said in a voice filled with disappointment.

Bee saw tears in her eyes. "D-don't say that. It's n-n-not true. You're the most talented and beautiful woman I've ever s-seen in my l-life," Bee declared sincerely, as she gently brushed the tears off Nicole's cheeks. "I've admired you ever since we first met at Sonia's Halloween party three y-years ago. You came dressed as Cleopatra. You were so beautiful. From that time on I was s-so jealous of Destiny. I remember that she didn't even wear a c-costume. She was in jeans and T-sh-shirt. I thought if I w-were her, I would want to go as one of your slaves or something like that." Admitting that, Bee, who was never known for her shyness, lowered her eyes bashfully.

"You remember that? You're so sweet." Nicole thrived on attention. Her concerns about Destiny vanished momentarily, as she basked in Bee's adoration. Bee's company was becoming more and more pleasurable to her. "I'm so glad that you're coming to LA with me. I really don't want to have to go to Sonia's house alone, to remove my things. So where are we staying?"

"Well, I have a little place at the edge of M-malibu. We can stay there. It's right on the beach. It's nice, but it's small. I've been thinking that if I s-s-start spending more time on the W-west Coast, I'll get r-r-rid of this apartment and find something bigger out there. M-maybe you could help me look." Bee was well aware of Nicole's love for the sun and fun of Southern California and she was willing to relocate if it would make her more attractive to the raven-haired beauty.

Chapter Seventeen

David took Andrie's coat from her and hung it neatly in the front hall closet. Without a word, he ushered her into the living room. There, Andrie suddenly felt as though she had been transported to the heart of the Orient. David had ordered in their dinner just as he said. The large, highly polished mahogany coffee table was set with platters of sushi and sashimi, an antique sake set and a variety of Asian condiments. Flanking the table were two large, gold-fringed pillows. "To rest our tired tushies on," he chuckled, as he pointed to them.

Andrie smiled weakly. She knew that the small talk would end shortly and David would begin his well-intentioned inquisition. She kicked off her shoes and sat on the pillow, readying herself for the onslaught.

"So, how was it at the office today?" he asked, as he handed Andrie a small glass of plum wine.

"Ann's hired Hal Gottfried to deal with this mess. He's convinced her to admit to everything and re-position herself politically. He said that if she apologizes for her hypocrisy and says that she's learned by her mistakes, blah, blah, blah, that he can make her into an entirely new political animal," Andrie said, staring into the glass of sweet wine.

"Darling, let's get down to brass tacks, I don't give a shit what happens with that witch. I'd like to throw a bucket of water at her and watch her melt. I want to know what's going on between you and Destiny. She's devastated," David said, plopping himself down on the floor next to Andrie.

She wanted to confide in him, but she was afraid that, in an attempt to help, he could cause more problems for her. "We're just not right for each other. I'm staying with Ann. That's where I belong." Just saying those words nauseated her.

"Are you out of your fucking mind? What are you saying? Don't try to bullshit me. I know you too well. I could see how you felt about Destiny . . . I saw it fifteen years ago," David screeched impatiently.

"It wasn't right then and it still isn't. What you see is a physical chemistry. That's not enough to build a lifelong relationship on," Andrie replied mechanically.

"Oh, I see, and what you have with the Dragon Lady of Capitol Hill is the stuff that dreams are made of? Right?" David rebutted sarcastically, as his frustration peaked.

"Ann's changing everything that was wrong with our relationship. She's openly acknowledging our love. I won't have to sneak around anymore. There won't be any marriage of convenience between her and Stuart Sottley. I have everything that I want. Can't you just be happy for me and let this go?" As she listed those points for David, the irony of it struck her. She remembered a time when she thought that those changes would have made her happy. But now she knew that she had been searching for a happiness that only Destiny could give her.

"Look at me." David's voice cracked slightly as he kept himself from crying. Disappointment overwhelmed him as he began to realize that he was powerless to stop his friend from ruining her life. He gently turned Andrie's face toward him with his hand. "I'm alone. Every night I go to bed alone. No matter how long and hard I've looked, I can't find the right person . . . and there are thousands of people out there in the world just as lonely as I am. But at least we all have hope because we're out there searching for the right person. You know that you had the right one and you're turning your back on her. You're locking yourself away with someone who could never care about you the way Destiny does. Fate, or God, or whatever you want to call it, gave you a love that few people are ever fortunate enough to find, and you're letting it go for nothing. . . . You have nothing with Ann. You know that." David's voice trailed off. His words were knotting in his throat until it became impossible for him to continue.

Andrie saw the love and concern in his eyes. She desperately wanted to tell him the truth. She needed to tell someone about the nightmare she was living. But David was too volatile. She couldn't trust his reaction. She feared that he would go to Ann, or worse, tell Destiny, who would sacrifice everything to be with Andrie. She couldn't let that happen. Tears filled her eyes and began to run down her face as she kept silent.

Seeing that, David thought that he had broken through to her. "Tell me. Who's making you do this? It's Ann, isn't it? What is she holding over you?" he asked with an intensity that was more than Andrie could handle.

"I can't do this. I have to go." She stood up and rushed out of the room. Then, taking her coat from the closet, she headed toward the door, but David chased after her and caught her arm.

"Andrie, let me help you . . . please," he begged.

"Don't try to look for mysterious reasons why I can't be with Destiny. It won't work. It's just not meant to be. Please. David, don't make this worse. You'll only be causing her more pain. Just accept it." With that, Andrie left.

Shaking his head as he looked back at the table-settings and the untouched food, David thought about the life of possibilities to which Andrie had turned her back. He was no longer sure of how to reach her. As he picked up the small stemmed glass of plum wine, he was certain of only one thing now . . . a life filled with love and happiness had been spread out before her by Destiny and Andrie had fled from it, just as surely as she had run out on this dinner.

Chapter Eighteen

The reporters clamored in the front office of Ann Capwell's New York headquarters early on Monday morning. They had been salivating at the idea of questioning Ann Capwell since the story had first broken on Thursday.

Hal Gottfried had been busy earning his fee by coaching Ann, her staff, and an unenthusiastic Andrie. He had also been trying to find the source of Ed Gold's story on Ann. That was an almost impossible task, because Ed Gold had refused to name the main source of his information and had subsequently gone out of town on vacation shortly after the story hit the stands.

Ann was nervously going over her notes in order to make certain that she wouldn't forget any of the points that Gottfried wanted her to address. She was wearing a navy-blue coat dress, which Gottfried had handpicked from her wardrobe. He was now orchestrating every move she made.

Watching her read the speech over to herself, he decided to go over its content with her one last time. It was agreed that she shouldn't look as if she were reading. He wanted it to appear as though Ann was speaking extemporaneously. Gottfried felt that she would appear more sincere that way.

"All right. The sharks have gathered outside. Are you ready?" he asked, seeing that she was still reading.

"Yes," she said, looking up from creased and dog-eared pages.

"OK. Let's just go over the main points one more time." Gottfried sounded like a coach instructing an athlete just before an important competition. "You start by apologizing for concealing the fact that you're gay. Then you explain that because you felt that prejudice and homophobia would have prevented you from serving your fellow citizens to the best of your ability, you chose to sacrifice your right to live openly with the person you love.

Remember to emphasize your commitment to serve and represent your fellow citizens. After that the new Ann Capwell makes her debut. You'll explain that what's happened in your life has caused you to become personally dedicated to combating prejudice against gays as well as other Americans who have suffered from bigotry. Stress your dedication to fighting for specific items on your new agenda . . . like the right to employee benefits for partners of the same sex, legalizing gay marriages, as well as discrimination in housing and employment. . . . Look apologetic, yet martyred. Remember, the public knows that the prejudice you're talking about exists. Your job now is to convince them that what has happened in your life makes you even more qualified to keep your seat in Congress. Remember, don't answer any questions when you're done. New York is a liberal town. There are going to be plenty of people out there who'll want to support the new Ann Capwell. I've invited a group of reporters to interview you afterward, in your office. Ray and I will be there with you."

This was only the beginning for the remade Ann Capwell. There would be a hard road ahead. She would need to use her power of persuasion, her connections, and her wealth to make this work.

Gottfried, Ray Dalton and Robert Capwell had met with the leaders of the more liberal opposing party. Currently that party didn't have a strong candidate for the upcoming election. So, they planned to convince them to endorse Ann, who was now joining their party.

This press conference would be Ann's first battle to regain her political viability. She needed to be more eloquent, more convincing, and more compelling than ever before in her career. Checking herself in the mirror, she seemed satisfied and certain that she would be able to exhibit the expected range of emotions that would be required to win over the hearts of her new constituency.

Before opening the door to the outer office, Gottfried reminded her not to answer any questions until the interview later that morning. Ann nodded, acknowledging his advice as she left the room.

*   *   *

Gottfried had decided that it would be best if Andrie wasn't around to be questioned. He felt it that it would only serve to complicate things at that point.

Andrie was relieved by his decision. She remained in her apartment with the ringer to her phone turned off, since reporters had begun calling her to get her version of the story. Gottfried had instructed her to leave her cellular phone on in case he needed to contact her.

Desperate to feel Destiny's presence in some way, Andrie looked around the apartment for remnants of her stay. She went into the room where Destiny had kept her things. Glancing around the room, there didn't appear to be anything left behind. . . . Nothing that she could hold on to as token of what was, or could have been. She retreated back to her bedroom where her only memento was the fragrance of Destiny's hair on a pillow there. Andrie had fallen asleep holding fast to it the night before. Picking it up again, she inhaled deeply and closed her eyes, momentarily picturing Destiny's face. Tears ran down her face, onto the pillow, as she tortured herself with thoughts of Destiny. Hopelessly, she held it closer, noticing that the scent was beginning to fade from it.

The cellular phone, which she had placed beside her bed, began to ring. Andrie knew that it was Hal Gottfried calling her. At that moment, she wished that she could let the phone keep ringing and just go someplace where no one could find her. But that was just a wish. She answered the phone. "Hello."

"It's me," Gottfried's voice replied.

"I know. Is it over yet?" she asked blandly, referring to Ann's public statement. She continued to hold the pillow to her while she was on the phone.

"Yes. I'd say it went very well. She'll be doing the Q and A in a few minutes. I just wanted to let you know that I discussed it with her and we both feel that it would be best if you moved into her apartment for a while. We want the public to see that she's settled and in a stable relationship. It makes her look less threatening to people that don't fully understand her lifestyle. So, throw a couple of things in a bag and I'll pick you up at your place tonight. I want to be with you if any reporters try to question you. Tomorrow, we can come by for the rest of your stuff. . . . OK? . . . Are you still on the line?" he asked, as Andrie's silence had become obvious to him.

"Yes . . . I don't think it's such a good idea. They'll be able to find out that I wasn't living with her all these years. So how settled will it really look?" Andrie tried to argue.

"That's OK. We'll just say that you wanted to live together all these years and that now, since everyone knows about you, you've moved in. . . . By the way, don't forget there can't be any further communication between you and Destiny Anderson. I'd better go. They'll be coming in here soon to interview Ann."

"I just want to know, how long am I supposed to stay there with her?" Andrie asked, afraid to hear the answer.

"I'm not sure right now. There are too many directions this thing can take. It will be at least until the election is over."

"I see," she said in a flat, lifeless voice.

"I'll pick you up about eight." With that Gottfried hung up.

Andrie put the phone down and looked out the window. It had begun to snow. She wondered what the weather was like in LA at that moment. Then, pulling an overnight case out of the closet, she started to pack. The first item she placed into it was the pillow.

Chapter Nineteen

Casa Pepino was a frequent lunch spot for Destiny and Maggie McBride, her manager. It was Maggie's favorite place, more because of the drinks than the food. Destiny was not terribly fond of either, but since the small Mexican restaurant was quiet and located near the recording studio, she found it a good place to discuss business with Maggie. Halfway through their meal, they were discussing how well the meeting with Rena had gone the previous Friday.

"They loved your songs. I asked Rena when she planned to release the movie, and she's considering next year at this time. There will be a simultaneous release of the soundtrack, which will be great for you. . . . Did you hear her rave about how you captured the sentiment of her story?" Maggie asked, as she motioned to the waiter to bring her another margarita.

"She showed me a rough cut of the film before I started, so I could get a feelin' for it," Destiny muttered, shrugging her shoulders.

Ever since Destiny had returned from New York Maggie sensed that something was wrong with her. She had seemed preoccupied and distant at the meeting Friday with Rena. At the time, Maggie attributed Destiny's lack of enthusiasm to jet lag, but as the week went on she had seen no improvement. It was time for her to find out what was going on, so Maggie initiated the conversation in her own definite style. "Do I know her?"

"What?" Destiny replied in a stunned tone.

"Who is the woman you've had on your mind lately? And don't bullshit me, I know that you haven't been thinking about your career since you got back from New York," Maggie probed.

"You don't know her," Destiny answered with the sadness of a lost child.

"Wait a minute. Is this the woman you stayed with . . . the one in the article?" Maggie asked, as her drink arrived.

"Yeah. Now let's drop this because I don't really want to talk about it. It didn't work out and so that's that."

"Des, honey, I have to tell you that I love seeing your pictures in the rags, but maybe you should start to settle down now. You've been running around with all kinds of women since Nicole left you. But it's time to calm down. There have been a few openly gay women celebrities over the past few years, but none of them were pictured in the tabloids every other day, locking lips with a different woman. And none of them got involved in political scandals. You're just moving too damned fast. You've got to give society a chance to catch up with you," Maggie advised as she sipped her margarita.

"Don't worry. You won't see me doin' that anymore. I was looking for somethin' then. I'm not lookin' anymore," Destiny replied pensively.

"If you found what you were looking for why do you sound so miserable?" Maggie asked.

"I lost it . . . again," Destiny said, with an angry, frustrated look as she leaned back in her chair and started tapping on one of the small red Christmas ornaments hanging on the wall just above her head.

"That's it; I don't care how mad you get at me, I want to know what's going on. Tell me what happened to you while you were in New York," Maggie insisted.

"All right. . . . Maybe you can help me make some sense out of it." With that, Destiny began to explain everything from the beginning, fifteen years before.

It didn't take long for Maggie to become totally involved in the story. "So, why don't you try calling her and get to the bottom of all this. It sounds to me like you had something special together. You should fight to keep it."

"I tried callin' her, day after day. There was no answer. I called David today and he said that she was all right. He saw her last

Friday and he spoke to her at work yesterday. She told him that she had taken her phone off the hook because of reporters callin' about the story."

"Well, OK. Call when that dies down . . . or better yet, fly back to New York and make her tell you what's going on," Maggie advised, as she became increasingly frustrated over the situation.

"I was plannin' to do exactly that, yesterday. I couldn't take it anymore. I had reservations for a flight last night," Destiny said, as she turned her eyes from Maggie, not wanting her to see the pain there.

"So?" Maggie asked.

"I was reading the *Times*, and there in front of me is an article that said that Ann Capwell came out publicly and that her lover of seven years had moved in with her, now that their relationship is out in the open. Until I read that, I still thought there was some hope for us. Now I know that it's over. She's still in love with Ann. I don't understand it. I don't know why she did this to me. I just know that I can't forget her," Destiny said, as she looked at Maggie, hoping for a solution.

"Well, honey, I think that you'd better come to terms with this somehow, before it really takes a toll on you. It's been my experience that not everything you read in the newspaper is true. Give this Andrie a call and see if she's really living with Ann Capwell. That way you'll know for sure."

"I did that this morning. But I got a recording that her number wasn't in service any longer. So I called David again. He couldn't believe it himself, but it was true. She moved in with Ann."

The discussion was over for Destiny. She got up from the table and told Maggie that she would wait for her outside.

*   *   *

Ann Capwell's Upper East Side apartment was large and elegantly appointed. Most of the furniture and artwork had been in her family for generations.

Despite the expanse of the apartment, Andrie felt trapped. It was little more than a well-furnished cage to her. By Friday, she felt that she was beginning to lose her mind. Gottfried had instructed her to remain in the apartment until the initial furor had dissipated. He had also informed her that she would no longer be working for Ann and, therefore, she was free to pursue any line of work that would not interfere with his plans. He even approved of Andrie returning to run her own marketing business.

The thought of going back into her own business and not working for Ann helped make the hell she was living seem more tolerable. It meant that at least a small part of her life wouldn't be dictated by Gottfried and Ann. At that point there was no comfort for Andrie. She was even finding it difficult and painful to speak with David or her family, since none of them could understand why she had chosen to move in with Ann.

Since Monday evening, when she moved into Ann's apartment, Andrie did her best to avoid, as much as possible, the woman who had destroyed her life. She spoke to her only when necessary and spent most of her time in the guest room she had been given. Ann barely acknowledged her presence, since she was too wrapped up with her re-election strategy. Andrie thanked God for that.

Although she had spent that whole week in New York because of the publicity, Ann had planned to return to Washington on Monday and remain there throughout the following week. Hal Gottfried would go along with her to trouble-shoot.

Andrie looked forward to their absence. She planned to devote the week to preparing her return to her marketing business. It had been a long time since she had dissolved LaStella Associates. Andrie knew that re-establishing herself wouldn't be easy, but since there wasn't much else in her life, she would have all the time and energy that she would need.

Chapter Twenty

Christmas and New Year's Day had come and gone quietly for Destiny. Harry and Elaine were still going back and forth from New York to LA. After reading the "page nine" article, they pleaded with Destiny to tell them what happened between herself and Andrie. She eventually explained everything, after which both Harry and Elaine had become more than close friends to Destiny. In many ways they were like surrogate parents. It truly distressed them that things worked out so badly for her and Andrie.

Although the Sterns had been supporters of Ann Capwell ever since she started the Women's Way project, they were never admirers of her personality or many of her other political views. It was a puzzlement to them that Andrie would choose Ann over Destiny. They had both seen a change in Destiny since it happened. She had thrown herself into her work, with little time for much else. Except for Harry, Elaine, and Maggie, she saw few people socially.

In mid-January Elaine Stern needed to go to Paris to visit her father, who had suffered a mild heart attack. Before leaving she told Destiny that she was very worried about her husband, Harry. She explained that although Cobra Records was doing well, Harry was downhearted because he was no longer its sole owner. He blamed himself for the bad investments and tax problems that forced him to sell more than half the company to Stuart Sottley. Elaine feared leaving Harry behind without someone to give him moral support in her absence.

"I'm only going to be gone for a few days. My father probably won't even see me when I get there. Harry's told you the story. . . . My parents wanted nothing to do with me when I married Harry, because his mother wasn't Jewish. My family was very strict about those things. I was their only child and they wanted what they thought was best for me. My father wouldn't talk to me at the unveiling after my mother died. But I still love him, so I need to do this. I guess it's not so different from how your family reacted to you being gay. I told Harry that I didn't think that it would be a good idea for him to come with me. I don't want him to go there with me, just to be shunned. So, I'd love it if you could kind of keep an eye on him . . . you know, maybe have dinner with him a couple of times," Elaine asked Destiny, knowing that she would be happy to help. It had also occurred to Elaine that since Destiny had been working day and night on her third album, an occasional dinner with Harry would at least provide her with some diversion as well.

No matter how busy her work kept her, or how many diversions were planned by well-meaning friends, Destiny could not escape her need for Andrie. The worst part was going to bed at night. That's when the emptiness inside her would scream out for Andrie and recurring dreams of her would cause Destiny to wake up nearly drowned in tears and sweat.

*   *   *

By late January, the stir about Ann's hidden homosexuality had calmed considerably. It seemed that Hal Gottfried's strategy was working out successfully. There were a few follow-up articles in the mainstream press and then nothing more was said.

Since Ann had admitted to everything up front, interest in the story quickly waned. She had switched parties and was winning the endorsements she sought. Her new agenda was becoming evident . . . and more and more liberal publications were interviewing her on the issues. It was here that Gottfried planned to reshape Ann's career and build new strongholds of support for her.

Meanwhile, Andrie was taking advantage of the fact that she could again walk freely down the streets, without worrying about being harassed by aggressive reporters. She had even begun to look around the city for just the right office space to restart her

marketing business. Her days were spent making preparations for
that, while most of her nights were spent endlessly tossing and
turning as the image of Destiny's face would haunt her through
closed eyes.

She thanked God for all the time Ann was spending in
Washington. It made living in the congresswoman's New York
apartment more bearable. As the weeks went by, Andrie saw less
of David. Most of the time she would come up with an excuse for
why she wouldn't be able to meet him for lunch or dinner. Since
he had not given up on trying to find the truth behind the reason
she decided to stay with Ann, being with him had become difficult
for Andrie.

After one of the infrequent occasions when they met for lunch,
David insisted that they take a walk. He missed spending time with
Andrie and he needed to tell her that.

"Sweetie, I'm not stupid. I know that you've been avoiding me,
because you're afraid I'll ask you too many questions about what's
really behind this thing with you and Destiny and Ann . . . and
when this first happened I was doing that, because I thought that I
could help you. I know now that you really don't want me to pry
at you about this. So here's my offer . . . I still don't understand
what you're doing with your life, but I promise not to ask you any
questions or interfere with your decisions, if you just let me be
there for you. Please, I really miss you . . . a lot." David's eyes
were glazed with tears as he appealed to his friend.

"I love you and I've missed you too. . . . Thanks . . . I'd love
for us to see more of each other. I just couldn't take the pressure
you were putting me under," Andrie said, hugging him tightly.

"Can I ask you a question?" Andrie inquired, as they continued
to stroll the streets of SoHo.

"Sure."

"How is she?" Andrie's concern was obvious from her tone.

"She's hurting still. She doesn't understand what happened, but
she wants you to be happy. She knows that you're living with Ann
now. I talk to her a couple of times a week. She always asks

about you. What else can I say?" It was difficult for David to keep his agreement and not ask any questions when he discussed this subject. But he managed to suppress that urge.

As they continued down Prince Street, they stopped to listen to a young street musician playing her guitar and singing. It reminded them both of when Destiny first started out, but neither of them mentioned that. Andrie noticed a vacant storefront, with a "for rent" sign, across from where the young woman was singing. The door was locked but when they looked through the window, Andrie could see that the size and configuration of the space was perfect for what she needed. As she copied the phone number from the sign, she noticed a gray tabby cat on the other side of the glass window. For a moment she looked into its yellow-green eyes and the small animal seemed to make a connection with her.

Chapter Twenty-One

Ever since Elaine had returned from Paris, she had felt particularly indebted to Destiny for, as she called it, "Babysitting my big baby." She had also begun to confide in Destiny that she had been worried about Harry ever since the deal with Stuart Sottley.

Harry was trying his best to raise the money to buy back majority ownership of Cobra, but no matter how hard he tried, he couldn't seem to get a loan for the kind of money he needed. He had even considered multiple investors all having a small piece of Cobra, just to avoid losing the company to Sottley permanently, but the contract he had signed wouldn't allow for that. He was beginning to conclude that he would probably not be able to raise the money that he needed within the two-year time frame, and therefore faced losing Cobra. The Sterns had no idea that it was Ann Capwell who had purchased most of Cobra and that she had used her connections to prevent Harry from raising the funds to buy back control of the company.

Ironically, as Destiny provided Harry with a sympathetic ear about the situation, she had no idea of how personally it had impacted her own life.

* * *

Looking around at the dusty, vacant space she had rented, Andrie rolled up the sleeves of her light blue denim shirt. She began to rummage through a large box of rags and cleansers that she had brought with her, until she found a small dish and a can opener. Then, opening a brown paper bag, she removed a can of cat food. The little gray tabby had insisted upon remaining in the office. As she emptied the contents of the can onto the plate, the small cat began to meow and circle around Andrie, affectionately rubbing against the leg of her blue jeans. It seemed to be welcoming both the food and the company.

"So you probably don't even have a name. What can we call you?" Andrie asked in a low gentle voice, as the tabby alternately ate and looked up at her, as if it understood what she was saying.

"How about *Blue,* since that's how I'm feeling. My little Blue. That's kind of cute. I like it, how about you?" With that, the small feline left its plate and walked over to Andrie, who was kneeling down a few feet away. Picking it up, Andrie stroked its fur as she began to assess what she needed to do to get the space ready for business.

* * *

While Andrie was preparing to reopen her marketing and public relations business in New York, Hal Gottfried was in Washington, working hard on revamping Ann's public image. He had arranged a number of interviews with the press and television appearances on political discussion programs. He planned for her to discuss both domestic social issues, as well as current international matters. Gottfried was using every tool at his disposal to bolster Ann's public image. Robert Capwell had continued to add his influence to Gottfried's efforts. He was even responsible for the idea that Ann's old party should consider the endorsement of Phil Massey, a former prosecutor and Assistant United States Attorney, who was neither well known nor thought of as a strong candidate. Capwell was able to manipulate party bosses to endorse a relatively unknown and weak candidate with the use of information he had on their private lives and business dealings. Although he was retired and ailing, he maintained a good deal of political clout and savvy, which he was now using to save his daughter's career.

Capwell blamed Andrie for everything that had occurred. He considered it her fault that Ann's career was in jeopardy. He abhorred the fact that Andrie was living with Ann and only tolerated it because Hal Gottfried felt that it was necessary to look as though Ann was in a stable, long-term relationship.

Whenever Capwell visited his daughter's apartment, he went out of his way to be as unpleasant as possible to Andrie. Since his visits were infrequent and mostly announced in advance, Andrie did her best not to be there when she knew he was coming. She spent as much time as possible at her office, rarely returning to the apartment before 10 or 11 o'clock at night. As the months went by, her business benefited by her long hours. LaStella Marketing Inc. was beginning to get clients. There were even some old clients who wanted to meet with Andrie when they heard that she was back in business.

In the past Andrie had always enjoyed working to make her business successful, but now the hard work was simply a way to keep herself from thinking about the pain inside. So many of the things that used to give her pleasure had lost their meaning.

So many miles away, Destiny also struggled with her work since it no longer provided her the pleasure it once did. Yet she too used her work to ease the pain of her loneliness. She produced and recorded her third album and had decided to call it *Brownstone Blue*. That was the title of one of the tracks. It was a song she had written one night when all she could do was think about Andrie. At first, she thought that she would keep it for herself, but later she decided to release it. It would be a way of telling Andrie how she felt. Music was all Destiny had left. It was the only friend whose company she sought.

Chapter Twenty-Two

The office was calm. Blue, the little gray tabby, was lazily stretched out in front of the window, soaking up the warmth of the mid-May sun. Friday was the least hectic day of the week for Andrie. It was a welcome respite, since her client list was growing every day. It was clear that she would soon need to hire someone to help with the typing and phones.

A new client was coming in later that afternoon, but for the moment she could relax a bit. She noticed that the morning paper carried a small article about the closing down of the Women's Way project. For months Andrie had appealed to Ann not to let Women's Way die, but her efforts were to no avail. Women's Way had never truly been a concern of Ann's.

Andrie felt that she had failed the women in the program, because she wasn't able to prevent Ann from terminating Women's Way. She had spent most of May trying to help as many of the woman as possible find jobs and housing. Although finding them work wasn't an adequate replacement for the Women's Way program, it could at least help some of the women keep from returning to abusive partners because of financial reasons.

Even David had helped by trying to find jobs for some of the women. Of the twelve women still in the program, only three remained unemployed, but Andrie hadn't given up hope. David's cousin, Sheldon, who owned three rather large pharmacies, had been looking for two people to work as clerks in his largest store. On David's recommendation, his cousin agreed to interview two of the three remaining women. They had been scheduled to meet with him that morning. David had promised Andrie that he would call her as soon as he found out the result of the interviews.

Sipping a cup of mint tea as she leafed through the newspaper, Andrie waited to hear from him.

Her restful wait was disturbed when Blue, having finally had enough of the sun's rays, leapt up on to her desk. Then, almost knocking over the tea, he jumped into her lap, where he curled up and began purring.

"Someday, I'm going to take you home with me, so you won't have to always be alone at night," Andrie told the gray tabby, as she cuddled him close. Ann refused to let her bring Blue to the apartment, ever since the day she came by Andrie's office with Hal Gottfried and Ray Dalton. The three had stopped by the office simply to have Ann be familiar with it, in the event anyone were to ask about Andrie's business. Blue had taken an instant dislike to Ann and hissed at her throughout the visit. At one point during that visit she tried to move Blue off a chair in order to sit down, and the little gray tabby scratched the politician's hand. After that, Ann made it clear that Andrie was never to bring Blue home with her.

As Blue climbed up and put his head on Andrie's shoulder, the phone rang. It was David and he sounded triumphant. "Sweetie, Sheldon thought both of your Women's Way ladies were wonderful. He said they can both start on Monday morning. His wife, Susan, is going to teach them about the stock and all the other things they'll have to know. Susan was a big supporter of Women's Way. Sheldon said that she told him to hire them, even before they arrived. Isn't that great?" David said exuberantly.

"I can't believe it. It's wonderful. Now, if I can find work for Nancy Hogan. I don't know how to give her enough confidence to go on an interview. And the ironic thing is that she's the most talented of all the women that we helped to place. She worked for an ad agency for seven years; she's really experienced on computers, as far as using word processing and spreadsheet software, and she's the nicest person you'd ever want to meet. She's just been abused for so long, she has very little faith in herself."

"Did you say she knows computers and she worked for an ad agency?" David asked, as the wheels turned in his head.

"Yes, that's why . . ." Andrie was quickly cut off by David as he broke in again.

"Didn't you say things were starting to get too busy for you?"

"Yes, but I thought that I'd wait a while longer before I hired someone . . ." Andrie's voice trailed off as she started considering the idea. Then, suddenly, it seemed to make perfect sense to her. "You're right. That could really work out well and I think that she'd like it here. I've got to call her. Bye hon." With that, Andrie abruptly hung up and called Nancy to offer her the job. By the time she hung up with Nancy, it was agreed that she would start work on Monday.

That night Andrie arrived at the apartment at the usual time, about ten o'clock. Since Ann always spent Friday evenings in her study, catching up on paperwork, it was odd that she wasn't home that evening. Andrie had little wish to think further about Ann's absence. She simply appreciated the fact that she hadn't yet arrived at the apartment.

Wishing to avoid Ann's eventual arrival, Andrie took a quick shower and went to bed. Predictably, Destiny's face appeared in her mind the moment she closed her eyes. Memories of her touch and her voice tormented Andrie, as she prayed for sleep to come. Thankfully, within a short while, her eyes fell shut and she drifted off.

After several hours of merciful sleep had passed, a current of Saturday morning's sounds drifted in through the slightly opened window. Rather than the usual noises of the heavy city traffic, Saturday's sounds were more subtle and peppered with the frequent barking of dogs being taken out for longer walks than on weekdays. It never ceased to amaze Andrie that on the twelfth floor of the high-rise, she could hear so much of what was happening on the street below.

The noise and sunlight worked together to wake her. She had plans to meet David around noon and spend the day with him, but first she decided that she would throw on her sweats and start her morning with a brisk walk. Just as she was about to leave for her walk, Ray Dalton arrived at the apartment. As soon as he walked in, Andrie could see by his face that something was wrong.

"What's happened?" she asked, realizing that Ann had still not returned to the apartment.

"Robert Capwell died last night . . . I think the stress of everything that was happening with Ann finally took its toll on him. Ann and Hal were with him when it happened. They were there to discuss strategy. He had been helping us out by calling in some favors with people that owed him from the past. Hal said that he looked pretty worn out and he complained of indigestion. Then in the middle of the meeting, he started to sweat and his lips turned bluish. They laid him down right there on the couch in his study, while they called for an ambulance . . . but he was gone by the time they arrived. The paramedics tried to resuscitate him but it was no use. . . . I'll tell you, he was one tough old bird. Before he would let them call the ambulance, he sent Hal out of the room because he wanted to talk to Ann in private. . . . Anyway, Hal sent me over to tell you what happened and to let you know that we're going to need you to stay close to Ann until after the funeral. You'll need to look supportive."

"So, how is she taking it?" Andrie asked, out of curiosity rather than concern.

"Ann is Ann. She's holding up fine. All I can say is, she's her father's daughter," Ray replied.

Hearing Ray say that suddenly reminded Andrie of Lilly's prediction. The tall Austrian's words came back to her with crystal clarity. . . . *There is a very wealthy man who will be passing from this earth, sometime within the next twelve months.* . . . Andrie felt a chill go through her. She had never trusted in psychics or their predictions. But she was so starved for the smallest crumb of hope that she found herself questioning whether this could be the death that Lilly foretold. And if it was, then which path had been chosen? she wondered.

"So, what do you want me to do now?" she asked Ray, trying to maintain an appropriately somber tone.

"Well, I guess that you should change your clothes and come back to Capwell's house with me. We're also going to need a change of clothes for Ann, since she's staying there today," he suggested.

"OK. Give me an hour to shower and change . . . and I'll put some of her things in a bag," Andrie replied as she started to head out of the room. She wanted to be alone for at least a few moments, so she could gather her thoughts about what was happening. It was difficult to discount the fact that Lilly had predicted this several months ago. The possibility of having something to hope for made Andrie come alive inside.

The radio was on as she began to undress for her shower. She called David and left a message on his machine, explaining that she couldn't meet him because of Capwell's death. As she hung up, she suddenly recognized Destiny's voice on the radio. She was singing "Brownstone Blue."

Andrie stopped what she was doing and stood still as she listened intently to the words of the song. Tears filled her eyes, as it became clear to her that Destiny was still thinking about her. Remembering Lilly's prediction, she wondered if this would be the turning point. Perhaps Robert Capwell had chosen the path that would bring Destiny back to her. Only time would tell.

Chapter Twenty-Three

The following Tuesday was dreary. It was raining heavily and the weather was colder than normal for mid-May. Nancy Hogan had been rescheduled to start work that morning, since Andrie had kept the office closed on Monday in order to attend Robert Capwell's funeral.

She had sectioned off the front part of the office with a partition. It would give Nancy some privacy and allow Andrie to work undisturbed by people dropping in. Blue was a little confused by the furniture rearrangement. He spent the morning meowing and following Andrie around the office.

It was about five minutes to nine when Nancy arrived. She wore little makeup to add color to her pale complexion. Her long blond hair was collected in a plain tortoise-shell barrette at the back of her neck. And although inexpensive, her light green skirt suit was meticulously neat. There was an awkwardness to her, as though she felt that she was in the way wherever she stood. Andrie already knew this about her, so she did her best to make Nancy feel comfortable and to let her know that she was going to be an important part of LaStella Marketing.

"How about some tea? I have a pot of water boiling," Andrie asked, as she showed Nancy around the small office.

"Only if you're having some. I'll get it ready if you'd like," Nancy replied in a timid voice, as she scanned the office for the boiling teapot.

"Oh no. You just start making yourself comfortable and settle in. We'll have tea and I'll explain how everything works and what you'll be doing. After that, you may want to start typing some letters that I need to send out. OK?"

"Sure," Nancy responded in a shy but eager-to-please tone.

Something told Andrie that, given the chance, Nancy Hogan could become a very capable assistant.

"How do you like your tea?" she called out to Nancy, as she filled two unmatched china cups.

"Just a little milk, if you have it. . . . Otherwise, it's fine plain."

"It's OK. We've got ·plenty of milk . . . Blue wouldn't have it any other way," Andrie laughed, as Blue began to meow upon hearing the squeaking sound of the refrigerator door opening as Andrie removed the container of milk.

"I hope you like Darjeeling; it's all I have today," Andrie said, as she set the two cups and a plate of shortbread cookies on the small round table in the back of the office.

"That's fine. Is there anything that you'd like me to do?" Nancy asked, walking toward the table.

"Not right now. Let's just have some tea and get to know each other a little. If that's OK with you."

"OK," Nancy replied, sitting down across from Andrie.

"Well, we already know a little about each other from Women's Way. I know that you're from Ohio originally, right?" Andrie said.

"Yes. I came out here with my husband, Matt, about four years ago. We started out in Ohio, but then we moved to Seattle because he heard that it was the place to be for musicians. He's a drummer and he sings. After a few months, he decided that Seattle was too *alternative* for him and his chances were better in New York, so that's why we came here. But ever since we arrived, nothing seemed to go right for him. He couldn't find a steady day job and he never got called back from any of the bands he auditioned for. That's when things got bad. I guess he always had a mean temper, but as the situation got worse, he got even meaner. He started drinking and then taking drugs. If I even suggested that we should go back home, he'd start punching me and kicking me. I ended up in the emergency room twice. That's where I found out about Women's Way. It got to the point that I knew I had to leave, if I didn't want him to kill me. So, I was lucky that I could go there to get away from him. We're all supposed to clear out of the Women's Way building by Thursday. I'll be staying with a friend in Queens until I can afford an apartment myself. Which reminds me . . . I know I thanked you on the phone, but I really want to tell you in person how grateful I am for this chance."

"I really needed some help here and you seemed like just the right person for the job . . . so, thank you, too. I guess this is where I should tell you a little about myself. I used to run this same type of business, up until about seven years ago, but I gave it up to work for Ann Capwell, the congresswoman. I don't know if you read the papers . . ."

"I did read them and I want to tell you how awful I feel about what's happened. I think people's private lives should be respected and it plain irks me when I see what some of these reporters can do to a person's life. I never met Ms. Capwell, but I know that she started Women's Way. . . . So, as far as I'm concerned, she helped save my life and so did you, and it don't make a stitch of difference to me if you're gay or straight . . . and I'm sure that any decent human being walking this earth would agree with me."

Nancy's sincerity touched Andrie. Talking with her convinced Andrie that she had made an excellent decision in hiring Nancy. Andrie could see a very basic strength and integrity in this somewhat timid, yet open, woman, and Nancy saw kindness and compassion in Andrie. Eventually they began the day's work. Nancy caught on quickly to her duties. By the end of her first week, she had proven herself to be an indispensable asset to Andrie's business and was becoming a good friend as well.

Chapter Twenty-Four

Bee sat at the side of the pool, bathing in the warm sun as she waited for Nicole to return from the hairdresser. This was the first time she was alone in her new home. Nicole had fallen in love with both the forty-year-old Italian villa-style home in the Hollywood Hills, and Bee, about the same time.

As Bee had thought, the Malibu beach house she had been renting was too small for Nicole's tastes. It wasn't long before Nicole had her meeting with realtors to sell her New York apartment and find something in Los Angeles.

For the first time since she had inherited her substantial fortune, Bee felt that she was enjoying her money. To add to that, the movie rights to two of her books had been purchased by a major studio, and Nicole was her lover. There was one word that came into her mind as she thought about her life now . . . contentment. She was totally and unbelievably content. She wasn't alone anymore. She was living with Nicole Bonham, the kind of woman she never thought she was capable of attracting.

She had never intended for Robert Capwell to drop dead under the stress of his daughter being outed. And, although it seemed like poetic justice because of what he had done to her father, the outcome provided her surprisingly little comfort. Even the fact that Ann seemed to be winning the battle to save her career was not something Bee cared to dwell on. Something had been changing inside of her ever since she and Nicole had become lovers. The pain and loneliness which she had felt yet failed to acknowledge was fading and along with it the vengeance which had plagued her since her father's death.

Hearing a car pull up to the back of the house, Bee sat up in the lounge chair. Seconds later, she saw Nicole walking toward her, wearing a soft white sundress.

Without taking her eyes off Bee, Nicole began slowly slipping out of it as she came closer.

Bee smiled a broad contented smile.

*   *   *

For Andrie, each day of living with Ann was more difficult than the last. Since the death of her father, the manipulative congresswoman had grown more devious and power-hungry than ever. Andrie had resigned herself to the fact that if Lilly's prediction had indeed come to pass, then Robert Capwell had chosen not to learn the life lesson of which she spoke.

Sitting in the living room and listening as Ann chattered on about how Hal Gottfried was managing her political resurrection, Andrie could only conclude that the dying Capwell imparted no great message of moral or ethical value to his daughter before his death.

"I haven't had a chance to tell you, but for the last six weeks or so, Hal's been arranging a big-name fundraiser to kick-start the Haven Program. He thinks that Haven should help dispel any of the questions that come up about me not doing all I could to stop the Women's Way project from closing down. . . . And since Haven's going to be a privately-funded grant program, it will have the same appeal as the Women's Way project. But Haven will award money to several different, high-profile community programs. So, since I'm chairperson for Haven, I'll be getting some great press locally. Meanwhile, I'm gaining new pockets of support in the district everyday. It looks like Hal was really able to turn things around. . . . Although I don't think it would have been possible without my father's help, he knew whose buttons to push to get the support we needed. So it looks like we should be coming out on top in November," Ann boasted, appearing oblivious to the disgust on Andrie's face.

"Do me a favor, never include *me* when you say the word *we*," Andrie told her, as she watched Ann mixing herself a vodka martini.

"Well, as distasteful as the thought may be to you, we are a *we*, until I no longer need us to be," Ann answered, as she approached Andrie and put her hand on her shoulder.

"It's well beyond distasteful, it's actually quite revolting," Andrie responded, as she recoiled from Ann's touch. Then, standing up, she continued. "You know, this is all my fault. I realize that now. We wouldn't be living this lie right now if I had been honest with myself seven years ago. I wanted someone that fit a bunch of screwed-up criteria I laid out . . . well-educated, good job, fine tastes . . . someone who I thought would make me feel secure. Someone stable and serious about life. You seemed to fit the bill, so I thought that you were the right one for me. I guess, in a way, I convinced myself that I loved you. I thought love could happen that way. I spent seven years making excuses for you and hoping that you would change. I made excuses for why you didn't want to live with me, for why we never went away together, for why you never accepted my family. Now that I know what love is, I can't believe how I could have fooled myself for so many years. So you see, in a way it's my own fault that I'm living in this hell now," Andrie said, hoping that Ann was able to feel loathing in her words.

"So living in a million-dollar Upper East Side penthouse is your definition of hell, hmm?" Ann asked, as she slowly swirled her drink around in its glass.

"If I'm living in it with you, yes," Andrie nodded.

"It wouldn't be nearly so hellish if it was Destiny here, instead of me. But since that will never be the case, I suggest that you become a bit more adaptable to your circumstances. Lately, I've been considering the idea of forgiving you your indiscretion and perhaps continuing our relationship. But, even if I decide against that, and don't want you around anymore, I'd still consider it a breach of our agreement if you try to start up with her again. . . . And I still hold the controlling interest in Cobra. Do you understand what I'm saying?"

"This is so sick. Why would you even care at that point? . . . I don't even understand why you would care now. You don't love me, so why not just let me go, so you can find someone else?" There was an innocence to Andrie's question that caused Ann to give a twisted smirk.

"Have you ever seen me lose at anything . . . a game . . . an election . . . anything? I don't lose . . . not even people. My father taught me that. He always said, *Do whatever it takes to win, always and in everything.* In fact those were also his last words to me."

"Somehow that doesn't surprise me. I understand now. You had no choice but to grow up a complete sociopath. . . . You're insane." With that Andrie turned to leave the room.

"The party for the Haven program is next week. We'll be attending it together and it's formal," Ann called out, causing Andrie to stop.

"In that case, you should get yourself a chiffon straightjacket," Andrie responded as she left the room.

Chapter Twenty-Five

The next morning, Andrie arrived at the office late. It had been one of those nights that sleep refused her its refuge. Nancy, who had been at her desk since about eight-thirty that morning, noticed the dark circles under her eyes as Andrie walked past her, trying to avoid a conversation.

"You look like hell. Are you feeling OK?" Nancy asked.

Andrie wanted to scream the truth . . . that she wasn't OK and that she had been living in hell since December. But instead she smiled and said, "Yes I'm fine. I just had a lot on my mind last night and I didn't get much sleep. I'll be fine after a caffeine fix." She began to sort out the papers on her desk. Andrie had resigned herself to the fact that she would have to keep her pain to herself for now and get on with her life as best she could.

"OK, I think that this is a coffee morning for you, so give me a few extra minutes," Nancy called out as she pulled the glass pot from the coffeemaker and began to rinse it out.

"As long as it's hot and full of caffeine, I don't care," Andrie called back as she searched the pile of papers on her desk. Then after a brief silence she again called out, "Nan, have you seen the proposal for Rae-Dee discount stores? I need to copy it and send out the original to Bill Rae. I should have done that yesterday."

"Relax. I dropped them off myself the day before yesterday. Mr. Rae seemed like the anxious type so I didn't think that we should keep him waiting. . . . In fact, I have some news that may help you get through the morning. His secretary called a little before nine this morning and said that he loved your ideas and he was agreeable to the costs. They want us to send over a contract as soon as possible," Nancy announced, as she turned to answer a phone that just started to ring.

"Thanks, Nan. I don't know what I'd do without you," Andrie

called out, thinking to herself how much she appreciated Nancy's ability to handle clients and assess their personalities so well. Andrie had come to depend heavily on her new assistant as the business grew. Nancy had even found an apartment that was walking distance from the office, just to make sure that she could always be close by if needed.

There was an open, friendly warmth to Nancy Hogan. It was a quality that Andrie's brother, Nick, had remarked about when he had stopped over to see the office recently. He and Nancy hit it off so well that day that Andrie had begun to hope that they might start seeing each other socially. At Andrie's request, Nick had even gone over to Nancy's apartment once, to hang a small oak shelf Nancy had bought to display a series of collector plates she had.

It was difficult for Andrie to believe that this was the same timid, shy person she had first met at Women's Way. She remembered the relationship Nancy had left and how the abuse robbed her of her self-esteem. It bewildered her to think that there were people who could, without regard, destroy the mind and body of the person they claimed to love. That thought made Andrie wish that someday the Women's Way program could be revived.

Nancy had just hung up the phone and the coffee was ready. Within a few moments both women were seated with cups of the stimulating hot brew in front of them. They began to talk about what was scheduled for that day and soon enough the conversation had turned to some other small talk. But throughout both conversations Andrie noticed that Nancy suddenly appeared nervous and preoccupied. The change seemed to occur after she had hung up the phone.

"Is everything OK? Did a client give you a hard time on the phone, just now?" Andrie inquired.

"No. Everything here is fine," Nancy replied, still visibly upset by the phone call.

"I'm not trying to push or be nosy, but I want you to know that I'm here if you want to talk," Andrie said, looking straight into

Nancy's eyes. She didn't want to pry. She knew how it felt to have that done to her.

"It's Matt. That was him on the phone. He found out from a friend that I was working here. He wants to meet me. I told him no at first, but then he started crying. He begged me. He said he was sorry and that he just needed to talk to me. I couldn't just tell him no. I'm meeting him tonight after work. We're going to dinner." Nancy seemed ashamed, even apologetic, about agreeing to meet Matt.

"Do you really want to meet him?" Andrie asked, blowing lightly on her coffee to cool it down.

"I don't know. I'm getting along OK and I'm starting to make a new life for myself, but as sick as it sounds, there's a part of me that misses him. It wasn't always bad. We did have some good times. There were times when Matt did very sweet things for me. He'd buy me flowers for no reason, and all kinds of things like that. Please Andrie, don't be angry with me for this. It's just something I have to do."

"Nan, you know me better than that by now. I'm not angry and I understand what you're telling me. It's just that I'm worried about you. You did leave Matt because you feared for your life."

"I'm meeting him in a public place, for dinner. After that we go our separate ways. He won't have an opportunity to get crazy, even if I say something he doesn't like. I have to deal with this like an adult. I shouldn't have to hide from him," Nancy said, sounding as though she were trying to convince herself that this was the best thing to do.

"I don't think that it has anything at all to do with being an adult. The fact is, he's a danger to you. Look, I know that it's none of my business, but I wish that you wouldn't go. You're doing so well now. I'm just worried about what could happen if you meet with him." Andrie's concern for her friend had overshadowed her own problems for the moment. She had a bad feeling about what would come from this meeting, but Nancy could not be dissuaded.

Chapter Twenty-Six

A warm breeze glided over Destiny's skin, as she lay sleeping on a lounge chair by her pool. She hardly stirred as it caused strands of her light brown hair to dance around, tickling her face. She was thoroughly exhausted from six weeks of touring and talk shows to push *Brownstone Blue.* Her efforts were paying off well. The title track off the album was in its fourth week at number one and CD sales were going through the roof. Nevertheless, Destiny felt empty. She wasn't enjoying the things that her hard work and talent brought her. Without Andrie nothing had the same meaning. Maggie had finally convinced her to begin going out again with her friends and attending parties once more. She had told Destiny that isolating herself wouldn't bring Andrie back into her life and could be potentially damaging to her career. Maggie's argument was valid and Destiny knew that, but it didn't make socializing any easier.

Being Destiny Anderson meant being the object of many women's desires. There was hardly a party she attended where someone didn't try to seduce her. Politely smiling and declining advances was becoming tiresome. There were times Destiny wanted to scream and run away, but she managed to remain cool and keep her distance in a pleasant, acceptable manner.

Since Maggie saw how devastated she was over what had happened with Andrie, she did her best to keep Destiny's spirits up. Most of the time that was an impossible task. The only time she seemed really alive was when she was performing. Knowing that, Maggie had proposed a fourteen-state tour that would start the last week in August. The performance halls were smaller than the ones to which Destiny had become accustomed, but this tour was a rather spontaneous idea and there wasn't enough lead time to get booked into most of the larger venues. Maggie thought the more intimate settings would also mean less pressure.

Sitting up, Destiny reached for the bottle of mineral water on the table beside her. She wondered if this tour would really be the therapy she needed. Just then the phone rang. "Hello."

"I'm sorry, Des. Were you sleeping?" the voice on the phone asked.

"Maggie?"

"Of course, who else has such shitty timing?" Maggie replied, believing that she did indeed wake Destiny.

"It's OK. I really wasn't asleep. I was just lying by the pool relaxing. So what's up?"

"I got an interesting call this morning, so I thought that you would want to hear about it as soon as possible."

"What is it?" Destiny inquired with casual interest as she stretched to wake herself fully.

"You were invited to a fundraiser being organized by none other than Ann Capwell."

"What? Are you joking?" Destiny asked, pulling herself up from the lounge chair.

"I'm dead serious. You see, she's involved in something called Haven or the Haven project . . . or something like that. It actually seems like a very good cause. Anyway, this morning I got a call from Stuart Sottley's office at Cobra. So I'm thinking that the call has something to do with the tour. Instead, it's Sottley's assistant telling me about this fundraiser that Ann Capwell's throwing in New York. I can't remember the exact date now . . . it's next month, July seventeenth, I think. . . . Anyway, she strongly suggested that you attend and I really mean strongly. I have to tell you that I don't like this Sottley jerk at all. He thinks that he owns everyone that's signed to his label. He knows nothing about the industry, and he's probably going to run Cobra into the ground, given enough time."

"I know. Harry's worried about that too. So tell me about the phone call," Destiny urged Maggie.

Without hesitation, Maggie continued. "Well, I got the distinct impression that this shindig is a big thing for Ann Capwell and I thought that if she's gonna be there, so will Andrie. . . . Who knows, maybe if she sees you and that dried-up, crow-faced Capwell hypocrite in the same room at the same time, she might wake up and realize what she's missing." Maggie saw through the new Ann Capwell image. She knew that her political rebirth was the machination of a very competent spin doctor.

Destiny placed the bottle of mineral water down as she took a few moments to assimilate the information. There was no doubt in her mind that she would attend the event, if it meant she might see Andrie.

"So, are you going?" Maggie asked

"You know that I want to see Andrie. But, I wonder why Ann Capwell would want to invite me to anything, considering the fact that she probably knows about me and Andrie."

"Look, she's a politician. If she thinks using your presence will get her more publicity for something that she's involved in, then she'll use you. Or, maybe she figures that showing that she's friendly toward you, would dispel any of the lingering rumors that Andrie had an affair with you last December. She has a reputation for using people. . . . But that's immaterial. If going to this means that you'll get a chance to see Andrie and talk to her again, what do you have to lose. . . . Besides, until I get a feel for this Sottley creep and what's going on at Cobra, I don't think we should rock his boat," Maggie reasoned.

"I don't give a damn about Sottley . . . but the idea of seeing Andrie again . . . tell them that I'll be there." Saying that, Destiny ended the conversation. Then, walking over to the pool, she stared into the crystal clear water as if she were trying to see what the future held for her. Her thoughts were only of Andrie and they sparked a fire that fled through her veins, finding its way throughout her body. Then, as if to assuage that heat, she tossed herself into the cool calm of the pool.

Chapter Twenty-Seven

The River Club sat at the edge of the East River and from its deck, the evening view of the river added to the magic of the city. Inside, the buzzing of conversation and the chime-like clinking of glasses being filled with champagne provided the festive atmosphere for which Ann had hoped. She sauntered about, making well-calculated small talk with the guests. She was an expert at working the crowd. Her graceful manner and polish had always allowed her to push all the right buttons on people in a most inconspicuous way. It was a talent that served her well in her political life, especially these last few months. Circulating through the enormous room, she subtly searched for any sign of Destiny's arrival.

"Her manager did say that she was coming?" she muttered in a hushed tone to Stuart, who tilted his head sideways in an effort to hear her better.

"Yes. I had my secretary reserve her a suite at the Plaza. She checked in a couple of hours ago. She'll be here," he assured her, then inquired as to why it was so important to her to have Destiny attend this event.

"A number of reasons," Ann replied, and began to explain as they strolled around the room. "It will suggest that she is a friend of both Andrie and myself. That should help our image as a happy faithful couple. . . . I have a more personal reason as well. I think that if I handle things just right, it might make Andrie begin to see that I'm all she really has."

"Are you telling me that you're in love with her after all that's happened?" Stuart asked incredulously.

"I'm saying that I want her. I don't know for how long, but I do want her for now. . . . And when it's over, I'll be the one to end it. I try not to employ the use of expletives if I can avoid it, but if it helps you understand, let me put it this way: I want to fuck her, in *every* way that I can," Ann whispered to him, as she flashed a chilling grin.

"I still don't see how throwing them together like this is going to accomplish that," Stuart replied, still puzzled by her tactics.

"I want that ill-bred, vulgar, Kentucky hillbilly to see that I've won. I want her to see Andrie and me as a happy couple. I want to enjoy the look on her face, as I touch my lover in front of her. After that, I'm sure Andrie will be out of her system. . . . And I think that it will help Andrie realize that her only future is with me," she explained with malicious glee that would have appalled anyone except Stuart Sottley. He had been an informal protégé of Robert Capwell's for years, and therefore quite willing to accept cruelty as a method by which to accomplish one's goals.

From across the room Andrie was observing the congresswoman and Sottley as they continued to talk. Watching them, she got the distinct feeling that she was the topic of conversation. Just the idea of them discussing her in any way gave Andrie a cold sinking feeling in the pit of her stomach.

Lately, Ann had been demanding more and more of her time, insisting that they attend functions together. As far as Andrie knew, tonight was no different. She had no idea that Destiny had been invited.

Realizing that Ann had finished talking with Stuart and was headed her way, Andrie began to feel even more uneasy. There was something about the way Ann was smiling at her that was alarming. She had seen that smile in the past . . . just before the congresswoman was about to destroy a political opponent.

"I noticed you watching Stuart and me, while we were talking. . . . You really should try to conceal your feelings a little better. I could read your face from across the room. I know that you don't want to be here, but this is one of the necessary evils you'll have to endure as long as you remain my loving partner," Ann said, through a clenched grin.

"'Even in jest, that thought sickens me," Andrie replied with disgust.

"I'm not jesting . . . you really *are* my partner, so you really shouldn't act so resentful toward me. You know, I still care for you . . . on some level," Ann said, smirking as she took a glass of champagne from a passing tray. "All I've done was prevent you from wasting your life with a woman . . . and I use that term loosely . . . who would *eventually* ruin your life. Yet, you act like I've murdered someone."

"You're killing me . . . a little bit at a time. . . . Every hour. Every day. As far as I'm concerned, that is murder," Andrie said, looking Ann dead in the eye.

"You've always had such a flair for the dramatic. That's what I miss most about you writing my speeches. I think they lack that quality now," Ann replied dryly.

Andrie was unable to endure another second alone with her. "Look, you wanted me to be here, to play the part of your loving partner. Now, let me start mixing with the guests, so they could see how happy I am to be here with you," she replied sarcastically as she started to turn away.

"Why don't you begin over there," Ann said, nodding toward a group of guests who had congregated around one of the entrances to the large room. Andrie craned her neck and peered into the heart of the crowd to see what Ann was referring to. There, in the center, dressed in a black leather jacket and blue jeans, stood Destiny, who had obviously just arrived.

Because of a column that stood between them Andrie was able to remain out of her sight.

"How could you do this? . . . Why?" she demanded, her eyes fixed intently on Ann.

Ann's self-satisfaction was obvious as she responded to the question. "It's so important to get celebrities to attend these things. They seem to make people more generous and they attract more press about the event. That's why Stuart invited your little friend to come to New York and be here tonight. . . . Of course she agreed. Apparently, either she, or her agent, or both of them, know how important Stuart Sottley is in her life, especially if she wants her career to keep going the way it is. . . . Besides, I thought that it would be good for you to see that I truly do pull the strings that control Destiny Anderson's future." Saying that, Ann raised both her eyebrows and widened her eyes with a cold arrogance that made it nearly impossible for Andrie to control the hatred she felt inside. At that moment, only fear of Ann's subsequent anger being aimed at Destiny kept Andrie from physically attacking her.

"As repulsive as the situation is to me, I'm living with you. I've told Destiny that I didn't want to see her again and I'm telling the world every lie you and Hal Gottfried concoct. . . . What the hell else do you want from me . . . or from her?" Andrie seethed with animosity.

"Look over there," Ann told her as she pointed to Destiny. "She's gone on with her life. Her career is important enough to her that, when Stuart asked her to attend, she said yes . . . and here she is. She was told that I was putting this party together, so she had to expect that you would be here too . . . I would think that if she had any lingering feelings for you, it would have been far too painful for her to chance seeing you here with me, your lover. . . . But take a look, she seems very comfortable."

Andrie's attention was divided between looking at Destiny and listening to Ann's venomous rhetoric. Her eyes absorbed Destiny into them, having starved for the sight of her for so long. Time had only served to make her love for Destiny stronger. She knew now that Ann intended to torment Destiny with this meeting. Andrie could only prevent that by leaving.

"That's it. I've really had enough for one evening. I've made my appearance here, so my work is done for tonight. I'm leaving," Andrie announced and began to turn away again, but Ann stopped her before she could take a step.

"You're not going anywhere yet. You'll leave when I think it's appropriate and that may mean leaving with me at the end of the evening. So for now, I suggest that we greet Destiny together, as a couple."

That was something Andrie couldn't do. She froze inside. She knew how painful that would be to Destiny.

Just then, Ray Dalton rushed over and informed Ann of an urgent call from Washington. Before leaving with him, she warned Andrie, "If you're thinking of leaving while I'm gone, consider this. . . . Would you rather that I ruined Destiny's evening, or her career?"

Andrie didn't answer. As soon as Ann had gone, she walked out onto the restaurant's sweeping deck. It was relatively uninhabited, since guests were still arriving and greeting each other inside. The sun had just set, leaving the sky with a quickly fading crimson hue. She walked to the far corner and stared down into the water. Watching the shimmering reflection of the lights on the river's edge, she fell deeper and deeper into thought, becoming mesmerized by the water's glow. Somehow there was a feeling of temporary comfort there on the empty deck, away from the crowd. It would be so easy, she thought to herself, to remain there the rest of the night watching the lazy current travel by below her. Just as she finished that thought a feeling came over her, and suddenly drew her back from the hypnotic influence of the river. Andrie knew instantly that she wasn't alone; she felt familiar eyes on her. Without turning to look, she knew that Destiny had found her.

"Why are you here?" she asked, as she continued to stare at the river below. There was no need to confirm with her eyes what she knew in her heart.

A brief silence followed her question. Then the voice she had expected, answered her.

"I was invited."

Andrie turned to see Destiny standing near. Her dark eyes were still as piercing and passionate as ever, and abundant waves of her chestnut hair were being tossed by the breeze that cooled the river's edge. For a few moments, they simply gazed at each other. Then Destiny once again broke the silence.

"How have you been?"

"Fine . . . and you?" Andrie responded, trying her best to conceal her emotions.

"You look . . . that dress is . . . beautiful." Destiny was overcome by the sight of the woman who occupied her mind every minute of every day and who was now standing there before her. She had rehearsed what she would say if they saw each other, but all those words were lost, as Andrie stood there bathed in the soft light of that red evening sky.

"It's good seeing you again," Destiny said, as she summoned up every ounce of self-restraint she had to keep from taking Andrie in her arms and kissing her over and over without stopping.

"It's good seeing you, too," Andrie replied, smiling again, as she prayed for the strength to resist her needs. Then, looking at Destiny, who had momentarily gazed out onto the river, she asked, "Why did you come here, really?"

"Why do you think I came here? It was the only way I knew that I could see you face to face again. Do you think that I could go on, like nothin' ever passed between us?" Sparks flew from Destiny's eyes, as she turned to Andrie. ". . . You said that you loved me and that you wanted us to be together, forever. Then, before I knew what hit me, you say that you're still in love with Ann. It's like history repeating itself from fifteen years ago. You lure me in and make yourself my whole world and then you decide that I'm not right for you. How could you be so cruel to someone that loves you the way I do?" Destiny's voice weakened and began to crack. She turned again toward the river, which was growing black as dusk was becoming night around them.

Andrie was afraid to answer. If she spoke now, she wouldn't be able to hold in her tears. Instinctively, she put her hand on Destiny's shoulder.

Destiny's head turned sharply and her dark eyes fixed on Andrie with a look that seemed as though it could melt steel. Filled with anger, love, and pain, they pierced Andrie to the soul. They compelled her. It was impossible for her to look away. She knew that their stare could eventually break through the barriers she had set up to protect Destiny.

The swarthy red sky was growing darker as they stood silhouetted on the deck. With Andrie's hand remaining on her shoulder, Destiny's expression slowly began to soften. Her eyes swelled with tears as she tilted her head to one side, touching Andrie's hand with her cheek. "I love you. I'll never stop loving you . . . and I know you still love me. I can feel it." Destiny's voice was now soft and low. As her cheek remained on Andrie's hand, the warm breath of her words traveled along Andrie's fingers, sending a tingling sensation up her arm and into her head, where it had an intoxicating effect.

"No. I can't let you do this." Andrie's words, which were more of a warning to herself than to Destiny, rushed from her mouth as she pulled her hand from Destiny's shoulder. Stunned by the sudden retreat, Destiny straightened up and took a step toward Andrie, who was now breathing heavily with a combination of anxiety and desire.

"Why? Why are you doing this to us?" Destiny demanded to know, in a hushed but angry tone.

Before Andrie could answer her, a third person walked out onto the deck. Tall, thin, gracefully draped in a gray silk evening dress, she walked directly toward them. It was Ann, smiling widely as she observed before her the painful scenario which she had orchestrated. Coming upon them, she slid her left arm around Andrie's shoulder and extended her right hand to greet Destiny, who stood frozen and without response, until Ann was forced to drop her hand back to her side.

"I'm so glad you were able to come here tonight. Andrie and I were concerned about how you might feel seeing us together like this, but then we felt that enough time has passed and your presence would really be helping out a very worthy cause," she said, grinning at Destiny.

Destiny looked on in pain and disbelief at the sight of Ann with her arm around Andrie. At that moment, Andrie saw her own agony reflected in Destiny's face.

"It's so nice to know how concerned you both were," Destiny responded, glaring angrily into Andrie's eyes. Then, turning back to Ann, she continued, "I'll be leaving now. I gave a check to Stuart when I came in, so I don't think I need to stay any longer." With that Destiny flashed a last bitter look at Andrie, and walked away.

Andrie immediately pulled away from Ann, who was still grinning with satisfaction at what she perceived to be a victory.

"Why was this necessary? What sick satisfaction do you get from manipulating people's lives like this?" Andrie demanded to know.

"I'm just keeping a tight rein on everything that affects my life. You happen to be part of that . . . and you've involved Destiny Anderson in it as well." She continued to talk as she guided Andrie to the opposite side of the deck, which overlooked the semicircular driveway in front of the restaurant. "I'm just keeping everything under control. You see, eventually Destiny will have someone new in her life and you'll be nothing more than an uncomfortable memory for her. Maybe then, you'll realize where you belong."

As always, Ann's timing was impeccable. As they reached the end of the deck, Andrie looked down to see Destiny getting into the back of a dark gray limousine, which promptly exited onto the service road and quickly disappeared. Andrie's heart sank as she looked on, certain that she had now pushed Destiny beyond the limit of pain that any love could tolerate.

Chapter Twenty-Eight

Nancy looked up to see Andrie pushing open the door of the storefront office with a worn look and downcast eyes. "You don't look good," she observed, in a sympathetic voice.

"I didn't have a very good weekend," Andrie replied, with the memory of Destiny's anguished expression still fresh in her mind.

"Well, maybe this will make you feel better," Nancy said, waving a small blue and white telephone message sheet under Andrie's nose. Andrie ignored the gesture as she put her briefcase on her desk and walked over to the teapot.

"Aren't you even curious?" Nancy prodded in a perky voice.

"I'm sorry. Of course. Tell me about it. I could use some good news," Andrie said, as she blew into the mug of tea she was holding.

"Well, Rae-Dee Discount stores loved the ad campaign you did for them and Mr. Rae apparently talked you up so much that his brother-in-law wants you to do his advertising, too."

"That's nice," Andrie replied, still unsure of the reason for Nancy's enthusiasm.

"Well, don't you want to know who his brother-in-law is?" Nancy chirped excitedly.

"Who?" Andrie's tone remained flat as she sipped the hot tea.

"Rennietti auto dealerships. He owns thirty-seven car dealerships, up and down the East Coast. We're talking big-time here," Nancy said, trying to stir some excitement in Andrie.

Andrie nodded her head. "Oh."

"Oh? Is that it? Oh?" Nancy mimicked in bewilderment.

"No. That's great. I know," Andrie added, with a forced, yet still weak, enthusiasm.

"OK. That's enough," Nancy said, grabbing the mug out of Andrie's hand and plunking it down on the table behind them.

"Tell me what's going on. I had a funny feeling that something was wrong with you last week, but I didn't want to pry. I can see now that whatever it is got worse since then. I don't know if I can help, but sometimes just talking about things to somebody can make you feel a little better. Whatever this problem is, have you talked to David or your brother Nick about it?"

"No."

"OK. Then I'm gonna give you a choice. You either call one of them right now and let them help you with this or you use my shoulder. It's up to you, so make up your mind."

Nancy was right. Andrie had contemplated the idea of confiding in her before. As Nancy stood before her, awaiting an answer, Andrie made her decision.

"All right. I'll tell you what's wrong, but you have to swear to me that you'll never mention any part of this to anyone. Not even David. . . . Swear to me."

The worried expression on Nancy's face became even more pronounced, as she swore to Andrie in a solemn voice, then walked over to her desk and switched on the answering machine so they wouldn't be disturbed.

"We'd better sit down," Andrie said softly, as she pulled a chair out from the table and began her story. She took Nancy back in time to when she first met Destiny. Nancy sat opposite Andrie, listening intently, and occasionally reaching across and placing her hand on Andrie's, as though she could, in some way, share the burden of pain that her friend was suffering.

Nothing would ever be quite the same between them, after this. The special bond women know when they share a friend's deepest secrets and fears was formed between them. It was a platonic commitment of emotion, almost as nurturing and protective as a mother's love.

*   *   *

The blazing August sun flooded the sparsely decorated living room, as Destiny sunk into the massive leather sofa and put her feet up on the sturdy glass and pewter coffee table in front of her. It had been three months since that night at the River Club, but the picture of Andrie standing there with Ann's arm around her remained in her mind. She could do nothing to erase it or dull the intensity of the pain it caused her. She reached for the cordless phone, which had been sticking out from between the sofa cushions since the last time she used it, and pushed the speed dial button for Maggie's office.

"Hello," Maggie's voice answered at the other end.

"Hi, it's me," Destiny responded.

"So how's everything going?" Maggie asked. She could tell that there was something on Destiny's mind by the sound of her voice.

Destiny had no good answer to Maggie's question, instead she told her why she called. "Mag, I need you to do me a favor. Can you get a realtor? I wanna sell this place. It's too damned big for a single person. It's startin' to bother me. I figured they can come in and see it while I'm on tour. I want somethin' smaller. I may not even want to own it . . . maybe I'll just rent some small house outside of LA." As Destiny spoke she stood up from the couch and began to pace the expanse of the immense living room like a caged jungle cat.

"You really need to get away, don't you?" Maggie asked, already knowing the answer.

"Let's just say I can't wait 'til next week, so I can start the tour," Destiny said, sliding open the huge French door and stepping out to the palm-tree-lined patio.

"By the way, I hired Tom Ganz to be your tour manager. Harry recommended him. He knows his stuff and he's been around for a while. He met with the band and the crew already. I wish that I could be with you when you start the tour . . . but from week two on, I'm all yours. I'll be flying out there to meet you. Tony will have to get along without me," Maggie said in an apologetic tone. Maggie's husband was Dr. Anthony Cerretti, a quiet, reserved obstetrician. He had delivered three of her children by prior marriages. And, together they had two more. He had injured himself a couple of days ago, when he playfully tried to carry Maggie into their bedroom. Now, he was scheduled for hernia reduction surgery the same week Destiny's tour was to begin.

"Don't worry about it. Stay with Tony as long as you need to. I'll be fine. Besides, the last time you came on tour with me, you had motion sickness the whole time. You're really not made for bus travel," Destiny told her as they both laughed, recalling the episode. Not unlike many other performers, Destiny and her band traveled in a specially customized bus when they were on tour. It was not one of Maggie's favorite modes of transportation.

After hanging up with Maggie, Destiny went back inside where she began to pack for the tour.

Chapter Twenty-Nine

"Is it money? Because if it is, maybe I can try to help you," Andrie offered in a loud voice, so she could be heard by Nancy who was in the next room changing into her shorts and sneakers. They had begun a regimen of brisk walking twice a week after work.

"It's not money. You just gave me a really good raise . . . and I have a great little apartment for a reasonable rent. So stop worrying," Nancy called back as she sat on the bed, tying the laces of her sneakers.

"Then what is it? Why do you want to start up with him again?" Andrie persisted in her questioning as she folded her arms and leaned back on the counter of Nancy's impeccably neat, but tiny kitchen.

Walking back into the room, Nancy stopped in her tracks and looked directly into Andrie's troubled face. She could see how concerned Andrie was about her safety. She knew that there would be no way to convince Andrie that having Matt move in with her was a good decision. She realized that it was time to tell Andrie about her reason for her decision. "I'm pregnant," she said as she reached for house keys, which sat on the counter next to where Andrie was standing.

Andrie grabbed the keys out of Nancy's hand and plunked them back on the counter, loudly. "What? . . . Did I hear you right?" she asked in disbelief.

"Right now, you remind me of my mother, with that disappointed, judgmental expression on your face," Nancy replied, momentarily regretting having told Andrie.

"I'm sorry . . . I don't mean to sound like I'm judging you, but come on now. . . . How am I supposed to react when you tell me that you're letting Matt move in with you and that you're pregnant

by him? This is all wrong. You know what he's like. I'm afraid for
you." Andrie's affect was indeed maternal.

"Matt's changed. He really has. When I agreed to start seeing
him as a friend, I told him that I was happy without him and that I
had no intention of getting back together, but as we saw more of
each other I realized that he really had changed. I also realized that
I still loved him. I know it sounds crazy, when you think of what
he's done to me in the past, but not all the time we had together
was bad. There were lots of happy times, too. Did I ever tell you
that we had always talked about having children? Back then, Matt
wasn't sure if he was ready. That's one of the changes he's made
. . . he really wants me to have this baby. . . . Please, Andrie, try
to be happy for me. I really believe that we have a chance this
time."

Andrie remained stone-faced as she listened to Nancy's argument. She knew that Nancy was making a mistake, perhaps a
life-threatening mistake, but she also knew that there was little she
could say without alienating Nancy at that point.

"I love you and I'll always be here for you no matter what, but I
think that you're making a dangerous move. That's all I can say. I
just can't say what you want me to." Even those words were
difficult for Andrie to get out.

"It's OK. I understand . . . I'm glad that you're not angry with
me. I really need you as my friend," Nancy said, hugging Andrie
and picking up her keys at the same time. Andrie was uneasy. She
felt that Nancy was heading for disaster and she had no way to
stop her.

"So how far along are you?" Andrie asked, trying hard not to
sound as alarmed as she felt inside.

"About six weeks. I took one of those home tests when I missed
my period. It came out positive, so I went to my gynecologist and
he confirmed it. I've even started crocheting a baby blanket . . .
see," Nancy replied, cheerfully pointing to a small knitted square of
yellow wool on the living room couch.

Walking through the living room toward the door of the

apartment, Andrie noticed an ashtray with several cigarette butts in it. The sight was inconsistent with the unadulterated tidiness of the small apartment. Knowing that Nancy didn't smoke, Andrie asked, "What's with the dirty ashtray?"

"Oh, that's Matt. He's trying to quit, but it's hard for him right now," Nancy explained in a matter-of-fact tone.

As they left, Andrie felt a foreboding chill travel up her spine.

*   *   *

Ann remained on hold as Stuart Sottley's call was being put through to her private office phone. Tapping her well-manicured nails on top of the cluttered cherry wood desk, she waited impatiently.

"It's about time. . . . What is it? I'm up to my waist in committee work," she bristled as she heard Sottley's voice greet her on the other end of the line.

Hearing Ann's mood, he got right to the point. "I thought that you might be interested to know that Destiny Anderson is going to be in New York next week."

"Why? Why is she coming here? For what?" Ann responded nervously, as she straightened up in her high-backed chair, suddenly forgetting about the work in front of her.

"She's starting a concert tour. I just came from a meeting with Harry Stern. That's how I found out."

"Where will she be staying while she's in the city?" Ann asked, as her mind began to race.

"That's the funny thing. She won't be in the city at all. She's playing a lot of smaller concert halls in outlying areas. Stern told me that the whole thing was arranged at the last minute, so they only booked these small venues."

"Let me know if she has any plans of coming into the city. I want to know if she tries to see Andrie," Ann ordered.

"I have a copy of her touring schedule and from the look of it, I doubt that she'll have the time for that. Meanwhile, I met with Mr. Tamashi from Cortronics. He's already purchased two other

American record companies. So, I had a letter of intent drawn up, which states that once I have one hundred percent control of Cobra, I plan to sell it to Cortronics at no less than the price they offered at the meeting in May," Stuart informed her.

"Good," Ann said. Her tone had improved slightly.

"Listen, I don't know anything about running a record company. If you want to hold on to this after you get re-elected, you're going to need someone who knows the business, and I don't trust Stern. He still wants to buy back his company."

"Don't worry about him. He could never afford to buy it back. Before we know it, his two years will be up and I'll own all of Cobra. Just let him keep running things. He knows what he's doing and as long as Cobra keeps making money Cortronics will want to purchase it at a very nice profit to us," Ann advised him.

"I'll keep you posted on Destiny Anderson," Stuart promised dutifully before hanging up.

Chapter Thirty

At 2:30 on a Tuesday afternoon, the small corner cafe was almost empty. David sat at a sidewalk table and nursed a glass of Chablis as he waited for Andrie to join him for a late lunch. Looking up, he saw her heading across the street toward the restaurant. As she came closer, he found himself admiring the way she carried herself, as the afternoon sun shone down, making her auburn hair shimmer in its warm glow. Her outfit was simple, a white skirt and sleeveless blouse. Yet there was a casual sensuality about the way the fabric looked against her slightly tanned skin. In the past, David had always seen straight men turn their heads as Andrie walked by them. At that moment, he almost understood how they felt.

It was ironic and senseless to him that someone as vibrant and caring as Andrie would choose to give up a woman like Destiny and live with anyone as cold and self-absorbed as Ann. All these months, David had silently hoped that Andrie would eventually come to her senses. Despite his promise not to question or interfere with her decision to stay with Ann, he had seen very little of Andrie over the three months that had passed. Between her new business and the schedule of functions she needed to attend with Ann, she seemed to have almost no time to socialize. Those months were made harder on David, knowing how torn apart Destiny was by all that had happened.

As Andrie neared the table, he told himself that he would keep the conversation light and pleasant, for both their sakes.

"Sorry I'm late. I just couldn't get out of the office," she said, as she sat down across from David.

"It's OK. I only got here a few minutes ago myself," David said, as he flagged down a passing waiter so that Andrie could order a drink. After the waiter left, he tried to listen with his usual attentiveness as Andrie began to make small talk about how hectic her day had been, but he couldn't stop himself from wondering what had been going on inside her these past months. Andrie's voice seemed to fade off into the distance, as the questions in his head became more pronounced. Finally, in an effort to satisfy just a bit of the curiosity that preoccupied him, David interrupted her with an ostensibly innocent question: "So how are things with Ann these days?" he asked.

The abrupt shift in conversation took Andrie by surprise, but she knew David well enough to know where he was headed. "She's doing well with the campaign. She's established a new constituency and somehow, with Hal Gottfried's help, she's even managed to keep a portion of her old supporters too. It's actually pretty amazing, when you consider that newspaper article appeared only eight months ago."

David could see beyond the counterfeit cheerfulness of Andrie's reply.

"Was it only eight months? It seems so much longer," he remarked, attempting to appear as casual as possible.

"It's the end of August now and that was the end of November." As she recalled the months that had gone by, the expression on Andrie's face changed so slightly that only someone who knew her as well as David did could detect it. Seeing it, he knew instantly that Destiny had come into her mind.

He couldn't resist seizing the moment and bringing up Destiny's name. "How time flies. Destiny's supposed to be coming to New York the first week of September. I didn't realize how soon that was coming up . . . it's next week. I told her that I'd hook up with her while she's here," he said, then paused to give Andrie an opportunity to respond.

She glanced up at the waiter as he placed the glass of chilled white wine and the menus on the table before disappearing back into the restaurant. That interruption had afforded Andrie the time to formulate a response that would allow her to appear only marginally interested.

"Didn't she just finish a tour?" she asked, as she put the glass of wine to her lips.

"Yes, I asked her about that when I talked with her a couple of weeks ago. She said that she wants to get back on the road right now to clear her mind. She just doesn't feel like staying in one place right now."

Andrie knew she was the reason for the way Destiny felt. It was clear to her that David knew that too. When she thought about what Destiny was going through, she wished that she could somehow hold her and comfort her even for just a moment. She had to change the conversation before David began his line of questioning.

"I have to tell you something. Nancy is letting Matt move in with her," Andrie said somberly.

"What? You mean the guy who abused her? Why?" David's voice now elevated in pitch as he switched the focus of his thoughts to Nancy.

Andrie's idea worked, at least for the moment . . . but she wasn't just using the news about Nancy to change the topic off of herself. She was truly upset and confused by Nancy's decision to have Matt move in with her. She desperately wanted to help Nancy see the mistake that she was making. She thought to herself that discussing the situation with David might ease some of the tension it was causing her.

"She feels that it's the right thing for her to do now . . . since she's pregnant," Andrie explained.

"Oh my God. Is she sure?" David asked, running his hand back over his head.

"Yes. She's always wanted to have a child, so she's thrilled about it."

"Well, if she wants to have the baby, it doesn't mean that she needs him around. . . . Does it?" David asked, almost unsure of what the answer should be.

"Of course not, but we've discussed this over and over since she first told me about it and she feels that the baby needs its father."

"Even if the father is a lowlife son-of-a-bitch that beats women and takes drugs? . . . Is she serious?" David was clearly disturbed by the news. Although he had grown up without a father figure himself, he knew that there were some men who should never be allowed to influence their children's lives. Matt Hogan was definitely one of those men.

"I can't get through to her. She thinks that Matt's changed. He's convinced her that he's not taking drugs anymore and he promised that he'd never get violent with her again, but I don't trust him. Do you know what it's like for me to have to stand by and watch someone I care about ruin her life like this?" Andrie's question was rhetorical, but David couldn't let it go.

"Yes. I've been doing that with you." Suddenly the conversation halted as they stared into each other's faces, both unsure of what would happen next.

Andrie gradually straightened up in her chair and took a long deep breath. "Maybe if you had a life of your own, you'd stop trying to live mine," she said, as she took the napkin off her lap and placed it on the table.

"I forgot what a bitch you can be at times. But now that the gloves are off, why don't you let me in on the reason you're destroying yourself and Destiny?"

"Months ago you made a promise to me that you wouldn't pry away at me about this, but you just couldn't stick to it, could you?" she whispered angrily, leaning across the table.

"Could you keep a promise like that if I were destroying my life?" he said, smiling back at her.

"I have to get back to the office," Andrie huffed, standing up and turning from the table.

"Whether you like it or not, I'm your friend and I'm always going to be here for you with the truth," he called out just loud enough for Andrie to hear as she walked away. Watching her disappear down the block, David shook his head in frustration as he poured the remaining wine from Andrie's glass into his own, and swiftly downed it in one swallow.

Chapter Thirty-One

It was well after midnight as the rain pounded on the roof of the motor coach that was carrying Destiny from state to state. She had flown out to the East Coast and met up with her band and the bus in Virginia, where she had started the tour three days before.

Lying on her bed in the back of the bus, she stared out the window as the stormy, black night swept by. She was on her way to New York, where she would do two concerts in auditoriums well north of the city. Over the past two days she had spent hours in the rain signing autographs and talking with the fans who gathered outside the concert halls after her performances.

In the darkness of the small mobile bedroom, she could see the signal bars go up on the cellular phone next to her. It had been over an hour since the signal was this strong. She had wanted to call David for a while and this seemed like the right time. She quickly punched in the numbers and waited for him to pick up.

"Hello," he answered. The sound of his voice made the dismal night less lonely for her.

"Hi. I'm on the road headed for New York," Destiny told him as she tucked the phone under her chin and changed from her blue jeans into a pair of black sweatpants.

"I can't wait to see you. I'll be heading upstate in the morning so I'll probably get to you by early afternoon, if you're free then." David's voice was filled with excitement. He was looking forward to seeing Destiny.

"Yeah. That should be fine. . . . So, anything new lately?" Destiny asked.

"Not much . . . I almost had lunch with Andrie the other day," he answered with a chuckle.

"Almost?"

"We were having a glass of wine and talking, then I asked her why she was ruining her life. So, she got pissed and stormed out of the restaurant," David explained.

"Some things never change. . . . Listen, we both know why I had to get on the road and do this tour . . . I couldn't stay home and think about her anymore. So let's talk about her as little as possible for now, OK?" The pain came through as Destiny spoke. David agreed and immediately changed the subject. "So the whole Destiny Anderson menagerie is on its way to New York."

"Actually, no. Right now its just me, my bus driver Pete, and Tom Ganz. He's the new road manager that Maggie hired. The equipment truck and crew are probably about an hour behind us and I'll bet everybody else is almost there already. Darlene, my bass guitarist, is driving up with her boyfriend. They wanted some alone time, so they rented a car. Frank, my drummer, is from New Jersey, so his brother drove down and met him and they planned to drive to New York together, since they haven't seen each other in a while. Then they convinced the rest of the guys to go with them, since I had stayed behind for a while to sign autographs and meet some of the people who waited around after the show. That took me over an hour, so they'll all be settled in and doin' their things by the time we get to the hotel. I like it quiet like this, though. It gives me time to breathe."

"So where are you right now?" David asked.

"That's a good question. Hold on and let me ask Pete." With that David could hear Destiny asking her driver about their location. He could also hear the tinny sound of Pete's answer coming through over the intercom at her bedside, informing Destiny that they were on the New Jersey Turnpike, just past Cherry Hill.

"Did ya hear that?" she asked David.

"Yes. It sounds like you have every comfort of home in that bus," David joked.

"Believe me, I'm not spoiling myself. It's just that I have to spend so much time in this damned tin can, that I had to try to make it as comfortable as I could. It's my home for . . ."

Suddenly, David heard Destiny scream, with the loud noise of shattering glass and a sound as if her phone had been thrown against something. Then silence. In a frightened shaking voice he called into the phone, "Destiny . . . Destiny . . ." but there was no response. David could hear that the phone connection was still live, which made the silence that much more terrifying. Seconds went by as he became paralyzed with fear, gripping the phone tightly. It was his only connection with Destiny. Again, he called her name into the phone. This time he screamed it . . . but still there was no response. He scanned his living room for his cordless phone. Spotting it, he reached for it without letting go of the receiver that was still in his other hand. With the cordless he was able to run out of his apartment to get help. He went into the hall and began banging wildly on the doors of the other apartments.

The late hour made it more difficult for him to get anyone to open their door. Then, from behind one door he heard the sound of a series of locks being turned. Finally, a blond man who was about David's age opened the door and asked if he needed help. Almost incoherent, David told him that this was an emergency on the phone and he needed to call the police. The man responded by opening his door all the way and waving David in. He pointed to the wall phone in his kitchen. David's hands were shaking as he dialed 911 and frantically proceeded to explain what was happening. Hearing what David was saying, the man began to understand the situation. He motioned to David to hand him the cordless phone. Hesitantly, David released the phone to him, while continuing to answer the emergency operator's questions. The man gave David a reassuring look as he put the cordless to his ear and in a calm voice, asked if anyone could hear him on the other end.

Without disconnecting David, the emergency operator contacted the emergency dispatcher for the precinct which she felt was nearest to the area of the accident.

Beads of sweat dripped down David's face and neck as he leaned against the wall waiting for the operator to return. He felt his heart pounding throughout his whole body.

In the next room he could hear the plaintive voice of the blond man whose apartment he was in. "Hello, can anyone hear me?" The concern in the man's voice emphasized the horror of the situation for David.

The sound of Destiny's scream and the shattering glass kept playing over and over inexorably in his head. It terrified him to think that Destiny was lying amidst the wreckage of a crashed bus miles away, in the unforgiving darkness of the stormy night.

Eventually, the operator returned to tell David that an emergency vehicle and personnel were already on their way to the scene. She went on to explain that a motorist who witnessed the accident had already phoned the local police.

"Is she all right? Did the witness say if she was all right?" he asked in desperation.

"Honestly, I gave you all the information I have. The only thing that I can suggest is for you give the police there a call. But wait a few minutes. Give them a chance to get to her. They'll be able to tell you where they're taking her." She gave him the phone number of the precinct. As David thanked her and placed the receiver back on the hook, he heard the blond man talking to someone on the cordless phone.

"Who am I speaking with? . . . Is the woman all right? . . . Can you at least tell me which one? . . . Thank you . . ."

With that, David rushed into the room and grabbed the phone out of the man's hand. "Hello . . . hello . . ." he yelled into the receiver.

"I think they hung up . . . but he told me the name of the hospital that they're taking them to," the blond man said, as he took the phone out of David's hand.

"What did they say? Is she OK?" David asked in a frenzied tone.

"They would only tell me where they were taking them . . . nothing else," the man said, shaking his head.

"Where are they taking her?" David asked impatiently.

"Benedict Memorial Hospital. It's in New Jersey, just outside of

Cherry Hill," the man answered, as his face showed concern for David's situation.

"Thanks for your help. I appreciate it . . . I've got to get to the hospital now," David replied as he turned to leave.

"How are you getting there?" the man asked as he followed David out of the room.

"I'm driving down," he replied as he continued out into the hallway.

"Wait. . . . Listen, you're in no frame of mind to be driving a car, unless you want to get into an accident yourself. I know where Benedict Hospital is. I interviewed some of their doctors for an article I was writing, just a few weeks ago. Your friend is in one of the best hospitals around, you should be grateful for that. Now, give me a minute to put on my shoes and I'll drive you. . . . I don't have a car but I'll drive yours, OK?" the man offered confidently.

"I couldn't ask you to do that."

"You're not, I'm volunteering. Get what you need from your place and I'll be ready in a sec, OK?"

"Thanks," David said, with sincere relief.

"By the way, my name's Alan," the blond man said as he extended his hand.

"David. . . . And thanks again for what you're doing," David replied, shaking the man's hand.

"I knew that I was the only one who could hear you when you were knocking on the doors. Everyone is away except for Mrs. Russo and she's deaf as a doornail. . . . I'll be right back," the man said, hurrying back inside to get his shoes. David hurriedly returned to his apartment and gathered up his wallet and car keys. His fear was growing with every passing second. Silently, he prayed to God for Destiny to be all right.

* * *

Although she had fallen off to sleep at about 10:30, exhausted from a hectic day at work, Andrie found herself wide awake only two hours later. She was unable to return to sleep. She wrestled around in her bed before getting up and going over to the window. As she stood at the window a flash of lightning fleetingly lit up her room. Rather than alarm her, it somehow brought back the memory of Destiny bursting into the brownstone apartment where they made love for the first time. The storm outside the window was strikingly similar to the one that night, when Destiny, rain soaked, held her, making her so thoroughly wet.

As Ann slept in the next room, undisturbed by the storm, Andrie remembered how it felt to wake up next to Destiny, after having spent most of the night making love with her . . . and how she believed all their mornings would be like that, from then on. She wondered what life would be like at that moment, if fate would have allowed her to remain with Destiny.

Suddenly, another bolt of lightning and the crack of thunder. This time Andrie's reaction was different. She was struck by an uneasiness which seemed to overwhelm her. She tried to shake the feeling, but it seemed only to grow more urgent. She quietly stole into the kitchen and made herself a cup of tea, which she immediately brought back to her room. She spent as little time as possible in any of the other part of the penthouse apartment and even had most of her meals alone in her room.

Slowly sipping from the steaming cup, she tried in vain to calm the wariness she felt inside. Unable to finish the tea, she set the cup aside on the nightstand.

As the storm continued relentlessly, Andrie remembered that Ann had an early flight to Washington in the morning, and Andrie wanted nothing to prevent her from leaving. Ann's presence had become unbearable to her.

Wide awake and wracked by a sudden anxiety the cause of which still puzzled her, Andrie looked at the clock next to her bed. It was 2 a.m.

As a little girl, she had always found comfort reading the twenty-third Psalm when she felt lonely or frightened. Lately she had begun reading it again, finding a small measure of comfort in its hope. But tonight it didn't seem to help dismiss the feeling of unrest that kept her awake. It was too late to call anyone . . . except David. He never got to sleep before 3 a.m. on a Friday. Reaching for the phone, Andrie made the call, but was surprised to hear his answering machine pick up. Disappointment was in her voice as she left a message. "David, it's me. It's about two in the morning and I just needed to talk. I woke up at 12:30 and I can't get back to sleep. I have this weird feeling like something's wrong. I know that it's probably just something stupid that'll pass, but call me when you get home, no matter what time it is. Thanks."

Then, hanging up the phone, Andrie slid down into the bed. She tried to force herself to sleep, shutting her eyes and trying not to listen to the thunder that reverberated around her. It took hours before sleep would come.

Chapter Thirty-Two

The storm had long faded into the night and David was able to steal some sleep on an unforgivingly firm couch in the hospital's visitor's lounge. He had received the hope he had prayed for . . . Destiny was alive.

Just as he had arrived at the hospital's emergency department, he met up with the police who were leaving. After explaining to them that he was on the phone with Destiny at the time of the accident, David was able to learn that an eighteen-wheeler had skidded out of control during the storm and had hit Destiny's bus. She was the only survivor of the accident.

By 6:00 a.m., inconsiderate, effulgent rays of sunlight assaulted David's bloodshot eyes, as he focused closely on the surgeon who woke him to inform him of Destiny's condition.

"Hi, I'm Dr. Penza. Your friend, Ms. Anderson, is out of surgery and she's doing fine. I guess that you know she was the only survivor of the accident," said the tall, slim, fiftyish man, whose voice and mannerisms were gentle and subdued.

"I know. The police told us that when we first got here. . . . How was the surgery? . . . Will she be OK?" David inquired, squinting as he was besieged by the sun flooding the dayroom through the three immense windows surrounding it. Before falling asleep there, he and Alan had spent most of the night drinking coffee and waiting for information, which seemed only to come in small spurts delivered by a kindly nursing director. He considered himself fortunate that it was Alan who had answered when he was banging on those doors. It seemed that both the hospital staff and its physicians were very gratified by his article, and because of that, he was given as much information as was available on Destiny since her admission.

But now, David stood listening to the very man who had spent hours in an operating room, using his skill and experience to repair Destiny's injuries.

"There were some abrasions here and there and some lacerations on her face and shoulder, which required suturing. All of that was all taken care of in the ER. She also had a right tibial fracture, which basically means a broken leg. We've reduced the fracture and put her leg in a cast. The worst of her injuries is a compound fracture of her right ulnar bone. That's more complicated than a simple broken arm. A compound fracture is when the broken bone actually breaks through the skin. That was why we needed to take her into surgery. Surgery is the only way to repair that type of injury. The arm is going to take more time to heal than the rest of her injuries and she'll need some physical therapy after it heals and the cast is removed. Right now she's in recovery. She should be transferred to her room in about an hour or so," said the doctor, who had not yet had time to change out of his green OR scrub-suit.

"She'll need to stay here for at least a few days, so we can keep her arm completely immobilized. Right now, we have to make sure that she doesn't develop an infection. We have her on IV antibiotics, so there's not much of a chance of that," the doctor added.

As David listened, he suddenly held up his hand as if to halt the surgeon from speaking further. Then he asked, "What about the instruments she plays when she performs? When will her arm be good enough to play again?"

"We'll have to take one step at a time. She's had a considerable amount of damage to the bone and surrounding soft tissue, so she's going to need some physical therapy. I believe that she'll eventually be able to do everything she did before. That reminds me, before we brought her into the ER last night, she asked me to call two people, yourself and . . . a Ms. McBride in Los Angeles. Ms. McBride seemed very upset when I spoke with her on the phone. She said she would get here on the next flight out. If you have any way of contacting her, I'd appreciate it if you let her know that everything went well. Once we get Destiny out of recovery to a room, I'm going to leave for a little while. The nurses know to call me if there are any changes, but I'm sure she'll be fine. I'm only about five minutes from here and meanwhile, my associate, Dr. Aaron, will be here with her."

As they spoke, Mrs. O'Neil, the nursing director, a small-framed woman with red hair, wearing a dark blue skirt suit, walked over to them, smiling as she recognized the look of relief on David's face. She was about the same age as the surgeon and seemed to share some sort of invisible bond with him.

"Well, I guess Dr. Penza told you that Destiny is in the recovery room. I just wanted you to know that her vital signs are good and she's starting to wake up. It won't be long before we send her down to a private room. Right now, there are a few things we need to discuss," she said.

"Sure," answered David, glancing over to Alan with a thankful expression. Alan patted David on the shoulder as Mrs. O'Neil continued.

"Reporters are beginning to call us. They find out about accident cases rather quickly, especially when a celebrity is involved. Actually, we were lucky that the storm bought us a little time last night. I think it slowed them down a bit. There were so many accidents and power outages that this incident sort of blended in. Anyhow, this morning our lobby is swarming with reporters. I wanted you to know about it before you tried to leave. If they have any reason to believe you're a friend of hers they'll bombard you with questions," she warned.

"I hadn't thought of that. Thanks," David said. In his concern, he had overlooked the fact that Destiny's fame was going to complicate the situation.

"The police called the families of the other two men who were in the bus with her, as well as the driver of the truck that hit them. They were all dead by the time help arrived. It's a miracle that she's alive and her injuries aren't more serious. The police think it helped that she was in the back of the bus and that the mattress she was lying on protected her from some of the impact. By the way, we haven't told her about the others on her bus yet. When she asked about them, we just told her that they weren't taken to this hospital. It wasn't the time to break that kind of news to her," Mrs. O'Neil explained.

"Well, since her manager should be here sometime today, I think that she would be the best one to break that news to Destiny. I contacted her band and crew. They were expecting her to meet them at a hotel in upstate New York. They'll probably be here soon, as well," David said, in a tired, drained voice.

"You both look like you could use some rest. Why don't you relax here until . . ." The nursing director stopped mid-sentence as she was interrupted by an obnoxious buzzing sound from one of the two beepers which protruded from the right pocket of her suit jacket. Looking down she pressed a button on the noisy little piece of black plastic, then, excusing herself, she walked over to a house phone on the wall behind her and punched in a four-digit number. David couldn't hear what she was saying, but he had a feeling that it had to do with Destiny. Sure enough, when she returned, she informed them that Destiny would probably be leaving the recovery room for a private room in about a half hour and that Dr. Aaron had just seen her and was very pleased with her condition.

"Will I be able to see her when she gets to her room?" David asked anxiously, looking back and forth from the nurse to the surgeon for an answer, as they glanced at each other before answering him.

"Only for a minute, she needs to rest," Dr. Penza replied, looking into David's face for assurance that he understood what he was told. He then added, "She's heavily medicated, so she'll probably be asleep until sometime this afternoon."

"You won't really be able to talk with her very much, if at all," Mrs. O'Neil added, in an effort to reinforce what the surgeon said. They had been through all this countless times before.

What was important to David was that Destiny was going to be fine and that he would be able to see her. It didn't matter if it had to be a short visit or if she would be asleep for it. He closed his eyes for a second and thanked God.

*   *   *

Stepping out of the shower, Andrie wrapped the fluffy white terrycloth robe around her body. Then, using a small hand towel, she wiped the mist from the fogged-up mirror until she could see her face. She studied her reflection, searching for the reason she had been unable to rid herself of the uneasy feeling that woke her during the night. Still puzzled about it, she tried to comfort herself with the fact that it was morning and she was grateful that Ann had left for Washington and the storm was just a memory.

She ran a brush through her dripping hair, causing drops of water to run down her neck, under the soft white robe and down her back. It reminded her of the way Destiny's wet hair felt on her naked body. Andrie tried to get the thought out of her mind. It didn't even mix well with the unexplained anxiety that she was still feeling.

As she opened the door to let some of the steam out of the bathroom, she heard the house phone ringing. She ran into the kitchen to answer it. The doorman's voice on the other end was far too brisk and cheerful for Andrie this morning. "Good morning, Miss LaStella. How are you today?" his voice blared.

"Fine. What is it, Bob?" Andrie replied, trying to conceal her impatience.

"A Miss Hogan is here to see you." He waited for a reply. There was a short silence. Andrie couldn't imagine why Nancy would be coming there to see her, especially on a Saturday. Again he prompted her, "Miss LaStella?"

"Oh. I'm sorry. Yes . . . of course, send her up," she finally replied. It occurred to her that there was probably trouble with Matt. As she waited for Nancy to get to the apartment, the apprehension began to build. Suppose he hurt her? Andrie thought to herself, hoping that Matt hadn't done anything violent. She jumped for the door, pulling it wide open when the bell rang. As

Nancy entered the apartment Andrie took an overall look at her, making sure she was all right. She seemed physically fine but very nervous and distressed.

"What happened? What did he do?" Andrie asked with her anger toward Matt building, as she guided Nancy through the front hall and into the living room.

"What? . . . You mean Matt? . . . No, that's fine. Andrie, is Ann here?" Nancy asked, as she glanced around the expansive room. She couldn't help but notice the lavish furnishings.

Andrie saw the astonished look cross Nancy's face and acknowledged it. "It's still just a prison to me. . . . Anyway, Ann's gone. She left for DC this morning. Why?"

"You haven't had the TV or the radio on yet this morning, have you?" Nancy responded, ignoring Andrie's question.

"No, why?" Andrie asked.

Answering her, Nancy forced the words out nervously. "I heard it on the radio a little while ago. . . . It's Destiny. . . . She was in an accident last night. She was taken to Benedict Medical Center, it's in New Jersey."

Andrie gasped loudly. "No. Oh my God. No," she cried out. Nancy put her arms around her and tried to calm her, but Andrie bolted out of the room.

"Where are you going?" Nancy yelled after her, as she followed behind.

"Please, call me a cab and tell them to find out where that hospital is. . . . Please, Nancy, hurry," Andrie replied as she moved about at a feverish pace, putting on the first articles of clothing she could find: a pair of blue jeans and a plain white cotton blouse. She was praying just as feverishly: *Dear God, please make her be all right. . . . Please God, I'll do anything. . . . I won't ever even ask you to send her back into my life . . . just let her be all right. Just let her live.*

With tears rolling down her face as she emerged from her bedroom with her hair still wet, Andrie grabbed her tan leather purse and headed for the door.

Nancy had already called the cab and it was on its way. "I'm going with you," she told Andrie firmly. Seeing the love that left her friend's eyes so desperate and tearful, Nancy understood why living anywhere without Destiny would be a prison for Andrie.

Chapter Thirty-Three

Andrie stared silently out the cab's window as it pulled into the hospital grounds. The driver proceeded to make his way up the path toward the front entrance of the broad, four-story gray building as Andrie's head suddenly snapped back. "Stop. Please, stop here."

The driver pulled the cab as close as he could to the curb, in order to let other traffic by, as Andrie hurriedly exited and ran across the path and into the visitor's lot.

Nancy sat dumbfounded in the back of the cab for several seconds before realizing that Andrie had spotted David standing next to his car, speaking with three other people.

Running toward them, Andrie noticed that one of them was dressed in a white lab coat. A doctor, she thought to herself, but she didn't recognize the other man, or the woman standing with them.

As David spoke with Dr. Aaron, he noticed a figure running toward him. A second later he realized that it was Andrie. Her previously wet hair had dried wildly. Her blouse hung half out of her faded jeans. He immediately walked toward her as she approached him. He saw the look of fear and panic on her face.

"It's OK. She's all right," he said with assurance, embracing her as they reached each other.

Hearing those words, Andrie seemed to give up what strength and control she had maintained to make it to that point. She went to pieces in his arms.

"Thank God. Thank God," she sobbed as she clung tightly to David.

"She broke her right leg and her right arm. The arm needed surgery, but everything went well. She's going to be fine," David said, trying to calm her.

Andrie tried to control her tears and trembling so she wouldn't miss anything David told her about Destiny.

The woman who had been talking with David and Dr. Aaron was now discreetly observing Andrie as she reacted to the news.

Meanwhile, Nancy had reached them and added her arms to David's, as they both tried to lend Andrie what strength they possessed at the moment.

"I have to see her . . . please," Andrie begged, wiping the tears from her eyes with a handkerchief that David handed her.

"She's asleep, honey. They gave her a lot of medication," he explained.

"Did you see her?" she asked, searching his face with the look of a frightened child.

"Yes, but she was asleep. She didn't even know that I was there."

"Please just let me see her. I just want to look at her," Andrie pleaded to Dr. Aaron.

"All right . . . but only for a minute. . . . I'll take you to her room," he said.

"Thank you." Never in her life did Andrie feel as grateful as she did to Dr. Aaron at that moment.

Suddenly realizing that Andrie had noticed Maggie standing with them, David introduced her. "Oh, this is Maggie McBride . . . Destiny's friend and manager. She rushed out here from Los Angeles as soon as she heard," he said, putting a friendly arm around Maggie, who in turn smiled warmly and extended her hand toward Andrie, who shook it instantly, thankful that Maggie seemed to care so much about Destiny.

Then, looking toward Maggie, David continued, ". . . and this is Andrie . . ." Before he could finish his introduction, Maggie jumped in.

"Destiny's told me so much about you. I feel like I know you already . . . I'm really glad that you're here. I think that having you here and finding out that she'll be able to be back on stage as soon as she heals up, is going to make our girl feel a lot better," she said warmly. Maggie's keen instincts told her that, no matter what had passed between Destiny and Andrie, the attractive, albeit tear-stained and disheveled young woman in front of her truly loved Destiny with her whole heart.

Andrie smiled at Maggie, but before she could respond, David broke in. "Sweetie, I'll wait for you here and take you back," he told her.

"No. It's OK. Nancy is going to stay with me, and the cab will wait. Go home and I'll call you when I get back," Andrie said, kissing him on the cheek.

David looked to Nancy for assurance that Andrie would be taken care of. Nancy nodded in a way that told him that she knew enough of the history between Andrie and Destiny to handle the task appropriately.

David, Alan, and Maggie watched as Dr. Aaron led Andrie and Nancy from the parking lot to one of the hospital's back entrances.

"So, do you think that it's possible for something good to come out of all of this?" Maggie asked David, as she began searching her enormous leather handbag for her cigarettes.

David understood that she was referring to Andrie and Destiny. "I wish I could figure out what is going on in her head," he replied, nodding in the direction of the corner around which Andrie had just disappeared.

"Well, she could hide what she's thinking, but she can't hide how she feels," Maggie told him, noting to herself that she saw more than just worry or concern in Andrie's eyes. She saw the terror of someone who feared losing the person they loved most in the world. Then, pulling a cigarette out and lighting up, she inhaled deeply on it. The smoke seemed to assuage some physical need in her that had been exacerbated by the stress of the day.

*   *   *

Dr. Aaron escorted Andrie and Nancy down the long, brightly lit hospital corridor, skillfully managing to avoid the press and fans who were milling around the hospital's lobby.

"I don't want you to wake her if she's asleep," he advised, as they made their way closer to the private room that Destiny now occupied.

"I promise. I just want to see her . . . to see if she's all right," Andrie replied anxiously.

"OK, this is it," he said, pointing to the last room on their right as they reached the end of the hall. The door was open halfway. The partially opened door was the nurses' way of giving their patient privacy, while still being able to check in on her as they passed by. Dr. Aaron instructed Andrie to wait while he went to assess Destiny's level of consciousness.

He remained in the room for almost five minutes before reappearing to announce that she was very sleepy but awake and responsive.

"The effects of the anesthesia are wearing off. She's awake. I told her that she had a friend here to see her. She doesn't know that she was the only survivor of the accident yet, so don't bring that up. We're planning to let her know later today, when Ms. McBride comes back up here," he said.

"Don't worry, I won't say anything," Andrie assured him.

Nancy pointed to the dayroom and told Andrie that she would wait there for her.

As Andrie put her hand on the door and gently pushed it open, she felt her whole body begin to shake from inside with fear and anticipation.

Once inside, there was a small alcove where the closet and the bathroom were located, so she could not immediately see Destiny, who had drifted back to sleep as soon as Dr. Aaron had left the room. Andrie slowly walked further into the room until at last she saw Destiny. She gasped, startled by the sight before her. No one, not even Dr. Aaron, had thought to prepare her. In their relief that Destiny's injuries would heal and not be permanent, no one had mentioned how badly bruised and battered she was. Aside from the surgical dressing and splint on her right arm and the cast on her right leg, Destiny's face was severely bruised. Both her eyes were blackened and her nose was swollen and misshapen. There were small thin strips of paper tape on the right side of her forehead, her right cheekbone and her chin. The strips were almost transparent, so Andrie could see the sutures underneath them. The one on her forehead was about two inches long and the other two about half that size. A line of blood extended from the sutures on her right cheek to a crease at the base of her neck where it had pooled and dried.

Andrie couldn't hold back her tears, as she imagined the physical pain these injuries must have caused Destiny. She searched for some sign of the strength and electricity that were so much a part of the woman who now lay before her, so ravaged by the violence of the accident she had survived. The horror of the accident itself was an unbearable thought for Andrie. If there were a way of suffering the pain for Destiny, she would have gladly agreed to do it right then and there, but that was impossible. She was helpless to ease any of this for the woman she loved so much.

Through the blur of her tears, she saw Destiny's eyes begin to open and focus directly on her. Without words, Andrie rushed instantly to her side. Holding Destiny's face gently in both her hands, only a breath separated their lips.

With that one look, Destiny bathed Andrie in her love and let her know that there could be no physical injury, no pain, no brush with death, that could ever diminish what she felt.

Andrie kissed her lightly on the forehead. "Thank God you're all right. I was so worried," she said. Then without words or warning, Destiny used her left hand to pull Andrie to her, until their lips met, and held Andrie close, not allowing for any retreat. None was attempted. After almost losing Destiny forever, Andrie was unable to deny herself that brief taste of the lips for which she had so long hungered.

For Destiny, who was just beginning to realize how fragile life was, it seemed a mortal sin to have the woman she loved so close, without some consummation of her desires. "Just now, when I opened my eyes and saw you, I thought that maybe I died and went to heaven. You looked just like an angel, standin' there watchin' over me," she whispered, without loosening her affection-ate hold on Andrie.

"Don't say that . . . don't joke about death. Not now after what happened. I don't know what I would have done if . . ." Andrie couldn't even bear to finish the thought.

"It's gonna be all right, honey. Everything's gonna be fine. You're here, just like a dream." Although Destiny's voice was weakened by all she had been through, it seemed to regain a certain vitality that been lost for months.

At that moment, there was nothing that Andrie desired more than to remain with Destiny. Yet she knew that nothing had changed. Yielding to her love for Destiny was no less dangerous now than prior to the accident. She knew that her mere presence there could give cause to Ann to fulfill her threats if she found out about it. For a moment she questioned whether it was worth this much pain to protect Destiny's career . . . but at the same time she remembered that, from the very first time they met so long ago, Destiny spoke of her dreams for the future and how, even as a child, her one wish was for stardom. Since then, Destiny had spent years struggling and living in cold damp basement apart-ments, as she strove toward achieving her goal. She had worked so hard and sacrificed so much of her life for the fame and success that were now finally hers. She had forged a dream into a reality and Andrie would not allow it to be destroyed by Ann.

Standing back from the bed, Andrie drew upon the little fortitude she had remaining, to give one final performance. "Destiny, please, don't . . . I . . . I came here because I was concerned about you as a friend. I'm still with Ann. Please try to understand." As she spoke, Andrie was already beginning to hate herself for what she was doing to Destiny.

"That's not true. I know that you love me. It shows in your eyes. I feel it when I touch you. Why are you doing this? . . . What's going on inside you? . . . Tell me," Destiny demanded, grabbing Andrie's wrist tightly, almost fearfully. "Just now when I held you, you didn't feel like a concerned friend . . . you felt like the woman who loves me," Destiny said, without letting go of Andrie's wrist or turning her dark, delving eyes from Andrie's.

"You're wrong," Andrie replied, pulling her wrist free and stepping back from the bed. "Ann and I were going through a very bad time last November. I'm sorry . . . I was confused . . . I thought that I was falling in love with you . . . but. . . ." Tears filled Andrie's eyes as she delivered that final painful lie.

"No. . . . Look at me and tell me that's not true," Destiny said in total astonishment. An ugly silence pervaded in the room. It was the kind of silence that happens when something dies.

"I'm telling you the truth," Andrie responded in a voice that was barely audible. Her eyes closed for a beat as she watched Destiny's expression turn from one of bewilderment to one of anger.

"You were using me? When we were young, you used me because you were confused about your feelings for women. I forgave that. I even thought that I understood it, on some level. But now, you're telling me that you used me to get through a rough time with your lover. I loved you. . . . All this time, I've loved you. That's why I kept trying to see you. Somewhere inside of me, deep in my heart, I always had some spark of hope for us. But there was nothing for me to hope for . . . was there? I'll never let you do this to me again. I want you to stay away from me . . . I don't want your concern . . . I don't want your friendship . . . I just want you out of my life . . . for good." With that, Destiny turned her head away from Andrie and stared at the stark white wall.

It was over. There was nothing left for either of them to say. Andrie took a few moments to just look at the woman she loved, but knew she would never see again. Then she turned and quietly left the room.

As the door closed behind her, she touched it tenderly, knowing this was as close as she would ever again be to Destiny. Then, turning away, she walked toward the glaringly sun-filled dayroom.

Nancy noticed her approaching and walked toward her. By the

time they reached each other, it was obvious to Nancy that Andrie was devastated by the visit. So without saying a word, Nancy embraced her, expecting her to break down in tears, but there were no tears left to cry.

Andrie seemed to be in a trance. Her face was devoid of expression.

Frightened by Andrie's lack of affect, Nancy led her back along the way they had come, until they reached the rear exit of the hospital.

The cab driver saw the two women emerge from the building and pulled up to meet them.

Nancy, who was no stranger to emotional pain, might not have known exactly what transpired in Destiny's hospital room, but she recognized what was happening to Andrie. She knew that there were situations in which the spirit, the mind and the body could all at once suffer such agonizing despair, that all feeling may cease for a time . . . as though some mysterious opiates were released to numb everything, right down to the very soul.

Helping her into the back of the bright yellow cab, Nancy wondered if Andrie would ever really feel again.

*   *   *

By early that evening, with the assistance of Dr. Penza, Maggie had finished up with the press and fans who had been demanding information on Destiny's condition and prognosis. Later, she quietly entered Destiny's room to see if she was awake. Her view was obscured by flowers, fruit baskets, and stuffed animals, which by then were being delivered every couple of minutes by nurse's aides, who tiptoed in and out, quietly placing them wherever they could find space. The bright yellows, reds and lavenders of the flowers and gifts in the room seemed too ironically cheerful, resembling a celebration . . . like a birth. While the ugly truth was that Destiny's bus driver and tour manager had both been killed in the accident that put her in this room, and now it was up to Maggie to break that news to her.

The bright colors and adorable teddy bears, with their permanently happy little faces, made Maggie feel that, in some way, she was about to violate some temporary serenity for Destiny by breaking the news of ,the men's deaths. She had no way of knowing that Destiny was already mourning a different kind of loss.

Chapter Thirty-Four

Although the leaves on the trees were dying, never was their color so breathtakingly vibrant as in mid-October. Andrie had spent the weekend in upstate New York at a quiet little inn. She had been making this trip alone for the past five or six Octobers. Ann had no objections to the trip, since she knew through Stuart that Destiny was in LA, with no immediate plans to come to New York.

Andrie had decided not to return to the city until Monday. She treasured every minute she spent away from the confines of Ann's penthouse. That morning she traveled south on the Saw Mill Parkway, leaving the beauty and peace of the country behind her and heading directly to work.

As the city got closer, so did the reality of her day-to-day life. She needed to look for things for which she could be thankful. It was one of the ways she kept herself from losing her mind. The thing for which she was most grateful at that moment was that Ann had never found out about the visit that she had made to Destiny in the hospital.

The two-hour drive was over before she knew it. In no time at all, she was enjoying the brisk October air chilling her face, as she made the five-block walk from the parking garage to her office. Andrie had begun to appreciate such small and easily overlooked pleasures, since they were the only things left that Ann's vindictiveness could not affect.

On her way she stopped at a small bakery. As she perused the still-warm cookies and pastries displayed behind the glass counter, Andrie noticed that it was almost eleven. She was not in the habit of getting to the office this late, but she was confident that Nancy could manage everything well on her own. After choosing some raisin buns, she headed down the block to her office, toting her briefcase, purse and now a white bakery bag, made warm by its fresh contents.

Getting closer, she crossed the street and noticed that the gate was down on the office's front window. That gate was the first thing Nancy took care of every morning when she opened up the office. Then, reaching the door, Andrie saw that the office was still locked and Nancy hadn't yet arrived. Putting down her briefcase, Andrie rummaged through her purse for her set of office keys. Finding them, she unlocked the door and seconds later was checking the answering machine for messages, but there was nothing from Nancy.

She went back outside for a moment and glanced down the block to see if Nancy was on her way. The only person coming down the block was Kelly, the street musician, whose frequent habit it was to play guitar and sing on the sidewalk near the office.

"Opening up kind of late today, huh?" the musician noted in a friendly tone, as she rested her large black guitar case on the ground and opened it up.

"Yes. I guess so." Andrie's voice was troubled as she answered the slightly disheveled woman, who removed a highly polished acoustic guitar from the plush, red velvet lining of its case.

"Well, I'm a little early today. Sometimes, I just can't wait to get out here. This afternoon I'll be playing at the city hall station, on Chambers Street . . . the subway ya know," the young musician said, as she set up for her street performance.

"Good luck with it. . . . You never know who's going to hear you," Andrie replied in a polite but preoccupied tone as she excused herself and returned to the office.

Back inside, she flipped her key ring around until she came to a short, hollow-cored key, which she inserted into an appropriately shaped opening in a small outlet on the wall near the front window. Instantly, sunlight cascaded in through the clean clear glass, as the electric security gate outside rolled up, disappearing into a huge horizontal cocoon of steel mounted above. Andrie took a cursory look out the window, but there was no sign of Nancy.

Kelly smiled at her as their eyes met briefly. She smiled back, then turned and headed toward her cubicle in the rear of the office, where she phoned Nancy at home. As she waited for an answer, Andrie recalled how Nancy had reprimanded her for the condition of her desk before she left on Friday. Nancy Hogan's neat and organized style complemented Andrie's whirlwind and sometimes absentminded manner perfectly.

After several rings without an answer, she hung up and then tried again. Again the phone rang and rang without being picked up. Nancy's apartment was only about five blocks south of the office. Andrie decided to walk over to make sure that she was all right. It had been several weeks since Nancy's morning sickness had subsided, so she wondered what could be happening, as she reached for the office keys and her tan leather purse.

Locking the office door, Andrie started down the block. She couldn't shake the feeling that Matt was the reason for Nancy not showing up. She remembered that he had stopped by the office a few weeks before, so he could accompany Nancy on her visit to the obstetrician. He was polite and quiet, yet Andrie was disturbed by the fact that he avoided her eyes when they spoke. She recalled looking at his hands. They looked like two enormous hairy mallets. At the time Andrie had tried not to stare, as it occurred to her that he had so frequently in the past used those callused violent hands to abuse Nancy. Now, as Andrie headed in the direction of Nancy's apartment, the image of Matt's hands became increasingly prominent in her memory. They seemed so unlike her father Rocco's large, gentle hands that had always protected and comforted his family, or her brother Nicky's hands that had always been used to build and repair things. Matt's hands seemed vile and murderous. Their strength was destructive.

This is crazy. I have to stop thinking like this. She's late. That's all. Maybe she had an early appointment with her obstetrician and she forgot to mention it to me, Andrie told herself, unaware that she had sped up her gait and by now was almost running. Within a few minutes she found herself in front of the four-story, red brick building where Nancy lived.

Except for the roar of a city sanitation truck and the crashing of garbage cans being emptied into it, the block seemed peaceful and without much movement. Andrie began to feel silly for imagining that something horrible had prevented Nancy from showing up for work. As she began to climb the stairs to Nancy's second-floor apartment, there was no sign of trouble. Reaching the top of the stairs, she walked toward Nancy's door, with its twine wreath of dried wildflowers. She noted how much friendlier it looked than the three other doors on that floor. Even the fact that its brass knob had been polished to a luster gave it a more welcoming quality than the others.

Pressing the buzzer to the left of the door, Andrie stood there for about fifteen seconds, awaiting some movement, then pressed the button again. This time she tilted her head, almost putting her ear to the door. There was total silence on the other side. She turned to walk away, but then on a whim turned back and tried the doorknob. The cold, brass knob turned fully. It had not been locked. Opening the door, Andrie took a quick glance around the empty hallway, then quietly slipped into the apartment.

Once inside she gasped as she looked around her. She reached back and locked the door behind her, so she wouldn't be surprised by anyone else entering the apartment . . . particularly Matt. In the middle of the floor of the small living room was an odorous pile of dirty work clothes, boots and socks. She noticed that there was only one area which appeared to be kept in complete order, as if it were some type of protected place. It was a dark oak curio cabinet next to the kitchen entrance. Through its clear glass door, she could see Matt's collection of miniature sailing ships: cutters and schooners and a variety of others. Some of them were in glass bottles, and others on small display stands, but they all seemed to be painstakingly hand-crafted. Nancy had mentioned how much Matt loved his collection. It had been passed down from his grandfather to his father, and finally to him.

A wooden baseball bat was resting against the side of the display case as though to guard its contents. Andrie was infuriated by the idea that, within the chaos to which he had transformed Nancy's apartment, the things Matt cherished remained so well cared for and unscathed. What kind of hell had Nancy been living in for these past months? Andrie wondered to herself, remembering how much this once cheerful and tidy little apartment used to reflect the personality of its inhabitant.

She looked over at the dining table that she had given Nancy as an apartment-warming present. It was piled high with empty pizza boxes, newspapers, crumpled cigarette packages and other trash. All the windows were closed and the air was stagnant and thick with the stench of tobacco smoke and spilled beer.

All but two of Nancy's collector's plates were gone from the dark oak curio shelf that Nick had put up for her. Andrie walked over to the shelf, lightly running her finger along the bottom of it, as she thought to herself that the missing plates had either been sold or broken by Matt.

Again, she wondered where Nancy could have gone. It wouldn't have surprised her if she found that Nancy had run away from this hell hole. It was obvious, from the look of the place, that Matt had not changed in the way that Nancy had hoped. No one could expect her to bring her baby up in this kind of environment.

Andrie started to feel guilty for not having seen the signs of this earlier. She hadn't been in Nancy's apartment since the summer. It hadn't occurred to her until now that Nancy had avoided having her there, all that time.

The idea that Matt was probably being physically abusive toward Nancy continued to nag at Andrie. She strained her memory, trying to recall if there were any noticeable signs of violence. She couldn't remember any bruises, but then the weather had become cooler, so it was easier for Nancy to cover her bruises with less-revealing clothes. She had been wearing more pants and long-sleeved shirts over the last several weeks. The only thing that Andrie recollected was that Nancy's eyes had been slightly puffy on several occasions. When Andrie had commented on them, Nancy had attributed the puffiness to the hormonal changes from her pregnancy.

"My God, why didn't I see this?" Andrie said out loud, as she turned away from the wall on which the display shelf hung.

Suddenly, she was shaken by a resounding crash. She stepped back, gasping. Her heart began to pound away, the pupils in her eyes dilated as she felt herself start to sweat and tremble. At that moment, Andrie knew that she wasn't alone here. The noise came from the kitchen. She was paralyzed with fear and as much as she wanted to run from there, she stood motionless. She would have to pass in front of the entrance of the kitchen to get out. More sounds followed. These weren't as loud and seemed more subtle, like a rustling. Andrie could hear herself breathing heavily through her mouth, as she forced herself to take small, tentative steps forward. Then a loud bang, like an object being smashed against a hollow surface, rang out. She bolted toward the door and grabbed the knob, panicking as she turned it and pulled on it, forgetting that she had locked it when she came in. Then, a faint, gasping voice called out from the same direction as the other noises had come. "Help me," it cried.

Hearing it, Andrie stopped pulling at the door. She turned around and looked toward the kitchen entrance. "Nancy, is that you?" she called out, as she moved cautiously in the direction of the kitchen.

"Andrie . . ." The voice was even thinner and less audible now, but immediately, Andrie knew that it was Nancy. Rushing into the kitchen, she found her curled up on the floor. Her color was ashen. She was wearing yellow cotton pajamas, which had obviously been torn in some kind of struggle. Their short sleeves revealed large purple bruises on both her arms. Her pajama bottoms were bloody and a large utensil drawer from the kitchen counter lay upside down next to her. Knives, forks, spoons and other kitchen tools were scattered about on the floor. Andrie realized that the

crashing sound was probably from Nancy pulling on the drawer to
lift herself off the floor. She bent down and touched Nancy's head.

"Oh my God. Nancy," she said, her voice shuddering at the
amount of blood that surrounded Nancy's menaced body.

"My baby . . . Andrie, I'm so scared . . . my baby." Nancy's
voice was weak and she was short of breath. She grasped Andrie's
hand as though it were her only link to life.

"Stay still. Just stay calm, honey. I'm going to get help," Andrie
tried to assure her as she gently removed herself from Nancy's grip
in order to look for the phone. She scanned the cluttered,
half-demolished kitchen, with a wild look.

"The phone . . . where's the fucking phone?" she said aloud.
Then, remembering that Nancy's phone was located on the kitchen
counter, she began frantically tossing off the items that had
accumulated on it. Finally finding the telephone cord, Andrie
anxiously reeled in the phone from the heap of newspapers,
magazines, plastic cups and other junk under which it had been
hidden. With quick nervous fingers, she dialed 911, but as she
waited for it to ring, she realized that the call hadn't gone through.
She began to feel like she was caught in a nightmare. She hung
up and immediately tried it again.

"Thank God," she sighed, as she heard the phone ring the
second time. Andrie anxiously rattled out Nancy's address and
apartment number the instant that the emergency operator answered. She begged the anonymous voice on the other end of the
phone to send help as quickly as possible.

After being assured that an ambulance was on its way, she knelt
down next to Nancy, slipping her arms under her and cradling her
close.

"Nancy. I'm here and I called for an ambulance. It's going to be
all right. They'll be here any minute now," Andrie said, attempting
to keep her friend as composed as possible.

"I'm afraid. I think I'm losing the baby," Nancy whispered
urgently, her eyes widening with fear, as she searched Andrie's face
for some kind of deliverance.

"The ambulance will be here any minute. We're going to get you to the hospital soon," Andrie responded, as she continued to hold her friend in her arms like a child. She felt Nancy's body growing weaker and beginning to shiver. She was going into shock. Andrie looked around her for something to keep her warm, but she could find nothing in the kitchen. Gently laying Nancy's head back down, she ran back into the living room. Remembering that she had locked the door behind her, Andrie hurriedly unlocked it so it would be open when help arrived. She picked up a small, pale yellow, knit blanket that was draped over one arm of the couch and raced back into the kitchen.

There was just enough of the small blanket to cover Nancy's curled body. Andrie tucked an end of it under Nancy's feet. She noticed that it appeared to be unfinished. Lifting Nancy's head, she held it gently in her arms as she looked at the clock on the wall. It had only been three minutes since she hung up with the emergency operator, yet it seemed like hours.

Please God, make them get here soon, Andrie prayed silently, as tears rolled down her cheeks. She had never felt as powerless as she did right then. All she could do was hold Nancy and feel the life drain from her limp body as they waited for help.

Just then, the door abruptly burst open. Andrie was instantly filled with relief.

"Straight ahead. We're in the kitchen," she called out, hearing the heavy footsteps entering the apartment. But her hopefulness turned to terror as she looked up to see Matt standing over them. His glassy, bloodshot brown eyes were wild and hateful as he saw her, crouched down and holding Nancy's battered body in her arms.

"What the hell are you doing in my house! Get out . . . now!" His voice exploded at Andrie, spreading the vapor of his alcohol-laden breath throughout the tiny kitchen. Then, directing his hostile glare toward his wife, he added, ". . . and you get off the floor. Don't start exaggeratin' everything, like you're all hurt. . . . Get up!" he yelled again.

Andrie looked down at her friend, who was as defenseless and vulnerable as a child, lying there, wrapped in the small yellow blanket, and suddenly realized that this was the blanket that Nancy had been making for her baby. But now, as it covered her, the pale yellow wool, soaked with her blood, looked more like a shroud than anything else. That grotesque realization triggered an angry strength deep within Andrie. A fierce, threatening look came over her, as her fury began to erupt. Glaring directly into Matt's glassy eyes, she slowly stood up.

"Get out," she demanded. Her voice was ominously . . . threateningly calm, as she held back the sheer vengeance that had taken hold of her.

"Listen, you fuckin' dyke, you're the one that's leaving . . . even if I have to throw you out the fuckin' window. You put all kinds of crazy ideas into my wife's head, about how she don't need me. I know what you're tryin' to do. . . . You're tryin' to turn her into a dyke like you. . . . I'm tellin' you now to stay the hell away from her . . . understand? I'm her fuckin' husband and she's having my baby. I don't want no degenerate like you around my family, so get the fuck out of my house. . . ."

Then, looking down at Nancy's motionless body, he continued, "And you get up now, ya hear me . . . now." He spat his demand in a loud brutal tone, oblivious to the fact that Nancy was bleeding and barely conscious.

His behavior convinced Andrie that there was more than just too much alcohol circulating through Matt's veins. She remembered Nancy telling her that he had used speed and cocaine heavily in the past.

Again, he yelled, "I said get up!"

"Matt, please . . . I can't," Nancy begged in a frail, indistinct moan, which seemed to drain her of the last bit of strength she had.

"Don't bullshit me. I said get up," he repeated as he moved toward Nancy's limp body, waving a clenched fist in her direction.

It was clear that he was ready to continue the vicious beating that he had begun earlier that morning.

"No!" Andrie shouted, seizing a carving knife from its block on the counter and holding it out in front of her. "If you take one step closer, I swear I'll kill you . . . so help me God," she threatened through clenched teeth, as she stepped forward toward Matt, determined to keep him from hurting Nancy. As Andrie advanced, Matt retreated, until they were both outside the kitchen.

"Leave. I want you to leave now," she ordered, still holding the knife out in front of her. Her heart was racing. She knew that Nancy was in very serious condition and that if Matt got his hands on her again, she would certainly be finished. She and that knife were all that that stood between Nancy and certain death.

The thought of having to plunge a blade into someone, even someone as vile as Matt Hogan, nauseated Andrie. It had only been four or five minutes since she called 911, but it seemed like an eternity. She was flushed and her hands were shaking. She saw Matt look at the glinting blade of the knife, as it seemed to waver in her grasp. The sunlight it reflected flickered around the room as Andrie tried unsuccessfully to control her fear. For a split second she looked toward the door, as she prayed for help to arrive. That was all the time Matt needed to knock the carving knife out of her trembling hands.

With one powerful back-handed blow to the right side of her face, Matt sent Andrie reeling through the air like a rag doll, and she landed on the floor, next to the display cabinet.

"Dyke bitch," he spewed, as he walked past her on his way back to Nancy. "I told you to get up!" he yelled as he crouched down over Nancy and grabbed a fistful of her hair, yanking her head back to see her face. Her level of consciousness had severely diminished from her loss of blood, so she had little reaction to the pain he was inflicting.

Andrie, still half dazed and now bleeding from the right side of her mouth, realized that Matt was in the kitchen with Nancy. She was less than six feet from the kitchen entrance, but as she lay crumpled on the floor outside, it seemed like six miles. She saw the baseball bat still in place leaning against the side of the oak cabinet, where Matt's precious miniature ships were kept. Pulling herself to her feet, she took hold of it and swung it as hard as she could against the glass door of the cabinet. The sound of the glass and wood exploding in all directions prompted Matt to come running back from the kitchen. Andrie had destroyed the top two shelves of miniature ships. He stopped dead in his tracks as he saw the scattered pieces of wood and glass all around him.

"If you take one more step, I'll demolish the rest of them," Andrie said, as the sound of sirens on the street below got louder and closer, giving her hope that she would be able to maintain this standoff for at least another minute or two.

"My ships . . . they were my father's . . . you fuckin' bitch," Matt screamed, his voice cracking as though he were about to cry. As he took a step toward her, Andrie pulled the bat back, ready to swing again.

"No. Please. That's all I have left of my father," he pleaded as he froze in place. Andrie stared angrily into his eyes, as he begged her to stop destroying his most cherished possessions.

Just then, they could both hear the police announcing themselves as they entered the small building and rushed up the steps. Andrie began to lower the bat, since she knew that the police were approaching the door and Matt was no longer a threat. Then something stopped her. It was the way Matt had just pleaded with her to not to destroy the things that meant so much to him.

It made her wonder just how many times Nancy had pleaded with him to stop brutalizing her. A sudden urge overcame her, and without warning Andrie swung the bat one last time, demolishing everything that remained in the display cabinet.

The police bounded into the apartment with the sound of the shattering glass, as Matt fell to his knees sobbing and cursing.

Andrie quickly led them into the kitchen. Just then, the emergency medical team arrived and immediately began treating Nancy. There were three EMTs, all clad in dark green pants and long-sleeved white shirts decorated with badges and emblems. An Asian woman in her early forties appeared to be leading the two other EMTs, who were both men around her same age.

Watching as the three sets of hands busily ripped open packets of gauze, needles, tape and tubing, Andrie heard the Asian woman say that Nancy's blood pressure was dangerously low and that she was in shock.

"She's pregnant," Andrie informed them, looking on as they worked feverishly over Nancy.

As the Asian woman prepared to insert an intravenous line into Nancy's arm, she acknowledged Andrie's statement fleetingly, with a somber, sympathetic expression. Andrie knew by the woman's response that there was little hope for the baby.

The blood-stained yellow blanket had been removed from Nancy and was lying on the floor along with the discarded plastic and paper wrappings from the medical supplies. Andrie picked it up and held it, as she watched them prepare to lift Nancy onto the stretcher.

The situation was under control now. The police were there and Nancy was safe from Matt and getting the medical attention she needed.

Andrie followed as they wheeled Nancy out of the kitchen and toward the apartment door. Then, stepping ahead to hold it open, she reached out and lightly stroked Nancy's forehead as the stretcher wheeled past.

Opening her eyes briefly, Nancy's face was a gray, expressionless mask, almost completely sapped of life. Yet, a single tear appeared at the corner of her eye when she saw the bloodstained blanket in Andrie's hands. It rolled down the side of her cheek and into the small pillow on which her head rested. At that moment, without words, both women had begun to grieve for the baby that had been lost.

Chapter Thirty-Five

Tuesday morning Andrie picked up her phone messages and returned calls from the previous day. She also rearranged her schedule for the rest of that week, since Nancy would be in the hospital. She was physically exhausted, having spent most of Monday giving statements to the police and then waiting at the hospital for Nancy to come out of surgery.

By Tuesday afternoon, she was on her way to visit Nancy, who had been sent from the recovery area to a regular patient room during the night. As she approached Nancy's hospital room, Andrie wondered what she could say to comfort her friend.

"Ms. LaStella." A voice called her from behind the nurse's station. It was the doctor who had operated on Nancy the day before.

"Dr. Bristoe?" Andrie was only half sure that she remembered the name.

"Yes. And I'd like to speak with you if you have a moment," answered the diminutive blond woman, hurrying toward her.

"Of course. Is Nancy all right?" Andrie inquired as she stopped and waited for the doctor to catch up to her.

Reaching her, the doctor smiled and explained, "Physically, she'll be fine. She knows that she suffered a spontaneous abortion; we also had a long talk and I told her that the injuries that caused it won't affect her ability to maintain future pregnancies. She lost a lot of blood yesterday, because her uterine artery was damaged. We were able to repair it and we gave her three units of blood. She got here just in time . . . but I'm concerned for her emotional status. From what she told me, I know that she doesn't have any family in New York . . . and I just want to make sure that she has some form of support system. I've seen too many other women in similar circumstances return to bad situations, because they feel like they have no place to go." There was sincere concern in her voice as she spoke with Andrie.

"She has me and some other close friends. I'll do whatever is necessary to help her. 'She won't be going through this alone," Andrie answered, without hesitation.

The doctor smiled again, this time with relief. She saw that Andrie was ready to do all she could to help Nancy. Then she asked her, "Did the police talk to you about any of this?"

"Yes. I gave them a statement yesterday, after the ambulance took Nancy to the hospital. They've arrested her husband, but they need her to give them a statement. They said that they would be sending an officer who handles cases like this to talk with her. Do you think that she can handle that?"

"Yes I do. She's a strong person and I think that she'll be fine. The hardest part of all this is the loss of the pregnancy. Before she's discharged, I'm going to suggest that she see one of our psychologists. I think it might be helpful," Dr. Bristoe explained as she was interrupted by the beeping sound of the pager in her lab coat pocket. "It's the emergency room. I need to call them. We'll probably be discharging Nancy the day after tomorrow. You can page me if there's anything else I can do," she said, shaking Andrie's hand, then started back toward the nurse's station. Just as she reached it, she turned and called to Andrie. "It's a relief to know that she has someone who cares about what happens to her."

Andrie responded with a smile. She was relieved that there were people like Dr. Bristoe in the hospital.

The door to Nancy's semi-private room was fully open, so Andrie just knocked lightly as she walked in. Nancy's head was turned away from the door. She seemed to be staring out the window, which was just beyond the vacant bed next to hers.

"Nancy," Andrie whispered softly, as she came closer to the bed.

Nancy slowly turned and looked at Andrie. Her eyes were swollen and filled with tears. Her face, which had been too weak to show expression the day before, now had the strength to reflect her grief.

"My baby. Andrie, I lost my baby," she began to sob.

"I know, honey, I know," Andrie said, unable to suppress her own tears and feeling Nancy's pain, as she held her tightly. It made her wonder why pain, and loss, and death had to be so much a part of life.

Chapter Thirty-Six

Maggie noisily rummaged through the myriad of containers, jars and bottles which filled the shelves of Destiny's well-stocked refrigerator.

Meanwhile, Destiny sat at the kitchen table clumsily trying to peel an orange without the use of her injured right arm. "Shit," she yelled out, as the orange rolled off the table and landed on the floor. Spotting where it had landed, she kicked it, sending it across the kitchen. "I can't stand this anymore. I want this cast off now," she grumbled, as she reached into the fruit bowl for another orange. Her leg had healed well and the cast on it had just been removed. The cuts on the right side of her face had left her with three tiny scars, none of which seemed to lessen the random beauty of her dark dramatic features. Even if they had, it would matter little to Destiny, who had never cared about her physical looks anyway. What concerned her was regaining full use of her right arm and hand, so she could continue performing again.

"Well, you have another two weeks before that comes off. So shut up and learn to be ambidextrous, for now," Maggie answered her, then turned back to the refrigerator and continued her search. "Where the hell is the tonic? I can't make myself a gin and tonic without the tonic."

"Look on the top shelf or on the door," Destiny suggested, as she concentrated her attention on the second orange she was attempting to peel.

"OK. Here it is," Maggie announced, pulling the large clear plastic bottle of tonic from the top shelf. She began to mix herself a drink as she spoke. "I'd really miss these late night get-togethers if you move. This is such a great house. I remember when you bought it. You couldn't believe that you could actually afford to look at a place like this, because you were still living over that little

Japanese restaurant in East LA. And now, not even two years later, you want to go back to another hole in the wall."

"I just want someplace that doesn't look like I should be sharing it with somebody. This is too big for me," Destiny told her. As she spoke, she hoped that Maggie hadn't noticed the stack of pictures and the listing of the sprawling Montana ranch, which she had left on the kitchen's center island.

"I know it's a month away, but do you have any Thanksgiving plans?" Maggie asked, with the intention of getting Destiny to spend the holiday with her and her family.

"I was supposed to spend it with Harry and Elaine, but I don't know if they're going to be back by then. Elaine's father is in pretty bad condition, so they just left for Paris and they aren't expecting to return right away. They don't know how long he has. Harry said that the doctors told Elaine that it could be a week or it could be a month."

"So Harry went there, too, this time. I thought Elaine's father hated him because he wasn't really Jewish or something?" Maggie's attention was split between her question and tasting her drink. She smiled. The drink was perfect.

"Somethin' like that, but Harry doesn't want her to go through it alone," Destiny replied. Then, with half the orange peeled, she started to pry off an exposed wedge. As she did, the juice shot out from the fruit and hit Maggie in the face. Destiny slammed the fruit down on the table in defeat.

"Give me that . . . I'll take it apart for you . . . and don't get so frustrated. You've always been a sloppy eater, even when you used both hands," Maggie admonished, grabbing the orange and proceeding to pull it apart quickly and neatly. It was something she had done many times in her life, as the mother of five. She knew that Destiny didn't care about peeling the orange. She was worried about how her injury would affect her music. Both Maggie and Destiny's doctors were confident that she would be able to play just as well as she did before, given enough time and therapy. But Destiny was impatient and anxious to get busy once again.

"Elaine's father is some kind of multimillionaire, isn't he?" Maggie asked, as she handed back several bare wedges of the fruit to Destiny.

"Yeah. He owns all kinds of commercial property in the heart of Paris. He also owns some big food exporting company and who knows what else," Destiny answered as she picked up an orange wedge and stuffed it into her mouth.

"I don't want to sound crass, but what happens to all that money, when he goes? Elaine's an only child, right?" Maggie asked, as she took a long drink of her gin and tonic.

"Who knows. Elaine was never interested in that. She just wanted her father to love her and accept her husband. I always respected her for choosing the person she loved over money and family pressure. It's funny how human beings always seem to complicate love. That's plain wrong," Destiny said, chewing another wedge of the orange. She wasn't just referring to Elaine and Harry . . . and Maggie knew that.

"I haven't mentioned this since you've been back from the East Coast, but when I went out there to see you in the hospital, I met Andrie. That woman loves you. She was out of her mind with worry. I know that she saw you that day. What happened?" Maggie asked.

"Nothin'. Look, I know that you care. I went through this same conversation with David. I told him the same thing I'm gonna tell you. She chose Ann. There's nothing I can do about it . . . I've tried. So, if you care about my feelings, you won't torture me about this," Destiny answered abruptly. There was sorrow and bitterness in her voice.

"Why are you buying this place in Montana?" Maggie asked, sensing that it had something to do with Andrie.

"To have a place to escape to from time to time," Destiny said, keeping her explanation as brief as possible.

"Maybe you wouldn't need to escape if you just tried talking to Andrie again. . . . Maybe you could straighten things out with her," Maggie said as she finished what was left in her glass and began mixing a second drink.

Destiny threw down a wedge of orange that she was about to eat. "Damn you and everybody else. Y'all think that it's all up to me. She's not in love with me. She's with Ann. Every day, every night, it's Ann that she feels next to her . . . touching her. Do you know what that does to me inside? Don't make me talk about this anymore . . . because if you do, you'll find out that nothing is the same for me anymore. Not even my music. Even *that* doesn't make me feel like it used to, but it's all I have left." Destiny stopped talking and looked away. She had to. She didn't want to cry anymore.

Seeing that, Maggie abruptly changed the subject. "I talked with Rena Samuel yesterday and she said that all the postproduction work is completed. She's getting things ready for the premiere in New York on December 23. You know Harry and Elaine are planning to be there," Maggie said, then paused to see if Destiny would tell her whether or not she planned to attend the premiere. But Destiny avoided committing herself one way or the other.

"The soundtrack is on the Cobra label, so of course he's gonna be there with Elaine, if they're back from Paris by then. . . . Speaking of New York, did I mention that David has a new lover? It's his neighbor, Alan. The guy that took him to see me at the hospital. They've been seeing each other every day since then," Destiny announced, hoping that Maggie would forget about talking her into attending the premiere.

"It's about time he got himself somebody. I was starting to wonder about him." Maggie held up her glass, as though she were toasting David's new relationship.

"Why are you so hell bound on seein' everyone that you know paired off? There are some people in this world who can get along damn well without bein' yoked to someone else." Destiny's drawl seemed to add emphasis to the point she was trying to make.

"Sorry babe, I don't know any of those kind of people," Maggie replied, further irritating Destiny.

"Mag, that's enough for tonight. I'm not in the mood to deal with your naggin' me about how I'm handlin' my life," Destiny replied, looking at her watch to see that it was one-thirty in the morning. "It's late, I'm goin' to bed. Why don't you call your house and tell Tony that you're stayin' over. Those were pretty strong gin and tonics you were makin'." Saying that, Destiny got up from the table and waited for an answer.

They were both tired, but the drinking had had little effect on Maggie, who eventually left. She could tell that Destiny needed to be alone. Maggie failed to realize that Destiny already felt as though she were alone. It didn't matter who, or how many people were with her . . . she would always be alone without Andrie.

Chapter Thirty-Seven

All the windows were open to allow the brisk November air to circulate throughout the apartment. Andrie, with the help of David and her brother Nick, had given a whole new look to Nancy's ravaged apartment. They had painted, repaired and redecorated the entire place.

After Nancy was released from the hospital, Andrie arranged for her to stay with David for the two weeks that followed. She didn't want her to return to any ugly reminders of what had happened. Andrie had even explored the possibility of finding her another apartment, but Nancy preferred to remain there.

It took the entire two weeks to finish the work, and it was planned as a welcome-home surprise for Nancy. As Andrie waited for David to arrive with her, she watched Nick hang a colorful print of a countryside on the living-room wall. She had seen it in a small shop near the office and knew immediately that Nancy would like it.

"Nicky, thanks for doing helping me with this," she said, kissing her brother on the cheek.

"Hey. I like Nancy. She's a nice person. Whatever I can do . . . let me know. But how about you?" he asked, as he turned and slipped his hammer back into the tool belt around his waist.

"What about me?" she asked back.

"Mom and Dad are worried about you. You hardly see or call anybody since you moved in with Ann. If you think that we're mad about all that stuff that was in the newspapers months ago, we're not. We just want you to be happy." He paused for a moment, then continued hesitantly, "Andrie, I never told you how to live your life and I'm not gonna start now, but I have to tell you what I see. I see my sister, who I love, living with somebody that doesn't seem connected to her. Isn't the person you love supposed to become part of your family? We all accepted your lifestyle from the beginning, yet that never happened. . . . I know that this sounds dumb, but it's almost Election Day and I feel like Ann is going to make you an even smaller part of her life if she gets re-elected." Nick ran his hand through his thick, dark brown hair as he tried to express his feelings. "I got one more thing to say. . . . It's about Destiny. That one night that I saw you with her at Mom's house, you looked happy. I saw something there with you and her. I don't know the whole story between you two. I know that you were mad at her for a long time . . . and I saw the picture of her in the paper with that woman, when she was staying with you . . . but I . . . I don't know. . . . Forget it. Just remember that we all love you, Andrietta, and we want you to be happy." Nick put his arms around his sister and held her. She couldn't continue lying to her brother about her reasons for living with Ann. She was running out of strength for that, so she simply rested her head against his chest, and silently she thanked God for her family . . . especially for Nick.

A knock on the door alerted her that David and Nancy had arrived. She turned from Nick and glanced around the room to see that everything was in place.

"OK, I'll be right there," she called out, then turned to Nick, "Get the welcome-home cake out of the kitchen while I get the door."

As Nick went to retrieve the cake, Andrie opened the door. "Welcome to your almost-new home," she announced to Nancy, guiding her into the living room.

Then, hugging Nancy, David added, "And it isn't a moment too soon. Nancy darling, I've grown to love you dearly, but you're even neater than I am, and you're making me look bad to Alan."

As Nick brought out the cake, complete with candles, Nancy's eyes widened with astonishment.

"I can't believe that you did all this for me. I don't know what to say," Nancy bubbled, as she wrapped her arms around Andrie.

"Is it really OK? If there's anything you don't like . . . anything that's not your taste . . . we can change it. Just say the word," Andrie told her, eager to make her as comfortable as she could.

"It's perfect . . . and you're all perfect," Nancy gushed with tears in her eyes. There was never a time in Nancy's life when anyone showed her the caring and love that Andrie had given her.

"Hey, isn't she supposed to blow out the candles now?" Nick asked, as he eyed the cake.

"You and that sweet tooth," Andrie chided him, then turned to Nancy. "So, do you want to make a wish?"

"OK. But I want to say something first," Nancy replied as everyone stood around the rectangular, white sheet cake, whose sugary *welcome home* letters were somewhat distorted by the fifteen candles which protruded from it. There was one for each day it took to re-decorate the apartment, and one extra for good luck.

"Thank you, Nick and David, for doing all that you've done for me, even before today. I hope that someday I get a chance to return all your kindness . . . and Andrie, thank you for today and for giving me so much love and support. You didn't just give me your friendship, you've shared your friends and your family with me. You invited me to spend Thanksgiving and the holidays with you and your family. I'm looking forward to that because I have so much to be thankful for. . . . So, now I'll blow out the candles," Nancy said with tears in her eyes.

"Don't forget to make a wish, hon," David reminded her, as he watched her take a deep breath and blow, until each candle had been extinguished.

"So, what did you wish for?" Nick asked, handing her a long cake knife.

"For happiness," Nancy answered with a hopeful smile.

"You deserve a lot of that, after everything that you've been through," he replied with unmistakable compassion in his voice. Like his stepfather Rocco, Nick LaStella had a sturdy, rugged appearance, but a gentle and loving nature.

The four friends enjoyed each other's company well into the evening. Andrie had even arranged to stay over, so Nancy wouldn't have to be alone on her first night back.

Chapter Thirty-Eight

The penthouse apartment was silent, except for the sound Andrie's fork made as it occasionally hit her plate of cappellini with garlic and olive oil. It had been Nancy's first day back to work since being discharged from the hospital. A fatigued, but satisfied smile crossed her face as she remembered how surprised Nancy was when she entered her re-decorated apartment the day before.

Leaning back in her chair, Andrie rolled up the sleeves of the white silk robe she had slipped on after taking a hot bath earlier in the evening. Then she pulled her legs up and tucked them under her, Indian style, and stared into the barely eaten dish of pasta. Pushing the pasta around the plate with her fork, she recognized the fact that she had no appetite. She had prepared the meal merely as a way to occupy herself. Most of the time she avoided eating dinner at the apartment, since it presented the possibility of being joined by Ann. But tonight, Ann was scheduled to be interviewed for a segment of a local news show and afterward she planned to have dinner with Stuart. She wasn't due home until sometime after 10:00 p.m., which gave Andrie close to two hours of time to herself.

Giving up on the idea of eating, Andrie took the plate into the kitchen, where she emptied it. Just being in Ann's apartment seemed to rob her of so much more than just her appetite. She wondered how the outcome of the election would change things for her. Once it was over, no matter what the outcome was, there would really be no reason for Ann to persist in forcing her to live here. The charade could end. Ann would no longer need to pretend that she was in a happy and settled relationship. No one would be looking at her as closely as they had during the campaign.

Andrie knew that there had to be some sort of post-election

strategy devised by Hal Gottfried and Ray Dalton. But she wasn't sure how it would affect her. She had avoided even thinking about the future until now, but it suddenly became clear to her that she needed to confront Ann and find out what was going to happen. No sooner did that thought enter her mind than she heard voices coming from the living room. Ann had arrived home early and she was with Ray and Stuart. Andrie could hear them discussing the interview Ann had just given. They were congratulating themselves and sounding pleased with the way things had gone.

Just as Andrie began to think that they would be staying for a while, she heard the conversation winding down. She could hear Ray ask Ann if she was certain that she didn't want to join them for dinner. She responded that she would rather relax tonight, since tomorrow was Election Day.

Andrie remained in the kitchen, listening as Ray and Stuart gave Ann some last minute words of encouragement about the election on their way out.

The sound of the door closing and the silence that followed told Andrie that she was alone in the apartment with Ann. As much as she dreaded it, she knew that this was her opportunity to talk with her about what was to happen after the election.

"Ann?" Andrie called out, as if she were wondering who was moving around in the living room. She felt unsure as to how to approach Ann, but she had no time to consider her options.

"I'm in here," Ann's voice answered, now sounding as though she had moved from the living room into some other part of the expansive apartment.

Andrie followed the sound of the voice. After finding that Ann wasn't in the living room or the study, she again called out, "Ann?"

"I'm in here." Ann's voice now emanated from her bedroom. Without hesitation Andrie left the study, crossed the wide, dimly lighted hall and approached the half-open door to Ann's bedroom. She knocked softly on the door as she walked into the room. Ann was looking into a dresser mirror as she removed her makeup. Her back was to Andrie, but each could see the other as they began to speak to each other's reflection in the glass.

Andrie felt an odd safety zone as she made eye contact with Ann's glass image. For some reason it seemed to make it easier for her to begin the conversation. "I need to talk with you about us and what's going to happen after tomorrow," she began, as she stood just inside the doorway.

"What do you want to happen?" Ann replied in a leading tone, as she picked up a brush and ran it slowly through her short mahogany-colored coif, without losing eye contact with Andrie.

"The election will be over by tomorrow night. You're way ahead of Phil Massey, so you know that you're going to be re-elected. There really isn't any need for me to pretend to be your partner after tomorrow. I don't have to move out immediately. I know that it wouldn't look right to do that too soon, so maybe . . . we could arrange it to look gradual, even if it takes a couple of months."

"I don't think that would be a very good idea," Ann said, putting down the brush and turning around to face Andrie directly.

The safety zone that the mirror had provided was suddenly gone and Andrie felt every one of her muscles tighten, as she wondered what Ann meant. "What bothers you about it? Do you think that a couple of months will still seem too soon?" Andrie asked in a cautious tone.

"No. I don't want you to leave . . . at all," Ann said flatly.

"You can't possibly want to continue this game of us pretending to be lovers," Andrie blurted, in disbelief.

"You're right. I don't," Ann answered with alarming conviction. "I want us to resume being lovers," she continued as she approached Andrie, who was struck momentarily speechless.

"I don't know why you're so surprised. I'm sure you can remember back to when I told you that I wanted to put your mistakes behind us and continue on . . . I meant that. You've kept your part of our agreement about Destiny Anderson for all these months now, and that's why I believe that somewhere inside, you've come to realize that your life is with me. I know that over the past year I've been preoccupied with damage control, because of my reputation . . . and of course getting re-elected. But all that is falling into place now and I'm ready to concentrate on us. I was going to tell you all this after the election, but since you've brought it up, I'll tell you now. I've decided that you should continue to live here with me and that our relationship should return to what it was. To my own amazement, I find that I'm still attracted to you and now I don't need to hide anything. That's what you wanted all along. It can be so perfect. My father always said that if I was smart and knew how to work the public, I could have anything I wanted. He was right. If I hadn't been so occupied by the whole damage control and my re-election, I would have told you this sooner. I've decided that I want to make love with you again." As she spoke, Ann came closer to Andrie, surveying her with the savor of a hungry predator circling its prey.

She had remained silent the entire time Ann was speaking, but Andrie's eyes betrayed her. They displayed every bit of the shock and disgust that she felt toward this manipulative and power-crazed woman. There wasn't a more nauseating thought for her than to touch or be touched by Ann.

"You're insane," Andrie said vehemently, unable to contain herself any longer. "How can you even think that there could be anything between us now?" she asked, with a look of disgust.

Ann seemed unimpressed by her outburst. "Let me explain this to you as simply as possible. I, myself, don't understand my desire for you, after all the trouble you've caused me. I shouldn't give a damn about you, but there's just something that I need from you. I don't know what to call it. I need to be with you . . . to feel you. You're something I want to enjoy. It might be love or lust or whatever, but I'm not ready to let you go . . . at least not right now," she told Andrie in a cool businesslike voice that lacked any emotion.

"You're completely twisted. But then, you never had a chance. Your father gave you his fortune and his lust for power, but he deprived you of the only thing that separates human beings from animals . . . a conscience," Andrie said, shaking her head as she turned to leave the room.

Suddenly, she was startled by a burning pain that spread down the back of her head, as her neck was arched back in a wrenching motion. She momentarily gasped for breath, as Ann gripped a fistful of her hair, brutally yanking her backward, then pushing her down onto the bed.

"I meant what I said. I'm not ready to let you go yet. It's time that you forget about Destiny. I still want you . . . now." Ann spewed the words into Andrie's face, as she held her wrists pinned down.

Still stunned by the attack, Andrie was unable to release herself from the hold. She felt Ann's mouth press against hers in an attempt to pry her lips apart.

"Stop it. Let me go . . . now," she demanded, but her words were muffled by Ann's mouth. Then Ann's thigh abruptly forced its way between Andrie's legs. The white silk robe had come open in the struggle, leaving Andrie all but completely naked as Ann released her left wrist. But before Andrie was able to react, she could feel Ann's hand forcing its way downward toward its objective. Grabbing Ann's wrist, she tried to pry it away, but it was only a second before the marauding hand broke free again.

Realizing that she couldn't restrain Ann, Andrie gathered up all the rage and disgust she felt, and with an open hand, hit Ann in the face, knocking her over to the side of the bed.

Then, springing to her feet, Andrie pulled her robe closed as she looked down at Ann, who remained on the bed, coiled up and temporarily stunned, holding her hand to the right side of her face where Andrie's fingernails had left a few unforgiving gashes.

"I'm leaving here tonight . . . and you can go to hell," Andrie told her in a breathless voice that was trembling with rage. Meanwhile, her eyes conveyed her loathing of Ann with undeniable eloquence.

"You haven't learned anything yet. You're still hoping that you'll get Destiny back. You think that you're saving yourself for her, don't you?" Ann asked with mocking scowl, as she stood up, still holding the right side of her face.

Still shaken and outraged by the attack, Andrie replied, "Don't worry. I know that I can't be with her. I'm sure that you'd carry out all your threats if I ever tried to break our agreement. I'm not leaving here to be with Destiny. I'm leaving to get away from you."

"Andrie, you're not leaving here at all. I've come to the end of my patience with this. Assuming that I get re-elected tomorrow night, I'll be taking an early flight to DC the following morning. I have a tremendous amount of personal business to wrap up regarding my father's estate and I want to complete that before the new Congress is in session. I should be getting back here in about five or six weeks, right around Christmas. When I return, I'll expect you to be thinking much more clearly about everything . . . especially our relationship. If I find that you haven't changed your mind about being with me, I'll have to believe that it's because of your lingering feelings for Destiny Anderson. In which case, I will consider it a breech of our agreement . . . and I promise you . . . I'll pull the plug on her so fast that she won't know what hit her. You know that I can cripple her career so badly that within a year or so, she'll be lucky to get a job playing at a mall opening." Ann was seething, as she spoke through clenched teeth. She would not allow Andrie to reject her again, no matter what it took.

"How could you want to make love with someone who detests you? It wouldn't even be making love."

"I know. It would be having sex, but wasn't that exactly what we used to do before Destiny came into the picture? I felt the need to enjoy you, so I would come to your apartment and we would have sex and then I would leave when it was over. At least this time, we would be living together. That should make it more palatable to a romantic like you," Ann said, as she turned toward the mirror to examine the scratches on her cheek.

"Do you really think that I would ever consider being with you like that again?" Andrie asked in total disbelief.

"Just remember that when I get back, if we are not together . . . in every sense of the word, I will consider Destiny Anderson the reason . . . in which case I will end her career. There's really nothing else to say on this subject. I suggest that you get a good night's sleep. I expect you to be with me at headquarters tomorrow evening, watching the returns, and of course the victory party should last into the wee hours. I assume that you will do your best to look cheerful and content." As she made her demands, Ann was preoccupied with the three long jagged red lines that marred her otherwise near-perfect complexion. "If anyone asks what happened to my face, tell them that that mange-ridden cat you keep in your office did this to me. By the way, if you ever try to claw me again, I promise I won't take it nearly as well as I have this time. Do you understand?" she cautioned with a menacing look on her face, but Andrie left the room, refusing to acknowledge the threat.

Chapter Thirty-Nine

The nightly news chattered on in the background about election results around the country, as Destiny sat slouched back on the sofa, exercising her right hand by squeezing a small rubber ball.

"So, what do you think of it?" she asked, while she waited for Maggie's reaction to a picture Destiny had just handed her.

"Nice. It's very nice, if you're practicing to be a forest ranger," Maggie commented, shrugging her shoulders as she handed back the picture of the hundred-acre Montana ranch Destiny had just purchased. "You should sell that to Rockefeller Center next Christmas," she added, pointing to the towering spruce in the foreground of the picture. The tree seemed to dominate the scene.

"It's beautiful, isn't it? It reminds me of a tree that Andrie had talked about, years ago," Destiny replied wistfully, as she put down the ball and reached for a guitar that was sitting next to her on the couch. She began to strum lightly on it, further obscuring the sound of the evening news.

Rolling her eyes with an incredulous expression and waving the picture at Destiny, Maggie begged, "Please don't tell me that you bought a house in the middle of nowhere because there's a tree in front of it that reminds you of a woman who you're not with anymore."

Destiny's lack of response was more than Maggie McBride was willing to handle without alcoholic facilitation. Shaking her head in disbelief, she retreated from the room, only to return moments later with a bottle of white wine and two glasses.

"Look, I know we've discussed this before, but I want to remind you again. Next month is the premiere of *Riverside Drive*. Rena will be heartbroken if you're not there and I'll be really pissed. You can't stay away from this. Everybody is wondering how you're recuperating since the accident. The last thing you should want is speculation about why you've been so reclusive. It's not good for your career. Dammit, you've got to stop connecting New York with Andrie LaStella . . . that's sick. You don't have to perform. Just go and have a good time. What's so hard about that?" Maggie asked.

"I don't know, I'll have to think about it," Destiny muttered as she continued strumming. Playing the guitar, piano, fiddle, and flute were not only good practice for her return to performing, but appropriate physical therapy as well.

"How are the exercises coming?" Maggie changed the subject as she twisted the corkscrew into the bottle. She didn't want to distract Destiny from her therapy by arguing.

"Good . . . real good. The doctors say that in another month or so I'll be as good as new," Destiny replied as she continued playing softly on her guitar.

"Well, the second they give you the green light, we'll get you right back on the road. In fact, before your accident, Harry and I were discussing a European tour, since he was considering promoting your next album there. I hope that moron Sottley doesn't nix all that, now that he's involved in everything. I can't wait for Harry to get back from Paris." As she struggled a bit with the cork, Maggie was oblivious to the fact that Destiny had abruptly ceased playing. She continued to ramble on without noticing that Destiny was now standing in front of the television. "I remember when my first husband, Frank, broke his arm. It wasn't as bad as yours, but it put him out of commission for a while. He was an artist. . . . What that man could do with his hands. . . . Did I ever tell you about him? . . . Destiny?" Maggie got no response from Destiny, who had tuned her out and was staring intently at the screen. Surprise drove the memories of her ex-husband from Maggie's mind, as she glanced over at the TV in order to see what had sparked Destiny's interest.

As Destiny turned up the volume, her living room was filled with the sound of Ann Capwell's confident, polished voice, making a victory speech.

"The last time I saw a snake that big, I was watching a National Geographic special," Maggie commented, as she watched Ann making her victory speech.

Without taking her eyes off the screen, Destiny held up her hand to prevent further commentary. "Shhh," she hushed Maggie.

Los Angeles news programs didn't make a practice of devoting air time to New York politicians' victory speeches, but this was an exception. Ann Capwell had become a national symbol for gay activism, ever since the account of her outing had unfolded. Hal Gottfried was more than successful at adding the right spin to her story and to her campaign.

Looking alternately from the TV to Destiny's face, Maggie noticed that Destiny's gaze wasn't at all fixed on Ann. She was occupied with the left corner of the screen. Squinting to see, Maggie was struck with a vaguely familiar face. It was Andrie. She stood in the background, to Ann's right. Her expression was gracious, but it seemed to lack the exuberance one would expect of a woman who was part of such a triumph. As the speech came to an end, Ann turned to Andrie, taking her hand and lifting it up in a show of victory. As Destiny watched the gesture, it was as though her heart were being crushed in Ann's upheld fist.

The news report continued on, but suddenly the sound of the television seemed overpowered by the silence that rang out from Destiny. Her eyes turned cold. The darkness that came from them eclipsed everything around her. Before a word could be said, she bolted from the house and took off in her car.

Maggie cringed as she watched the dark green Mustang tear out of the driveway, with its wheels screeching much of the way. Since it was almost eleven-thirty at night, and she was worried about Destiny's state of mind, she decided to call home and let her husband know that she planned to stay there for the night. She made herself at home as she waited for Destiny to return. Over three hours passed before Maggie heard the loud hum of the Mustang's massive engine in the driveway.

Destiny came through the front door, appearing to have calmed down during her drive.

"How are you feeling?" Maggie asked softly as she walked into the front hall to meet her.

"I'm going," Destiny answered decisively.

"Going? Going where?" Maggie asked, almost afraid of what the answer would be.

"I'm going to the premiere in New York. You were right. I was avoiding New York because of Andrie. I'm not going to let that happen. She's with Ann and she's happy in her life and I'm going to be happy in mine . . . without her."

"Whatever it is that will make you happy . . . I hope it happens. I really do," Maggie said as she leaned forward and hugged Destiny. "Come on inside and have a drink with me before I go home. Tony thinks that I'm spending the night here. But, if I leave here in the next five minutes, I'll still have enough life in me when I get home to surprise him with a little kinky sex in the middle of the night." With that announcement, Maggie turned and headed back into the living room.

Destiny started to follow her in, but stopped for a moment to look into the hall mirror. She saw the silver maple leaf dangling from the chain around her neck. Staring at its reflection she grasped the small, glimmering charm in her hand and closed her eyes, as she readied to rip it from her neck. The seconds were passing, but she was unable to find the strength to go through with it.

"Get out. Get out of my heart," she whispered in a strained voice, while inside she realized that she was fighting an impossible battle. She opened her eyes again and slowly released the trinket. As she walked away, she could again feel it, lying in place against her chest. Inexplicably, that sensation comforted some part of her.

* * *

Phil Massey had made his concession speech at about eight o'clock in the evening. Having received over two-thirds of the votes, Ann had won a resounding victory over the political newcomer.

After the victory party at campaign headquarters, Hal, Ray and a few of Ann's most important supporters had come back to the penthouse to continue celebrating. For the sake of appearance Andrie was forced to host the small gathering, which lasted until well after dawn. It was a champagne-popping, cigar-smoking celebration, throughout which Hal Gottfried and Ray Dalton gave each other non-stop congratulatory pats on the back. Andrie actually saw it as a blessing in disguise, since she didn't have to spend the night alone with Ann.

By the time the last of the guests had left, Ann was packed and ready to leave for her early flight to DC. As she waited for her car to arrive she took the opportunity to remind Andrie of her ultimatum.

"Don't forget that when I get back I'll expect things to be as they were before that Destiny Anderson affair of yours. If not, I will be fully prepared to consummate my threat. Do you understand?" she hissed.

Before Andrie had an opportunity to respond, the house phone rang and she answered it. A broad smile crossed her face as she shortly after hung up. "Your car is downstairs waiting to take you to the airport," she announced, still grinning as she left the room. Then, she groggily headed into the shower to purge herself of the night.

The stale, nauseating stench of cigarette and cigar smoke had permeated her hair and clothes. As she undressed, Andrie realized that even her skin smelled of smoke. Now alone in the bathroom she saw her naked reflection in the mirror. She was no longer grinning. She knew that the clock was ticking and it wouldn't be long before she would have to respond to Ann's ultimatum. There was no doubt in her mind that the callous politician would carry out her threat if Andrie refused to resume sleeping with her.

Chapter Forty

The melodic theme from the film *Exodus* filled the house as Destiny exercised her hand by playing the piano. Her favorite part of any movie was its music. That was one of the reasons she had jumped at the opportunity to write for Rena's film.

Taking a short rest, she stared out the rain-spattered window at the gray sky overhead. Her mind wandered from one subject to another as she tried to think of anything but Andrie. She remembered the phone call she received from Harry the week before. He wanted to let her know that Elaine's father had died and that they would probably not return from Paris until sometime shortly before the premiere, but that he and Elaine would still be attending. She knew that it was Harry's way of gently urging her to be there as well. He didn't know that Destiny had already decided to go.

Her mind then drifted on to Elaine's losing her father. After so many wasted years of bad feelings between them, in his last days, Elaine's father had opened his heart to his daughter and made his peace with her.

Destiny remembered hearing the emotion in Harry's voice as he explained how Elaine's father had summoned up what little strength he had left to extend his trembling, but contrite and loving hand to his son-in-law. She was touched by Harry's tears when he told her of the peace and grace that came to the old man in his last days and how much his forgiveness meant to Elaine.

Neither success nor time had brought Destiny any closer to her own family, with whom she maintained only the most minimal contact. She was certain that it would have been much different had her father not died when she was a young girl.

As she began to play again, she wondered why it was so difficult for human beings to find that peace throughout their lives. The music was softer now, as she continued to gaze out the window.

*   *   *

The sun's rays permeated the fractured canopy of trees that shaded the walking path of Washington Square Park, providing intermittent blotches of heat and light to those below.

"I must be getting old. This weather is really getting to me," Nancy complained, digging into her black leather purse in search of her gloves as she and Andrie strolled the walking path.

"They say that it's supposed to be a cold winter. I was reading that we might actually get some real heavy snow right before Christmas," Andrie said, then paused as her expression saddened. "It was snowing the first time I met Destiny . . . and last year when she turned up at Ann's fundraiser . . . it was snowing that night, too. Come to think of it, on both those occasions it snowed before Christmas. This time will break the trend, snow before Christmas and no Destiny . . . unless there's some kind of miracle." Andrie's eyes were misty, and she seemed momentarily caught up in some distant point in time as Nancy listened.

"Well, I believe in miracles. I believe your coming into my life was a miracle. If it wasn't for you, I might still be living with Matt. If he didn't kill me by now. But look at my life. I have a good job, a beautiful apartment and. . . ." Nancy stopped herself in mid-sentence. Her expression was that of someone who was about to reveal some happy secret. Then she saw the shrewd grin on Andrie's face. "You know, don't you?" Nancy asked with a sheepish smile, as she slowed her pace to a full halt.

"About you and my brother, Nick? . . . Of course. I could see something happening between you at Thanksgiving. Honestly, I don't know what took him so long. I knew that he was attracted to you, even before we had that party when you got out of the hospital. Now, don't you dare ask me how I feel about it. You should know the answer to that already. I just hope things between you two develop to the point where I get to play Aunt Andrie to a whole bunch of new little LaStellas. . . . Get my drift?" Andrie finished with a wink and resumed walking.

"Thanks for making me comfortable about this. We've only been dating for a few weeks 'and Nick wanted to tell you right away. I asked him to wait a little while, though. You've been going through so much . . . I was hoping things would get better for you first." Nancy felt awkward and Andrie heard it in her voice.

"Listen, what you told me was the best news I've heard in a long time. Whatever I'm going through has nothing to do with the way I feel about you and Nicky and your happiness. Don't ever be afraid to share that with me. Right now, seeing you two happy is the closest I can get to happiness myself. Don't deprive me of that," Andrie told her.

"I won't. I promise. But it hurts me so much to know that you could have the love you need, if Ann wasn't holding all that crap over your head. There's got to be something that you can do. . . . You can't go on living this way. Maybe you can call her bluff. If she owns Cobra, then she profits when Cobra profits, so why would she want to destroy the career and earning potential of one of its most popular artists? . . . I think you should fly out to LA and tell Destiny the truth about everything," Nancy advised, as she linked arms with Andrie, as much to comfort her as to keep warm.

"Number one, if Cobra went under tomorrow, Ann would hardly feel it financially. Number two is that power means more to her than money. That's the reason she's in politics and it's why she won't let me go. It's a sickness with her. Ann's not normal. She would think nothing of destroying everything Destiny has worked so hard for all her life. . . . I know what that would do to her. I can't let that happen."

"Don't you think that Destiny would rather have you more than anything else in the world . . . including her career?" Nancy's voice was tinged with impatience. She loved Andrie as much as if they were sisters and she was frustrated by Andrie's immovable attitude.

"She finally has what she always dreamed about. I can't be the cause of her losing all that."

"It's December fifteenth. Ann will be back in about a week, right?" Nancy asked.

"Yes," Andrie replied.

"So you told me that she wants to start sleeping with you again. Can you really agree to that, feeling the way you do?" Nancy stopped walking and held on to Andrie until she stopped, too.

"I don't have a choice. I don't even care, anymore. I'm numb to everything now. Anyway, what difference will it make?" Andrie said, feeling that she had lost track of the person she used to be.

"The difference is that you love Destiny," Nancy said in a voice loud enough that a woman who was across the path, walking an assortment of unruly dogs, turned to look at her. "How can you sacrifice so much of yourself; why do you have to be a martyr?"

"I'm not trying to be . . . I have to tell you something that I've been keeping inside. Do you remember when Destiny had that bus accident and you drove me to the hospital to see her?" Andrie asked her, in a voice that was begging to be understood.

"Of course, I remember," Nancy answered.

"Well, when we were on our way there, I was praying for her to be all right, but for a fleeting moment, there was another part of me that was thinking . . . well, maybe, if she isn't able to perform anymore, we could finally be together, since she wouldn't have a career for Ann to destroy. . . . So, do I still sound so self-sacrificing?" There were tears in Andrie's eyes as she made her confession, and waited for her friend's response.

"You're a human being, not a saint. That's a normal thought. But what you're doing now . . . I just don't know. Sometimes, I would like to just write a letter or something and tell Destiny what's going on, myself."

"No. Don't you ever do that. Please promise me that you'll never do that and you can't ever tell Nick, either. That would destroy my trust in you and our friendship." Andrie's voice was desperate and angry. There was an intense panicked look in her eyes.

To Nancy, it was as if Andrie was so possessed by fear that for a few seconds she became a raging, irrational stranger.

"OK. I promise. My lips are sealed . . . they are," Nancy vowed, as it became clear to her that no matter how well-intentioned, any interference on her part would likely destroy her friendship with Andrie. The thought frightened Nancy, since she loved her friend and didn't want to lose her. She was also falling in love with Andrie's brother and was afraid that betraying Andrie's trust, even for the right reason, might complicate her relationship with him. A pang of guilt tugged at her from deep inside. Nancy was never one to think of herself first, but she valued her new life, and Andrie's friendship, too much to lose either. She would keep her silence and pray for some miracle to happen in her friend's life.

They continued walking until they were out of the park. Although the conversation had turned to lighter subjects, both women's thoughts remained far more serious, as they made the long walk back to the office.

* * *

The rattling of the office's steam heat radiator, and the aroma of the cup of mint tea that Nancy placed on her desk, provided Andrie with a small measure of temporary comfort for which she was grateful as she returned to her work. Blue had jumped up on the desk and ensconced himself contentedly between a stack of files and the computer with which she was working. He began to sniff at her teacup, so Andrie scooped him up and plopped him on her lap as she continued what she was doing. It was a familiar and comfortable arrangement for both of them.

Too involved with her work to hear the phone ringing, Andrie found it a disquieting surprise when Nancy informed her that Ann was on the line waiting to speak with her.

Nancy watched Andrie from across the office, observing the

expression on her friend's face as she picked up the receiver and reacted to what Ann was saying.

At one point, she saw Andrie's body stiffen as she slowly lowered Blue to the floor. Even the little gray tabby seemed to be reading her face as she continued listening to Ann on the phone. He sat at her feet tilting his head to one side.

After several minutes of a conversation that was inaudible to Nancy from where she sat, Andrie hung up and leaned forward on her desk with her head in her hands. Blue managed to jump back into her lap and rub his head just under her chin, as if to somehow comfort her.

"What is it? What does she want from you now?" Nancy demanded to know, as she walked quickly toward Andrie. Her voice betrayed the fact that she was reaching the limit of what she could witness her friend endure. She put her arms around Andrie as she waited for the answer to her question.

It took several seconds for Andrie to look up at her and speak. "She's coming back on Christmas Eve. She wants me to be packed and ready to leave for Europe with her, at that time," Andrie said.

"Europe? Why? What's going on?"

"She's planning for us to have what she's calling a sort of honeymoon. She won't even tell me what country we'll be going to. She said that she wants to keep that a surprise," Andrie explained, still stunned by Ann's announcement.

"You've got to do something. Can't you see how wrong all this is?" Nancy pleaded.

"I tried to say no, but she brought up Destiny again," Andrie replied. Her expression was one of defeat and her voice was drained and lifeless as she continued, "I have no choice. I have to go with her." She was resolute.

"You've got a week before she comes back. Can't you try and think of anything that can get you out of this in that time? Don't you know anything that you can hold over her head? Maybe some kind of embarrassing stuff that would affect her political life?"

"I've thought of that already . . . and so did Ann. She told me that if I did anything to damage her politically, that she would still hold the controlling interest in Cobra and the first thing she would do is destroy Destiny. She's too rich, she's too powerful and . . ." Andrie's voice trailed off. She didn't want to finish her explanation, so she left out the most important fact. Ann would do whatever was necessary to have what she wanted or keep someone else from having it. That philosophy was just part of her father's legacy to her.

Chapter Forty-One

Fresh flowers and sunlight filled the suite as Maggie stood at the wet bar mixing herself a gin and tonic, while Destiny reclined on the couch with a bottle of mineral water.

"Did you make sure that David got those passes to the premiere?" Destiny asked as she lazily sipped from the bottle.

"Yes, and the invitation to the party afterwards. By the way, you'd better start getting ready soon. We have to be at the theater by two p.m. I have a car coming at one-thirty to pick us up. I can't believe that they made this thing so early. Rena said they had to, if they wanted everyone to attend on Christmas Eve. A lot of people are catching evening flights back to LA," Maggie said, looking at her watch as she taste-tested her mixture. "Time's really flying. How long will it take you to be ready?"

"I won't need more than a half hour. All I have to do is shower and jump into my clothes," Destiny replied nonchalantly.

"Wait a minute, now," Maggie screeched, stepping out from behind the bar. "You're not thinking of attending this in jeans and that beat-up old leather jacket, are you?" Maggie's dismayed tone was one that she routinely employed when dealing with any of her five children.

"I'll be wearin' a brand new pair of boots, though." Seeing Maggie's furious expression, Destiny continued, "Mag, why do we have to have this conversation every time I go to some function? You've gotta know by now that gettin' me to dress up is like tryin' to get a rooster to lay eggs. I tell you what. You dress real pretty and sexy and we'll let the press think that you're my date," Destiny joked.

"Oh, that's real funny. Go ahead and wear what you want. I give up. I guess I should be grateful that you're even going. . . . Could you at least dry your hair after you shower?" Maggie beseeched in frustration, as she left the room to call home.

Destiny laughed. She found it funny that her habit of going out with her hair still wet from the shower caused Maggie such concern.

Alone in the room, Destiny stood up and walked over to the tremendous window across from where she had been sitting. The view was one that overlooked a good portion of Central Park. She thought back to the day that she and Andrie walked along its paths a year before. Now, standing at the window, she noticed that it was beginning to snow. It reminded her of that day all the more, since it was snowing then, too. She started to think about the week she spent with Andrie and the night they made love. These were the memories that Destiny thought she could avoid by not coming to New York. Yet, no matter where she was, she would be unable to resist savoring the memory of the taste, the scent and the feeling of being in love with Andrie. It was something she took with her everywhere, the same way she always wore the silver maple leaf.

As she watched the snow drift slowly down to the city streets below, she remembered how Andrie looked the first time they met. She could still recall how the snowflakes landed softly on her hair and face. Then, melting from the heat of her body, they made her skin glisten with their dew.

Now, looking out over the snow-covered city, Destiny wondered where Andrie was at that very moment. A light tap on her shoulder suddenly drew her from her thoughts.

"I'm going back to my room to get ready. You'd better start too," Maggie told her in a soft voice, the kind she used when waking her children up in the morning.

As Destiny turned to acknowledge her, Maggie detected the slightest trace of a tear in the corner of her eye. Walking to the door, she spoke without turning back toward Destiny. "My first husband always said that memories of lost loves were the only scars he couldn't fix. He was a plastic surgeon. . . . Don't forget, dry your hair." With that Maggie pulled the door closed behind her.

Destiny glanced out the window one last time, as though

somehow she could find Andrie in the city below. Then, pressing a small button on the right side of the window, she turned away as the curtains drew shut.

*   *   *

Holding Blue in her arms, Andrie stood behind the window of her storefront office, watching the snow as it turned the pavement white. Kelly, the street musician who was usually installed on the sidewalk directly outside the office, was packing up her guitar so she could wait out the snow in a dry venue, like the nearest subway station.

Andrie had brought her luggage into the office that morning, since Ann was to be coming by to pick her up at the end of the day. She hardly spoke all morning. At lunch, she read that Destiny was in town for the premiere of *Riverside Drive*. There was no picture of her, just a mention of her name, among many others who would be attending.

"You're thinking that she's here in town somewhere and you want to see her. Aren't you?" Nancy asked, as she stood next to Andrie and stroked the furry stripes between Blue's ears.

"I couldn't see her. That would be impossible. It would hurt too much. David told me that she'd be coming in for this. I just forgot that it was today, until I saw it in the paper. I must have blocked it out of my mind," Andrie answered with a faraway look in her eyes.

"Maybe it's an omen. Don't you find it an odd coincidence that she's in town the same day that Ann's making you leave the country with her? Maybe it means that you're supposed to do something . . . like go to Destiny and tell her that you love her."

"No. I can't do that. You know what Ann is capable of doing to her. . . . Remember when I told you about that woman Lilly, and the prediction she made?" Andrie asked.

"You mean about the man dying and how it would affect you and Destiny?"

"Right. Well, ever since Ann's father died, she's become even more obsessed with keeping Destiny and me apart. I guess as far as signs and omens go, I already know how things are going to turn out for me."

"So you're determined to go through with this and waste your life with someone you hate," Nancy said, taking Blue out of Andrie's arms and placing him on the floor, so Andrie would have nothing to distract her from what Nancy was about to tell her. "What you're about to do is emotional suicide. As your friend I'm begging you not to give in to Ann's threats and demands. Please, go to Destiny and tell her everything . . . please."

"I love you and I appreciate what you're trying to do, but I don't want to discuss this anymore," Andrie said, dismissing Nancy's advice.

"This is crazy. It's Destiny's career, versus your life. Isn't your life more important?" Nancy argued impatiently, as she felt precious time slipping away.

"Destiny *is* my life. I won't let Ann do anything that would destroy her happiness."

"Don't you see? She already has," Nancy replied, shaking her head as she walked back to her desk. It was obvious to her that Andrie had turned a deaf ear to her warnings. "Listen, I don't want to be here when Ann comes for you. I don't think that I could trust myself if I saw her. . . . Anyway, I'm supposed to meet Nick at your mom's house. I'm having Christmas Eve dinner with them. So, I'm going home in a little while," Nancy announced as she began shutting down the copy machine and her computer.

Andrie returned to her desk in the back of the office. "I'm still working on the proposal for Franklin Pharmacies, so don't turn off the printer," she instructed Nancy, as she typed away at the keyboard.

"Sure . . . oh, by the way, I'm sure that you're aware of the fact that Nick and the rest of your family are worried sick about you, since they can't figure out why you've distanced yourself from them over the past year. They know that it has something to do with Ann. Do you know how I feel, keeping all this a secret and watching you do this to yourself?" Nancy fumed as she buttoned her coat.

Andrie stood and turned sharply toward her. "Whatever you do, don't make me sorry that I trusted you with this." Her expression was at first angry, but it softened almost immediately, as she looked into Nancy's eyes. "Please, Nan, try to understand; I'm doing the only thing I can do for now," she explained in a milder tone. Then, pulling a small, brightly wrapped rectangular box from her desk drawer, Andrie handed it to Nancy. "Oh, here, I almost forgot. Merry Christmas," she said.

"Should I open it now?" Nancy asked.

"No. Why don't you wait until tonight at Mom and Dad's. I had the rest of my gifts for everybody shipped there. You can open it when they open theirs," Andrie suggested. In the box was a watch she had seen Nancy admire once when they were window shopping.

"All right. By the way, my gift for you has been sitting on your desk since this morning." Nancy pointed to a gold foil-wrapped box, topped with a generous red velvet ribbon.

Andrie looked at her desk, and for the first time noticed the ornately dressed box, perched atop a stack of drab manila folders. "That's been there all day? . . . I'm sorry. I guess my mind's been somewhere else," she apologized.

"I know that. I wanted to tell you to open it this morning, when I saw that you weren't wearing anything red for Christmas, but you didn't seem like you were in a mood to open any gifts . . . Andrie, are you sure that you have to do this?" Nancy asked, referring to the trip with Ann.

"I'm sorry. I know this is a burden for you and that you're worried about me, but please just let it go. There's nothing we can do about this. I'll be OK. Now get out of here and have a Merry Christmas. And don't forget to give my love to Nicky, and everybody, tonight." With that Andrie smiled, put her arms around Nancy and they embraced.

Seeing beyond Andrie's forced smile to the desperate loneliness inside, Nancy was angry with herself for not being able to help this dear friend who meant so much to her. Again she pointed to the gold box on Andrie's desk and reminded her, "Don't forget that now."

"Whatever is in that box, I promise that I'll put it on before the end of the day. Now take Blue and go home," Andrie replied in a kind but instructive tone, as she picked up the affectionate ball of gray fur and handed him to Nancy. Sensing Nancy's misgivings and reluctance to say good-bye, Andrie opened the door and led her through, patting Blue on the way out. She watched from the doorway until Nancy disappeared around the corner.

The snow seemed to be letting up and Andrie knew that it wouldn't be long before Kelly would be back in front of the office, strumming her guitar and singing for loose change from passersby. The delicate layer of white that had covered the sidewalk was fading rapidly from the tracks left by pedestrians and cars as they traveled down the street. She returned to her desk, where concentration eluded her as she continued to work.

*   *   *

The second Nancy opened the apartment door, Blue jumped out of her arms and headed for his favorite room, the kitchen. The friendly little cat spent all the weekends and holidays at Nancy's apartment, since Ann refused to let Andrie bring him into the penthouse.

Nancy removed her coat and headed into the kitchen where she filled a small bowl with milk and placed it on the floor for her four-legged house guest. Then, walking over to her answering machine, she pressed the play button and after a series of clicks and winding sounds, Nick's voice filled the kitchen. *"Hi sweets. It's just me. I can't wait to see you tonight. I'll probably be getting to Mom's house a little late. They just mentioned something about a special detail assignment. Anyway I'll see ya later."*

As she listened to his message, Nancy was filled with a feeling of warmth and belonging. She was looking forward to spending the holidays with Nick and his family. She knew that he was the right one. There was something about him that struck her as special from the first time Andrie introduced them. Looking around her apartment she realized how very much her life had changed because of Andrie's friendship. Suddenly the sense of fulfillment she was feeling made her even more aware of Andrie's pain. There was no way she could stand by and enjoy her own life while her best friend continued to suffer.

Andrie's parting words to her amounted to the fact that there was nothing Nancy could do to help her. But her own conscience told Nancy something else. It told her that Andrie had one chance left for happiness, and that Nancy was it. But she would have to violate Andrie's confidence and risk losing the very friendship that had not only saved her life, but made it worth living. She thought to herself how ironic it was that just when her life was turning out so well, she would have to make a decision that might cost her a friend she loved so much. Nancy never had much in the way of family or friends. All her life, her dream was to belong somewhere and have a family who cared about her. Andrie had helped that dream come true for her.

"It's my turn to give something back in this relationship . . . even if it destroys it," she said out loud, as Blue looked on from his spot in the kitchen. Rushing out to the living room and riffling through her small, dark brown leather briefcase, she pulled out her address book and a copy of the newspaper with the article on the premiere. She nervously flipped through the pages of the book until she found Andrie's mother's home phone number. Grabbing the phone, she quickly dialed the number. After only two rings, she heard Maria's cheerful voice on the other end.

"Hello."

"Hi, Maria. It's Nancy."

"Oh, Nancy honey. I'm just getting dinner ready for tonight. Is everything all right?"

"Yes, But I may be getting to your house a little late. I need to do something for a friend. It shouldn't take long, but I just wanted to let you know."

"Don't worry, sweetheart. You do what you need to do. Nicky is going to be a little late too. He's on some special duty. It doesn't matter if you come late. Just come hungry."

"OK. I'll see you as soon as I get done." Hanging up, she then reached for the newspaper and began searching feverishly for the article on the premiere. Finding it, she tore out the page, put her coat on and ran out to the street to find a taxi.

She impatiently looked up and down the street for a cab. Then, checking her watch, she saw that it was a quarter to four. She pulled the tattered newspaper page from her purse. It mentioned that the time of the premiere was unusually early, about two in the afternoon. Figuring that the movie itself was probably about an hour and a half, Nancy could only hope that a premiere would take longer than that. She felt her heart racing as she remembered that Ann would be arriving at the office by five o'clock to pick up Andrie and leave for Europe. As she began to calculate how many minutes she had to accomplish her task, Nancy saw a cab. She frantically flagged it down. It had barely stopped before she pulled open the door and jumped in. She rattled off the address of the theater and directions to it in one long breath, then craned her head forward to see if the driver had understood her. The cabby appeared to be a foreigner, so she quickly added, "Do you understand where I need to go?"

"I think you want to go to the movies. Huh?" the swarthy, mustached driver replied in a heavy Arabic accent. He seemed amused by Nancy's concern for whether or not he understood her instructions.

"I'm sorry if I sounded like . . ." Nancy started to apologize for her patronizing tone.

"Don't be sorry, lady. I learned English and studied street maps of the city, so I could do a good job. I know not everybody does that. . . . You got lucky to get Mohammed as your cab driver. I'll get you there fast and safe," he said with pride.

"Thank you, Mohammed. I appreciate that," Nancy replied, as she moved back in her seat and allowed him to negotiate his way through the heavy, cross-town traffic. She no longer felt the need to monitor the cabby's facial expressions for a lack of comprehension; she was confident that he knew what he was doing.

It took close to thirty minutes for them to reach the Upper East Side from Nancy's West Village apartment. As Mohammed attempted to turn onto the block of the theater, a policeman approached the cab. "You're gonna have to go two blocks down, if you need to make a left turn. This street's temporarily closed to through traffic," the officer informed them in a polite but firm tone.

"What's going on?" asked the curious taxi driver.

"There's some big movie premiere that's finishing up and we can't let any cars through until the Mayor and the other guests have left. You gotta move now, OK?" said the young blond cop, as he waved them on.

"Pull over there," Nancy instructed Mohammed in a hurried voice and pointed to a spot halfway up the street. The driver did as she requested. She thanked him as she handed him a twenty-dollar bill for her ten-dollar fare, then rushed down the block. "Lady, lady your change," he called after her. But she had no time to wait for change.

"Keep it, Mohammed," Nancy shouted back, without slowing her pace. As she turned the corner, she saw that some of the limousines were pulling away and others were moving into their spots to pick up the guests as they exited the theater. She prayed that Destiny hadn't left yet. Reaching the theater, she became immersed in the crowd of fans who had gathered on either side of the entrance, blocked off from the celebrities' path by blue and white police barricades.

"Has Destiny Anderson come out yet?" Nancy urgently asked a young woman who was being thrust against her by the movement of the enthusiastic crowd.

"She was never in the closet," the woman quipped back with a wink. Then, turning more serious, she told Nancy that Destiny hadn't left yet. Nancy thanked her and continued to push through the throng of celebrity watchers as she attempted to get at least as far as the police line. She was hoping to be able to get Destiny's attention as she passed by on her way to her car. There seemed to be a short lull in the activity. Nancy hoped that the woman was correct about Destiny not having exited yet.

Without warning, another wave of celebrities paraded out to their limousines, some of them stopping to shake hands or wave to shrieking onlookers as they made their way to the sanctuary of the waiting cars.

Nancy suddenly felt her heart begin to race when she heard a group of what were obviously Destiny Anderson fans begin to scream her name, having sighted her just inside the lobby of the theater. *"Destiny . . . Destiny . . . Destiny,"* they roared, almost hysterically, as a sandy-haired figure in a brown leather jacket and faded jeans appeared.

Nancy had made it up to the police line, but she was standing close to the curb. She wouldn't be able to catch Destiny's attention until right before the singer reached her limousine.

Realizing that by then her voice would probably be drowned out by the rest of the crowd, Nancy decided to take immediate action. Destiny was halfway to the curb and had momentarily stopped to chat with some fans who had successfully caught her attention, so Nancy crouched down and came up on the other side of the wooden police line. Without a split second delay, she dashed toward Destiny.

"Destiny, Destiny!" she called out. But before Nancy could get close enough for Destiny to hear her over the noise of the crowd, two vigilant police officers closed in on her. They quickly flanked her and pulled her back behind the police line, despite her protests.

"Please. I have to talk with Destiny Anderson. It's important," she insisted, as the two officers stood shoulder to shoulder, facing her and blocking her from another attempt to cross the barrier.

"Lady, half the women here want to tell her something important. Now, why don't you just calm down, and admire her from afar like they're doing. OK?" The policeman's tone was more bored and fatigued than condescending, but it was clear that he had no intention of letting her near Destiny. As he spoke, Nancy saw Destiny heading toward a waiting limousine.

"Destiny!" she screamed as loud as she could. Her voice seemed to climb above all the others. Just before entering the back of her car, Destiny turned instinctively toward the source of the call. Her eyes met Nancy's. She smiled at her, then disappeared into limo.

In one last, futile attempt, Nancy tried to push her way through the towering blue wall that the two policemen had formed. Their patience almost exhausted by then, the police officers pulled her back to restrain her from running toward the car.

"Let me go. I need to talk to her," Nancy demanded and continued to call out to Destiny.

"Lady, calm down or we're gonna have to arrest you," the older of the two cops cautioned her. She was oblivious to the warning, as she continued to call out to Destiny, whose car had now pulled away from the curb.

"That's it lady. We better take you someplace where you can calm down," said the younger officer, as he pulled Nancy away from the line and began to escort her toward a nearby patrol car parked at the curb.

"Nancy, Nancy," a voice called out from nearby, as a third officer suddenly appeared on the scene. His tall broad form was familiar to Nancy, as was the sense of warmth and protection she felt from him. "What's going on here?" he asked, putting his arm around Nancy's shoulder.

"Nick, is she a friend of yours?" both cops seemed to ask in unison.

"She's my fiancee. Now what's the trouble?" Nick asked in a perturbed tone.

Nancy knew that Nick was exaggerating the nature of their

relationship simply to ensure that there would be no further trouble. Yet the sound of his lie was appealing to her.

"Nothing, really. She just got a little overexcited about one of the celebrities, that's all," the older cop answered, not wishing to pursue the subject further.

"What are you doing here? Is everything all right?" Nick asked as he turned to her.

Curiosity got the best of the two police officers, who had been about to arrest Nancy prior to Nick's arrival. They remained in place waiting to hear her response as well.

"We need to get to Destiny. It's important," she told him, uncomfortably aware that the two nosy police officers were listening to her.

"Come with me. Do you know how lucky you are that I pulled special duty as part of the Mayor's escort while he was at this shindig? Those guys would've probably arrested you as a public nuisance if I hadn't come along," Nick admonished as he ushered Nancy toward the patrol car, which remained parked at the curb. "So, what's so important that you almost got arrested?" he asked as they reached it.

"I know what's been wrong with your sister. I've known it for months now, but she swore me to secrecy. . . . Only I can't keep the secret anymore because I'm afraid that if I don't say something now, she's going to ruin her life."

"Nancy, what are you talking about?"

"Do you know where Destiny is headed?" Nancy asked, too impatient to continue with explanations.

"I know that they invited the Mayor to some big party at the Plaza, but he couldn't go because of an emergency budget meeting. She probably went there. . . . At least give me an idea of what's going on," Nick persisted, as his curiosity heightened.

"Andrie is in love with Destiny and Destiny is in love with her. Now we need to get to Destiny right away, or your sister is going to do something she'll regret forever," Nancy hurriedly explained.

"Get in the car. I'll be right back." Nick pointed to the parked patrol car. Then he ran over to a group of police officers who were in the lobby of the theater. He returned moments later and jumped behind the wheel of the patrol car.

"OK. I have one hour to be back at the station to sign off. Now, tell me everything from the beginning," he said, turning on the flashing red lights and starting off toward the Plaza Hotel. The car made its way swiftly through the city streets, while inside it, Nancy revealed everything that Andrie had confided in her. As she spoke, she knew that she had made the right decision. She only hoped that she had made it in time.

*   *   *

Inside the Plaza's ballroom, the atmosphere was festive. Everyone agreed that *Riverside Drive* was sensational, and that Rena Samuel had truly captured the flavor of New York City in her film. Destiny's music was acclaimed as having intensified all the emotions that the story intended to stir. It was obvious that the soundtrack would be a tremendous hit.

Between the compliments and congratulations, Destiny surveyed the room for Harry and Elaine. She had seen them at the screening and Harry had said that he needed to speak with her later. But as she stood there looking around the room, she could find no sign of him or Elaine. Then, a familiar voice came up from behind her.

"Des, Des. There you are. Some *pretend date* you turned out to be. You walked away from me the minute we arrived here," Maggie complained, as she approached with a gin and tonic in hand.

"I'm sorry. When you stopped to talk to Stuart Sottley, I didn't want to hang around. You know how I feel about that guy. So I figured I'd hang out and wait for David and Alan," Destiny explained apologetically.

"Well, you walked away from me for nothing. He barely started to talk when Harry interrupted us and asked if I would excuse them for a while. So, here I am . . . and if you walk away from me again, I think I'm going to get a complex." Then, hearing the music wafting in from the next room, she continued. "Rena went all out with this. She had them re-create the dance club that was in the first scene. You've got to go in there and see it," Maggie said, pointing in the direction from which the music was coming. Then she added, "Although no one is using it to dance. Who the hell wants to dance at four o'clock in the afternoon? I'm amazed that anybody would even want to attend a party at this hour. Sometimes I think Rena is crazy, but I guess that she's one of those crazy-like-a-fox types." As she spoke, she was distracted by a well-built young waiter with a broad smile and steel blue eyes, who came by with a tray of hors d'oeuvres. She continued to stare admiringly at him as he circulated through the room.

"Will you stop staring at that poor guy," Destiny snapped, nudging Maggie with her elbow.

"I can't help it. He reminds me so much of my fourth husband," she replied without losing sight of the waiter.

A befuddled look came over Destiny. "But you've only been married three times," she noted.

"I know," Maggie answered with a mischievous grin.

Destiny shook her head and laughed. She knew that Maggie was as happily married as anyone could get, particularly anyone in the Hollywood scene.

"By the way, did you see Nicole yet? She's here with Bee," Maggie whispered, as she scanned the room to locate them. Suddenly, her eyes widened with shock as she grabbed Destiny's arm. "Oh my God! I can't believe it!" she gasped.

"What?" Destiny asked, in an only half-interested voice.

"Sonia. It's Sonia."

"Where?" Destiny's reaction became significantly more concerned with Maggie's discovery. But, before Maggie could reply, Sonia had seen them and was headed directly toward Destiny.

The tall, lanky blonde's face wore a rather solemn, sheepish expression, which grew more remorseful as she got nearer. Destiny stared squarely into her unadorned green eyes. Sonia was once one of her closest and most trusted friends, until she stole Nicole from her. Yet any bitter feelings that Destiny might have harbored toward her then, were now long forgotten.

Much to Maggie's surprise and relief, as Sonia came upon them, Destiny greeted her with a clement smile. It was clear that Sonia was deeply touched by her old friend's forgiveness. Tears were not something easily shed by the carefree, womanizing Swede, but this time she could do nothing to control them. They rolled down from her face, following the paths of the lines and crevices left there by time, sun and a fast lifestyle. "I missed you so much!" she exclaimed, as she enveloped Destiny in a huge bear hug. "I want you to know how sorry I am for what I did to you and to the friendship we had. I was an ass . . . I was worse than an ass. I was a brainless, soulless, heartless ass! I would give anything to have our friendship back."

"I'd like that, too. What happened between you and Nicole isn't even something I think about anymore. So let's just take it from here. . . . A fresh start. OK?" Destiny's offer was sincere and she had no desire to discuss the past. Too much had changed in her life since then.

Grateful for Destiny's forgiveness, Sonia hugged her once again as Maggie slipped off, unnoticed, to mingle with the other guests. The two friends remained in the middle of the room getting reacquainted with each other.

"So, are you just in town for this premiere or is there something else?" Destiny asked.

"I'm just here for the premiere. I don't know if you've heard this yet, but Rena and I have been seeing a lot of each other, so it was important to me to be here for her."

"You and Rena?" The idea of Sonia in love with Rena Samuel was amusing. Although Rena was fashionable and elegant in appearance, which was something Sonia always looked for in her women, she was also in her early fifties and was well known for her "all business and no bullshit" philosophy. Destiny couldn't help but grin at the thought of Sonia and Rena as a couple.

Catching her expression, Sonia began to explain, "I know what you're thinking. You're thinking that this could never last, because Rena is a lot older than me and she's a very strong woman with a lot of power. But I'm tired of being used for my power and my money. I don't want to be with anymore air-headed, *user* types, who want to build a career off my fame. You know the kind just as well as I do." Then leaning forward she whispered, "Don't look now, but Nicole is standing a few feet behind you. It looks like Bee is about to learn about that type, too."

Destiny chuckled, acknowledging Sonia's observation.

"Somebody mentioned that you were looking for a place in Montana," Sonia mentioned, as she remembered the rumor.

"Actually, I just bought the place. It's beautiful . . . really peaceful," Destiny said, wishing all the while that she could share that peace and beauty with the woman she loved.

As Destiny spoke, Sonia recognized a change in her. The observant Swede couldn't quite focus in on what it was. But she decided that this wasn't the time or place to question her old friend about it. Instead she just joked about Destiny becoming a mountain woman.

Just then Destiny spotted David and Alan. They had seen her first and were working their way through the crowded room to get to her. Finally reaching her, David threw his arms around Destiny, kissing her loudly on the cheek.

"Hi, honey. Let me look at you. Oh look, those cuts left you with little tiny scars. We can put a little concealer on that and they'll completely disappear and, while we're at it, maybe a little blush and . . ." he said, gently touching Destiny's right cheek with his finger.

"No thanks. Give it up. After all these years, you should have learned that you're never gonna get me to wear makeup," Destiny cut in, taking his hand in hers and chuckling at his persistence.

David began to laugh. In all the time he had known Destiny, she had resisted every effort ever made to change her rather boyish style. "Well, you can't kill me for trying. . . . Anyway, the movie was wonderful and your music as always was beautiful . . . perfect. It brought out such emotion, I started crying right there in the theater. I can't wait until I see you on stage again. That reminds me, how's the arm feeling?"

"It's fine. It's almost completely back to normal," Destiny answered with a proud, relieved grin, as she reached for Alan, who was quietly standing behind David. She pulled him toward her and kissed him hello. "Sonia, you remember David, you met at my birthday party a couple of years ago . . . and this is his partner, Alan."

"Of course I remember David," Sonia said as she extended her hand to him, but David was holding a drink and made no effort to respond to her overture. She then proceeded to shake Alan's hand, as David dealt her a cold stare. Unlike Destiny, he was not ready to forgive Sonia for what she and Nicole had done. He had clearly made her uncomfortable.

"Destiny, I'd love to talk with you or have lunch soon. So let's hook up when we both get back to LA," Sonia stammered awkwardly, as she tried to maintain her poise.

"Sure, I'd like that too . . . really," Destiny said, earnestly attempting to compensate for David's behavior. They hugged each other briefly before Sonia excused herself and returned to the table where Rena was seated.

"Now what did you go doin' that for?" Destiny chastised David.

"Because I don't like what she did to you and I'm not ready to forgive her yet," David responded in a petulant tone, as he stirred his Bloody Mary with his finger.

"Can't you do somethin' about him?" Destiny joked in exasperation to Alan.

"He's in one of his Bette Davis moods. It's better to just ignore him until it passes." Alan's reply was that of someone who was intimately aware of David's few shortcomings and patiently accepted them.

Destiny could see that Alan was obviously very much in love

with her friend. She was happy for David. For years, she had wished that he would find someone like Alan.

"David, don't get too obnoxious. You've got a really nice guy here," she advised, giving a friendly wink in Alan's direction.

"Don't worry about me. . . . Unlike you, I'm smart enough to know when I found the right one," he answered.

Destiny understood the message in David's response. "I told you, weeks ago, I don't want to hear her name. OK?" she reminded in an impatient tone.

"Who mentioned her name. All I said was . . ."

"Enough." Destiny cut him off. "Now, let's drink or eat or dance or whatever the hell else you want to do. We don't see each other that often. Let's make the most of it."

"You're right, I'm sorry. Let's go dance." David's apologies regarding that subject were always halfhearted. He was a slave to his emotions. He knew this would not be the last time that he would break Destiny's rule about mentioning Andrie. So did Destiny and Alan. As they all turned and headed for the next room where the dance floor was, Destiny accidentally bumped into David, causing the drink he was holding to spill onto his black silk trousers.

"I guess I'm still as graceful as ever, huh? See, that's one good reason why you'll never see me in anything like that," she said, referring to the impeccably tailored Armani suit David was wearing, as she looked around for a stray cocktail napkin.

"I'm going to run into the men's room and clean this off. Try not to spill anything on my boyfriend while I'm gone, Calamity Jane." With that David disappeared into the crowd.

Destiny turned to Alan and smiled. "There's a look about him that I haven't seen since we were in college. He's really happy," she observed.

"I'm happy too. It's like I was waiting all my life just to meet him." Alan's soft blue eyes glowed when he spoke of David. And Destiny understood exactly what he meant. She understood all too well.

*   *   *

The patrol car pulled up to the main entrance of the elegant
hotel. Nancy and Nick jumped out and ran up the front steps. Her
determination made Nancy look every bit as official as Nick did in
his uniform. Reaching the top of the steps, they were approached
by a doorman, ready to provide assistance in what to him
appeared to be some sort of police emergency. "Can I help you,
officer?" he asked eagerly.

"We need to find Destiny Anderson," Nick replied.

"Destiny who?" It was obvious that the doorman was not an
avid fan of Destiny's music.

"She's a guest at the big party that's taking place here," Nancy
said.

"OK. I'll have to call the manager's office to get permission for
you to go up there." With that, the doorman led them into the
lobby, where he picked up a phone, dialed a four-digit number,
then appeared to be put on hold.

"We're never going to make it. We're losing too much time,"
Nancy sighed, tapping her foot, with annoyance.

"We don't really have a choice, Nan," Nick said, as he put his
arm around her. Just then the elevator doors slid open and out
walked David. He was on his way outside for a few minutes,
hoping that the cool air would dry the large wet spot that was left
on his pant leg after he had washed off the stain.

"David," Nick called out to him as he headed toward the door.

David turned to see Nick and Nancy standing there with worried
expressions on both their faces.

"Oh my God. What's wrong? Is Andrie all right?" he demanded
to know as he rushed toward them.

"Yeah, she's fine," Nick said in a hurried but assuring voice.

"No she's not," Nancy broke in. "Ann is about to take off for
Europe with her and she's still in love with Destiny."

Although Nancy hadn't told him the whole story, David heard
enough to know that he needed to get them to Destiny instantly.

From behind him, David heard the elevator doors open and people coming out.

"Quick, come with me, she's upstairs." They followed him into the elevator, leaving the doorman, who was still holding on the phone.

On the way up, Nancy quickly explained what had been going on in Andrie's life over the last several months. As they filed quickly out of the elevator and directly toward the ballroom one of the plainclothes security guards approached them. David pulled the invitation from his breast pocket and announced that Nick and Nancy were with him. The man recognized David as a guest and allowed them through.

"I'll bet he thought that you were an actor in a cop costume," David said, as he craned his neck to see where Destiny and Alan were. None of the guests seemed particularly concerned by the presence of a uniformed police officer in their midst.

"There she is. She's standing at the bar," Nancy told them, as she started toward Destiny.

"Des, Des!" David called to her, as he ran ahead of Nancy. As difficult as it was for him, Nick followed behind, slowly and calmly. He knew that if he rushed through the room the guests might think that there was something wrong.

"You've got to come with us right now!" David said, grabbing hold of Destiny's hand as he reached her.

"What?" she exclaimed, bewildered as to what he was up to now. Then, looking over at Nancy who was standing next to him, Destiny asked, "What's going on?"

"I was the nut screaming for you today as you left the theater," Nancy replied.

"She's Andrie's friend," David added.

Then, Destiny saw Nick as he stood towering above David and Nancy. Suddenly, she felt the blood drain from her face as she saw the three people close to Andrie staring at her. "Oh my God, it's Andrie. . . . What's wrong?" She grabbed David's arm and demanded to know in a frantic, alarmed voice. All her defenses were momentarily down, as her eyes widened with fear.

Alan, who was standing with Destiny, immediately put his arm around her.

"She's OK," David assured her.

"Then what's going on?" she demanded.

David nodded to Nancy. "Tell her. You're the only one who knows the whole story."

Without hesitation Nancy started. "Andrie's still in love with you."

Hearing that, Destiny's expression turned to one of anger. "What is this? David, this is it. Look, I don't know what's going on here, but if Andrie put you up to this because her little life with the congresswoman is getting boring again and she thinks it's time to pull me out of her past, you can just tell her to . . ."

"No. My sister loves you and you love her, but time and again things have been keeping you apart. Just shut up and listen. Please," Nick said, breaking his silence in a way that was unusually forceful for him.

Hearing him, Destiny turned to Nancy, ready to listen to what she knew now would be the truth.

Again, Nancy picked up her story. "Ann has been forcing Andrie to stay with her for the past year. Last December, when Andrie told her that she was in love with you and that she was leaving, Ann said that she would never let her go. She told Andrie that if she left, Ann would ruin your career by not promoting your albums or letting you tour and stuff like that. And that if you tried to get out of your contract, she could keep you in court for enough years that no one would remember who you were by the time she got done with you."

"Look, Ann may be close with Stuart Sottley, but he's not gonna let her make decisions for him about his business," Destiny said, her voice still laced with skepticism.

"That's just it, Sottley doesn't own his share of Cobra Records. Ann does. He's just a front for her. She uses him to run all the businesses she owns, so she can avoid being accused of conflict of interest or impropriety, as a member of Congress. None of that matters now. . . . Andrie loves you and the only reason she's not with you is because she wanted to protect you from Ann. She said that she couldn't let Ann take away everything that you've worked all your life to achieve," Nancy explained excitedly.

"All this time, Andrie was with Ann just to protect my career? I don't give a damn about my career, if I can't have her. Where is she now?" Destiny asked, as she began walking toward the door with the small entourage close behind.

"She's either in her office or . . ." Nancy began to hesitate.

"Or what? Tell me," Destiny demanded, as she stopped and looked at Nancy for a reply.

"Ann is supposed to pick her up at the office at five o'clock. She has a private chartered jet waiting somewhere to take them to Europe, for what she's calling a *honeymoon*. She hasn't even told Andrie where they're supposed to be going," Nancy explained frantically.

"Andrie's not going anywhere with her," Destiny exclaimed, as she grabbed Nancy's hand and rushed out of the room. Her heart was pounding with joy and urgency at the same time.

Following behind them, Nick called out, "I'll take you there in the patrol car. It's on my way back to the station and I can get you there faster than a regular car. "

"Come on. I only have twenty-five minutes," Destiny urged, as she reached the elevator and hammered repeatedly on the down button.

Standing by the elevator, deep in conversation, were Stuart Sottley, Harry Stern and two other men carrying briefcases. It seemed as though the men with the briefcases worked for Harry.

Seeing them, Destiny interrupted their discussion. "Excuse me, Harry, I just need to talk with Mr. Sottley, or should I call you Congresswoman Capwell," she said sarcastically, as she stared Sottley squarely in the eye. "You can take my recordin' career and shove it up your ass. I know the whole story and nothin' short of

God himself is gonna keep me away from Andrie." Then, pushing her finger into Stuart's chest, she finished, "Understand?"

"Destiny, sweetheart, what's wrong?" a dumbfounded Harry asked.

"I'm sorry, Harry. I love you and Elaine. But I'm finished with Cobra. In fact, I'm finished recording," she told him as she hopped on the elevator the second its doors opened, followed by David, Alan, Nick, and Nancy. Just as the doors began to close, Harry jumped on too.

"Destiny, were you serious?" Harry asked.

"Harry, Sottley doesn't own the controlling percentage of Cobra, Ann Capwell does, and she's been holding on to Andrie by threatenin' to destroy my career if Andrie left her for me," she explained, as the doors opened and she headed through the lobby to the front door.

"You're wrong. That's not true," Harry said with an air of authority.

"What do you mean?" she asked, stopping momentarily, as she reached the patrol car.

"Sottley doesn't own Cobra, and neither does Ann Capwell. I do . . . or actually Elaine does. Me, and my legal eagles upstairs, just declared the contract null and void. I paid Sottley in full, as per our agreement, and he signed Cobra back to me on the spot. We took him by complete surprise. You see, Elaine's father left her enough money to buy Cobra fifty times over." With that, Harry handed Destiny a manila envelope he had been carrying. "Take this. It's a copy of all the dirt my guys uncovered for me over the last couple of weeks. They were looking into Sottley, but they came up with plenty of stuff about the congresswoman. . . . So, you go be with Andrie now and tell her not to worry about your career. She's a good girl. I always liked her," he said, kissing Destiny on the forehead as she got into the patrol car.

"Harry!" Destiny called out.

"What, sweetheart?"

"Can you do me a big favor?"

"Anything," he answered sincerely.

"I need your car and your driver for the rest of the evening. Do you know where Andrie's office is?"

"Yeah, I went there to congratulate her when she first opened up."

"Have it meet me there as soon as possible. Oh . . . and the company jet . . . can it take me to Montana tonight?"

"With pleasure. It'll be waiting for you at Kennedy . . . and tell Andrie that I bought back the Women's Way building too. Elaine is going to start up the program again in her father's name."

Hearing that from the back seat of the patrol car, Nancy blew a kiss in Harry's direction. She, more than anyone else, knew how important the Women's Way program was.

As the patrol car pulled swiftly away from the curb with its lights flashing and its siren blaring, Destiny was consumed by a single purpose, to reach Andrie before she had sacrificed anymore of herself to Ann.

Nick maneuvered the car briskly through the late afternoon traffic. On the way Destiny ripped open the envelope and glanced at the information inside. It was all there: proof of everything Ann owned, her dealings with Cortronics and even her illegal campaign financing. Destiny tossed the documents onto the floor of the patrol car angrily, as she realized the kind of woman who had been tormenting and threatening Andrie for the past year.

Within minutes, the car had crossed town and arrived on the West Side, headed toward SoHo. As they turned onto Lafayette Street, they suddenly found themselves in bumper-to-bumper traffic. Even the patrol car siren was unable to clear the cars in front of them quickly enough to get to Andrie's office in time.

"I know this area, just tell me where her office is," Destiny demanded, as she threw open the car door and stepped out.

"It's on Prince Street between West Broadway and Thompson. It'll be on your right. . . . The sign says LaStella Marketing Inc. . . . But it's at least ten blocks from here and it's almost five o'clock now; you'll never make it by foot," Nancy called from the back seat, in a pressured tone.

The unassuming Kentuckian glanced back at Nancy with determined eyes, then slammed the door behind her and bolted out of sight.

*   *   *

Andrie had changed into the red lambswool sweater that had been nestled between piles of flaky thin tissue paper in the gold foil box. On a card that was attached to it, Nancy had written a short note: *Dear Andrie, You are my closest friend. I so dearly want to wish you a Merry Christmas, but I know how you're feeling right now and how you'll be spending this holiday. So instead, I will wish you, with all my heart, a Christmas miracle. One that brings you all the happiness you deserve. Love, Nancy*

If only that wish could come true, Andrie thought to herself, as she glanced at the card again. Then, walking over to the front window of the office, she looked to see if Ann's car had arrived yet. It hadn't. There was little activity on the street aside from Kelly, the street musician who had returned soon after the snow had stopped falling. Andrie couldn't hear her, but she watched her lips move and her facial expressions change as she stood under a broad-brimmed, cowhide hat and sang to some imaginary audience, more than to the few passersby who dropped money in her open guitar case. Watching her reminded Andrie of Destiny. They had something in common. A dream. For Destiny, the dream had come true. But for now, Kelly was still only seeing that dream in her mind's eye. She remembered the way Destiny told her how not being able to perform would be like not being able to breathe. Continuing to stare out the window with that memory in mind, Andrie was suddenly assaulted by the sight of Ann's black stretch limo as it slid up directly in front of the office. She saw the driver open the door and Ann's tall gaunt figure emerge. Wrapped in a black sable coat with a mask of bitter intolerance on her face, she strode onto the sidewalk. Andrie noticed that Ann seemed annoyed at the presence of the street musician, who, conversely, seemed indifferent to the arrival of the congresswoman and her limousine as she continued strumming away.

"Oh, God, please, if you could, give me that Christmas miracle that Nancy wished for me," Andrie prayed in a quick desperate little whisper, as the bitter mask advanced in her direction.

As Ann entered the office, so did a cold gust of air that promptly blew Nancy's note off the table and out the door, taking Andrie's hope with it as it disappeared. Ann immediately began rushing Andrie. "Are you ready to leave?" she asked, with poorly disguised impatience.

"Yes. Just give me a minute to turn the phones over to voice mail," Andrie answered.

"Is this everything?" Ann asked, pointing to two brown tweed suitcases and a small, tan leather overnight bag that Andrie had earlier placed by the door.

"Yes."

Ann then opened the door and motioned for the driver to come and take the luggage. Within seconds the luggage was stowed away in the limo's huge trunk.

"So, where are we headed?' Andrie asked in a lifeless tone as she tied the belt of trench coat and searched its pockets for her gloves.

"You'll see when we get there. I find surprise to be one of the more zestful experiences in life. Don't you?" Ann said, smiling smugly.

"I can't find my gloves," Andrie said, choosing to ignore Ann's remark.

"Try your purse," Ann huffed, as she opened the door in an effort to push things along.

"There they are, on my desk," Andrie said, spotting the pair of brown leather gloves. A familiar numbness had overtaken her. It was as though she had begun to move robotically. Then, turning off the lights, she walked out the door past Ann. Once outside, she saw that it had begun to snow again. A fleeting sensation of warmth touched her heart, as the snow reminded her that Destiny was somewhere in the city. Locking the door, Andrie turned toward the street.

On the sidewalk, halfway to the car, Ann took hold of her arm and stopped her. "Wait. Before we get in the car, I want to make something clear. I'm planning a wonderful time for us. I expect this trip to get our relationship back on track. I'm sure if you cooperate, we'll accomplish that. Which means that I expect you to put Destiny Anderson out of your thoughts, for good."

Infuriated by the demand, Andrie pulled her arm free and pointed her finger in Ann's face, as she responded to the coercion.

"Listen to me. I want to make something clear to you now. I don't love you. What you're forcing me to do turns my stomach. You know that the only reason I'm here with you is because of your threats to destroy Destiny. So every time you look at me, remember, I'll be thinking of her . . . every minute, every second . . . I'll be thinking of her. That's the only thing that will keep me from leaving you." Andrie's voice and eyes were filled with hatred and disgust.

"You *will* forget Destiny Anderson, I'll make sure of that. You'll see," Ann vowed, with a predatory smugness.

Andrie looked away from her, distracted by the street musician's guitar playing. The melody was strangely familiar to her. It was just music and no words. It haunted her, as she searched her purse for the envelope with the twenty dollars she had planned to give to Kelly for Christmas. Finding it, she walked over to where the young woman was standing. Kelly's head was down as she continued playing, and the wide brim of her hat prevented her from seeing Andrie waiting there to wish her a Merry Christmas and ask about the tune. It appeared that the young musician was once again in a daydream state, playing for hordes of imaginary fans. Andrie didn't want to disturb that dream. She preferred to wait for her to look up on her own.

Again, Ann took hold of Andrie's arm, urging her to hurry up.

"Come on. We haven't got all day," Ann insisted, as she huffed impatiently.

"Merry Christmas, Kelly," Andrie said softly, as she dropped the envelope from her hand. It seemed to glide down to the open guitar case in slow motion, as did the snowflakes that fell along with it.

Looking down to see it land, she suddenly realized why that melody being strummed by the street musician was so hauntingly familiar. It stirred a vague, almost ancient memory of a time when she stood in a Brooklyn basement listening to Destiny play the piano. Andrie's eyes shot up, and there, standing only inches away, smiling at her from under the broad brim of that cowhide hat, was her whole world.

"Merry Christmas, baby," Destiny said, with the same tender, loving, dimpled smile that Andrie had fallen in love with sixteen years before.

"Destiny," she cried in a soft voice as passion and confusion mixed to dizzy her senses.

"I know all about it. She can't keep us apart anymore," Destiny said, taking Andrie into her arms. The snow drifted down around them as their lips met in a fervent, hungry kiss. From that moment, in both their hearts, which had long ago become one, they knew that this time would be forever.

Ann looked on in shock and anger. "Your career is as good as dead now, Anderson. I swear it. You'll be singing in the streets for real by the time I finish with you," she spewed furiously.

Still holding Andrie tightly in her arms, Destiny answered, "I don't think so, Ann. Harry Stern took Cobra back this afternoon and he knows everything. He knows that Sottley was your front man with Cobra and he knows that you sold the building that Women's Way was in to Cortronics. . . . I guess it would come as no surprise to you now if I said that he won't be supporting any more of your campaigns. . . . That's if you have anymore campaigns, after you face ethics violation charges. . . . Harry's got proof that your father funneled over two million dollars into your re-election campaign, when the legal limit is a thousand. . . . Oh. One more thing, even if things hadn't worked out this way and you still owned Cobra, you couldn't have kept me away from Andrie forever. She's my soul . . . I can't live without her . . . and no threat to my career, or even my life, would have mattered."

The feelings that Destiny spoke of were foreign to Ann and therefore held no meaning for her. She glared hatefully at the reunited lovers, knowing that she had no weapons left to keep them apart. Then, sickened by her own powerlessness, Ann stormed into the back of her limousine. It was time for her to focus her energies on Destiny's allegations. No matter how true they were, she would not allow them to derail her political career. Her driver closed the door for her and walked around to the other side of the car to get in. But just before he did, he glanced over to Destiny and Andrie, giving them a subtle approving smile. It was clear that he knew the congresswoman well.

The long black car disappeared down the street like some retreating monster who had been driven back into the darkness, defeated by the forces of fate and love which proved too powerful to overcome.

"How . . . how did you find out?" Andrie asked, as tears of joy ran down her cheeks, mixing with the snowflakes that were sprinkling down upon her.

"Your friend Nancy explained everything to me. I'll tell you all about that later. Right now I just want to hold you tight," she said, drawing Andrie closer to her as though she needed to convince herself that this wasn't a dream. Then, staring for a moment as she drank in the sight of the woman she loved, Destiny added, "I want you to know that there isn't anything in the world I love or need more than you . . . not anything."

"Me too," Andrie replied softly as she put her lips to Destiny's, healing the wounds of time lost.

The calm, soothing snow covered the tracks left behind by Ann's limousine and cushioned the street around them, dulling the uglier noises of the city until it left only the sound of nearby church bells playing "The First Noel." Hearing that, both Destiny and Andrie suddenly felt as though some higher power was smiling down at them, satisfied that they had found their way back to each other. But before they could put words to that thought, Harry Stern's stretch limo pulled up next to them.

"What's this?" Andrie asked, nodding curiously toward the uniformed driver, who had emerged from the second limousine and seemed to be dutifully waiting for them.

"That's Harry's driver and car. Now, don't move," Destiny answered, removing the silver maple leaf necklace. "I've waited sixteen years to give you this," she said, tenderly slipping it around Andrie's neck. With that, she pressed her lips to Andrie's in a brief but passionate kiss and led her to the waiting car.

As she got in, Andrie noticed Nancy's card lying open in the snow. She quickly whisked it up and took it with her. "Where are we going?" she asked, not really caring what the answer was, as long as she and Destiny were together.

"Remember that perfect Christmas tree you used to wish for? . . . Well, I found it," Destiny announced proudly, her dark eyes sparkling like diamonds and her face radiating everything she felt for Andrie.

As the car pulled away, Andrie glanced down at Nancy's Christmas card and the note inside it. Then she looked back up at Destiny, who began to kiss her slowly and tenderly with a love that touched her soul. At that moment, she believed in miracles.

The End

About the Author

Before writing fiction, **Juliet Carrera** had a successful career in the field of women's health. While Director of Women's Services at a major hospital in New York City, she was elected to the board of directors of the National Association of Women's Health Professionals.

Juliet received numerous awards as well as national recognition for her work in women's health. During that period of her life she produced and hosted *Health Update,* an award-winning cable television talk show in New York. The television show seemed a natural outgrowth of Juliet's degree in nursing and her brief stint in modeling and acting. Juliet attended the prestigious American Academy of Dramatic Art in New York City.

Currently, Juliet is working on a medical thriller novel with what she describes as one of the most offbeat and controversial themes ever to be offered to the reading public. For those who enjoyed *Inside Out,* she is also planning a sequel to it and a novel about the early life of one of its main characters, Destiny Anderson.

Juliet lives with her partner Laura, whom she calls the center of her universe, and their English springer spaniel Bosco. They divide their time between their apartment in the city and their home in upstate New York. When she is not writing, Juliet makes herself available to women's groups, speaking on health and related topics. She is also becoming increasingly active as an advocate for gay marriage and domestic partnership rights. Juliet is donating five percent of her royalties from the sale of this book to the Human Rights Campaign. Visit Juliet's Website at <http://home.att.net/~/julietcarrera/index.html>.